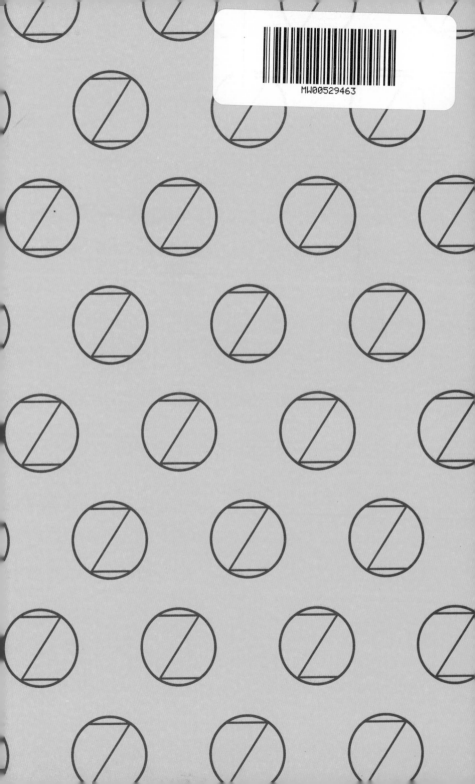

MEET THE AUTHOR

TEASERS,
TRAILERS & MORE...

Pearce Oysters

"As gritty, complex, and nuanced as the eponymous bivalve at its center. Takacs is as skilled at portraying the bayous, swamps, and bays of Louisiana's coastline as she is exploring all that is unpredictable about the human heart. It's a remarkable novel."

—ADRIENNE BRODEUR, author of *Little Monsters*

"*Pearce Oysters* tears back the veil and reveals the crude realities of the biggest oil spill in history. Takacs shows extraordinary talent . . . eye-opening and compelling, I couldn't put it down."

—MARY ALICE MONROE, author of *The Summer Girls*

"A vivid, intimate portrait of a disaster the world has forgotten, even though for families along the Gulf Coast it has never ended. An impressive, big-hearted debut."

—NATHANIEL RICH, author of *Losing Earth*

"With lyrical prose, sly humor, and endless empathy, Takacs balances the intimate with the global, showing us the Pearce family in all of their flawed complexity. An essential novel for our time."

—GWEN E. KIRBY, author of *Shit Cassandra Saw*

"There's nothing I love more than a family drama steeped in love and complication, and *Pearce Oysters* delivers it note for note. It also reminds us of what . . . it means to fight for a legacy, and why we stay together in the midst of our fiercest trials. Full of wit, grit, and longing, this novel captured my whole heart."

—AMY JO BURNS, author of *Mercury*

Pearce
Oysters

Joselyn Takacs

ZIBBY BOOKS
NEW YORK

Library of Congress Control Number: 2023946568
Hardcover ISBN: 978-1-958506-50-9
eBook ISBN: 978-1-958506-52-3

Cover design by Vi-An Nguyen
Text design by Neuwirth & Associates, Inc.

www.zibbymedia.com

Printed in the United States of America

10 9 8 7 6 5 4 3 2 1

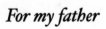

For my father

Author's Note

What follows is a work of imagination. The characters and town of Golden Vale were invented, and the geography of Louisiana has been altered slightly. I based the novel on true events in the aftermath of the 2010 *Deepwater Horizon* spill, though I've taken occasional liberties with chronology. The names of some real people and companies appear, but they are applied to the events of this novel in a fictitious manner.

⇥ One ⇤

2010

J ordan Pearce had left the boat's cabin just as his father had arranged it, as if Al might step in from the heat and tell him where to head next. It was a good old oyster boat, built to purpose in 1972. A sixty-five-foot shallow-draft boat—a barge, really—designed to cruise in two and a half feet of water while ferrying forty sacks of oysters on the broad face of its front deck. Jordan's grandfather built the boat with profits from the family's oyster reefs, inherited from his father, who established the first reef behind his fishing camp on Chênière Caminada, a peninsular arm reaching into Caminada Bay. There, the oysters quickly grew fat and briny in the warm, brackish waters so near the Gulf of Mexico. He leased his plot of water bottom from the state of Louisiana in 1919 and built up the reef with spent oyster shells, which he dumped by the boatload, year after year, down to the mud.

So began the Pearce Oyster Company.

In 1975, the boat passed to Jordan's father as a wedding gift. At the time, it was called *Fortuna*, after the Roman goddess of fortune. His father re-christened the boat *May's Day* in blue paint on the stern after Jordan's mother, not that May would spend any time on it. For the next four decades, *May's Day* dredged the same oyster reefs in the Barataria and Terrebonne Basins, and in those years, except for changing captains, fortunes, and too few coats of paint, the boat had changed hardly at all.

On the wall opposite the galley kitchen were pictures Jordan's father had pinned up with thumbtacks—redfish dangling on the line, Jordan and his brother Benny, young, each holding up a crab pot, and the old-timers: his grandfather, father, and uncle. Here they stood in a row—corralled, Jordan guessed, by his mother behind the camera—with their hands in their pockets, their caps casting shadows on their square faces. Even while they lived, even while somewhat young, they had looked to Jordan like men out of photographs, like leftovers from some older way of the world now gone.

The dashboard held old papers, maps, and curios bleached from sun. At one end was a hula girl swaying on her suction cup when the waves picked up. On the other end, a figurine of the Virgin Mary glued in place. A string of Mardi Gras beads hung around her ankles. In the cabinet below the dash was a framed and jaundiced *Times-Picayune* with a quote from Jordan's father that read: "You pluck one thing out of nature, and you find it's tied to everything, everything in the universe."

His mother had framed the article, though Al never got around to hanging it. It was about the oyster die-off of 1993. When a season of excessive rainfall threatened to flood New Orleans, the state flushed the Breton Sound with fresh water from the Mississippi River, drowning thousands of oysters in the estuary east of the river. The oyster shells flapped open, releasing the dead oysters. Putrid oyster meat floated on the water's surface, stinking up the area and sickening the seabirds. Dolphin deaths spiked that year. Shrimp and crab populations faltered. Beachgoers in Mississippi developed skin rashes and diarrhea from toxic algae blooms. All from the fresh water. The oystermen sued the state of Louisiana for damages. They won their lawsuit. Al was chairman of the Louisiana Oyster Task Force then.

Al had been gone five years and the maps on the dash were historic, all of them drawn before Hurricane Katrina had swiped the trees from the lower parish. Louisiana had been losing its wetlands for eighty years, visible enough in Jordan's lifetime that he could see the marsh disappearing, the cypress forests of the lower parish skeletal where they stood in the water. Now there was nothing to interrupt the long, empty draw of the Gulf, except for the oil platforms gloating over the horizon.

Jordan was twenty-nine years old when he inherited the business. He had started culling oysters on his father's oyster lugger the summer he was eight and worked every summer into his college years, before he dropped out. He knew the boats—the family owned three, two of which now sat on tires in the high grass. He knew the reefs, and their buyers. He'd thought he'd have more time to learn the business end. They'd both thought that. First, a stroke ended his father's time on the water, and just when it seemed he was regaining his strength, his heart gave out.

Katrina was the biggest loss their company had ever sustained, and Al Pearce was not there, with his cigarette and his pageboy cap, to tell Jordan that this was a loss the company could survive.

What Jordan learned about hurricanes was that, although they destroyed, they also renewed. Some oyster crops were buried, other crops—long submerged—were unearthed. It takes two to three years for an oyster to reach market size, and in the same span of time, Jordan taught himself to run his father's business. Five years after Katrina, it was looking to be a windfall year again. The hurricane generation was ready for harvest.

Jordan motored down Bayou Lafourche before dawn, toward his oyster reefs in Caminada Bay. His three deckhands sat up watching as the houses along the bayou slept with darkened windows, the shallow peaks of their roofs outlined against the early light. An egret sailed by with the silver leaf of a minnow in its beak.

He felt most reverent about these mornings on the boat. The gold sunrise pulling back the curtain on the day and the water's buttery softness. Green elephant ears lining the bayou bobbed in his boat wake. Turtles perched on cypress roots. A silvery nutria slinked into the water from the saw grass, and a water moccasin skittered across the gleaming surface. The churning motor, the smell of coffee and his first cigarette. That morning, Jordan caught himself repeating the word *splendor*, *splendor*, and rolling the word around in his mouth because he didn't want to be heard.

The bayou looks like a slough of muddied water to an outsider—loitering and shadeless and smelling of marsh rot. It could be homely to a whole crowd of people, but for him, it could flash silver and call the seabirds to fly low. He longed to find this private beauty off the water. He was thirty-four years old, broadly built but already prone to stooping, growing thicker in the middle in the year and a half since his fiancée left. When he thought about the condition of his reefs or the disarray of his office, he knocked on his chest as if trying to dislodge a blockage in a pipe.

Doug Babies, his longtime deckhand, came into the cabin, took a pack of cigarettes from his shorts, and shook it lightly.

"You forgot these out on the culling table last night," Babies said. "Got all rained on." He removed a cigarette and set the pack on the dashboard. The color bled from the tipping paper and the brown of the tobacco showed through the stem.

"You don't have to smoke it," Jordan said.

"Bet it won't even light."

But it lit fine. When Babies exhaled, he frowned, looking at the cigarette between his fingers.

"This doesn't even taste good to me right now," Babies said.

They called him "Babies" because it rhymed with his last name, Davies. And because he had the doughy physique of an overgrown baby. This had been true in high school, when they played football together, and it still was, seventeen years later.

"I guess it wouldn't," Jordan said.

"It's the hypnosis," Babies said. "I've been to a hypnotist to stop my drinking. He asked me—my hypnotist—he said, 'While we're quittin' habits, maybe you want to quit that one too,' and pointed at the pack I had in my shirt pocket. I told him to work his magic."

"You never mentioned it." Jordan took one of his own cigarettes.

"He speaks right to my subconscious. I'm dozing on the couch, and he says to me, 'You don't have to drink. You don't have to smoke anymore either.'"

"Huh," Jordan said.

"I woke up feeling pretty good, actually. There's something to it, maybe. I'm only smoking because I'm bored. That's all. Or I want to take a break."

Babies came to work for Jordan four years ago, and he'd tired of being a deckhand. Jordan knew Babies wanted to run his own boat. One of the Pearce family boats.

"You know, I can tell you're nervous," Babies said.

"What?"

"About seeing Benny tonight. I can see you talking to him in your head."

"My mom told you he was coming?"

"She said the dinner was just for family." Babies said this with some bitterness. He considered himself family. Jordan's mother had encouraged him to, but she probably suspected that Benny wouldn't want to see Babies. In high school, Babies was in a crowd that Jordan's younger brother looked down on. But then again, Benny looked down on most of his classmates. That was a hard place to start friendships from.

"She's crazy about this dinner," Jordan said. "He probably won't even come."

"You think so?"

"He'll cancel at the last minute. She'll make excuses for him. He's a genius just because he can play the piano."

Babies laughed, leaning forward to grind his cigarette into the ashtray.

"I think he's a genius too," Babies said. "He's sleeping right now and still getting a paycheck. We're the fuckers going to work before sunup."

Jordan pulled on his cigarette in response. He did not like being reminded that he paid Benny a salary. Their father's succession plan passed on the family business to Jordan and Benny as partners. Babies said it only to needle Jordan. In this way, Babies was more his brother than Benny was.

Babies shrugged and walked off to join Alejandro and Manuel on the deck. Jordan thumped on his chest. Most of the time he tried not to think about his brother, who was the front man for a band whose music Jordan did not like. Benny hadn't been home in two years, though he lived only an hour and a half away in New Orleans, saying he was a "full-time musician."

By midday, Jordan's crew had dredged thirty sacks of oysters from Caminada Bay—a good haul for a morning. The new deckhands, Manuel and Alejandro, were fast learners. They'd shown up together, both on work visas, three weeks earlier. Neither one of them had ever so much as held an oyster hammer. Manuel had never even eaten an oyster. But Babies had shown them what to do. Every two minutes, Jordan pulled the winch to lift a dredge full of oysters from the reef below, and the deckhands spilled the oysters on a steel table and attacked the pile like they were born to do it, breaking up clusters into singles and bagging them for market. They were already faster at culling than Babies, who dragged the hundred-pound sacks into the shade and tied them up.

Jordan preferred the harvest days, tiresome as they were. Driving a heavy-bottomed oyster boat in wide arcs in the bay was like driving a mower over a lawn. It was good work if you liked to live in your mind. The boat rolled portside as the dredge, a great steel-toothed cage, scraped the reef below. He could feel it, as if the whole boat were an extension of his body, knowing where to be gentle, where to leave the reef alone. He had to sense when it was full.

When Jordan was young, he heard his father say, "No matter where I am, I can see my oyster population in Barataria." This made sense to him now. Jordan had a map of all his family's oyster leases in his mind—each in its own stage of production. It was like closing your eyes, with great stillness, and sensing the various lengths and angles of your own body. He saw the leases in Caminada Bay he would harvest until July, and the leases he was soon to plant. He saw the leases that weren't producing, fallow for any number of reasons: freshwater intrusion, predators, poachers. The leases had been passed down through the years—plots of water bottom they leased from the state to build their reefs on. Each generation did what it could to add to the family's holdings. The most important thing was to ensure what they passed on was larger than what had been passed to them.

The sun grew livid and pitiless over their shoulders, tempered only by the occasional breeze on the water. Babies ducked back into the cabin for another of Jordan's cigarettes, then stood there smoking for a while and looked reluctantly out the window, though it was hardly cooler in the shade.

They both watched as the new deckhand Manuel dragged another full sack of oysters next to the others. That made sixty sacks before lunch. Jordan couldn't believe it. He gave Manuel a thumbs-up. Manuel stood, stretching his back, and looked away. None of Jordan's workers liked him much, except for Babies. "They're not your friends," his father had said about the deck-hands. "They'll take advantage. Can't hold it against them but can't forget it either."

"I was thinking," Babies said, "more about our conversation earlier."

"What conversation's that?" Jordan asked.

"About your brother."

"Oh."

"I've been thinking about what I'd do if I didn't have to work," Babies said. "I'd buy a motorcycle with a sidecar, and I'd drive all over the fucking country. I'd see the shit out of this country."

"Yeah, well . . ." Jordan said, and then trailed off while muscling the winch handle. The topic of conversation grated on him.

"Meanwhile, that's your brother's situation," Babies said.

Jordan, annoyed, yanked the winch into gear. The winch whined as it lifted the dredge. Manuel leaned on the taffrail before the culling table, staring off into the distance over the water, waiting to empty the dredge with Alejandro. When the dredge smacked the steel railing of the culling table, it produced, somehow, a pierc-ing human shriek. It took Jordan a moment to see it was Manuel who had issued the shriek, and it took another moment to under-stand what he was shrieking about. Alejandro jolted forward and pushed the dredge off the railing. Manuel snatched his hand to his chest, his face twisted in pain, and stomped a few paces down the deck and back, cursing in Spanish.

Dumbfounded as Jordan was, action did not occur to him until Babies ran out of the cabin to look. But Manuel guarded the hand at his chest and wasn't giving it over to Babies. Jordan joined them on the deck.

"Did the dredge catch your hand?" Jordan asked.

Manuel cradled his hand, cursing in Spanish.

"Let him see," Alejandro said.

Manuel extended the gloved hand.

"I'm going to take off the glove," Jordan said.

Manuel nodded, steadying the hand with the support of his good one as if it were a stranger's.

Jordan gave a tug on one finger of the glove and Manuel jerked the hand back, sucking in air.

"You'll have to cut the glove off," Alejandro said.

Babies went to find some scissors.

"Was it the fingers or the hand?" Jordan said.

"The hand."

Jordan nodded, knowing the day was over. Manuel was rocking back and forth slightly, and Jordan steadied Manuel's hand before he brought the scissors to it. When he did this, he felt the bones floating in there like twigs, not attached to anything. He would never forget it as long as he lived.

The scissors were dull, which made the job harder. Sweating and pallid, Manuel stared up at the sky, mouthing curses at God, or Jordan. Alejandro spoke to Manuel soothingly as Jordan cut along the palm down the center until the glove was loose enough to be taken from the hand. He tried to be gentle and quick. The glove slapped to the floor, and the four of them stared at Manuel's index finger, hanging straight down at a horrific angle. It was just the skin and the muscle that kept the finger from dropping to the deck where the split glove lay at their feet. His palm was broken. Jordan didn't know what you could do for a hand like that.

"That hand," Babies said, thinking it over very carefully, "is fucked as can be."

"Let's get you to the hospital, then," Jordan said, turning toward the cabin.

"He won't go to the doctor," Alejandro told him.

"Hell he will," Jordan said, "if he plans to use that hand again."

Alejandro shook his head. "It's too much," he said.

Jordan's mind jumped to the question of obligation. Because they were day laborers, he had no contract with them, but he did not know what that meant about payment.

Jordan said again that Manuel had to see a doctor. He'd need surgery, or the hand would lose function. Then he couldn't work at all. He ought to think about that, Jordan said, before not going to the doctor. Again Alejandro said that he wouldn't go. It was a short, unproductive discussion, and Manuel did not contribute.

"Well, we're going in anyway," he said to Manuel. "You can think on it."

Through the streaked cabin window, Jordan watched as Babies conferred with the other deckhands. The morning's splendor was gone. The water was sheet glass in the sun. Jordan turned up the radio to drown out the discussion on the deck and had them coasting toward home. No one had ever had his hand crushed by a dredge on one of their boats. It was Manuel's fault for leaving his hand where it shouldn't have been.

The left speaker buzzed, so Jordan smacked it, which had no effect at all. On the radio, the reporter talked about an explosion on a BP oil rig offshore in the Gulf. He'd heard the news about the explosion a few days ago. Eleven men were missing. The Coast Guard was combing the Gulf for them. The rig, the size of a football field, burned for nearly two days, and then, laden with the seawater they used to douse the flames, the rig sank.

Manuel appeared in the doorway of the cabin. Jordan turned down the radio.

"Look at this," he said. The palm ballooned up like the abdomen of a spider, and the fingers curled stiff and lifeless. "Just when I found work," he said. "It's stupid."

"If I could get you back any faster, I would," Jordan said.

"I'm not dying," Manuel said.

"You'll have to go to the hospital, you know," Jordan said. "Want a cigarette?"

"I don't smoke," he said, looking down the bayou.

They passed a couple of old men in a skiff who were fishing for bass. The men each waved with one hand occupied, and Jordan waved back. They wouldn't catch anything at this hour.

"That's a cemetery," Jordan told Manuel.

Manuel huffed, as if Jordan had made an unfunny joke.

"No, it is," Jordan said. "Underwater. It's a fishing spot now, but when the tide goes out, you can see the tombs."

Manuel seemed to be listening to the radio, as faint as it was. The reporter explained that there was a growing slick around the drill site, but they were unsure if the oil was from the rig or if the well had failed. He flicked the radio knob off then, not wanting to hear any more. Every other year, sometimes more often, there was an oil spill offshore. He had no space to worry about that—or even the missing men, terrible as it was. In front of him was a hand obliterated by a dredge. A harvesting day cut in half, which meant buyers to call. A brother bleeding his business from New Orleans.

It was stupid, as Manuel had said, but fate works on us stupidly.

"Listen," he said. "About your hand. I'll take care of it."

→ TWO ←

It was Benny's coming home that brought on the project of house excavation. May Pearce vacuumed until everything appeared a new color, the couch browner, the baseboards whiter, the carpet creamier. She flapped rugs in the front yard. She beat clouds of dust out of the couch cushions in the steamy afternoon until her underarms were wet. She took a toothbrush and bleach water to the base of the guest room toilet. She raged through a week's worth of cleaning in two days, and in the cleaning, she felt a yearslong burden lifting from her. She glimpsed her life in that house again as if she were returning from a long trip away.

In the old days, the Pearce Oysters Compound, as her good friend Lucille called it, was comprised of three vinyl-sided ranch homes in a densely packed 1960s-era neighborhood. There was the main house—the beating heart of it all, a buttercream three-bedroom charmer; the "office," which faced the bayou and the dock, where Al received potential buyers and the men drank beer at night; and the old house belonging to Mee-maw—Al's mother—which shared a driveway with the main house. They were the only family in the neighborhood to own more than one house. Their little compound had once pulsed with activity all day long. Mothers stopping by to look for their children. Workers coming and going. Mee-maw, that old Cajun witch, casting cat food in the driveway to her flock of feral cats as though they were chickens. The boys scampering around, sunburnt and scabby with mosquito bites. A collection of neighborhood kids' bikes strewn in the front yard. Mee-maw's friends popping by at inconvenient hours expecting sun tea. Al sauntering among the houses laughing, sometimes hollering, at deckhands or oyster shuckers, always with a cigarette in his mouth. And May had been in the middle of it—complaining with glee to Lucille about someone's bad behavior, about Benny's backtalk, about the feral cats screaming when they mated.

Al had bought two of the houses in the eighties, one of the best decades for oysters, prosperity they had not seen before or since. A period like her late teens, when May was an Alabama beauty queen and was accepted by the University of Alabama, where she was invited to all the parties, and she stole her friends' boyfriends. A period when she could ask anyone for anything because the answer was always "Yes." Until five years ago, she'd viewed her life with about as much concern as a piece of antique furniture in her joyfully cluttered home—so upright and reliable it didn't warrant a second thought. It held her morning mug of coffee, and then, suddenly, it didn't.

When she vacuumed past Al's closet in her bedroom, she parked the upright vacuum, engine still roaring, and opened the door. Pressing her face into his hanging shirts—some of which were clean, others he'd worn just once or twice before the stroke—she smelled him alive again. Burnt earth, sweat, and the arboreal kick of his cologne—the scent of the arm that would search her out in the middle of the night. A man she once loved so much that her body produced his name as her heart circulated blood.

This door had long remained closed. She feared some barely sutured wound would burst. This happened from time to time. Last week she'd been in the grocery store and looked down at the bottom of her shopping cart to see a tube of Metamucil she had no memory of grabbing. Metamucil for Al. Then there were tears in the grocery store—for Al, who'd tried, in his way, to be healthy, despite the cigarettes—but also tears for herself because of all the other husbands who were fat and struggled to lumber out of their easy chairs, and yet were somehow still alive. He was only fifty-six when he passed. Why should it have happened to her?

The cashier had been a swimming, watery apparition when she forced herself into the checkout line. So what if she was crying? She was a widow. Let her cry if she wanted to. She hated how quickly people were overwhelmed by her grief. They gave her a few months, and then they expected her to talk about something else. Their eyes slid to the floor if she brought up Al in conversation. They gave her no time at all.

In half an hour, she'd emptied the closet and hastily taped up the boxes of clothes still on their hangers, except for one shirt she set aside for Jordan. He'd put on some pounds in the past year; she couldn't help but notice. May wasn't certain that Jordan would still fit in Al's shirt, but it was worth a shot. Jordan's room held some troubling signs of late bachelorhood: the smell of unwashed clothes, plates crusted with food on the carpet by the bed, lotion pump on the night table. She laid the shirt on his bed and left his mess alone. Jordan and his great privacy.

Lucille had appeared in the kitchen yesterday, bearing the requested fistful of parsley from her garden, and was puzzled by May's housecleaning project: "Even if your kids stay close, it doesn't solve anything. They're still people with problems, and they still resent you for enrolling them in baseball camp or for fixing their teeth or for not fixing their teeth."

What May knew, however, was that people were not inflexible. Even the most stubborn characters could change and soften in love like clay in water. When Benny called to tell her he was in love, she was thrilled with the possibility of Benny finally moving back home, tidy new wife in tow. They would tack a new roof on Meemaw's house, long ago ravaged by Hurricane Katrina, and they'd become the Pearce Oyster Compound once again. Al had always intended for his boys to run the company together, and his will reflected as much.

She couldn't tell all of this to Lucille because she couldn't stand to see the who-are-you-kidding look, or the I'm-worried-you-don't-see-the-big-picture look. The worst was when Lucille just said her name in exasperated pity.

After Al passed, Benny had pledged to come home every week when May was so bereft. Months of paralysis she couldn't recall without some disgust. A nubby pink bathrobe and Xanax for her nerves that she liked a little too much. One pill turned down the volume of her feelings, and two pills sent her wheeling through afternoons like a hawk in the sky.

Benny's weekly pledge dissolved into monthly visits, dissolved into never coming at all. He'd not been home in two years. May went to the city, to New Orleans, when she wanted to see him, and he did not look well. The way he lived—she couldn't understand it. For all his talk about being a musician, and all his talent, he looked as though he spent more time drinking in bars than performing in them. She talked to him frequently on the phone, though. She called him to talk about anything at all, to tell him she was planting begonias that spring. Benny had always listened to her. For all his problems, he was the son who seemed interested in her feelings.

When he was in college, taking classes in philosophy at the University of New Orleans, he'd said he was too busy with school to visit. Then it was music management. Then Benny had called home and said, "The whole money side of the music industry, it just makes me sick. I'm really not into music as a business." May felt Al's muscles tensing up like a compressed spring, and she grabbed his knee to stop him from speaking. "Then what will you study, Benny?" she asked. "I'm figuring that out," he said. Al stood and left the room. Benny dropped out of college his sophomore year and started working as a barback at a club in the French Quarter. He'd been in one band after another for the past ten years with little to show for it. She hoped that one day he would realize, regrettably, that Al had been right.

There had been so many false promises about visits that May no longer bothered to start cooking for him when he said he was coming. The last time he said he'd visit, five months earlier, he'd called that same afternoon claiming he was on the side of the highway with a blowout. It broke her heart to admit he was lying.

"I'm sorry, Mom. I've just been really busy here lately," he said. "With activism."

"Activism?" she said, slumping into Al's easy chair.

"I'm organizing a protest against the destruction of public housing."

"Public housing?" She could not feign interest.

"The projects. All these people are going to be displaced," he said. "This city is waging a war on the poor. The city is out to get them. We saw it during Katrina, and it's happening again."

"Son," she said, in the tone that she rarely took with him as an adult, "your brother needs your help here."

This brand of foolishness offended her. It seemed a petulant disavowal of his responsibilities, and she suspected it could be traced to a new influence—a woman. And she was right. A month after Benny shared his new interest in activism came the phone call that he was in love. Now Benny wanted everyone to meet Kiki.

May decided to cook oyster étouffée, a kind of rich gravy served over rice, though it was a winter dish and a fuss to make the roux. It meant browning the flour in butter until it became the color of caramel. But Benny loved étouffée.

She wanted fresh oysters for the dish, which meant fetching a tub from Hoa and Linh in the garage. Al had converted the business office garage into a shucking station with stainless-steel tables and a walk-in cooler. Every day that Jordan had oysters to sell, Hoa and Linh were out there shucking a portion of yesterday's catch, prying the shells open with knives, and plopping the oyster meat into tubs for the restaurant market. In the summers, Jordan ran an industrial fan so loud the women wore earplugs to protect their hearing. The fan kept the flies down. Hoa and Linh had worked for the family for twenty years at least. Women May's age who'd known her children since they were young. They did their work and left most days without a word to May—their lives on elliptical orbits that never crossed.

May walked across the driveway to the garage. Late April, and she already felt the heat in her lungs. Her car needed a wash. New weeds had invaded the flower bed by the office. Louisiana was so fertile it seemed the plant life wanted the land back. May paused outside the door. Inside, she heard the women chatting in Vietnamese, the clinking of oyster shells on the steel tables. Should she knock first? She didn't.

Hoa looked up, just the briefest annoyance passing over her face at the interruption, and then she smiled. She was surprised to see

May, who rarely spoke to them—often just a wave from the kitchen. Things had been easier when Al was alive, loud and jocular. Hoa's daughter was about Benny's age. She and Benny had been friendly as kids. The women had more to talk about then.

"Hi," Hoa said.

The garage was smaller than she remembered. The air thick with the smell of the marsh, and a hint of funk from the oysters.

"I should have knocked," May said. "I need some oysters. Benny's coming for dinner."

"Ah, Benny!" Hoa said. "You must be very happy."

"Yes, very happy," she said, feeling, instead, a bit defensive. Was she hinting at Benny's long absence?

"It's been a long time!" Linh sang.

Well, it was true enough, though she didn't like thinking they were keeping score. Hoa's daughter—what was her name?—she lived in California now. She was in law school. Linh did not have children.

"How much you need?" Linh asked.

"Just a tub," she said. "Benny is bringing his girlfriend for dinner. We'll see if he finally settles down."

"Oh." Hoa laughed, snapping the lid on a tub of oysters. "Good luck with that, Mama!"

"Benny was such a funny boy," Linh said fondly. "Is he well?"

People said that about Benny, that he was funny, though sometimes they meant something else. Hoa handed May the tub. She wished she remembered Hoa's daughter's name.

"We'll see how well he is," May said. "And how is Annie?" Thank God. The name came to her.

"Too busy to date," Hoa said. "That's what she says. With law school."

"That only means"—Linh massaged her gloved palm, kneading her arthritic joints—"that she doesn't want you to meet him."

"It does not," Hoa said. She said something else in Vietnamese, but May detected no edginess in Hoa's tone. Linh laughed.

Their husbands were shrimpers. Ever since Al passed, Hoa and Linh presented May with a cooler of shrimp at the start of each season as an offering in Al's memory. They'd seen May in her pink-bathrobe days, and once found her sleeping in her car in the driveway. She was in the driver's seat and woke to Linh's tapping. Their two faces peering down at her, a picture of concern. She said that she must have been sleepwalking. In truth, she'd just overshot the mark with the nerve pills and could remember, like it was a dream, leaving her bed for her car in the middle of the night. It had seemed at the time there was someplace she desperately needed to go.

"Well," May said, in the tone that meant she was leaving. She hugged the tub to her chest. "Thanks again for the oysters. I'll tell Benny you said hello."

→ Three ←

It was a shock to see Jordan home early from harvesting oysters. It could mean only that there had been some problem on the boat. He stood in the doorway in his socks, shoes in hand, with that hangdog look on his face that meant he didn't want to talk. He resembled Al when she'd first met him—filling up a doorway with those broad shoulders, his deep tan, the hooded eyes and thick brows that traced back to the family's Scottish ancestors who came to Louisiana before the turn of the century. But Al had been particular about his appearance, and Jordan presented as though he didn't own a mirror, dressed in cargo shorts and a T-shirt given to him for free at a car wash.

"What's going on?" she asked finally, when he didn't explain why he was home.

Jordan sat down on the arm of the easy chair to pull off his socks. "New deckhand got his hand smashed by the dredge, so we hauled in early."

"That's terrible," she said. She gave the roux a stir. It was browning too quickly. "He's going to be all right, though?"

"Hand hurt to look at," Jordan said. "But he'll live. Strangest thing. I've never seen a guy put his hand there before. I wouldn't even think to tell him not to put a hand there. It's just so obvious."

She pulled the pot off the burner. "If your father could lose a finger to a silly infection, then I'm prepared to believe anything can happen."

"The house looks nice," he said, looking around at her cleaning efforts without seeming too pleased about it.

"Are you excited to see Benny?" she said, and then regretted it. She'd been thinking, I wish you were excited to see Benny. He gave her the look she expected, and she quickly changed the subject.

"How much did you give the deckhand?"

"Two thousand," he said, walking toward the shower. "Never saw a hand like that before."

She smiled to herself as she scraped the garlic and onions from the cutting board into the roux. That's how Jordan was. Two thousand dollars. She'd think he was made of stone, but then he surprised her.

A few hours later, the living room was styled to her liking. The rice was ready. The étouffée was simmering on low. She'd wait until the last minute to stir in the oysters. May heard Hoa and Linh chatting in the driveway. They ought to have gone home by this time. And then May heard a new sound. It was a young woman's laughter, clear as a bell. She shoved the tongs into the butter lettuce and flew to the window overlooking the driveway, and there was Benny.

Benny lifted the petite Linh into the air in their embrace and spun her around, a move that surprised everyone, but most of all Linh. When he put her down, she wailed and slapped him playfully on the biceps. A very tall, striking Black woman in her early twenties stood next to Benny and smiled at the scene. May was annoyed that the oyster shuckers had hung around just to see Benny. Of course, the old busybodies.

May shrieked Jordan's name—shrieked, she realized, because the four of them in the driveway turned in alarm at the sound of her voice. May tugged her apron off. The young woman cocked her head as they made eye contact. Then she noticed how oddly the woman was dressed.

Kiki wore a yellow gingham dress that she'd hacked up with scissors. She'd sliced the skirt off so that it came mid-thigh, unhemmed, with threads dangling at the level of her black biker shorts underneath. She'd ripped off the sleeves of the dress, drawing the eye to her toned arms. She'd torn the collar open to expose sharp collarbones. The overall effect was not unlike a victim of shipwreck. Around her neck she wore a red bandanna, jauntily tied. Her heeled boots brought her three inches taller than Benny. She looked stately and aloof, and the whole outfit was so confident in its disdain for propriety that it seemed to lend her a kind of power. May was cowed.

Jordan emerged grudgingly in the living room, aware that the buttons on his father's dress shirt were pulling apart at his stomach, to see his mother latched on to Benny for a moment too long. When she finally released him, she was swiping away tears. The girl with Benny looked on, smiling. Jordan noted first the girl's figure, rousing, and then the odd dress.

"Benny, you're an absolute skeleton!" May cried. She laughed to make light of her emotions. She gave Benny's shoulders a shake. "I'm so emotional today."

Benny had transformed in the past few years. When they'd last seen each other, Jordan had an inkling of where his brother was headed, but he still had the baby face then, round as a plum—the same timid young man. But the person in the doorway was not timid. He wore some kind of old-timey hat, cocked at an unreasonable angle, with the nub of a ponytail at the back of his neck. He used a dirty shoestring for a belt and his threadbare shirt had holes crawling up one side. There was a pack of cigarettes tucked into his sleeve. He looked sallow and underfed. What's wrong with your pockets? he wanted to ask Benny. I know you can afford to buy a belt. I'm paying you a salary, for chrissake.

Benny shrugged May off and inched closer to his girlfriend, touching her elbow with an air of possession. "This is Kiki," he said.

Kiki smiled and held out her hand, which May swept past, hoping they might quickly become familiar, as she so desperately wanted the woman to like her. She hugged the tall, beautiful figure and felt her body stiffen in her arms like a mannequin.

"We hug around here," May said when she let go, nearly an apology.

Jordan decided that his brother was addicted to drugs. Benny had always been different, but this was a flirtation with squalor, a symptom of a life so carefree that he had time to announce his difference from everybody else. Jordan should have known. It was what happened to people who didn't work yet still had their needs met. They bought motorcycles and started sharing needles.

Benny turned to Jordan, smiling and flushed with happiness. "Hey, buddy," he said.

People warmed in Benny's attention. Jordan felt this, even as he resisted it. Something about Benny was still as innocent as a child. This quality had once made him an easy target for ridicule. Kids used to smell it on him. Now Benny sidled over to him—he'd developed a way of walking that was all hips—and knocked Jordan lightly on the shoulder.

"Good to see you, man. It's been a while." Benny screwed his face up as he gave Jordan a once-over. "Older. You look a few years older. A little distinguished. Stepped into Al's shoes nicely. Is that Al's shirt?"

Jordan looked down, as if to verify, and smoothed the taut buttons again. He couldn't read his brother's tone. "It's clean," he said.

"A little tight there, isn't it?" Benny said.

"I went through your father's closet today—a little spring cleaning." May thought that Benny was jealous. But, Benny, his clothes wouldn't fit you, she wanted to tell him. Benny would look like a child in Al's clothes. She glanced again at Benny. Were his small shoulders hunching prematurely? He had wrinkles at the corners of his eyes. So soon?

She then turned hopefully to Kiki. "You know what it's like when you're going through the closets!"

Kiki did not smile like the good sport May had hoped she would be. May believed that women, first and foremost, needed to be good sports if they were going to limp along in life.

"It freaks me out a bit, to be honest," Benny said. "Can you take it off?"

"Are you joking?"

"I know, I know, it's crazy." Benny took off his fedora, turned it over in his hands. His hat left a little band of sweat in his unwashed hair. "But I'm gonna feel like Al is at the dinner table all night."

May didn't like Benny calling Al by his Christian name. He'd never done that before, to her knowledge.

"Maybe you should change, baby," May said.

"I'm not changing," Jordan said.

"Jordie," May said, and she looked again at Kiki, who had folded her arms and assumed a polite disinterest.

The cordless phone in the kitchen rang, which meant it was either some telemarketer or Lucille. Those were the only people who called the home phone. They stood blinking at one another while waiting for the answering machine to pick up.

It was Byrdie, the family lawyer. His voice was broadcast into the living room: "Hello, Jordan. Hello? This is James Byrdie calling you back. If my Alice got you right, you wanted to talk about day labor laws . . ."

Jordan rushed across the room to the receiver. "Byrdie, hold on a minute. Just a minute, Byrdie." He cradled the phone to his chest as he walked back to his room, avoiding eye contact on his way out.

They were off to a rough start. May knew Jordan would be in a mood for the rest of the night. She looked at the couple, who were standing so close together that their elbows were touching, and she felt a pang of envy. The total self-sufficiency of a young couple in love. It was in the way they looked at each other. Kiki seemed to be sending messages to Benny with her eyes.

"Well, something smells wonderful," Kiki said, trying to clear the air. And May remembered her role. They needed drinks. They needed to be coaxed into sitting down. They needed to relax. Everyone needed to relax, so that she might wordlessly convince them to visit often.

The couple perched on barstools at the kitchen island overlooking May's pottering. Benny stroked Kiki's forearm absently.

As she poured them tea, Benny told her about an alligator that they'd seen dead on the side of the road, a sixteen footer. It was the first alligator Kiki had ever seen, which meant she wasn't from Louisiana. She'd screamed, Benny told her, thinking it was alive.

"It sure looked alive," Kiki said, "with the way it was lying, its snout right up to the edge of the highway."

"But that was some hick's idea of a joke," Benny said.

The way Benny said "hick" had an air of contempt.

"I'm sure Benny told you he had pet gators," May said to Kiki. "Babies only. And two or three of them. He was a real critter kid. What was the one that you loved so much—Meatball?"

"Meatball," he said. "They have personalities, you know.

Meatball was the best of them. He liked to swim with me in the pool. They're like feisty lizards. And then, well, there comes the time when you part ways because . . ."

He tickled Kiki's abdomen. It seemed to delight and annoy her simultaneously.

This loosened her up a bit, and they chatted about the oyster étouffée, and what the Cajuns called "the trinity" in Cajun cooking—bell pepper, onion, and celery. May lifted the lid on the étouffée and playfully waved the steam of the simmering roux in their direction. When May showed Kiki the tub of oysters, she peered with interest.

"They look like the inside of something. Like the intestines of an animal," she said, not in disgust, but as a lover of precision.

"Where are you from, Kiki? I don't hear it."

"New York State, the Hudson Valley."

Benny announced with a little too much eagerness for May's liking that Kiki had gone to Cornell. An Ivy League pedigree was evident in the way she held herself. This bothered May. She likely appeared uncultured to Kiki. And it already seemed doubtful that this girl would be moving into the house next door.

"My parents said I was crazy for moving to the South," Kiki said. "But I told them that New Orleans isn't what they think. It isn't Alabama. It's like the northern capital of the Caribbean."

May straightened up. She was from Alabama. "Plenty of nice folks live in Alabama."

Benny laughed, touching Kiki's hand.

"Mom was an Alabama beauty queen." He hopped off his stool and went around the kitchen island to his mother. He put his hands on May's hips and spun her around while talking to Kiki. "You're looking at Miss University of Alabama 1974."

"I'm sorry," Kiki said, and she did seem sorry.

They commenced a waltz so naturally that May's feet knew what she was doing before her mind did.

Benny waved it off. "You didn't know."

He waltzed May around the kitchen. "Mom taught me how to dance. She learned in finishing school. I used to think, My mother is the best-looking mom in the neighborhood. I was always so proud when she came to pick me up from school."

Kiki watched May melt in Benny's arms. His movements were slightly exaggerated for play, but this was not play for his mother. Her cheeks flushed pink, and when he twirled her, her housedress belled. Kiki could imagine May as a southern beauty queen. She had the gray eyes and heart-shaped face that editors put in magazines to sell wholesome things like orange juice. Benny was thirty, so that meant May was likely in her fifties, Kiki thought, though she looked even younger. But things like May's accent, dress, and decorum made her seem old-fashioned. A certain kind of white woman, Kiki had noticed since she'd moved south, seemed preserved in amber, with ideas of the world just as fixed. And yet, watching them dance, Kiki felt tender toward May. No doubt she was the reason Benny was gentle and sympathetic when the bullying could have turned him cold.

There was something about watching a man make his own mother blush that was magnetic to women, Kiki decided. Despite all the Oedipal murkiness, this was a beacon of future familial bliss, and she was not immune to it.

When Jordan reemerged from the hallway, holding the phone gingerly, he presented himself to Benny as if to say, Are you happy now? He'd changed from Al's dress shirt into a T-shirt with a cartoon of two amorous oysters in an oyster shell bed. Below, in bubble letters, it read: OYSTER LUBBER.

May knew he chose the worst shirt on purpose.

"What'd Byrdie say?" she asked.

"He just wanted to tell me something I already know."

"Do you want some tea?"

He shook his head, and he plopped on the couch.

"Do you want a Coke?"

"I'll get something if I want it." He flipped through the *Good Housekeeping* magazine on the coffee table so casually that they all could tell he was feeling anything but casual.

"Hey, chief," Benny said. He moved across the room and perched over Al's old easy chair in a gesture of reconciliation. "How's the oyster business?"

"You ought to know," Jordan said. "You're part owner."

Benny winced and turned to look at his girlfriend, whose face betrayed that this was news to her, but she didn't say anything. Jordan realized that Benny was pretending to be poor, for some reason.

The sky outside was violet after the sun went down and the cicadas turned on their whirring. Even indoors the air felt tropical. At that moment, a squall was tottering toward them from Texas. The four of them took a seat at the dining table, each with a perfect hill of white rice steaming up to their faces, and after the scuttling of chairs on the linoleum, there was a long moment of silence. Al's chair was empty. They so rarely ate in the dining room that Jordan seldom noticed the absence at the head of the table. His mother had her hands knitted so tightly in her lap she could crack a nut between them. She was waiting for someone—Jordan—to offer up grace. Well, he didn't want to bless Benny's homecoming. Benny reached for his beer.

"Our Father who art in heaven," she began testily. "Hallowed be thy name."

They all bowed their heads obediently.

"Thy kingdom come, thy will be done—on earth as it is in heaven. Give us this day our daily bread and forgive us our trespasses." Here, she paused dramatically, for Jordan's sake. "As *we* forgive *those* who trespass against us, and lead us not into temptation, but deliver us from evil."

Then, as was their tradition, she went off script. Jordan's stomach whined as he smelled the étouffée, and he realized he'd not eaten all day.

"Thank you for this food before us, the bounty of the sea. And thank you for Jordan's oyster haul. Thank you for bringing Benny home and for our beautiful guest, Kiki. Please watch over us all in the week ahead. In your name we pray."

She paused, signaling that she was finished.

"Amen," they said.

His mother gave the table a little pleased pat and stood to serve everyone, ladling the oyster gravy into a brown moat around the hill of rice on their plates.

"It looks incredible," Kiki said.

May peppered Kiki with questions about how she met Benny. In her eyes, there was nothing more thrilling than the story of Benny courting a young, beautiful woman. Jordan tried not to let this trouble him. His mother had liked Ashley, his ex-fiancée. When he'd come home from work once to find them together on the couch with wine coolers, watching a show about plastic surgeries gone awry, he'd been surprised and pleased, but that was when Ashley still looked at him with interest. There was no wrongdoing on Ashley's part before she called it off. All of a sudden she was bored by him. She said that Jordan never wanted to do anything. When he asked her what she wanted to do, she wailed that he didn't understand her.

For all of Ashley's faults, at least she wasn't pompous. Jordan thought that Kiki was a little too impressed with herself when she talked about her work with "formerly incarcerated youth." He didn't understand what a girl like her was doing with Benny. Did she know he was a college dropout? Kiki chewed on her cuticles and said "curious" when most people would have just said "interesting." He sensed some condescension in her politeness, and it bothered him, but not as much as his brother's second mention of gentrification in New Orleans. Jordan didn't know what this meant, but he wouldn't give Benny the satisfaction of asking. He barely knew the person across the table, wearing a dirty fedora and draining his second beer at a rapid clip. After their father's stroke, he'd sit at this table with his coffee, laboring over the words to ask Jordan where he'd harvest that day. Meanwhile, Benny was nowhere to be found. Al never told Jordan that he'd will them the business as partners, so Jordan never knew when or why he'd made that decision, which had made it sting more.

Kiki told them all the story about Benny coming to the café where she worked. He played ragtime music on the piano, which all the young employees hated. But he impressed them when he played old pop songs—Mariah Carey or Sheryl Crow. And he impressed Kiki when he began inserting her name into the lyrics. The staff, apparently, ate that up. Everyone enjoys being audience to a courtship.

"Is Kiki your real name?" Jordan said. He hadn't spoken in a long time. They all turned to him as if he'd just appeared.

His mother frowned into her fruit wine.

"Yes and no," Kiki said, trying to be patient, nibbling on her pointer finger. "My parents named me Katherine, but my sister couldn't pronounce it. She called me Kiki. And it stuck."

"I didn't know that," Benny said, his eyebrows raised, mouth drawn in a smirk. His face said, I want to know everything.

"So," Kiki said, straightening up, and turning her big, intelligent eyes on Jordan. "You took these oysters out of the bayou today?"

"Yesterday, from Bay Courant," Jordan said. "Hoa and Linh shucked them today. Some restaurants like to buy them shucked."

She nodded as if she knew what this meant. She was interesting to look at, but seemed unable to keep judgments from sweeping over her face. He imagined his brother felt proud walking around New Orleans with his tall, sharp girlfriend.

"You must be worried about the oil spill," Kiki said, in her clean northern accent. He'd heard this accent all his life on television. "After the explosion on that rig."

"I'm not worried," Jordan said evenly.

Her eyes widened briefly with surprise, and then she nodded again.

"Those poor men!" May put her napkin on her plate. "Almost all of them with children."

"We see a spill every year," Jordan said. "Oil companies are always going to cut corners. Always have. Gulf's been oiled since they found it."

"'It'?" Kiki said.

"Oil in Louisiana."

"It's true," May said. "Oil spills happen all the time. You can't pay them much mind."

Kiki fixed her attention on Jordan.

"It could be a huge spill, though," Kiki said.

"Can't afford to worry," Jordan said, cutting her off. "As a farmer, my job is a lot of wait-and-see."

"But why make excuses for the oil industry," Benny said, "when they killed the coast? Everyone around here used to be a fisherman. Now it's all oil. They own state politicians."

"I know that," Jordan said. "I wasn't defending them. I'm just saying I've seen oil spills before."

"And it happened so far away, dear," May said. "It won't affect us."

"You can't know that," Benny said gently.

"Why do you want this to be so bad?" Jordan asked.

"I don't," Benny said. "I just feel like you're not acknowledging how bad it could be."

"The Coast Guard is saying that most of the oil burned up in the fireball on top of that oil rig."

Benny seemed unmoved. "Kiki and me are planning a vigil for the men who died in the explosion."

This didn't make sense to Jordan. Benny wasn't religious.

"You're planning a religious service for the offshore oil men?"

"Not religious." Benny set a spoon on his plate. "It's a protest, but we're going to honor the dead."

"What are you protesting?" Jordan asked.

"Corporate negligence," Benny said. "That cost workers' lives."

May's chair raked the floor and they turned toward her. She seemed to be willing them all to be quiet. She circled the table, collecting plates. Kiki offered up her plate without making a gesture toward helping May clear the table. Jordan clocked disapproval in the humming sound his mother made.

"Did you hear that Hoa's daughter is at Stanford Law now?" Benny said, trying to settle the tension. "Annie at Stanford Law. She was in high school when I last saw her."

May clanked the pile of dishes in the sink.

"Hoa never fails to mention it," she said, and then, regaining her composure, "Who wants key lime?"

Benny belched loudly, patting his stomach. "After a minute."

To Jordan's surprise, Kiki didn't bat an eye.

"If you couldn't oyster, would you miss it?" Kiki asked.

"It's a point of pride in this family," May said. She had a beautiful key lime pie in her hands, with whipped meringue on top. The tufts of it were toasted. "Al was the most well-known oysterman in

Louisiana. He was always in the newspaper if there was an oyster story. People always wanted to talk to him."

"I have the most beautiful office in the world," Jordan said, and regretted it immediately. It sounded phony, and he didn't like Kiki smiling at him the way she was, disbelieving.

"Curious."

"Jordan doesn't have friends," Benny explained.

Kiki seemed unsurprised.

"I work seven days a week," he said. "I sleep five hours a night to run a business that pays your rent."

Kiki looked at Benny. She hadn't known this.

Benny shrugged. "Nobody asked me what I wanted."

"Dad took care of you, but, hey, if you don't want your share, let's just forget it."

"Nobody made you stay home and be a good boy," Benny said. "You did that to yourself."

"Boys, stop," May said, her motherly voice activated. "Kiki's here."

She set the key lime pie at the head of the table and flipped her head to dislodge a curl of blond hair that had gotten stuck in her lipstick.

Benny was looking at his mother and seemed to be thinking of something else. "He wasn't a saint," Benny said.

"Your father?" May said dreamily.

"Don't talk about him." Jordan pushed himself up.

Kiki gasped. Her hand jumped to Benny's arm.

"Don't you talk about him," Jordan said. He was pointing at Benny. "You have no right."

"Good lord," Kiki said. She seemed to be afraid of him.

Outside, Jordan's dog, Cypress, was barking, wanting to be let in the office before the storm.

Benny laughed and stood up too. "All right, chief. I won't." He stuck out his hand toward Jordan.

"What?" Jordan's chest was blocked, that familiar tightening, and he wanted to thump it.

"What?" Benny said, mocking him. "Shake my hand, for fuck's sake."

"Why?"

"Let's be done with it. We'll talk about it later."

"Go on," May said.

Jordan reluctantly took Benny's hand and shook it.

"Oh, come on," Benny said, gripping tighter. "Shake like you mean it."

Jordan gripped back and gave his brother's hand a firm yank.

Benny then put a hand on Kiki's back and announced that he was going out for a smoke. Kiki stood wordlessly and joined him. She glanced apologetically in May's direction as she tucked her chair back in. May slung a dish towel over her shoulder and watched them go. She looked utterly defeated. Jordan felt no responsibility at all for her unhappiness. She was most to blame for Benny's arrogance. In order not to tell her this out loud, he sank himself into the couch and turned on the news. The survivors of the explosion had returned from offshore and were now just thirty minutes down the road at Port Fourchon. He watched a tearful reunion of a soot-smudged man and his pajama-clad daughters. Then they showed footage of the burning rig again, which burned so furiously that looking at it must have felt like looking at the sun.

His mother smashed around in the kitchen behind him.

"Jordan, *please*," she said, and he turned it off.

→ Four ←

Not long after Benny and Kiki went outside to smoke, Jordan stood from the couch and walked into the evening after them. On the phone, Byrdie had assured him that he was within his rights to stop paying Benny. There were no stipulations in his father's succession plan that required Jordan to pay his brother a salary if he wasn't working. And especially not with the meager profit he'd been making. Jordan heard the thunder churn in the distance, and overhead he saw gray steamroller clouds whipping up from the wide-open Gulf. The spring sun cooked the water's surface and sent the offshore storms to the coast. A lightning bolt zippered across the sky.

He needed a cigarette too, after that dinner and before he asked Benny to speak in private. So Jordan went to the bayou-facing house, which was the business office. Through the front windows, he could see Benny on the dock by his oyster boat. Benny had refused to set foot on a boat since he was fourteen, but at that moment he was showing off to his girlfriend.

Just hours before, Jordan had been in the office with Manuel and his busted hand, while Alejandro and Babies unloaded the day's oyster sacks. Manuel scanned the pictures on the walls, mountains of oysters from good harvest years and framed newspaper clippings about his father. "I wonder what childhood sin I'm paying for," Manuel had said. "An accident at the beginning of the season." His eyes widened when Jordan slid the stack of bills toward him. It was more than he'd expected to receive. Jordan knew little about Manuel, only that there was a family in San Salvador. Manuel did not look him in the eyes when he took the money. But that's what a gift of money did to people—embarrassed them into resentment.

Jordan stepped out on the front porch of the office to light his cigarette. Benny and Kiki were engrossed in discussion and did not notice him. The wind had just picked up, suctioning Kiki's dress even tighter around her backside and belling it in front of her like a sail filling up. Kiki was animated, her voice was raised, and she spoke with her burning cigarette in her hand. He waved to get their attention, but they didn't notice. Benny shredded seed husks from the tall unmown grass as he listened. She took another drag on the cigarette, which on closer inspection did not look like a cigarette at all, but a joint. A cloud of smoke issued from her mouth.

A truck trundled by on the road between him and the couple. Benny reached for her joint, and she yanked it out of his reach, smiling. Then they were latched on to each other, Benny looking like a little boy hooked onto a big, beautiful woman—his hands moving up and down her backside like kneading dough. Kiki held the burning joint aloft over Benny's shoulder. He'd never seen such fervent public kissing. And right on the side of the road, as if daring people to watch. He hadn't handled anyone like that in years, maybe not since high school. Jealousy whipped through him.

When Jordan hollered to them, they disentangled and looked at him—completely unabashed—as if he were brazen for interrupting.

"Looks like a storm," Jordan yelled, pointing at the sky.

They looked up and then back at him.

"I need a word with you, Benny."

When they crossed the street toward him, they held hands, pausing momentarily as Kiki ground the joint under her bootheel.

Jordan stopped Kiki from following them into the office. "It's family business," he said.

"I see," she said. "I'll make myself scarce, then."

"Would you mind checking on Mom?" Benny said to her, with some remorse in his voice. He pressed his cheek on the doorframe, halfway in the room. "And if I don't come back, tell Mom I love her."

Kiki skipped toward the main house, calling back, "You think I'm on your side, huh? I'm about to help Jordan toss you in the bayou."

Benny stepped into the office with a smile on his face and surveyed the room.

"Sofa's new," he said. "I guess it'd have to be, after Katrina. But the decorations are all the same. You put everything up just like it was."

This didn't sound to Jordan like a compliment. Benny walked from picture to picture around the room, as Manuel had hours before. Oversized photos of all three generations of Pearce oystermen standing astride mountainous oyster harvests. In this office, their father had received potential buyers. They used to sit at the conference table and toss oyster shells with increasing inaccuracy onto a pile that mounted toward the ceiling light.

Jordan looked around the room. Why would he want it to look any different? "Our customers like to know that things stay the same."

"Chief," Benny said, preempting him, "I know it's probably been hard for you here. Mom told me you had a breakup last year. That you were engaged and everything."

"Yeah, it's been hard," Jordan said. "We're down to fishing with only one boat when we used to run three. As you know."

Benny threw himself onto the couch and hooked his legs over the arm of the sofa. "And Mom seems good. Better now."

"She's fine, but she's more forgetful lately. Misplacing things, forgetting names, conversations we've had."

This caught Benny's attention. "I haven't noticed that. She's too young for anything to be serious." He'd plucked a framed photo of their father from the side table. Al in his pageboy cap, big cigar in his teeth, crooked grin. "That stupid hat," Benny said. "You know, Dad used to say, 'You're not dressed unless you're wearing a hat.'"

Jordan did not remember his father saying such a thing.

"He wore that hat every fucking day. It irked me. I told him so. I was being a shit. To his credit, he said, 'I'm not making you wear it.' This was on the way to New Orleans. He was driving me to art class, but the only reason he drove me was because he wanted to see his girlfriend. She was a singer. Did you ever meet her?"

"No," he said. "I didn't."

"A blues singer. Really corny stuff. They'd act like I was an idiot and didn't know."

"You never mentioned it."

"You were in college, or maybe not yet. I don't know. We never talked anyway."

That was true enough. They'd never talked much when they were teenagers. Jordan could remember a time when Benny, age five or six, dogged Jordan and his friends wherever they went. Even when Jordan was cruel—throwing a Coke can at him for the amusement of his friends—Benny wouldn't go away. But as a teenager Benny became sullen, and lost interest in following Jordan. They'd been embarrassed around each other, if not outright antagonistic.

"It's like you all remember a totally different person than me. The way she talks about Al and everything. It's a fantasy. It makes me crazy—as if she didn't know he was a cad."

"She didn't know."

"Of course she knew."

"She didn't."

Benny turned his head to face Jordan. He had been addressing the ceiling. His eyes were big and dreamy. "Maybe I'll tell her."

"You won't."

The threat in his voice was clear to both of them.

"You're right," Benny said, nonplussed. "I won't. No point in it."

"Are you stoned?"

"Not really."

"You shouldn't have—" Jordan sighed. "Well, whatever. Do what you want. This isn't New Orleans."

"I know this isn't New Orleans," Benny said, in that mocking way he'd developed over the years.

Outside, a crack of thunder. Benny pushed himself up to peer out the window. No rain yet, his face said, and then he sank back down onto the couch.

"Benny," Jordan said. "I'm hardly making a profit. I can't pay your salary anymore."

"You can't cut me out." Benny sounded bored. "It was in Al's will."

So he knew, then, or had expected, what Jordan would say.

"I've been over it with the family lawyer. I have no obligation to make pro rata distributions—to pay you. I've been underpaying myself for years. I can't figure why except that Dad wanted it that way."

"This is my inheritance we're talking about," Benny said. "I have just as much a right to it as you."

As the seriousness of Jordan's announcement dawned on him, Benny swung his legs to the floor. It wasn't an inheritance; it was a business. Jordan went on. "Besides, it's not good for you. Look at you." Jordan's hand swept the air, inviting Benny to look at himself. "You look terrible. What are you doing with your life?"

"Never mind how I look," Benny said. "I have my rights. It's in the will."

"You never came back to work, Benny," Jordan said. "Do you want to come back to work?"

"And live here?" Benny scoffed. "Even Dad knew I hated it here."

Jordan shrugged. There were things he could have told Benny about their father, but Benny wouldn't listen. He never did.

"You can't just decide to cut me out," Benny said. "I'll get a lawyer."

"That's fine," Jordan said. He was pretty sure things would work out in his favor. Byrdie explained it to him over the phone. He'd paid Benny for five years in his father's memory. He'd been charitable, but charity was wasted on Benny.

"I know you resent sharing the profits, but I never asked to inherit the business with you." Benny stood up and started pacing the room. His voice went higher in pitch. "Am I supposed to want this for my life? In this shitty town?"

The room seemed smaller and hotter around Benny as he paced. His pettiness came as a relief to Jordan. It was easier than he'd thought. He could have done it years ago. But first he needed to see how low Benny would get. His shirt so threadbare that a strong wind might rip it off his body. That knock-kneed saunter of his. He'd fashioned himself into a tough guy.

Benny's eyes shot around the office. "This place is a fucking mausoleum," he said, and tore out the back door.

Inside the house, May was brewing decaf coffee and gleefully assumed that the approaching storm was a hand dealt in her favor. She found that Kiki had warmed to her in the interim. It was like a different person had flounced in the door. "Let's have some pie!" Kiki said, laughing heartily to herself. They ended up on the couch together, cupping mugs of coffee. Kiki sidled up so close that her thigh touched May's, and she turned to face her the way schoolgirls do. Here was the long-lost good sport May had dreamed up for Benny. Kiki gushed over the pink ibis she'd seen, and the Spanish moss draped from the limbs of imposing cypress trees. She ran her hand through her braids as she talked, flipping them to one side or the other every few moments, and May was enchanted.

"Benny told me about the bayou," Kiki said, "but he didn't tell me it was like this. I've never seen a landscape like it. But then, he didn't tell me he owned the oyster farm either." She smiled conspiratorially at May over her coffee mug, and May honestly didn't know what to make of this statement, or why Benny hadn't mentioned the farm. Perhaps Kiki thought she could explain Benny's behavior, but she couldn't. Despite talking to Benny often, most of his life was a mystery to her. Kiki sipped her coffee and changed the subject. "Anyway, it's beautiful out here."

"I didn't think so at first," May said. "I didn't want to move to Golden Vale when I met Al. To me, the whole world was in Alabama. But saying yes to Al was saying yes to here." But she was quick to add: "It is beautiful, like you say."

"How did you meet Al?" she asked. She had her fist propped under her chin, and looked like a sleepy child, but something about Kiki's eyes struck May as funny. They seemed unfocused.

"At a fundraiser in Mobile," May said. "Al was in town on business, and I was always invited to fundraisers back then. Like I was an attraction."

"An attraction?"

"It was the title," May said. "Miss University of Alabama."

"That's right," Kiki said. "Benny said that. I'd hate it, feeling like an attraction."

"I didn't mind. I think I liked the attention."

Kiki nodded, as though she understood, the sweetheart, and she may have. Just look at how she'd come dressed. May felt like grabbing her hand.

Then Benny threw the door open so it slapped the end table. He announced that they were leaving. He was sorry, but they couldn't stay any longer. He seemed agitated and was looking around like he'd lost something. What'd we bring? he seemed to be asking.

Jordan walked in behind, one hand in his pocket, untroubled.

"Don't be ridiculous," May said, confident now in the weather and Kiki's warmth. "The skies are about to open."

Benny couldn't be dissuaded. All her married life, she'd failed to dissuade her husband from an idea once he'd set upon it. Al became stone and was fond of saying she was too sensitive. An empty accusation, she retorted in private, considering all there was in the world to be sensitive about. Now here was Benny, like Al, made of stone.

"But Kiki looks so tired," she said.

"They're high," Jordan said, and when May did not understand what this meant. "They were smoking marijuana by the boats."

May regarded Kiki again, but this time like someone she'd never seen before. The funny eyes, of course. Kiki avoided looking at her straight-on. She couldn't understand why they would elect to smoke marijuana there and then. It seemed downright perverse. There are things a mother would rather not know.

"He exaggerates," Benny said. "Don't listen to him."

He sat on the arm of the sofa next to her. "Mom, I love you. I miss you. I'll come back again soon. You look like you're doing so much better, and I'm proud of you, but we've got to get out of here. Kiki has work in the morning. Come give us a hug."

"What's going on?" she said. Her Alabama accent came out.

"The storm's coming now. Kiki, get your things. Let's go."

It happened so quickly that May did not have time to get angry. She rushed a bag of Tupperware to the car. Kiki hugged her warmly, but May smelled the nutty kick of marijuana in her hair, and she was the one who stiffened. Jordan hadn't come out to wave goodbye. The car sounded awful starting up, as if it would never turn over. Then they were backing away, waving. Then they were gone.

The lights were on in all the houses, and the amber lamplight in her own house was tinged with blue from the TV that Jordan had turned back on. Again, the news and the oil spill. The frogs singing made her feel tender. A stray cat searched the grass for lizards. The sight of her own bronze car saddened her. They would not be moving into Mee-maw's house. She could have thrown a brick at it then—the sight of it was so despairing—with the new spring-green tendrils of the cat's-claw vine climbing up one wall. If she let the vines have it, they'd take the house in a few years—nature reaching up from the ground, refusing the brief designs man puts on it. Nothing steadfast on this earth. It was Jordan's fault, of course. He'd said something to Benny. She could smell the electricity in the air before the storm. All she had wanted was for everything to be entirely different.

→ Five ←

The marijuana left Benny with a dreamy fatigue, and as they thrilled along the highway after his escape from Golden Vale, he hoped that they would not arrive at the subject of his salary at the oyster company. He tried to steer her away from it—waxing about the landscape, the refineries, the state's politics. New Orleans was less than two hours away and yet an entirely different world from his hometown. Kiki said that the brackish marsh reached out from the highway like a golden green savanna. Driving U.S. 90 past herds of pumpjacks plunging the ground for oil, it was obvious that Louisiana was a land rich in mineral resources—a land that made a minority of people very rich. Benny was proud of this little turn-of-phrase in his narration to Kiki.

"Did you see the DON'T TREAD ON ME sticker on his truck?" Kiki said.

"Don't get me started," Benny said, hoping to avoid the subject of his brother. "I'm the worst version of myself when I'm there. Every time I go back I think it will feel different, and then it's the same. I'm twelve years old again."

"Dinner was tense."

"I'm glad we went," he lied. "I'm glad I introduced you to Mom."

The rusting oil derricks looked like quaint antiques next to the fortresses of refineries, which were so guarded and fenced and surveilled, they might as well have been military bases. The burning gas flares roared up like torches in the purple light. Kiki had never seen the "Deep South." She was drinking it up with a kind of rapt disapproval.

"It's so monstrous, it's almost beautiful," she said.

She was right. The oil refineries shone with lights, orange and white and blinking red, and it hurt him a little, this beauty. Benny told her, "When I was a kid driving around with my dad, I thought the refineries along the highway were New Orleans—all lit up and angular just like you see city skylines on TV. I just assumed that was what the city looked like in person."

"That's so fucked up," Kiki said, but she thought it was delicious.

Louisiana was one of the only subjects about which he knew more than Kiki, so he answered her questions in as much detail as he could muster, and he made up only a little bit where his knowledge was patchy. Exposure to toxic chemicals along Louisiana's industrial corridor was among the highest in the whole country. The cancer rates were so high that the refinery towns along the Mississippi River earned the title Cancer Alley, and disproportionately affected African Americans, who'd first settled along the river after the Civil War.

Kiki pointed to a billboard advertisement for offshore oil work. A picture of above-average-looking men and women smiling in their hard hats at a sun setting behind an offshore oil rig. JOIN THE WINNING TEAM, the billboard said.

"You don't need a billboard to see who's winning around here," Kiki said.

Benny forced out a laugh. Normally he was poised to dump on Louisiana. That's what she wanted him to do—demonstrate that he was hip to the forces at work there. Environmental racism, gender inequality, worker exploitation. All important, without a doubt. It was fine for him to disparage Louisiana, but when she did it, he couldn't help but feel that old seize of defensiveness.

Benny's own father used to chew washed-up tar balls on Gulf beaches as a kid like it was gum, or so he said. His father's cousins were in "the industry," as if the oil industry were the only industry that existed, though one-third of the nation's seafood came from Gulf waters and Louisiana estuaries. Commercial fishing was big, yet also a piddling business next to the oil interests doling out princely campaign contributions to local politicians. In any case, "plenty of good folks"—to use his mother's phrase—worked in the oil industry, and Benny knew this to be true enough. It was honest work that was bringing the planet to its knees.

Before Kiki, he'd never met anyone so lustily interested in knowing things. She acquired knowledge at a rate that spelled disaster for her sustained interest in him, especially given the number of admirers she had at the anarchist library—where they spent considerable amounts of time—who thought she was a goddess and that he was a joke. He'd tried to make himself read what they were reading—Emma Goldman's biography, a history of the Wobblies, *Assata*—but he couldn't open those books without a vengeful sleepiness befalling him.

"Here she comes," said Benny when the skies belched open and the storm rolled over them. The highway flooded within fifteen minutes. Benny explained that they were, at that moment, just a couple of feet above sea level and that the ground was slowly sinking.

"How slowly?" Kiki asked, surveying the rising water with increasing alarm.

"A quarter-inch a year or something. Slowly."

A couple eighteen-wheelers whipped by them and a tidal wave of water slapped the windshield. The lone working windshield wiper groaned with exertion. Kiki asked him to pull over, but he ignored her. The station wagon slid through the water like a boat. They felt the water slushing below the floorboards. The wind harassed the trees all around them, so the view on all sides was a fluid-green blur. Kiki demanded again that he pull over.

Benny told her that the road was higher up than the shoulder. It'd be like driving into a lake. The windshield wiper groaned back and forth but did little to improve visibility. She gripped the door of the Volvo so tightly he saw her bicep awaken.

"I can't swim," she said.

He tapped her thigh in reassurance. He asked her to roll a cigarette for him.

"No," she said. "You can't smoke with the windows closed. And the road . . ."

"It's for later," he said.

"I don't like liars," she said.

He knew nothing was in front of them, and that was all the knowledge he needed.

"Roll the cigarette," he said. "It'll distract you."

"You said you had an inheritance."

"I do have an inheritance."

"Your brother pays you. You said your brother was an oyster farmer. You never said you were the co-owner."

"My father left me half of the business. It was my inheritance, and now my brother is trying to cut me out. I'm going to have to sue my own brother."

"But why wouldn't you say that in the first place?"

"We don't get on."

"But why?"

"You met him, didn't you?" he said. "Would you get on with him?"

"I don't like liars," she said again. A wave of rain slapped the windshield. "Pull over, Benny."

He could tell where the road was because the rain smacked the pavement differently than it did in the median.

"I'm telling you we'll get stuck."

She begged him.

"Fine, let's get stuck, then." He steered off the road onto the shoulder, which was as soft as coffee grounds. They sat in the car, breathing heavily. A thunder crack and a brief light turned on in the distance. Kiki rolled the cigarette to have something to do with her hands. He ventured that they should not have gone to Golden Vale.

Until now, he'd been so preoccupied with what Kiki was thinking that he hadn't had time to consider what he'd do if Jordan could stop paying him. Jordan acted as though Benny's taking the money was an insult to his father, when in fact it was the other way around. Al passing on half of an oyster business knowing that Benny had no interest in oyster farming seemed, to him, one last act of disapproval of his life—his "fairy son." Al had actually said this, not to his face, but Benny overheard him saying it to friends at a crawfish boil. Benny felt profoundly misunderstood by his father—not that his father had been wrong about his sexuality. He'd had sex with several men over the years. But it seemed to hurt his father deeply that the parts of himself he liked most, he didn't see in Benny. His father, who'd lost a finger to an infected cut from a catfish wound and talked endlessly of storms he'd weathered. Al could have just given him some money and been done with it.

Benny had dug his own grave by bringing Kiki to Golden Vale. After the news of the explosion three days ago, everyone in Kiki's crowd was suddenly curious about the Gulf Coast, about the fisheries, and no one more than her. The month before, all they'd talked about was the defunding of the public school system. Then it was public housing. Now it was the Gulf Coast.

Kiki lit her cigarette with the car lighter. She exhaled, and the cabin filled with smoke. "My parents think I'm sabotaging my future here," she said, rolling down the window.

"And what do you think?"

"I just don't know what to do with myself. How could I? I don't know anything about this country. And, as a Black woman, understanding the South politically is important. Take your brother, for example. I've never had dinner with a Tea Partier before tonight."

"I'm glad it was educational for you," he said.

"That's not why I wanted to meet your family," she said. "But, like, big picture, I don't see how I'll make a difference if I'm sheltered in a university for another three years. They don't value community organizing. They don't see it as learning. The only learning they want for me is the kind that comes with a diploma and an internship."

She offered her cigarette to him, scissored between two fingers, and he took it. He cracked his window and the storm leaned into the car, wetting the side of his face. Cool air whipped through the cabin. Kiki eyed him with an interest that unnerved him, as if his family had made him more interesting to her for anthropological reasons. He was nothing like the boys she'd gone to school with, she'd said.

She leaned in and licked his cheek, long and slow, and when she pulled back, she was smiling. He could tell she felt triumphantly superior to him, and that turned her on. Then she gave him a mischievous look, and she unfastened her seat belt.

They had sex in the backseat as the worst of the storm raged over them, and then they smoked cigarettes with the windows cracked, letting the water drip inside the car.

Kiki knew her life had taken an unexpected turn, and maybe she was rebelling, as her mother had alleged when she'd missed deadlines for the master's in public policy program in the fall. She'd already been out of college for two years, and when she described Benny to her mother—a tattooed thirty-year-old white musician who stocked the shelves of a grocery store part-time—her mother had said, "Baby, are you mad at us about something?" And then later she said, "Well, you never seem to keep them around long anyway." This irritated Kiki. She cut the phone call short. Benny had delighted her for five months. He wore his intellect lightly, was content to play the buffoon, and she admired this, even though she knew the same trait would not be rewarded in a woman.

Benny held her wet back to his chest, arms wrapped around her waist. He rarely had sex sober before Kiki. He'd always engaged in the act at a distance from himself, with his faculties bludgeoned, and he often finished with some self-loathing. The last person, before Kiki, had been an accordion player, Jonathon, from a traveling band, who was so sharp and caustic onstage, and then so open and giving in bed. Benny had left in a hurry after they'd finished. Jonathon's wounded expression had only deepened Benny's anger at himself. What a relief, then, to hold Kiki's back to his chest—this bighearted, perfect physical specimen—and not wish to be anywhere else. The happiness was so intoxicating that he could do nothing but fear the day it would end.

The lovemaking had cleared the air, and they were able to circle back to Kiki's concerns about Benny's "obvious inclination for deception."

"There are lies by omission," she said. "And that's just as troubling as—"

"You already said that," he said. "Now you know all my secrets.

Except it's all beside the point because Jordan is cutting off my salary, or trying to."

"The way he narced on us to your mother!" she said. "I couldn't believe it."

"He's just lonely, and he takes it out on everyone."

"And the way they interact," Kiki said. "It's like they're symbolically a couple."

"Don't talk like that," he said. "Please. I can't think about it."

She reached up and stroked his unshaven chin.

"I'm just glad nobody said anything fucked up to you." And he was. Jordan easily might have said something offensive. Not blatantly racist—he wasn't a goon—but something ignorant.

Kiki said again that she was glad she'd met his family.

He drove back with mud itching his ankles because he had to get out and push. Kiki asked him to drive much slower than he needed to on the flooded highway, and it took an additional hour to make it back to New Orleans. As he drove, they cooked up plans about the vigil for the men who'd died in the oil rig explosion. After the vigil, they'd lead a demonstration, and they'd need some big props for dramatic effect. Should there be a giant prop pelican? A pelican dipped in oil? Maybe they'd have time to papier-mâché a giant seabird if they started tomorrow morning. It would be good for the cause to make it into the newspaper.

✦ Six ✦

The week after Benny's visit, May was still ignoring the calls on the house phone. It was Lucille, of course. They typically spoke every other day, but May had made a fuss about Benny coming to dinner, and now she was too embarrassed to talk about it. She'd decided to finish the work that Benny's visit had begun. She remembered Kiki's eyes surveying the living room and her amusement in the décor. All of it tacky, dated. She didn't know what her life was supposed to look like now that she was alone, but she no longer wanted all the memorabilia looming over her. Boxes were strewn all around the house, their box-mouths open and half-filled with things she'd donate to charity.

Finally, Lucille let herself in through the kitchen door. "What's going on now?"

"It's all these silly tchotchkes," May said. "I'm done with them!"

Lucille helped herself to tea in the kitchen. She was a few years older than May, with penetrating eyes and tawny brown skin. She had one gold tooth, a canine, that lent a mischievous flash to her smile, and suited her. Lucille sat on the couch, and a box slid closer to her. She peered in—Al's fishing trophies. She would wait until May was ready to tell her what had happened.

In the meantime, they spoke about the traffic. A week had gone by since the explosion, and May tried to ignore it, weary as she was of disasters—man-made or natural—but she couldn't ignore the traffic. In the week since, the state route through Golden Vale clotted with out-of-town cars headed south. News reports said this wasn't a typical "spill" from a tanker. It was an open oil gusher at the seafloor from the drilling pipe that had been connecting the wellhead to the floating oil rig. BP admitted the well gushed as much as a thousand barrels of oil a day. An oil spill cleanup center was down the road at Port Fourchon, which meant that all the traffic had to travel through little Golden Vale to get there. Faces of strange men bobbed in the aisles of the grocery store, and for the first time she could remember, there was a wait for checkout. Trucks carrying strange, elaborate equipment roared by with alarming frequency. Lucille's son, Roland, was a deputy sheriff, and he'd met his monthly quota of speeding tickets within just five days. Now, Lucille said, beaming, Roland was on his way to setting a department record.

"And did you hear the president is coming?" said Lucille.

"Which president?"

"*The* president," Lucille said. "Obama!"

"Oh lord," May said, not wanting to get into it. Lucille's besotted smile telegraphed everything. She loved Obama. His official portrait loomed over her kitchen table. She had filled her yard with Obama signs during the election, which had made her unpopular in the neighborhood. She used to be a republican like the rest of her neighbors. May suspected that Lucille was more attracted to the man than to his politics.

"What a circus," May said, hoping to elude further discussion of the topic.

"How is Benny?" Lucille asked, finally.

May issued rote pleasantries about the dinner, saying how nice it was to have Benny back at her table, while avoiding Lucille's gaze. When Lucille asked about the girlfriend, May began with the positive: "She's a very smart girl—she went to a fancy school up North—and pretty too. Tall, tall, tall. And she's Black. Benny didn't mention that at all. I don't know why. He only talked about how smart she was."

Lucille cocked an eyebrow at that, which May didn't like.

"But she's from the North," May went on. "You know how they can be."

Lucille made a knowing hum.

"On the upside, she seemed very much concerned with the plight of others. That's a nice quality. She mentors boys who've been to juvenile detention."

"So, what's the problem, then?" Lucille said, stretching her legs on the coffee table.

"Well, she dressed strangely," May said. "As if she was purposely trying to degrade her good looks. Her dress was just torn to shreds." May was deciding whether to mention the marijuana. She knew Lucille would disapprove. "And—"

"Shreds?" Lucille asked.

"Shreds," May said. "And the boys argued at dinner. I can't understand why they never get along."

"What was the fight over?" Lucille didn't seem surprised.

"It wasn't a fight." May was ready to deny everything. "It's just—Jordan is so irritable. He was goading Benny from the start."

Lucille didn't believe her. May had always been soft on Benny, and people do not worship what they can rely on. She knew this to be true enough in her own life. "You're getting rid of Al's trophies?"

Trophies were only a thing worth keeping for a few years, May contended. And then she confided that she'd seen the way Benny's girlfriend looked around the house, with an expression that made May feel self-conscious. May wanted to have a house that made people feel rich when they were in it. At this, Lucille studied her short nails, her lips pursed.

"Doesn't everybody?" Lucille said. "So, remind me what you're doing for the shower?"

"Shower," May said, surprised. She hadn't thought of that yet, but maybe she ought to. "Well, I've always wanted a walk-in."

Lucille laughed, her gold tooth glinting in the light. "Not your shower, Cami's shower. You said cupcakes and then I don't remember what else."

"Oh, of course!" May chuckled, searching the carpet for the answer. She hadn't even bought a gift. It would be Roland's third child—and a surprise one. Not only had she forgotten about it, but she also couldn't remember what she'd agreed to bring. Lucille had noticed her little lapses, and May couldn't stand to give her friend more reason for concern.

"Ice?" she guessed.

"Roland's getting ice," Lucille said.

"Deviled eggs," May said.

"Good," Lucille said.

Then Lucille got a phone call from the elementary school because her eldest grandson had clocked another kid during a kickball game, and she had to go pick him up. Lucille was huffy with the secretary. "He doesn't hit," she said. May waved to Lucille from the driveway, consumed with jealousy. Ten years before, May would not have guessed she'd be jealous of Lucille, who lived alone after Earl had left her for a young teacher at the kids' school, which was embarrassing for everybody. Earl had looked so idiotic with the young woman that May could not understand how he did not die of shame—but Lucille's children had all stayed close to her, and they always remembered her birthday, and they always threw her a

party. And she got to see her grandchildren all the time. Lucille
even spent weekends in New Orleans with a smartly dressed
Moroccan man she met online who promised to take her to
Europe. May was supposed to be the one with the enviable family.
And now her sons couldn't have a peaceable meal.

The light was changing in the afternoon. May poured two fingers
of rum into her tea, and she felt the light changing in her body.
She sat down on the overstuffed leather couch that the men had
ruined with their sweat and peered again into the box of Al's
effects—fishing trophies, yes, but also a watercolor painting of a
cypress tree he did in grade school, which was surprisingly com-
petent for a young person. It had lived on the living room wall all
their married life; Al was more sentimental than his bravado suggested. No one would want it now, but she couldn't throw it away.
Why should it be her fate to manage the museum of Al?

The rum had gone to work, and she thought of the dwindling
supply of Xanax in her medicine cabinet. Dr. Jones had prescribed
them after the funeral. She couldn't sleep, and often woke clutching at her chest. There didn't seem to be enough air in the room.
She thought of mammals that died soon after their partners. But
there was nothing wrong with her heart, the doctor said. It was
panic she felt. And the pills helped. She'd come to rely on that
dissolving calm in her afternoon. Dr. Jones had kept refilling her
prescription, and then, during her last checkup, told her that he
was retiring. When she asked about her Xanax refills, Dr. Jones
looked at her evenly. He'd been their family doctor for twenty
years, but she felt pinned by his gaze in that moment, as if he knew
just how much she liked those pills.

"May," he said. "It's been four years. It's more for short-term
treatment. I wonder if we should find someone for you to talk to."

"About the prescription?" she asked.

"I was thinking of a therapist." It embarrassed him to say this. She could tell. "If you're still having symptoms."

"Oh," she said. "But I feel fine now!"

When he retired, she had three refills left. She'd rather die than ask another doctor for a prescription. She did wonder about long-term effects of the drug. She felt sometimes, quite pleasantly, that she was gliding through her afternoons like they were long, idle dreams.

The front doorbell rang, which meant it was a stranger. It was someone she hadn't seen in years—a big man in a Hawaiian shirt with a kind, dopey smile. Dr. Merritt, the oyster biologist.

"Doc," she said. Her first impulse was to think that he was bringing her bad news, but she couldn't imagine what. She hadn't seen the man since Al's funeral. He'd moved out of the area. May clutched the door. "Is everything all right?"

"Hello, Mrs. Pearce," he said. "It's strange, my coming by like this, but I passed your sign, and I thought, Why not?"

"Why not stop?" she offered.

"Why not check up on my old friend," he said.

Doc had been a friend to Al, but not to May. She thought she might have to tell him that Al was dead, but Doc knew this. He'd seen Al's body in the casket.

"Well, what a surprise!" she said. "Come in! I wasn't expecting anyone. The house is a mess. I'm doing some life cleaning."

She meant to say spring cleaning, but it came out wrong. He followed her into the living room, past the boxes.

"Life cleaning, huh? I could use a little bit of that myself."

Doc had put on weight, was grayer than the last time she'd seen him. But the Hawaiian shirt had always been a part of his wardrobe. His being in the house made her feel as though Al might flush the toilet and emerge in the hallway at any second.

"It's nice to see you, May," he said.

She felt more studied than she had in a long time. She hoped he could not tell she'd been drinking in the afternoon.

"Do you want some tea?" She turned to go get him some whether he wanted it or not.

"That's fine. I'm going to sit on your couch," he announced.

"I'm still so surprised to see you," she said. "What brought you to town?"

"I'm here because of the spill. I'm one of the local environmental advisers to BP. They just want a local biologist in the room for appearances. They don't want to listen to me. They don't want me to talk at all."

"Is the spill as bad as they're saying?"

"It's worse!" Doc said, strangely upbeat. "They're saying it's only a thousand barrels a day spilling, but it's much more than that." He sipped his tea and then grinned at her. "There's a reason they call it 'Mother Earth' and a 'man-made disaster.' Men," he said, shaking his head, "we're a plague."

May had no response. Was this comment out of character? She only remembered him as jovial.

"My ex-wife would agree, wouldn't you?"

May wrung the tea glass in her hand. "A plague? I don't think I'd say a plague."

So he got a divorce, May thought. It must have happened in the years since she'd known him. In the old days, she recalled that he was fond of saying, "I tell people I've been with my wife all these years because of oysters"—then he would give the listener a meaningful look—"and she says it's because I'm at the oyster hatchery five days a week." Then he'd laugh raucously. His wife lived upstate, which always struck May as strange. He worked in Grand Isle, and on the way back Doc would stop by and drink with

Al. More than once, he slept in the office bedroom because he'd gotten too drunk.

Doc went on: "I nearly killed some fool in the Coast Guard. I said to him: You're letting this oil company spray that chemical dispersant, and you're delivering that oil right into the ecosystem. It's toxic. They're dumping it by the boatload, by the planeload. But those stooges don't want me to talk. I'm a tool, and I did not get a PhD in order to be a tool for a gas company."

May made a mental note: look up *dispersant*. She knew Jordan would like to hear about it, but where was Jordan? He was hiding out in the office, most likely—doing God knows what—or he'd gone to the bar.

"So, why didn't you say so?"

"It's my job. The university wants me to do it. The new president doesn't care for my oyster hatchery. He'd defund me in a minute if I make waves, and then there's retirement on the horizon. Anyway, I didn't come here to bore you with my business. I came by to see a familiar face. I need a dose of sanity." He looked around at all the boxes. "So, May, how's the life cleaning?"

"It's fine," she said, looking at the carpet. She couldn't tell if he was making fun of her. "I suppose this BP thing is like putting a criminal in charge of the crime scene."

He sat back, looking pleased. "That's just it. That's just the problem."

May would not let on that she was just repeating something Lucille had said to her.

"You know, you're a beautiful woman. I always thought so."

"Oh," she said, smoothing her hair back. "Oh," she said again, and then recrossed her legs.

"I've always thought that," he said. "I hope my saying so doesn't make you uncomfortable."

"Have you been drinking?" she asked.

"Not much," he said. "I've made you uncomfortable. I'm sorry. I have this problem of saying what's on my mind these days, some-thing about getting older—not that I came here to tell you that. I came here to talk to Jordan, I guess, about the business. See how he's getting on now that Al's . . ."

"Maybe Jordan's in the office," May said. But Doc didn't seem interested in seeking him out.

His glass was empty. Should she offer him more tea? She didn't know if she wanted him to stay any longer. Or maybe she should be angry with him. He'd been friends with Al. But now he just smiled at her like this was all very amusing.

"May," Doc said. "Would you have dinner with me sometime?"

"I'm not ready," May said. "I'm sorry, Doc."

"Not ready to eat dinner?" he said. "We don't have to right now." She opened her mouth.

"I'm not funny," he said. "I understand. You're not interested."

"It's not that," she said. She didn't know what it was. Was Doc attractive? "I'm just not ready."

"I understand," he said again. "If you want a friend, I can be a friend, too. You know what I remember about you? You used to laugh a lot. You were playful."

Was that true? She couldn't be sure.

"I hate to see you so . . ." He searched for a word. "Diminished. You were once so full of life."

"I appreciate your concern," she said, "for my vitality."

"You're funny when you're annoyed."

"I'm not annoyed!"

He raised his eyebrows. His amusement annoyed her.

"I'm surprised, really," she said. "You used to be so polite."

"Dishonest," he said. "I used to be so dishonest." He leaned for-ward on his knees, and she was relieved that this gesture meant he might leave. "Listen, I went about this all wrong, but I would like to take you out. I'd show you a good time, and there'd be no expectations on my part. I mean it. I'll call you," he said. "Think about it. I could always use more friends, and I can be fun. In the least, we can have fun."

"You've been drinking, haven't you?" She felt herself smiling, which happened when she was nervous.

"I'll call anyway," he said, "because I know you're a nice lady and you'll humor me."

He smiled at her from the doorway, but she diverted her eyes and immediately set to work on the kitchen, wiping the counters, scrubbing the sink with Ajax. Her heart was twitchy like a teenage girl's—not because she was interested, exactly, but curious.

Seven

In a week's time, the oil slick in the Gulf had grown to the size of Rhode Island. Now it was a national news story. BP had to admit that a well-drilling failure caused the explosion on the oil rig. Jordan watched the coverage of the press conferences. There was a hubbub about a chemical BP was spraying near the site of the explosion — a so-called "dispersant" — intended to disperse the oil in the water column. People seemed to think the chemical was toxic. On TV, BP officials spoke about the difficulty of closing a failed deep-sea well, but not about how they were going to close it. In the meantime, they were working on containment, trying to save the coastline from incoming oil by burning it at the water's surface fifty miles offshore. Workers zipped into full-body suits set the Gulf on fire. The footage was unreal. From a distance, it looked like a boat on fire. But there was no boat. It was the water itself burning — a funnel unraveling into the sky like a coal-black tornado.

At that moment, on Jordan's wild-growing oyster reefs throughout the sheltered inshore bays, the oyster spawn was happening.

The male and female oysters released sperm and egg into the water column, where they'd meet and fertilize and drift back down to the reef. Jordan could hold an adult oyster in his hand and count one hundred black specks of larvae cemented to its shell. In two years' time, if they survived to adulthood, some of those black specks would grow three to five inches, and they, too, would be hauled up from the reef, culled by Doug Babies, bagged, and shucked by Hoa and Linh, or else driven to his distributer in New Orleans, where they'd be sent to a restaurant, served on ice with lemon and cocktail sauce, and drunk up by a tourist. Only, the larvae were remarkably sensitive. The slightest change in salinity would wipe out a whole generation. A season of extreme rainfall in the Midwest could do it. A state-ordered release of fresh water from the Mississippi, with its pollutants from heartland farms and factories, could too.

After Hurricane Katrina, Jordan and Babies visited every wild-growing reef he owned and took stock—counting the larvae specks on shells—to see what the future held for them. Though he'd lost half of his crops to the hurricane, the spatfall afterward was tremendous. He told Babies they were floating over a fortune in future harvests. He'd waited five years for it, and here it was. Babies and Alejandro bagged 250 oyster sacks that week—beautiful, briny oysters from Barataria. He was his better self when he had reason to think it'd be a good season, but also, superstitiously, he suspected his better self could bring about a better oyster haul.

On Saturday night, after locking up the cold storage, when he might have driven the mile to Bayou Bud's, he found himself slipping his truck keys into his back pocket. He would walk. It was a balmy night. A bat had swooped across the purple sky as Jordan strolled through his neighborhood of squat single-story houses in the twilight. The hiccups of children's laughter rang from the YMCA two streets away. He passed a driveway where a man's legs extended from beneath his car because people fixed their own messes in his neighborhood. Another bat zipped overhead. He felt swept up in an energy he couldn't place. It felt so unfamiliar. It was pleasure. He was vital, still young. He wished there was a beautiful woman around, so he might show her consideration and tenderness. He would like to take her out for a spin along the Gulf Coast. He would like to make a woman throw her head back and laugh while spearing a shrimp with her fork, just like in a local jewelry ad he'd seen. He enjoyed the crunching gravel under his feet and ground it with relish. He wondered how he might continue this pleasure—yes, with a woman. That's why he was going to the bar. Maybe the women would notice a newfound purpose about him—a leaner man since he'd cut the dead weight of his brother from the business.

As he walked, he thought how decent the small houses looked, and he thought of BP's CEO Tony Hayward, whom he'd seen for the first time on TV. Hayward, a slight British man with a beak nose, had a smug, harried look about him.

"This was not our accident," Hayward said about the spill, "but it is our responsibility to deal with it."

The houses Jordan walked past were full of people who lived small lives like him, dignified in their smallness and sacrifice. When Jordan had a wife, he'd move her into the bayou-facing office. They'd fix it up like the real house it was, not an office. He imagined hanging a sign on the office door when he was doing paperwork to keep the children out.

Once he reached the highway that bisected town, he saw a steady thrum of cars—far more than normal—were headed down the bayou toward the Gulf. Jordan had to wait five minutes, grinding pebbles under his feet, for a break in the traffic so he could cross. These were not vacationers on their way to Grand Isle. These were BP's people headed toward Port Fourchon, where the oil tankers docked. Out-of-town cars were congregating there—rentals for corporate men spearheading the operation to close the well—but it was also where local oil cleanup operations were based. Jordan knew he would worry over this later—what the facility's proximity meant for him—but he pushed disaster from his mind at that moment to listen to the Mexican polka music emanating from George Roy's garage. He suspected George was involved with his Latina housemaid, and this made Jordan smile.

When he arrived at Bayou Bud's, there were no women in sight, except Cyndi, the bartender, opening beers. It was dark, cigarette smoke billowed overhead, and the hum of the poorly working ventilation system battled with a classic rock song for priority. He chided himself for imagining a trove of single women in Golden Vale, where the generations skewed geriatric, and where unmarried women were as rare as wild horses in the marsh.

Doug Babies sat alone at the bar. "Hey-hey," he said.

Jordan gave Babies a pat on the back. Babies hadn't mentioned that he was going to the bar after work. Perhaps Babies even told himself he wouldn't go.

"I just can't overdo it," Babies said, indicating his beer. "I'm not the 'cold turkey' type."

Jordan told him it was okay. Nobody expected him to be the cold turkey type. Have a beer if you need one. Just don't get messy.

Cyndi stood a few feet away, leaning on her forearms while talking to a fisherman. She wore a scoop-neck top, so her cleavage was available to the eye, a half-moon of bayou brown. Babies called her Cyndi the Indian, because she was Pointe-au-Chien Indian, her parents from Montegut. She didn't look Indian to Jordan, but that didn't mean much—since his reference came from movies. Cyndi had a world-weary way of talking, and she talked that way most of the time, except when she was recounting some piece of delicious gossip. She might tell a story about a Catholic priest in Larose who gambled away the collections money every week at the bar's video poker machine. She could be filled with girlish enthusiasm then: "And the congregants are wondering why the roof still leaks!" A few loyal patrons brought in silver balloons for Cyndi's fortieth birthday over the winter. He'd been surprised to learn she was older than him.

She floated over to Jordan's end of the bar. "Jordan, did you get a haircut?"

"No," he said, and then proceeded to tell her that his brother was on drugs. "I had to remove him from the business payroll. I guess I'm partly to blame," he said. "It ruins a person to receive a handout."

"What kind of drugs?" Cyndi asked. But Jordan didn't know what kind of drugs.

"You wouldn't recognize him on the street," Jordan said to Babies. "He's so changed."

"I couldn't pick Benny out of a lineup anyway," Babies said. "The city does that to people."

In Cyndi's experience, you didn't have to be in a city to ruin your life with drugs. She went to refresh the drinks of the two out-of-towners. They were a breath of fresh air to her, this glimpse of the outside. She wanted to leave Golden Vale, and she periodically bought herself a vacation in some promising other city—the last of which was Miami—where she looked around at the baking tourists and thought, Why did I come? Nevertheless, she'd met a Cuban man, who was her boyfriend for a couple of days, and afterward, when people asked about her trip, she would mention the miracle that was fried sweet plantains.

The two strangers were milquetoast men in collared shirts—one old, one young—seated a few stools down the bar. Coworkers, Jordan guessed. Mostly it was the younger one who did the talking. He used his hands to express himself, and the elder of the two, white-haired and slightly bow-shouldered, watched the young man's hands between sips of his beer.

Jordan kept glancing over at the men. They weren't vacationers. He guessed they were working for BP in one way or another.

Cyndi came by and Jordan put his hands down on the bar for her attention.

"Another?" she asked.

"No, still working on this one," he said. Then he nodded discreetly in the direction of the two men, as if to ask, Who are these guys?

But Cyndi only mimicked Jordan with a similar nod.

"Who are they?" Jordan asked. "BP?"

"Be friendly," Cyndi said.

Babies tore up a bar napkin and told Cyndi about the sacks of oysters they'd bagged that day. The best day they'd had in April since before Katrina. Cyndi smiled, not to encourage him, only to acknowledge that he'd spoken. "Anyway, you might see a lot more of us."

"Why's that?" Cyndi leaned forward on crossed elbows, glancing in Jordan's direction.

"If they don't close that well, we'll be here every night crying into our beers."

"Then they better plug that sucker soon," Cyndi said.

"They'll close it," Jordan said.

Cyndi had one tooth that crossed over the other and only showed when she smiled widely. Jordan loved that, but it was hard to make her smile wide enough to show it. She was, in that moment, wearing a mischievous grin.

Cyndi turned to the strangers. "You hear that, guys?"

The elder man swiveled his stool to face Cyndi. "Excuse me?"

"I said, you better plug that well soon, or I'll be mopping up a lot of tears."

The man's eyebrows were black and expressive. "I don't understand," he said.

Jordan noted how different the man's voice was. Clear. He was from some place far away.

"They're fishermen," Cyndi said.

"Oystermen," Babies said, patting the bar. "We're oystermen."

Cyndi rolled her eyes. "They're oystermen."

Jordan watched the men tense. He wanted to see if they knew how bad things were going to get. When would BP close the well? Would the oil come inland? As bad as the spill looked, Jordan was not prepared to believe he'd be affected. It was still miles away, and reporters were always horned up to tell you the world was ending.

"That's not our job," the elder said, looking at Jordan, "but if it was, I'd try."

"We're not engineers," the young man said. "We're oceanographers."

It bothered Jordan that the man was younger than him.

"We're oceanographers," Babies said mockingly, and he took a long pull from his beer.

This aggression was registered, and the men resumed their conversation.

"What're you here for?" Jordan asked.

The young man, with slight annoyance in his eyes, held up his beer glass as evidence. "This."

"I mean, what're you, like, studying?" Jordan said.

"Where the oil is going, how it's moving," the young man said.

"So, where's it going?" Jordan asked.

"Can't say."

Jordan surprised himself with his tone. "Can't say or won't?"

"We're not weathermen," the elder said in a voice that was meant to end the conversation.

The younger wanted to be likable. "We're not at liberty . . ." he began, and then trailed off.

Jordan pulled a cigarette out of his pack. Both men watched Jordan light it. He saw he made them nervous, especially the younger one, as if he might initiate something physical. So much the better. He was content to leave them that way, with his smoking as a response. Cyndi emerged with an ashtray, which she tapped in front of him, saying, Don't you dare ash on the floor, with her eyes.

"Pencil neck," Babies said, down into his drink.

Babies was, and always had been, a big guy. Knocking kids on their backs for two hours a day after high school gave him a physical confidence he rarely put to use, but it remained all the same.

"Excuse me?" the elder man said. This time sounding like he was inviting Babies to correct himself.

"Pencil necks," Babies said, banging down his empty bottle. "Sitting in our bar and acting like you don't have nothing to say for yourselves."

"We're oceanographers," the young man started.

"Oh, here you go again," Babies said.

"We have nothing to do with oil or the spill," the elder man said.

Cyndi watched this all unfold, rapt, almost smiling, leaning her forearm on the bar, so her cleavage was at Jordan's eye level.

"I think we ought to leave," the elder man said, tapping the bar with his finger.

The younger man sat upright as if he'd been given instructions.

"Listen, guys," Cyndi said, addressing Jordan. "Leave them alone, would you? I don't want a reputation of being hostile to newcomers."

"Jordan here is going to occupy Doug," she said, smiling widely at Jordan with an interest he'd not yet seen. She turned to the older man. "And no one is going to bother you."

Jordan, seeing this as an opportunity, said, "Hell, I'll even buy your next round."

Cyndi winked at him. "See?"

"That's not necessary," the elder said.

"Don't make me look like a chump," Jordan said. "Cyndi, whatever they want is on me."

"We appreciate it," the elder said. "But no thanks."

The young man kicked back his glass and drained the remaining third.

"Take the drinks, honey," Cyndi said. "God knows this doesn't happen often. Jordan's tight."

"Hey, now," Jordan said, searching her face to see if that's what she truly thought.

Cyndi beamed at Jordan, crossed teeth showing.

"We're done here," the elder man said, looking sharply at Cyndi.

Jordan did not like the man's tone.

Cyndi nodded, and with a dissatisfied hum, she turned toward the register.

"I ought to keep my money, huh?" Jordan said. "What with that oil coming in."

The oceanographers stood, ignoring his comment, and pretended to be interested in the Christmas lights strung around the perimeter of the smoky bar.

Babies, seeing this, spoke even louder. "So what's this chemical dispersant you all are spraying? Are we all going to die, or what?"

He enjoyed playing the fool.

"It's soap, basically," the young scientist said. "Like Dawn dish soap."

"You hear that?" Babies asked Jordan. "Just soap. Do you believe that?"

Jordan shook his head and took another drink.

"My friend here doesn't believe you," Babies said.

The young scientist watched Jordan turn a cardboard coaster over in his hands.

"Well, I guess that's his business then," the young scientist said with something like pity in his voice.

For the first time since the explosion—maybe because of the young man's tone—Jordan felt fear bloom in his chest about the spill. It could come inland if they didn't plug the well. It made him hate the two men. Well-paid tourists who didn't really care if things turned bad. It wasn't their livelihood at risk.

"These guys are probably going to say there is no oil, or the water's fine! The fish are fine!" Jordan said.

Babies threw up his hands. "What oil spill?"

The elder scientist was fingering the bills in his open wallet.

"We do an honest job," the younger said, marshaling confidence. "We didn't cause the spill."

"You're a hired gun," Jordan said.

Cyndi edged in to overhear them, slipping a pen behind her ear.

The elder scientist shook his head. He put a hand on the younger's shoulder to guide him past Babies and Jordan.

"We did nothing to you," he said as they passed, and he sounded young, like a bullied child.

"It's your world," Jordan said. "You're just as bad."

Jordan registered pleasant surprise in Cyndi's face. There was a flicker of attraction he never thought he could elicit from her. A signal was sent, and a signal was received.

The elder picked up the pace to the door, ushering the young one out.

For once, a night had fulfilled all its promises. Bayou Bud's, which was often a place where Jordan went to put his life on pause, became a place where his life was unfolding. It was an over-chilled boxcar on its way to nowhere. The bar itself was laminate. The wood paneling on the walls was wafer-thin. It was windowless, and on the wrong kind of day, the hopefulness of the multicolored

Christmas lights had the opposite effect. On such a day, Jordan looked into the mirror behind the bar and was dispirited to see what time was doing to him. He was not married. His business was shrinking. But this night, he had one eye for Cyndi's sashay along the length of the bar, a sashay that she meant for him to watch. He liked Cyndi's coarse laugh, the unapologetic way she had of talking. Each glance she sent was a present he could unwrap, and it astonished him that he'd overlooked Cyndi's beauty, her wry kindness and good sense.

Babies was in high spirits, enjoying the camaraderie of the moment, and was moving about the room making friends with everyone. His new friends were buying him shots.

A man sidled up behind Jordan's stool and clapped him on the back. It was Rollo—a friend of his father's whom he'd not seen in a decade, a canny old Cajun with the bulging eyes of a deepwater fish and a bad leg that made a scuffing sound as he dragged it. At family barbecues, Rollo liked to tell the boys stories about the fistfights he'd won. At seventy, Rollo was still imposing, but his leg slowed him down. Jordan did not know Rollo well, but in this surprise meeting, they hugged like long-lost relatives. Rollo began by explaining to Jordan that a few areas deep in the Gulf had already closed down to fishing because of the oil. These were the first closures Jordan had heard of. Rollo said a group of New Yorkers had just canceled their chartered trip with him.

In addition to owning a bait shop with his wife on Grand Isle, Rollo, like most men of his generation, fished whatever was in season and was well priced—shrimp, crabs, oysters. Occasionally he did chartered trips for tourists, not because he had an especially nice boat but because he was such an odd old bird that people thought they were having an authentic Cajun experience.

Now he was mourning the loss of income from the New Yorkers

who'd canceled on him. "And I said, 'You think you know better than the feds? Because they tell me it's okay to fish.'"

Jordan was prepared to act as though Rollo's misfortune had nothing to do with him.

"You didn't see the Nazis," Rollo said, "trying to cozy up for drinks with Parisians when they occupied Paris."

"What?" Babies said, appearing next to Jordan, his face flushed.

"I'm saying those BP fuckers have a lot of nerve." Rollo looked into his beer bottle like he'd lost something in it. "You know what'd happen to me if I dumped a cup of oil in the Gulf of Mexico?"

"Yes," Jordan said.

"U.S. Fish and Wildlife Service would slap a fine on me that'd ruin my goddamn year."

Babies called to Cyndi at the other end of the bar. "Cyndi, precious, Cyndi-the-Indian, can we get a round of Rumple Minze?"

"I don't know why you'd want to," she said. When she upturned the bottle, she overpoured like an angel. "But why don't you try?"

Jordan wanted to kiss her. Then she flew off to serve someone else.

Rollo went on: "I'm thinking of signing up for that Vessels of Opportunity program with BP. They're hiring fishermen to clean up the oil."

Rollo looked on the verge of tears about it.

"I hear they'll pay beaucoup money," Babies said. "There's no shame in it."

"There's shame in it," Jordan said, staring at Babies.

Rollo nodded, dejected. "But I don't see what choice I've got."

"My brother-in-law is signing up with them," Babies said. "And he's going to make two grand a day. Can you believe it? You gotta make that money when you can. Who knows how long this'll last?"

Rollo was not heartened by Babies's statement.

"I couldn't stomach cleaning up BP's mess," Jordan said.

Babies tossed his drink back and then pushed off his stool. He lost his balance and pitched backward a step, and this seemed to genuinely surprise him.

"But you're not hurting for money. Are you, Jordan?" he said acidly, and lunged away toward the bathroom.

This left Jordan and Rollo alone together, and they watched the TV in the corner. BP was working on a containment dome that they would lower on the spewing oil leak. They were flying in scientists from all over the place. They showed a graphic of the dome, made of cement and steel, with a large tube projecting from the top. Once BP lowered the dome over the leak, they would pump the spewing oil onto a ship on the water's surface.

On the TV, a BP spokesman said, "That kind of dome-pump-pipe-ship system has been used in shallow water, but not in five thousand feet, so we have to be careful."

"What'd he say?" Rollo said. "I can't hear shit in this place."

"He said they'd need to be careful," Jordan said.

"Right," Rollo said. "Careful."

Cyndi was in front of him again, leaning conspiratorially on the bar. She told him that the keg of Budweiser was kicked and the lazy ass who had worked the night before hadn't brought in another one from storage out back.

He blinked at this news until Cyndi said, exasperated, "Well, could you help a girl out?"

Jordan gave Rollo's shoulder a squeeze as he left.

"See you, then." Rollo laughed.

Once they were both outside, Jordan took this as an invitation to back Cyndi up against the clapboard and kiss her, until she put some distance between them with her arms. "Let's take it easy, now." She was smiling. They looked at each other in astonishment that it had not occurred to them to do this sooner. He got in a good study—she was sweet when amorous. So often her face was set like she was digesting some bad news. She wore her hair pulled back too tight and he started to yank the ponytail out.

"What do you think you're doing?" she asked, catching his hand.

He put the elastic around his wrist and ruffled her hair. "I want to see you with your hair down."

"I like it out of my face when I'm working."

"It looks better when it's down," he said. He ran his fingers through it, feeling it, thick like a horse tail, black with some caramel in it. It smelled fruity, but a different kind of fruity than his ex's hair. They were savaged by mosquitoes in the humid night, but she seemed to enjoy this petting. Her eyes were closed.

"Your breath smells like mouthwash," she said.

"Babies thinks his wife won't know he's been drinking if he smells like mint."

She laughed, but it wasn't her coarse laugh. It was unguarded, girlish laughter, and he recalled how he'd begun the evening, walking in the balmy night toward the bar, and he felt as if he'd known this would happen.

Inside, Cyndi heard the beginnings of a mutiny in her absence. They bellowed her name, "Cyndi, Cyndi," and pounded on the bar.

"I'm so tired of them." She told Jordan to walk around the building and smoke a cigarette, and then come in the front door. "I don't want them knowing what we're doing." She tried to pull her hair back, but she didn't have the elastic anymore.

"You have some other boyfriend in there I should know about?"

"I don't have a boyfriend anywhere," she said, enclosing herself from him.

"Whatever you want," he said, backing away, hands up. He decided he would have to work on her.

Car lights swept the road as they passed Jordan, who stood smoking in the front of the bar. He whistled to himself. A few men exited, and Jordan offered a warm farewell. "Have a good night," he said. They didn't know what to make of this.

"Okay," one said.

When Jordan had been alone for long enough, he went back inside and found Babies sitting by himself, bashful as a child.

Cyndi told Jordan that he had to drive Babies home now. He had exhausted the bar's hospitality when he knocked over Rollo's beer. Cyndi's hair was down, and she had a big mosquito bite plumping up on her cheek. Jordan fished the keys from Babies's back pocket and tried to intimate to Cyndi that they'd finish what they started later. He did this solely with his eyes, prompting Cyndi to ask, "Are you all right to drive?"

In the passenger seat, Babies hummed something unrecognizable, slack-jawed, looking as though the booze had hit him all at once. His house was fifteen minutes down the road. Babies farted loudly and laughed. When Jordan rolled down the window, the warm air had a hint of the bayou in it.

"I didn't think this through too well," Jordan said. "I walked to the bar tonight. You think Regina will drive me home?"

"Regina's up," Babies said. "My wife is always up."

Jordan wanted to think about Cyndi. He wanted to take her home. He wanted to see where she lived. He wanted to take off her clothes. He wanted to know all about her. He wondered about her world-weariness. He wondered about the crossed teeth. He wondered about all the men who stared at her every night. He wouldn't like that—knowing all those men were staring at his girlfriend.

"You think you're some kind of cowboy, don't you?" Babies said.

"What?"

"'You're a hired gun'! That's what you said to those guys. Like you were a cowboy."

Babies whistled when he laughed, and this reminded Jordan of the high school kid he'd been—a linebacker, a boy hungry for attention, and an unsuccessful flirt. He felt affection for Babies that he rarely had access to. His life had been so full of difficulties of his own making that it was hard to sympathize with him. He knew Babies wanted a larger role in the oyster company than Jordan thought he could handle.

The headlights flashed the old seafood drive-through as Jordan turned into Babies's neighborhood. Doug's neighborhood was a collection of low-lying ranch homes, old Acadian cottages, and trailers hauled in by FEMA after Hurricane Katrina.

"What if I hooked up with Cyndi?" Jordan said, turning onto Babies's street.

"Never happen," Babies said. "Don't count on it."

"But why not?"

"I got a feeling it's not in the cards," Babies said. "But I've been wrong before."

There were children's toys in Doug's front yard, an overturned plastic tricycle, a snap-together fort. The lights were off in the home, and then they weren't.

It would take Jordan forty-five minutes, at least, to walk home.

"Babies, just 'cause you're drunk now doesn't mean you can skip work tomorrow." He was talking to himself as much as to Doug. "I'll see you bright and early even if you have to puke all the way down the bayou."

Doug had his forehead against the window, staring at his house.

Jordan gave him a hard shake. "What are you, sleepy? You're home now."

The front door opened and Regina appeared. She had her hand up, shielding her eyes from the truck headlights.

"Uh-oh." Doug laughed. "Look out."

Jordan cut the engine and Doug tumbled out of the truck cab. Jordan watched Regina say something low and cutting to Doug as he passed her in the doorway. He stumbled on the steps.

Regina walked toward Jordan in the truck. She was a petite woman with a squeaky, birdlike voice. She wore one of Doug's oversized shirts, and hugged herself in it, making her look even smaller. She'd been cute. He'd long liked and pitied her for putting up with Doug.

"Keys," she said—with her hand outstretched.

Jordan put the keys in her hand. There was so much contempt for him in her face. He didn't know where it came from. All the while, he'd been expecting a thank-you for driving Doug home, for saving him from hurting himself, for saving him from a DUI—and for employing him.

"I don't know why he keeps on thinking you're his friend. You've been nothing but trouble for him, but I can't convince him of it. I wish I could."

"I was trying to help."

"Help him get drunk?"

He said what Babies said, that it was fine for Babies to have a beer occasionally. He just couldn't overdo it.

"You know Doug still goes to AA meetings. He has a sponsor. He's trying to turn his life around, and then his 'friend' watches him get drunk."

"I don't make him drink."

"'I don't make him drink,' he says."

She wanted him to hear how shallow this was, and, well, he heard it. "What else am I supposed to do?" Doug had once said. "Lock myself in the house? We'll kill each other." Doug had been torn up about this. He didn't want to go home after work. He wanted to be around people. That's just how he was.

"I'm his boss," Jordan said, "not his babysitter."

"I told him you don't give one lick about him, but he doesn't believe me. He thinks I'm the bad guy."

Regina opened the truck door, inviting Jordan to step out of it. He did, and he felt weaker when he was on level ground with her. Their front door was ajar, and there was a small dog in the doorway. One of those dogs that looked like a teddy bear that he didn't remember them having.

Jordan felt unbearably sleepy then, like he could lie down right there on the dewy lawn.

"I need a reliable father for my kids," she said. Her voice quavered.

"It's none of my business," Jordan said. "I don't want to be involved."

Then he was off. Once he was out of Regina's sight, he slowed his pace, putting one foot in front of the other—past the lumberyard, past the helicopter pad that took the oilmen offshore, past the fenced-in parking lot where the oilmen left their cars while they were gone. Nice big trucks in there. Almost no cars passed him on the highway as he walked.

→ Eight ←

Jordan woke well after dawn to the sound of rushing water raking his window. It was bright out, the quality of light meaning that he'd overslept several hours in his drunkenness. The water wasn't rain. It was his mother with the hose. She was watering the begonias under his window. She hummed something to herself, the sound of which was a rare demonstration of cheer, but it fit his mood. He recalled the events of the night before—his triumph at the bar, Regina's telling him off, his calves sore from the long walk, and Cyndi. He could still feel the impression of her small shoulders in his arms. He felt bleary and giddy. She wasn't too pretty. She wasn't a spry twenty-year-old with everything ahead of her. He thought this meant she might be easy to please, even dazzle, that she'd have him; they might be a team—she'd handle the secretarial work of the business. He also thought of sex—she had to be molten in bed. He bet she was loud.

Outside, May was calling his name He pulled aside the curtain to see her facing the wrong direction. She thought he was in the office, not knowing he'd overslept. She was wearing an old pair of his father's trousers and a button-up shirt tied at the waist. She never wore his father's clothes like that, but something had come over her. For the past week, she got the idea to make over the house. She looked almost folksy in her outfit, and it suited her. The hose was kinked in her hand as she called him. When he knocked on the window, she jumped and dropped the hose, which briefly became animate—a snake spewing water. It doused her.

He was laughing, and she squinted at him through the window.

"Jordie?" she said. "You're in bed? Are you sick?"

"I'm fine," he said. "I just overslept."

"You don't oversleep," she said, squinting. "You look strange. Maybe you're sick."

"I feel fine!"

"Then come outside and tell me if you smell something funny. I woke up with a splitting headache."

It was seven-thirty in the morning. He hadn't missed any calls from Doug Babies, who should have been there at five. He called. No answer. He called again. Straight to voicemail. Finally, he left a message: "Babies, I know you're paying the piper right now, but it's time to go to work, buddy."

Outside, his mother was cranking the garden hose into a hose reel he'd gotten her for Christmas. It looked laborious, not all that helpful to her, though she'd never admit it. When she stood, looking him over, he could tell that she was studying him for signs of illness. She smirked, having come to a conclusion. "It must have been some night," she said.

"With all the boxes inside," he said, "it looks like you're moving out."

She ignored the comment. "Tell me what you smell," she said, looking up.

Cypress, his old arthritic dog, came to him, moving painfully across the driveway. She slumped down his leg, leaving her heavy skull on his sneaker. He squatted down to rub her. Tufts of burnt-orange fur came off in his hand. He murmured words of love, and she flipped to offer her stomach to him in weary ecstasy.

"I don't smell anything," he said, not looking up.

"I woke with the worst headache," she said.

He stood, stretching. Faintly, he smelled diesel, something chemical. "Is the truck leaking?"

She shook her head, looking relieved, but also incredulous. "It's the oil."

"No. That's impossible. It's fifty-five miles off. It's in the water," he said, not knowing if that meant you couldn't smell it.

"They've set the Gulf on fire. They're burning it, big black plumes." Her eyes were wide with the drama of it.

He knew this, but was surprised that she did. She had seemed to be willfully ignoring the news.

"I don't think you should go out today. I don't think you should go any closer to that oil. It can't be good for you. There's probably an advisory or something about it."

"I'd know if there was an advisory," he said, though this sounded false to him, and he could tell that it sounded false to her too.

"They closed down a few areas for fishing deep out in the Gulf," she said. She was looking at the sky as if she could see the smell. "A couple of dead dolphins washed up on Grand Isle. They might do an autopsy to check for oil."

"Sounds like a great use of taxpayer dollars," he said. "This will all be over in a week or two. Everyone is losing their minds about this accident."

"I hear it's even worse than they're saying," May said.

"Why?"

"I talk to people," she said hotly.

"Well, whatever, I'm going out as soon as Babies gets here. He's not answering his phone."

"Poor Doug," she said, which never failed to irritate him. She loved to lavish her sympathy on Doug and his predicaments. Babies came crying to her the first time he got sober. Jordan had walked in on them in the living room. She'd had an arm around his shoulder, and he was pawing tears away on his pink face. When he saw Jordan, Babies had coughed raucously into his fist.

The phone in his pocket started buzzing. It was Babies. He sounded groggy and cotton-mouthed. He had the crestfallen tone Jordan recognized. Regina had skinned him alive. Babies would likely offer up his favorite excuse of his unreliable truck starter, probably forgetting that Jordan had driven him home in his truck the night before.

"I'm sorry, Jordan," Babies said, "but I can't come."

"I know your truck is fine," Jordan said. "Let's just get going. I've been waiting for hours."

"I can't do that, actually. I can't come."

"Quit playing."

"I can't come because I'm gonna get in on that oil spill cleanup."

"Bullshit," Jordan said.

"You remember Regina's brother, Raymond? He's got his boat signed up in that Vessels of Opportunity program with BP. The one Rollo was talking about. Raymond's got room for me. Guys are already on waiting lists to enroll. They're all lining up to get a spot. The pay's good, Jordan."

"Babies, you're not thinking things through," Jordan said. "You're gonna leave your job for some day-labor gig. The spill will be over in a week or two. This is your job we're talking about."

"It doesn't look like they're stopping that oil tomorrow, if you ask me," Babies said. He sounded bolder than he normally did. "Besides, I've been thinking about making some changes."

"You think you're being fair to me right now?"

"How come you won't let me run one of your boats?"

"What?" Jordan said. "They're family boats."

He'd never turn one over to an outsider, let alone a man who regularly showed up late, bearing evidence that he'd had his big neck sucked on.

"See? That's just what I mean. I need to start looking out for my interests."

This sounded like a line from Regina.

"You're not in your right mind," Jordan said.

"Regina said you'd be like this."

"You don't seem to care too much about Regina after you've had a few."

Jordan never brought up Babies's philandering as a line of argument before. He knew Babies lived with a lot of shame and couldn't bear being reminded of it.

"You're out of line there," Babies said.

"You're right." Jordan walked over to a plastic chair his mother had wet with the hose and had a seat. "I'm sorry. I'm hungover too. Listen, we're both not thinking straight. Take a cold shower. Think it over. And then come over here, and we'll talk about it, okay?"

"I'm sorry about this," Babies said, and then he hung up.

May was scribbling a to-do list in the kitchen while waiting for the coffee to brew. When Jordan walked in she seemed to know that something was wrong. She put her pencil down. His worries mounted as he recounted the conversation. Who could he get to come out and work so late in the day? And then who would come tomorrow? This would cost him two days' worth of work. He couldn't fish with only one deckhand to cull oysters. He'd have to call his distributor in New Orleans. It was about the worst timing imaginable. His mother listened with her head propped up in one hand. The house phone rang.

He was annoyed that she answered it. She sounded surprised, and giggled nervously when the person on the other end said something. "I'm sorry, Doc. I'm in the middle of a conversation with my son right now. I'll call you back. Can I get you at this number? . . . Great. I mean, good . . . I'll think about it . . . Oh stop . . . I've got to go . . . Yes, 'bye." She sang, "'Bye" into the receiver and then hung up. She was blushing.

He checked his phone again. Babies hadn't called back.

"I'm sorry, honey," she said. She put the kitchen phone down and petted it absentmindedly. He noticed her nails were painted a glossy red when they were normally plain. "Doug has always had a tough go of things. You know what his family was like. But you're right. He's making a fool decision. Let me talk to him."

"Absolutely not," he said. "He's made his bed. If he doesn't show today, I'll fire him."

"Just give him another chance. He hasn't thought things through properly."

Jordan poured their coffees. He felt a headache present itself as a dullness at the back of his skull that radiated toward his forehead. He wondered if this was the smell outside or his hangover.

May was quiet for a moment, staring into her mug. Then she looked up. "Maybe your brother could help."

"Don't be ridiculous," he said.

"I'm serious."

"Benny is worthless."

"He's not worthless," she said. "What a thing to say about your brother."

All his life, she chided Jordan that he needed to look out for his little brother. He'd continued paying Benny out of that lingering sense of responsibility.

"On the boat, he's worthless. And besides, he wouldn't want to come. He's never worked a day in his life. He hasn't had to."

"I know he could use the money," she said.

So, Benny had told her, then, that Jordan was stopping the payments. The crybaby.

"It's not out of meanness," he said. "I'm not obligated to."

"I won't get in the middle of it. I never do get involved in the business. Lord knows I've seen some rows over the years."

Jordan groaned.

"I don't!" she said. "But I will say that Benny has a stake here too. And if you need help, you can ask him."

"You saw how he looks now. He'd be the last person I'd call to be a deckhand."

"Fine." She sighed. "What about the boy?"

"What boy?"

She put her mug down. "The deckhand. Tell me he hasn't been waiting for you all morning."

"Oh Jesus. I forgot all about him."

Alejandro was prostrate under the aluminum shade tent by the dock, not sleeping, though he looked as if he might be. His calves were covered in purple welts from mosquitoes. When Alejandro saw Jordan, he pushed himself up, but he did not look relieved. Jordan told Alejandro somewhat defensively that there had been an emergency. Babies couldn't make it today. He was sorry for being so late, but there was nothing to be done about it. They wouldn't go out at all that day. Alejandro watched him calmly as he spoke. He didn't know why his mother had called Alejandro a boy when he was in his late twenties.

"I'll pay you extra next shift," he said, "for your trouble."

Jordan hadn't planned to make this offer, and yet it came out.

"Okay," Alejandro said. He bent forward to study the mosquito bites on his legs.

"I need another deckhand. What about . . ." He could not recall the other deckhand's name. Jordan grabbed his own hand and massaged it in demonstration. "Your friend with the hand. Is he better? Could he work?"

"Manuel?"

"Yes, Manuel."

"I don't know what happened to him."

This surprised Jordan. They'd shown up at his deck together looking for work. He'd assumed they were friends.

"Is he okay or what? Don't you know?"

"His hand looked bad. He doesn't call me, though, so I don't know really."

"Do you know anyone else who could work?"

"I don't know anyone here," he said.

"All right, Alejandro. Thanks. I'll call you as soon as I've got someone else."

"No problem," Alejandro said. He pushed himself to his feet and walked down the bayou to wherever he stayed. He wanted nothing from Jordan in the way of further small talk or further explanation.

Jordan knew little about Alejandro or Manuel other than their nationality—both Salvadoran. Neither one spent much time with him in the cabin, like Babies did. One day, about three weeks earlier, they appeared at his boat asking for work just when he'd needed them, and they had been reliable, showing up on time, working without complaint or hassle. They had quickly become a part of the machinery of his operation. But he sensed Alejandro didn't respect him much, which bothered him. His father had always said that you can't be friends with your employees. And look at what Babies had just done.

Jordan checked his phone again. No missed calls. Then he sank down on his haunches in the shade of the tent and looked at *May's Day*. Back in the eighties, his father installed culling tables for the deckhands so the men could stand as they broke up the oysters. It was a kindness to the workers' backs, and it sped up production. His grandfather said it was a waste of money. He thought it'd make the workers lazy. The old man never could see outside of himself very well. Al caught him on the boat one night unscrewing equipment from the deck, intending to pitch the five-thousand-dollar tables into the bayou.

His grandfather still operated his own boat back then—the *Capt. Ellis*—which he'd steered through the hardscrabble years of the 1950s and '60s when fishermen across the parish left the water for high-wage oil jobs. He always said he'd die on the water, and he was right. His heart stopped one morning when he was harvesting in Bay Jimmy.

Nine

Benny wanted to be helpful to Kiki, but his body was trying to sabotage him in this effort. So many of the liberatory activities Kiki loved reminded Benny of detention. Anarchists aren't supposed to have leaders; they're not supposed to be organized by hierarchies. They're supposed to love and embrace disorder and difference. But what the ragtag gang of vegetarians loved, it seemed plain, was Kiki. Without her, nothing in that anarchist collective would happen. His girlfriend loved hand-raising; she loved facilitating; she loved the goofy hand signals they all used (finger waggling to indicate you liked a proposal), and she seemed to relish the interminable consensus-based meetings that could be prolonged at the whim of one wingnut property manager—a kind, dopey-faced man who dressed entirely in denim because he said his sweat would wet his clothes and then keep him cool. He smelled of onions. During these meetings, Benny felt his body drooping progressively in his chair.

What they were trying to do at the anarchist collective was model a new way of living. They were trying to be anti-capitalist, anti-racist, and anti-hierarchical, and he was with them in that. He shared their critique of society—the pursuit of owning more garbage, women treated as servants and depicted as sex objects, racism so pervasive that it could be measured in quantities of lead in the bloodstreams of children. The foundation that capitalism required—cheap labor, cheap goods, cheap "natural resources"—to increase profits for the few. However, a discrepancy remained, he thought, in how global capitalism might be overturned with a community menstrual calendar or radical puppet shows or even a dozen community gardens.

If Benny intimated these reservations in bed to Kiki, after they'd had sex and he was failing to read a zine on nonviolent communication, she would tell him that he was unwilling to care. That was his real problem. His cynicism was a way of protecting himself from caring and thus getting hurt.

It was unbelievable to everyone that Kiki had chosen to date him, though he'd vied doggedly for her affection. They'd met at a house party. She'd watched his band perform and came up to him afterward. Here was a tall, beautiful woman in combat boots smiling suggestively at him. He'd never seen her before, and he would have noticed.

"Do you read the Bible?" she asked.

He didn't take her for an evangelist in those boots.

"I can't say I do," he said. She kept smiling, which was encouraging.

"I wonder why you sing about it, then," she said. "That song."

"It's a cover," he said, "of Blind Willie Johnson. He was very worried about his soul, as you might guess."

"Maybe he had his reasons." Again, that smile.

"Are you new to town?" he said.

And so it went. When Benny had bent over his guitar as a teen-ager, practicing chords, he had a dim vision of just such a moment. When a Kiki would approach him after a set.

Their romance unfolded quickly. Kiki was overly serious for her age, only twenty-four. She was serious about what she ate, what she read, how she passed her time. At the end of the day, when they were in bed, she hugged her knees and worried aloud about the things she'd not yet finished. She could never get enough done to satisfy herself. But she believed, and this was rare in Benny's circle, that she would have an effect. He believed she would too.

Before Kiki, he hadn't known the anarchist collective existed. It wasn't that he didn't care about political issues. He just didn't think anything he could do would make a difference. Money made a difference. Kiki's activist friends smelled his poverty of spirit, his lack of radicalism. It was obvious to everyone, except Kiki, that she was dating him out of some self-destructive impulse. She was a beautiful woman with an elite East Coast education, and he was a musician, a college dropout from Louisiana, and what her friends dismissively called "a lifestyle anarchist," though he sometimes hoped that they were wrong.

One week after the disastrous visit to Golden Vale, Benny was on his way to deliver Kiki's sprout-and-avocado sandwich for lunch at the anarchist collective, where she was overseeing the completion of the dead pelican papier-mâché for the BP protest the following day. The warehouse held the anarchist library, a collective meeting space, and a bike cooperative. It was a big brick building in a quiet residential-industrial neighborhood near the Mississippi River and the train tracks that had once been a factory of some kind; little pieces of metal remained flattened into the floor. Five evenings a week, a church charity set up camp in an adjacent empty lot and washed the feet of the transients they fed hot meals to.

The anarchist collective rented the building for a steal after Hurricane Katrina. Many collective members were the college do-gooders who first came to New Orleans to help with hurricane cleanup and house rebuilding. Then they stayed. Benny had watched as these, mostly white, do-gooders poured in with their love and enthusiasm and their tireless energy for social uplift, and with this uplift, so went the rent prices. The library was stocked heavily with political theory and history, practical guides for fixing your own car, making a biodiesel VW, and healing your depression with herbs. It seemed to Benny the best the world could offer. Everyone doing the best they could.

But, much to everyone's shame, the collective failed as a genuine community space. The neighbors had no use for anarchism, and the neighborhood kids only came in periodically to steal the fishbowl of free condoms for fun. The collective was always happy to pitch in and restock it.

For the past week, the collective had pulsed with activity. The oil slick around BP's drilling site was growing. The collective members were furious and ready to pitch in. BP confessed during congressional testimony that the oil well was leaking five thousand barrels of oil a day. That was five times the initial estimate. The oil company was also using a chemical, Corexit, to disperse the oil in the water column. Kiki said that the chemical was banned in the U.K. for its toxicity and potential harm to wildlife.

Benny thought about Jordan and his mom in Golden Vale—how their lives were about to change and how they would be denying it up until the second shoe dropped. He couldn't imagine what they'd do if the oyster business closed. Jordan had likely been squirreling away money, but if that oil came inland, it would wipe him out for years.

When Benny arrived in the wide-open warehouse, there were two people struggling with the unwieldy, pulpy mass that would become a papier-mâché pelican for the protest. It was the size of a large inflatable exercise ball and did not resemble a bird in any way. He recognized one of the workers. Felipe was a narrow-shouldered guy who looked younger than his age—twentysomething—and often wore the same black bandanna around his neck. He waved his gummy, glue-covered hands at Benny and said something to him that he couldn't hear because Felipe was too soft-spoken.

Although racked with self-doubt, and rarely speaking up for himself, Felipe was as dedicated as they came; he'd papier-mâché all night long if anyone asked him to. Felipe told him that Kiki went looking in the storage unit for sign-making materials for the night's meeting. They would all write their best anti-BP slogans on posters. At the protest tomorrow, they would hand these out to anyone in the crowd who looked remotely interested.

Benny knew Kiki was nervous that no one would show up. Anarchist attendance could not be counted on. On his way to the storage room, he had to walk through the library and then the bike co-op, where half a dozen people tinkered with bikes hoisted in the air. At the helm of this operation was a handful of aging punks in too-tight pants that sausaged their beer bellies up on a platter. Benny liked them, even as they presented a cautionary tale of why not to marry yourself to an aesthetic.

Kiki was not in the storage unit. He found her outside smoking with two tall white men who looked like hip Bible salesmen—beige trousers, short-sleeved button-up shirts, wildly styled hair. They looked as though they'd just arrived from the future. As he got closer, he detected a Scandinavian accent, maybe Swedish.

"American protests are so funny," the taller one said. "Five people show up with posters and sit quietly. No wonder your government doesn't listen. Americans are too fat and happy to care about anything."

He was teasing her, flirting.

"Well, I don't know about tomorrow . . ." she began. "But historically, there's a real precedent—"

Benny interrupted her. "Yes, American protests are hilarious. You should join us tomorrow for a good laugh."

He handed Kiki her sandwich, and looped an arm around her waist, wheeling her away from the handsome Swedes. They sat down together in the library; she hooked her legs over his. She talked nervously at first, saying she'd been in touch with a reporter from the *Times-Picayune* who was interested in the protest but sounded noncommittal about covering it. She'd also called the local news channel and radio station, wrote to the anarchist LIST-SERV, reached out to the local socialists, the feminist reading group, the teachers' union, and she'd even posted flyers at four library branches.

"Eat," he said, petting her legs. "Everything is going to be fine, and even if no one shows up at all—which won't happen—this will still be worth doing."

When Kiki was touched, she squinted, almost as if flinching, before she smiled. He didn't know why she did this, but when it happened, he felt a world open in his chest.

A few hours later, Benny bought a pizza for the folks who showed up to help with the pelican and to make signs for the protest. There was a chalkboard on the wall where people spitballed protest slogans to write on the signs: BOYCOTT BIG POLLUTERS; BP LIES. THE GULF DIES; and, curiously, WHO LIVES IN A PINEAPPLE UNDER THE SEA? NOBODY! THANKS TO BP.

The pelican was finally taking a birdlike form. Benny tore up newspaper for an hour and helped a punk girl mold the head while she told him depraved stories about her family from North Carolina. By the time the evening meeting rolled around, Benny was about done with his service to the cause. He wanted to go buy a six-pack of tallboys and see who was at the speakeasy on Desire Street. He couldn't understand where Kiki's stamina came from. This last meeting's purpose was just to make sure everyone was on the same page as to the schedule. The feminists had shown up. So had a couple of straitlaced, exhausted teachers.

Benny groaned when two of the more seasoned protesters instructed everyone to write the phone number of a sympathetic lawyer with a Sharpie on an arm in case of arrest. Kiki seemed turned on by this idea too. It was hard to imagine getting arrested for stopping traffic for eleven minutes, which was their plan. Eleven minutes for the eleven oil rig workers who died in the *Deepwater Horizon* explosion. But it ennobled them to think so.

The meeting had devolved into the typical cant about the oil industry's crimes against the people of southeast Louisiana. One bespectacled young man raised his hand just to say, "The Gulf Coast communities have lived on that land for generations. It's an entire economy based on the fisheries—bait shops, fishing gear, ice shops. There's nothing else there. What's going to happen to them?"

"Let's remember who these people vote for," said another young man. "Oil companies come in, carve up the wetlands, drill and dump wherever they want. All the while, these people rally behind Bobby Jindal, who's in the pocket of these oil companies. What we need to talk about is: How do we help people who can't help themselves?"

Benny cut in. "Do you, like, actually know any of these people in the Gulf?"

The man blinked at him. "I mean, I've been to the coast. I talk to people."

"Benny," Kiki said, "you didn't raise your hand."

"Whatever," Benny said. "I just don't like to hear people . . . Most of the people in this room weren't born in Louisiana."

Kiki's eyes slivered with displeasure. He felt himself failing to be the kind of partner she wanted.

"I think appealing to nativism isn't the right attitude here." The man crossed his arms. "We're all in this together. Even in New Orleans, we're being poisoned too."

Benny opened his mouth to speak, but Kiki looked toward a guy in the circle who hadn't spoken yet. "You had your hand raised, but I think I skipped you."

The man was seated in the outer ring of their circle. Benny had never seen him before. The man stood to speak, making his comment seem significant. "I wasn't born here either," the man said playfully. The first thing Benny noticed about him was his classically beautiful face and then his accent—rural, but not Louisianan. "I just got to town. I asked around, and I was told to come here. I'm excited about what you all are doing, and I want to be a part of it. I'm AWOL from the U.S. Army after three tours in Iraq. I am on a bike ride across the country to protest the war. I'll be riding until the war stops. Maybe some people here want to join."

Benny saw Kiki's eyes flash with interest. "What's your name?"

"They call me Possum," he said, without irony. "I don't advertise my real name because I'd be court-martialed."

Possum was on the shorter side, but sturdily built. His forearms looked like they'd done some lifting. He had long black hair in a ponytail, a strong, square jaw, and soulful brown eyes. He was so obviously handsome that Benny was surprised he hadn't noticed Possum sooner. The group seemed to perk up when he spoke.

"I do a presentation," he said. "About my experience in the war and my decision to go AWOL. I'd like to do one here if people are interested."

"I'm sure we're interested," Kiki said, and then stopped herself. "I can't speak for the collective. But you should go to the general collective meeting. This is a meeting for the protest tomorrow."

Possum said, looking at Kiki, "This is what I've been looking for."

Kiki fingered her long braids absentmindedly in a way that irritated Benny. The meeting had gone on for an hour and a half at that point. Benny had now been at the anarchist collective for five hours. The meeting had accomplished little beyond nailing down a few additional logistical details for the protest. The rest of the talk might have happened over drinks in someone's backyard.

By the meeting's end, Felipe had volunteered to keep painting the pelican until it was finished. It looked like another five hours of work, but Felipe was glad to sacrifice himself. Kiki was talking to the overextended teachers. After Benny had lined up all the folding chairs into neat rows, he looked back at Kiki, still chatting happily. It seemed to fuel her. Benny was reminded of being a boy waiting for his mother to finish up at the grocery store. He felt a childish wave of indignation at his role, likely unfair, so he went outside to smoke a cigarette.

He rounded the building to the street where he could smoke in peace, but as he turned the corner, the guy who called himself Possum was there, looking up contemplatively. Benny turned on his heel to find another place to smoke, but Possum called to him. "Hey, man," he said. "What's your name again?"

Benny had to approach him to answer. He resigned himself. He took his cigarette from his ear. "I'm Benny," he said.

He half-heartedly clapped Possum's hand. Possum began to dig in his jean shorts for a lighter, but Benny waved him off. "I got one," he said.

Possum said, "So you're from the bayou, huh? Your people fishermen?"

Benny spit on the sidewalk by his shoe. "My dad was an oyster farmer."

"I didn't know there was such a thing. That you farmed them. I'm from farmers too, in Iowa."

"That so?" Benny said. His mouth felt acrid. He'd smoked too many cigarettes already that day.

Possum seemed not to care that Benny was aloof. He trusted his innate interestingness. "I was recruited for the Army in high school. I wanted to be a big man. I wanted to be a part of a brotherhood. I loved all of it. Then I went to war."

Benny could tell that the Army had shaped him. He possessed physical confidence rare in Benny's crowd. But Possum was too blandly good-looking for Benny to be attracted to him, and there was something virtuous about him that Benny distrusted.

"Sounds like you're doing a good thing now," Benny said, "with your bike ride and all."

"I'm hoping to get a bunch of people to join me. The more people, the more attention to the cause. Something to make the hell we've been through worth something."

A large cockroach flew by their faces, and they stepped back together.

"Fuck, man. I didn't know cockroaches could fly," Possum said. "First time I ever saw that."

Benny pitched his cigarette into the street. He looked back toward the warehouse. In the distance, they heard a steamboat playing a tune for the tourists on the Mississippi. A tune that reminded him of old carnivals.

"Do you bike?" Possum said.

"Yeah, sure. But I have a job."

Possum put out his cigarette on his shoe and then slipped it into his pocket. This was not lost on Benny. It seemed a reproach for littering.

"Taxpayer money pays for the war, you know."

"My job is under the table," Benny said, not wanting to get into it. "But I also have a band. We do shows and whatnot."

"I'm a banjo player, myself," he said. He became excited. "Want to hear a song I wrote?"

Benny did not and was embarrassed on Possum's behalf that he would ask. It was not impossible that Possum was flirting with him. Benny shrugged. "I'm just waiting for my girlfriend."

"Kiki your girlfriend?" Possum said. Benny couldn't read the tone—surprised or disappointed. "She's something else."

Possum galloped into the warehouse to pick up his banjo in a manner surprising for an Army man. Benny noticed that Possum had a turkey feather tied into his ponytail. Benny lowered himself to the curb. He hoped Possum would get caught inside and not return. Kiki was something else. He knew that, but he also thought that if he had to wait for her any longer, he was going to go to the speakeasy without her. A couple of svelte women biked by him. They called out his name, but Benny didn't recognize them. He'd stood up too late. "Hey! You going to the speakeasy?" he said to their backs as they zipped up the empty street. Their laughter pulled at his guts as they biked away.

Then Possum was beside him again, plucking at his banjo and humming. More turkey feathers dangled from the neck of his banjo.

"What did you do to that turkey?"

Possum laughed but didn't respond. Benny recognized Possum's stance as he plucked. He was a guy who'd watched a lot of YouTube videos of folk players from the middle of the previous century. In a way, Possum was almost doing an imitation of a folksinger, which was hard for Benny to watch. It was like someone was showing him something unseemly about himself that he hadn't noticed before. Benny looked around. This performance was only for him.

Possum began in the sing-talk style of Pete Seeger: "*Now, I'm just a farmhand from Iowa. There's a lot of things I don't understand . . .*"

Benny wasn't sure if Possum was talking to him or if this was part of the song.

"*Like why we send farmhands to shoot farmers in Afghanistan.*"

Benny liked that line. Possum won him over with it. His voice wasn't too pretty. It cracked and was low, and he went higher than he should have when he began to sing in earnest, but this was endearing. What Benny liked about the song was that it wasn't just an anti-war song; it was a confession of personal failure that gave way to his feeling betrayed by his country. And Possum really put his lungs into it. In his voice there was the tension that he might suddenly start to cry. It was transfixing. Possum nearly howled that he couldn't sustain a relationship and he couldn't hold down a job.

From the moment Possum stood up in the meeting, he had exuded an air of capability few collective members had. It should have mortified Benny that Possum addressed the flag as if the flag were a lover that had betrayed him, that he'd been a boy and didn't understand why he was going to war. But Benny couldn't help himself. He was moved. Not only that, but Benny felt petty and small-minded next to him—and undeserving of someone like Kiki. Possum was even a better banjo player than he was.

When Possum had finished, he looked down on the pavement with relief. Then he looked at Benny and knocked him on the arm in embarrassed gratitude. He called Benny "my brother."

Benny, mired in sudden despair, said he needed to go for a walk, and took off in the direction of the Mississippi. He walked unthinkingly, one foot in front of the other, until he arrived outside the speakeasy on Desire Street. The house was dark but alive with laughter inside.

The Desire Speakeasy, a dimly lit house with an L-shaped bar in its living room, opened whenever the old punk who owned the house felt inclined to host. It was in the Upper Ninth Ward, on a residential block of Desire Street where many of the shotgun houses had been boarded up after Katrina. Benny had walked himself over there without having made a conscious decision to do so.

It wasn't much of a speakeasy. There was an effusive drag queen in a metallic green dress behind the bar—rumor had it that this was the homeowner—pouring drinks, but most everybody had flasks tucked into their back pockets or tallboys in their shoulder bags. Guests had to enter through the back door, and it was so dark inside that the rooms could surprise you. Like an alcove off a hallway, where strangers sat cross-legged on pillows and weed smoke bloomed around them.

Benny had been there for a couple hours. He'd made friends with a couple of hitchhiking boys from Phoenix, who invited him to play a drinking game he couldn't understand. He'd helped them finish their bottle of rotgut whiskey and sometime after noticed that his phone had died.

The smell of dried sweat pervaded the rooms, but not the garden out back, an oasis surrounded by a tall wooden fence. There was a magnolia tree strung with lights. Brick pathways wound through wild palms and elephant ears, and cat's-claw vines climbed up the trees. This greenery hid congregations of wrought-iron patio furniture. The tall palms created nooks for sudden lovers, which was where Benny found himself, improbably, now that he'd rested a guitar against the bench and a girl, Maria, moved closer to offer him a skin-colored tablet in her palm.

"Let it dissolve under your tongue," she said.

"Too late," Benny said, and she laughed.

He couldn't remember if Kiki was on her way to the speakeasy or not. She might appear from anywhere in the party—through the back door or detaching from a crowd. He picked up the guitar from where it was leaning as he waited for the drug to take.

Benny was plucking an old blues song as Maria watched him, smiling, and he was alight in her attention. This he felt without drugs, but then the ecstasy kicked in and his body flushed with heat, flickering, and he felt the incredible dexterity in his hands, that they could do anything to the guitar. It didn't matter to him then that he didn't write his own music. He could bring the old songs back to life. *"Baby, please don't go back to New Orleans. You know I love you so . . ."*

Maria sat so close he could taste the cigarettes and whiskey in her mouth. What was she talking about? He couldn't follow it. The ecstasy made him thirsty. He finished the warm beer Maria produced from her bag, and though he had to pee, he didn't want to stand. It would close a window he knew was open, a window that he'd nudged, and there was some magnetic pull to her face.

She was talking about being from Cincinnati and how she had been riding freight trains most of the winter until she came to New Orleans. Then she was talking about how you have to touch someone; you just have to, or else the drugs were a waste. His whole body was alive to touch, and he told her so. She said, "Try this," and her finger hovered between his eyes, and he was nearly ticklish. It was a warm ecstatic feeling, emanating from her finger. He touched her neck, petting her collarbone, and she pulled her hair back in invitation. It was like a game to see so much pleasure in someone else's face; he wanted to see if he couldn't produce more. He had a hand down her shirt, cupping her breast, and she moaned. Her moan was loud and frightening. He shushed her. And then the taste that he'd already tasted was in his mouth, and he was thinking about the texture of her tongue, that it was smaller and rougher than Kiki's.

They were on the bench entwined like one body. He felt bad about it, but he also felt like it was just bodies and that it didn't have to be wrong. It wasn't love; it was ecstasy. And there was the strange sensation of his penis, springing with pleasure, but then soft again. The rest of his body flooding with this pleasure, as if he were a cup filling up and pouring over.

Benny was slightly aware that they were visible to others. A shadow or two had entered his peripheral vision and then faded. Some giggling. As they were intertwined, the talk faded in and out.

Maria said they should go, and somehow they were navigating the path to the gate. Benny felt his body had betrayed him, first his dick, then his legs. They were autonomous legs. He passed faces he knew on his way out—faces he could not read. He was certain people knew everything he'd done wrong. Not just that night, but always.

Ten

Benny woke to the opening of "Backwater Blues" coming from another room. The sound was familiar, and he thought his roommate, Stani, was playing it before he realized where he was. The girl's house. A mobile of bird feathers hung above the girl's bed, which was soft and smelled sweeter than his own. He hoped that she'd left, so he could slip away, but he heard rushing water and a clanking noise coming from what he assumed was the kitchen.

The girl's name escaped him, but he remembered some trouble with the condom and that he'd objected to using one. He'd felt nothing for Kiki in that moment, with the girl on top of him. But being in the girl's house made no sense to him now—he *loved* Kiki. He woke feeling his body had committed crimes he had nothing to do with. Now his head felt like it'd cracked open; he could feel his heartbeat in his forehead. His thighs were tacky with sweat and cum. His phone wouldn't turn on and he wasn't sure if he'd tried to call or text Kiki before it died; she could have been at his house that very moment.

The smell of fried eggs wafted into the bedroom, and it turned his stomach. He picked his nose and flicked the crust on the girl's floor, where he saw his underwear and pants. He tossed the sheets but couldn't find his shirt.

On his way to the kitchen, Benny passed through another girl's room. There was a fabric tent over the girl's bed that stretched to the ceiling, obscuring the bed and who might have been sleeping in it. The sun's insistence through the curtains told him that it was afternoon already.

In the kitchen, he was shocked by the girl's red hair, pulled up on the top of her head like it had been the night before. The hemline of his T-shirt stopped at her hip bones, just above her yellow cotton underwear. There was a slight smile on her freckled face, as if to say, Look what I've done! while she poked eggs with a spatula.

"Aw," she said cheerily. "You look like shit."

"Yeah?" He patted his pockets for cigarettes, but there weren't any.

"Are you hungry?"

"No," he said. He had a hand on his stomach. "But I'd give my right arm for a cigarette right about now."

"You smoked all of mine," she said. The spatula landed with a thud in the sink.

"My roommate smokes. You could probably roll one of hers." She pointed behind him. "Look in her room. A wooden bowl on the dresser."

Benny rummaged about the girl's dresser, lifting clothing and papers gingerly in case the roommate was still in bed, but he couldn't find any cigarettes. Then a brunette's face, puffy with sleep, emerged from the fabric tent. "What the fuck are you doing?"

He searched his mind for her name, but nothing was there. "Your roommate said I could have one of your cigarettes."

"Maria?" the girl yelled.

Benny stepped back toward the doorway.

Maria appeared, and Benny was stuck between them.

"What the hell, Maria?" The brunette sat up in bed. "You tell people they can go through my stuff?"

Maria blushed easily, something Benny hadn't noticed the night before. She stumbled on her words. "I thought you might be at Max's."

"It's my fault," Benny offered. "I asked."

"Who the fuck are you?" the girl said to Benny, though without any bite.

"No one," Benny said. He didn't want her to know his name, and yet she'd learn it eventually. "I'm no one."

The girl looked back at Maria for an explanation, sitting upright, her tank top so low Benny could see the shape of her heavy breasts. Maria was frowning at Benny.

"Your *no one* friends can't come into my room and take my stuff."

Benny could understand her annoyance, and yet he thought she was being a bit harsh with poor Maria. The layout of a shotgun house required one to walk through all the rooms to reach a bathroom in the back, or the kitchen. The layout necessitated some sacrifice of privacy.

He felt dizzy and tried to steady himself on her dresser, which rocked. A picture frame fell over.

"I think I'm going to vomit."

"Get out!" The girl flung back the covers, rising from the bed. Her legs were bare too. "Get the fuck out!"

He brushed past Maria, through the kitchen, and into the backyard. He was on his knees in the grass, dry-heaving. There was nothing coming up. It was like someone had a grip on his intestines and erratically squeezed. Eventually he quit trying and just lay down. The grass itched his bare stomach.

Maria appeared at the back door. "You don't want eggs?"

Benny turned onto his back, his forearm shielding his eyes from the sun. "I can't, thanks."

She slumped down on the back steps, and he crawled toward her in the shade and sat up. He was wet all over.

"I wish I could just throw up," he said. He looked over their sun-fried vegetable garden, the imprint of his body in the tall grass, and the chain-link fence separating her overgrown grass from the neighbors' cut grass on either side. He was sweating, and another wave of nausea hit him. It distracted him from his head, at least.

"I really need a cigarette."

"Are you serious?" she said.

"It'll help my stomach. Please."

He heard her stomp through the kitchen and exchange words with the roommate. He heard Maria say, "He's an asshole." That was fine. He didn't care. He hoped to never see either of them again.

Maria appeared again after a minute, shaking the bag of tobacco for him to see.

"Come sit out front," she said. "There's shade there." Then she disappeared inside again and left him to hoist his ruined body up from the grass.

The roommate was gone, he discovered, as he tiptoed through her room. He found Maria on the front porch in the only chair, her skinny legs propped on the railing. She'd put shorts on. Benny sank down on the porch next to her legs, which were downy with strawberry hair. The peeling paint of the railing itched his bare skin. He wanted his T-shirt back, but he didn't feel he was in a position to ask for it. Her fork clinked against the plate as she pierced scrambled eggs. He felt both desperate and unable to leave, as if he had already been discovered. Someone from the party saw him with her, most likely. His pride forbade him from asking her for the cigarettes again. He would wait until she offered.

"Can I have some of your water?" he asked instead.

They both noticed his hand shaking as he took the large purple cup from her. He looked away as he drank.

"That's not from the ecstasy," she said.

He squinted at her.

"I don't usually drink like that."

"Sure," she said. She tossed the tobacco pouch on the floor by him, and he could have kissed her skinny leg. "Yeah, me too."

"How late were we there?" he asked. What he really wanted to know was, How many people saw us?

"Pretty late. Almost four, I think. I've never been there that late, but there were still people around dancing. We danced. Here."

Yes, he slightly remembered this—realizing he was too drunk to dance, his stomach leaden, his feet like balls, or stilts, nothing to keep him upright. She held out a chunk of scrambled egg on a fork to feed him. He waved it off.

"You don't look like you're going to any protests today."

So he had told her about the protest, then. Did she know he had a girlfriend? Looking at Maria's narrow face, her wounded expression, he didn't get the sense that she knew about Kiki.

"I should go home," he said, rolling up the cigarette. "Where am I?" He licked the seal. The houses on her block were the same as the houses in all the old neighborhoods of the city. He could be anywhere. The cigarette tasted sour and wonderful. He felt it numbing his headache.

"Upper Ninth, Gallier and Urquhart Street," she said, watching him.

It was not far from his house, maybe fifteen minutes. But it was already in the wet nineties.

"You think you could drive me home?"

"No!" She laughed. "You can walk. It's only a hangover, friend."

He leaned back on the railing, exhaling smoke. "I'm just not meant to be in the world today."

"You know something?" Maria said. "You haven't said one nice thing to me all morning."

"I feel terrible."

"You were so nice last night." She took her feet down from the railing.

"I'm not myself." He hurried to roll another cigarette before she told him to go, which he sensed was coming. He slid it behind his ear.

She snatched the tobacco pouch from the floor and stood. "That's right," she said. "I forgot. You're no one."

Maria closed the door behind her, and Benny stepped down from the porch into the blinding afternoon, shirtless, and in the wrong direction.

The rest of the day unfolded like a hot nightmare. He was a bare-chested fool in a fedora trudging down Poland Avenue. As if summoned, a car full of teenagers slowed down next to him. A big girl leaned out on her forearms and called him "sweetcheeks." Her companions thought this was hilarious and beat their excitement on the side of the car. Then the driver pitched an empty soda can at him but missed. "All right, all right," Benny said, waving them on, and they trundled past. He loved New Orleans; he always had. But there was a ruthlessness to it that could overtake you on a shadeless day when you'd cooked your brain and wondered what kept you in this swampy hellhole.

He'd hoped and feared that Kiki would be waiting for him at his house, but she wasn't there. Neither was his roommate, Stani, whom

Benny had hoped he could unburden himself on. Stani had volunteered to deliver the papier-mâché pelican to the French Quarter in a truck. Benny had said he'd help too, but it was nearly two p.m. now, and that bird was already in flight. Benny's list of failures was growing so long he was tempted to go to bed and remain there until he could muster some feeling besides self-loathing.

His room seemed as hopeless as he did, the sheet a knot on his bed. An empty tallboy can on the floor with a cigarette snuffed out on the top. On his desk, a stack of flyers that Kiki had designed for the protest. Kiki's nubby blue sweater was draped across the shoulders of his desk chair. This was despair—the very sight of it. Where would he say he'd slept? He took her sweater to his bed with him, and he lay with it over his face, breathing her in.

Realizing he couldn't escape himself in sleep, he took a shower and decided he'd go to the protest and apologize. He had no idea yet what he'd say to her.

His hair was wet and cool as he biked to the French Quarter. This was the only part of his body that felt good. He biked by the run-down storefronts of St. Claude Avenue, past the mural that instructed passersby to READ, which some prankster had transformed into ANAL BEAD. As a teenager, Benny had fallen hard and fast for New Orleans. He'd felt the small-mindedness of his hometown constrict around him. In those years, his only reprieve was an after-school arts program in New Orleans. His father, when he drove Benny, would shake his head in disdain at the sight of the city's litter-strewn sidewalks and impoverished people clutching tallboys in the middle of the afternoon. This only increased the city's pull for Benny.

Benny knew that his father only drove him occasionally because he had a girlfriend in New Orleans, Rita, a blues singer of the corniest variety. Al had taken him to see her perform once and then insisted that this woman, who'd dedicated a love song to him, was an old friend he'd never mentioned before. After the set, Rita was bent on extracting compliments from Benny on her singing, determined to have Benny grant his approval, and his father had acted as if this were completely normal. Al called Rita a "loon" on the drive back to Golden Vale. Benny did not let himself interrogate this episode too much and even succeeded in dismissing it for a couple of years as a fluke. He had admired his father, even as he felt misunderstood by him.

Kiki had long ago warned him that she had no interest in dating the drunkest guy at the party. But among his set in New Orleans, Benny could always find someone drunker. Except he was discovering that he did indeed court self-destruction, and he couldn't understand why.

He slid between the cars on old oak-lined Esplanade Avenue and onto Decatur Street, the start of the French Quarter, past Balcony Music Club, where some old workhorse jazz musicians were already blowing their horns for a weak afternoon crowd. Tourists clotted up the street there—a quaint model of colonial life—all of it elegant and sullied. Moldering brick tenements were painted gaily—salmon, seafoam, buttercup-yellow—each skirted with tall iron balconies, saving the walkers from the pitiless sun. Ferns dripping water from balcony boxes onto the street below. Music—the boom of bass from cars, and the tinny whine of jazz in the shops and bars. Forest-green shutters on door fronts and windows. Antiques shops, shoebox markets, and French-style cafés. The sun baked the pavement, and the soap solution the city sprayed to deodorize the streets nauseated him. Benny had to dodge a group of grown men in straw hats who'd stopped mid-street to photograph the Mardi Gras beads looped on balconies, left over from festival season.

Before he reached Jackson Square, he heard Kiki speaking into a megaphone, asking a group of people to gather around. The sound of her voice pained him. The traffic clogged up right around Jackson Square on Decatur, and it slowed him down. Tourists and tour guides milled around the statue of Andrew Jackson on a horse. Benny had to dismount his bike and push it through the hordes of overhot families and fortune-tellers and men painted silver pretending to be statues and Black children tap-dancing with Coke cans tied to their shoes.

There she was—standing on a wooden crate with her megaphone—head and shoulders above the crowd. The wings of her shoulder blades above her tank top shone with sweat in the sun. He felt wretched, but the sight of her made his stomach seize up in guilt. She was sermonizing about the evils of the oil industry in general and BP in particular. There must have been forty people in attendance. It wasn't an impressive number, but nothing to be ashamed of. Benny recognized a dozen signs being passed out among the crowd—one he'd written himself: BP LIES. THE GULF DIES.

He waited for the crosswalk sign to change and jogged with his bicycle, locking it to an iron fence near Café du Monde. The line of tourists waiting for beignets extended toward the plaza where Kiki was, and some of these people turned with folded arms to hear what Kiki was saying. He joined the crowd and positioned himself in her eyeline, waving, smiling. She turned to face the opposite side of the audience, refusing to look at him.

"The people of southeast Louisiana . . ." She paused as she glanced down at a note card in her hand. He'd thrown her off. "Are exposed to some of the most carcinogenic air and water in the country; they suffer miscarriages at unheard-of rates in the United States. We allow this because we feel powerless, but we are not powerless. We're in a position to demand change."

On the periphery, he saw a bright red bun of hair belonging to a girl with hands on her hips, listening to Kiki. Benny almost vomited. It was Maria. She was still wearing Benny's T-shirt. Next to her was the heavy-chested roommate who hated him. Why had he told her about the protest? Had Kiki noticed his T-shirt on Maria? Had Kiki spoken to Maria about the T-shirt? He quickly looked away from Maria and hoped, in not looking at her, that Maria wouldn't notice him, and Kiki wouldn't notice her.

Kiki went on: "We're here to honor the lives of those eleven workers who died in the explosion on the *Deepwater Horizon* oil rig. An oil rig that missed sixteen safety inspections but was nonetheless allowed to go on drilling. These are lives that didn't need to be lost. This is an oil spill that didn't need to happen." She paused, peering over the crowd looking for someone. She seemed to have found who she was looking for. "We're going to honor these lives lost with eleven minutes of silence. Thank you for respecting this silence with us."

She turned off the megaphone and stepped off the crate. Benny thought this might be his chance to discern what she knew. Someone began passing out yellow packages that shook out into full-body suits. A dozen people zipped themselves into neon hazmat suits. This was a new development. Nobody at the meetings had mentioned hazmat suits. The suit wearers looked outrageous. Kiki too stepped into a suit as if it were pajamas, and she zipped herself up. The full-body suits were plastic. He imagined she would boil in it.

The hazmat-suit-wearers led the crowd of sign-toting protesters into the middle of Decatur Street, provoking polite car honking. Then the drivers realized that these people in the street were not going anywhere, and they began to lay on the horns. Benny watched as Possum straightened up as if he'd received an injection of iron. He trotted up to a driver's window and began speaking passionately. Those soulful brown eyes were doing their magic.

As the crowd of demonstrators walked into the street, Benny caught Kiki by her yellow plastic arm. Too hard, perhaps. Her arm was slippery with sweat under the plastic. She shook him loose. "Not now," she said, turning away from him.

Felipe, the faithful, was at her side, and looked at Benny with a territorialism that Benny didn't know Felipe possessed. Together, Kiki and Felipe sank to the pavement and lay down like corpses. It was a die-in.

The demonstrators spilled into both lanes of traffic on Decatur Street in front of Jackson Square. They lowered themselves down and lay back. Some held their signs aloft, others tucked them under their heads to save themselves from the asphalt, which could fry an egg, from the look of it. Benny stood amid the sea of bodies in the street. He could see the triple steeples of St. Louis Cathedral, often the postcard picture of New Orleans. Next to it, the stately old Cabildo, where the Louisiana Purchase ceremony took place. Tourists passing on the sidewalk slowed to read the protest signs and to make sense of it. From where he stood, he could see too the exasperation of the stalled drivers in their cars.

On the pavement, the protesters looked uncomfortable and determined, their faces shiny with sweat, eyes closed in the sun. No one had foreseen how hot the pavement would be. Then he spotted Maria, who was pointing him out to her roommate as they too sank to the ground and pretended to die. Benny realized he was the last person standing, and then he too sank to his butt. The pavement was scorching. He didn't have sunglasses and his eyes burned and watered. Here were fifty people lying in the street, quietly enduring the burning pavement, and Kiki had orchestrated all of it. She had lost sleep over this protest. She'd biked all over the city with a staple gun to put up flyers. And did she fancy herself a little too much as a result? Undeniably. But she seemed to be made of better stuff than most people. Benny didn't have the bandwidth to care about biodiversity in the Gulf. If he set himself on fire in front of BP headquarters, he couldn't affect the international corporation. And if this couldn't, what was the point of losing sleep over it?

As he lay there, he considered how to get Kiki's attention. If she would just look at him, he might know how much he'd have to grovel. She was a deeply prideful person. This was to her credit but also just the problem. It was the longest eleven minutes of his life.

Somewhere, a trumpeter began a funereal tune. People around him stirred, and Benny took this to mean the eleven minutes of silence were over with. When Benny sat up, the papier-mâché pelican had appeared. He wondered where it had been before. Four people in black held the bird overhead with sticks. It was the size of a small car with its wings spread. It looked more artful than Benny could have imagined. The bird's wings were dipped in black, signifying oil. It had black teardrops in its eyes too. The puppeteers were skilled. Their movement made it seem as though the bird struggled to fly.

Then a second line appeared, a full jazz band—a drummer, trombone, tuba, and trumpeter dressed in black suit jackets. Black men in their fifties wearing matching hats. It was the Preservation Hall Jazz Band. He couldn't understand how Kiki had gotten hold of them. These were professional jazz musicians—men who demanded a fee. They started to play "Down by the Riverside." Kiki had arranged a second line—a funeral march for the Gulf. This had been tossed out as a joke in one of the meetings, and she had actually made it happen.

The crowd was slowly swaying after the giant pelican and Kiki was lost somewhere within it. The march started up Decatur Street. He was one of the last people left in the street, and an irate driver had edged up so close to him that his bumper was a few inches from Benny's face. It was a license plate from Florida.

Benny stood and smacked the hood. The driver was a blond lady with a pink face who looked scared of him. "Just cool it, would you?" he said. "It's a protest."

"You all can't block traffic," she said, her voice hoarse. "Who the heck do you think you are?"

She grew more frightened when he walked around her SUV and leaned into her passenger-side window. They exchanged words, and Benny lost his temper. She said that if he cared so much about the environment, he ought to go scrub a sea turtle. He hated the woman. In this moment, she represented all of society's ills. Benny reached into her SUV and grabbed her Big Gulp of soda and dumped it on her passenger seat. She screamed and hit the gas, nearly running over his foot.

In the interim, the funeral march had continued up Decatur Street without him.

As he broke into a jog to catch the parade, Benny spied a news truck parking nearby. A cameraman popped out of the van and struggled to trot after the marchers with his gear on his shoulders.

The protest turned into the heart of the French Quarter, the pelican out of sight, and Benny wanted to run, but he felt too weak. He felt a thrum of nausea, and like a gift from an angel, a trash can was right where he wanted it to be when he emptied his stomach. The band was playing "Just a Closer Walk with Thee" now. Benny began to trot toward the marchers, but the distance was growing larger. He succeeded in catching up only to the cameraman, who looked anguished, out of shape, sucking air.

"What's their route?" the man asked. "Do you know their route? I need to get the front of the parade to get a good shot."

Benny was so hot that he wanted to die. The cameraman looked at Benny's shirt. He had vomit splashback on his shirt stomach.

The cameraman seemed to think Benny was just another drugged-up gutterpunk.

"Oh, of course. I'm sorry," said the man, realizing his mistake.

✦ Eleven ✦

After Doug bailed and did not call back, Jordan lost a full day's work. He sat in his office, the old swivel chair whining beneath him, and thumbed through his phone contacts for a deckhand to cull oysters for him. Good deckhands were scarce before the explosion. Matt Clark, newly on parole, said he'd already signed up to do cleanup work for BP. The Kovak brothers had too. He was incredulous by the time he got Eddie DeBlanc on the line.

"Have you heard of the Vessels of Opportunity program?" Eddie said.

"That's a cleanup job," Jordan said. "We're talking about a spot on my boat for the season."

"Ain't going to be a season," Eddie said, "when that oil comes in."

"We don't know it's coming in."

"Yeah, well," Eddie said.

"Bend over for BP like everybody else, then, that's fine," Jordan said. "I hear they're paying good."

"Take it easy," Eddie said.

Jordan hung up on him, not seeing a way to walk back what he'd said. On his office TV, the news showed a graphic of the four-story tower that BP planned to lower on one of three leaks from the underwater well. Once that tower was over the leak, they'd pump the oil to a ship on the water's surface. Eddie likely had no idea that they'd nearly finished the tower and that the big spill was almost over.

This was how he spent the afternoon before his first date with Cyndi, sweating over his desk, cursing Doug Babies to hell forever in his heart. Outside, a rainstorm swept up from the Gulf and cooled the afternoon. His oyster lugger sat idle in the bayou, pelted by a sideways rain. Jordan thought about canceling the date, but he knew Cyndi had a friend covering her shift just so he could take her out.

As he stood shaving in front of the mirror, he heard his mother moving around in the kitchen. He smelled butter sauce and knew she was making oyster spaghetti—butter, garlic, white wine, parsley, Parmesan. She made it, he noticed, when she was thinking of his father. This was his father's dish. He'd made it on the rare nights that she was away.

Jordan had forgotten to tell her that he had a date and would be out. He called to her.

She rapped on the bathroom door. "All right if I come in?"

"Yeah," he said, tightening the towel at his waist. His face was covered with shaving cream.

"You're shaving." She smiled, her cheeks flushed. She was holding a goblet of white wine. "Why?"

"I have a date. I forgot to tell you."

"You'll miss dinner?"

"Yeah," he said. "Sorry."

"I'm happy. You should go on dates, especially now. Keep your mind off things. Have you heard about the containment dome they're going to lower on the well?"

"The top hat?"

"Of course you've heard of it. Anyway, who's your date? Do I know her?"

"No," he said, smacking the razor on the sink edge. "You don't know her."

"Don't tell me, then."

"You don't drink wine."

"I think I like it, though," she said. "And I feel wasteful whenever I make oyster spaghetti. I keep it in the fridge and then I dump it out. You know who came over the other day to see you? Dr. Merritt."

The name meant nothing to Jordan.

"The oyster biologist. Your father called him Doc. He came to see you, but you were at the bar." She said this with some playful scorn. When he tried to picture the man, all he could see was a Hawaiian shirt.

"What'd he want?"

"You know what? He never said. But he asked me out to dinner. I think he'd been drinking."

"What'd you say?"

"Oh, I don't know."

"You don't know what you said?"

"I said I didn't know. I never thought I'd go on a date again."

In the mirror, she futzed with her hair, smoothing and tucking it. All his life, she had had variations of this haircut—her blond bob. The thought of her dating again, canoodling with some old man on the couch, flipped his stomach. She wasn't asking for his permission, but she did seem to want his approval. She wanted to hear him say he didn't think it was awful. She was waiting for him to speak. Well, he couldn't. Instead, he carefully worked the razor over his jawbone.

"Did Doug call you?" she said finally.

He flicked shaving cream from the razor into the sink.

"I can't believe it," she said. "Have you got someone to fill in for him?"

"It's tough right now," he said.

"I'll call Benny."

"Don't call Benny."

"I'm calling him!" She picked her wine goblet up from the vanity. This was tipsy behavior, out of character. "How will you make your orders? You have buyers to supply."

She reached for his phone by the sink.

"Don't," he said, more firmly.

"Then you call him," she said. "You need help."

He dropped his razor in the sink. Half of his beard was lathered still. "Fine, I'll call him right now, so you can see that he won't come."

She seemed oddly certain Benny would drop everything and come to work, despite having no reason to think so.

With Jordan's phone on speaker so his mother might hear, it rang once, twice. His mother smiled at him in the mirror, almost teasing. He hoped Benny wouldn't answer. Benny's voicemail picked up—his goofy singing voice.

"See?" he said, picking up his razor.

He let the song play to its conclusion as he brought the razor up to the other side of his face. Then the robotic voice that said the voicemail box was full.

"That's Benny for you," he said. She hummed when she was disappointed. She took her goblet with her back to the kitchen. He was sorry about the oyster spaghetti.

Jordan had to pass Bayou Bud's in his truck and then double back to park. He'd not expected the parking out front to be full. The bar had eight angle-entry parking spots, and these were each occupied. The nice trucks gleamed in the late day's sun like an affront. In general, oilmen owned newer trucks than fishermen did, and because President Obama had placed a moratorium on new offshore drilling in the Gulf because of the spill, Bayou Bud's was full up of seething out-of-work oil workers and out-of-towners working for BP in some form or another. Jordan parallel-parked on the side of the state route, which was bordered with saw grass. His passenger-side door was sealed with saw grass up to the window.

He heard the racket inside the bar before he opened the door—music, voices jockeying over one another. The din of hilarity teetering on the edge of becoming a ruckus. When he walked in, he couldn't see Cyndi behind the blockade of strangers, but he heard her laughter coming from the opposite end of the bar, and then he saw her bent ear-forward to hear a man's order. She spotted Jordan too. She had her eyelids painted silver just for him, and he thought what a fool he would have been for canceling. A fool who denied himself a good time just to heap punishment on himself.

Cyndi jogged over to his side of the bar like a young thing. He watched with some belly-felt pride as the heads of the men turned to watch her go. She put a beer in front of him.

"You don't want to miss out on all these tips for a date with me, do you?"

"People will still be drinking tomorrow." She shrugged, looking at the men, one of whom was waving her down for a refill at that moment, before turning back to Jordan. Her metallic eyelid paint shimmered in the bar light. "Besides, you'll make it up to me. At least, that's what I was banking on. I don't know when I'll get a moment to change." When she leaned toward him on her elbows, he smelled the fruity perfume and recalled holding her a few days ago. It turned him on to remember it. "Listen, you sit tight until Bob gets here to relieve me, and don't start any shit with the BP guys."

"Wouldn't dream of it," he said.

She smiled brightly for him, and turned at the call of a patron. He did not muster the confidence to say what he felt, and regretted not saying, The way you look tonight, I'll remember for the rest of my life. He'd not said it and had lost his chance.

The busyness seemed to animate her, and she flitted the length of that bar like a tennis pro. It was more than pleasing to watch. She was overextended but charmingly so, hair falling loose from her ponytail and a half-moon of sweat blooming on her lower back. She could wordlessly establish a cue of drink orders with a businesslike nod to three men. She upturned a bottle of Wild Turkey in one hand and levered a beer open with the other. She quipped and laughed and brushed off advances. She didn't just toss a beer bottle into the trash, she pitched it, and she knew he was watching her, and that excited him too. He'd had two beers before Bob showed up to take over.

All the while, Jordan kept to himself and listened to the conversations happening around him. Two oilmen were talking about the concrete cube that BP planned to lower on the open well.

"But the force of that oil coming up," said the ponytailed man next to him. "It's like six fire hoses of pressure at once."

A weaselly man tapped his beer bottle on the bar absently. "I don't know how much concrete you use to counter that kind of pressure, but I'm guessing it's a lot."

"It won't work," said the other.

Jordan had to step out of the bar while Cyndi counted her tips. The sun remained in the sky, saffron in the late day. The temperature was pleasantly warm and so humid that it seemed a living animal, like the air could breathe him. He smoked, feeling sorry for himself, and searched his mind for someone else to call who could cull oysters for him. He'd be hard-pressed to find someone more unreliable than his brother. But he might have to call Benny in earnest if he didn't find a deckhand with a pulse tomorrow.

Jordan drew deeply from the cigarette and then tossed it, watching the embers spray toward an expensive new truck. It bounced two times and landed next to what seemed to be a credit card. Jordan walked over and picked it up. The card belonging to someone named David Bolingsworth, a British name if he ever heard one. A platinum Visa card with a little BP logo in the corner.

Cyndi came out and found him, but she'd changed into a low-cut sequined top, and her lips were newly painted red. The large leather bag looped over her shoulder looked to have her work clothes and sneakers stuffed into it. She braced herself on the railing as she clicked down the concrete steps in her heels. She looked ready to go out dancing.

"Thought you'd run off," she said.

When he said that she looked great, she smiled as if she knew this to be true. He handed her the credit card. "This name look familiar to you?"

"Probably some BP guy." She frowned, examining it. "People like to lose their cards at the bar if they're going to do it. We cut up a few cards like this every month." It surprised him when she handed it back. "David's loss," she said. "I'm not walking back in there dressed like this. I barely made it out of there a virgin."

She was kidding, he realized, and because he didn't know what to do with the card, he pocketed it.

"I shouldn't have left without telling you," he said.

"Let's get stuffed on BP's dime," she said, surveying the parking lot. She was kidding again. It was obvious from the beginning that she was nothing like his ex, but for the first time, he began to feel that maybe he was in over his head. "So where are you taking me, anyway?"

"Where do you want to go?"

"You don't mean to tell me you haven't given it any thought, do you?"

He hadn't. "I thought I'd take you wherever you want to go."

"The only date places are on Grand Isle."

"There's a toll," he said. "It's forty-five minutes away."

"You've got something better in mind?" She crossed her arms and looked at the highway. "What, you want to go to the Chicken Shack? Or the Dirty Dozen? Or the one family-style sit-down restaurant in Golden Vale? Is that what you had in mind? I know that you're a fisherman, but goddamn, Jordan, don't you know how to date anybody?"

"Do you know any restaurants down there?"

"Let's spare no expense." She hooked her arm around his. "Which truck is yours?"

The women Jordan knew were occasionally playful, mostly in a goading way, but they did not joke. In the jokes Cyndi told, men usually ended up looking dumb. She frightened him a little, but this quickly registered as excitement. Just the way she looked excited him, and it wasn't merely the shortness of her skirt. As they cruised down to Grand Isle, Cyndi toyed with the radio dial until settling on the local country music station. The wind whipped papers around in the cab. There was never a reason to race to Grand Isle on a weeknight—where the vacation cabins for rent were as large as the houses in his neighborhood. Cyndi's knees pressed together in the passenger seat like two pretty apples gave him a reason. The old highway down to Grand Isle was once lined with oaks, but a succession of hurricanes and saltwater intrusion had wiped them out. A few skeletons of the trees were left with their swaying beards of Spanish moss. Cyndi surfed the radio stations in his car and talked so easily she seemed not to need much from him in the way of conversation.

They passed a derelict boat warehouse that the marsh had claimed for itself and that fishermen had turned into a monument. The warehouse was skeletal now—wood pilings and a roof—forty feet from the state route in the water. The road that had led to it was underwater with the wetland loss and the sea level rise. Back in the eighties, the marina's wood pilings became a community memorial for fishermen who'd died. Families started to tack up life preservers and ring buoys to honor them. To Jordan's chagrin, offshore oilmen had started to tack up hard hats too. The memorial had held a fascination for him when he was a kid, but he hadn't thought of it in years. Catching it, as they were doing, in the early evening, with the ring buoys silhouetted in the purple light, it seemed a dignified monument to lives spent on the water, and he reached over and put his hand on Cyndi's thigh. She seemed to welcome this and then leaned forward to see where he was looking.

"My father loves to brag about the storms he's been through on his shrimp boat." Cyndi shifted her legs in his direction as she talked. "It's dangerous just to mention a storm. He'll go off on some story that you think is about someone else, but it always comes back to him being a hero."

She turned the volume dial down, so they could talk.

"The best date I've ever been on—and I'm telling you this so you know what you're up against—the best date I ever had was blindfolded."

"Was he that ugly?"

"I don't date ugly men," she said. "At least not physically."

"He blindfolded me before we got to the restaurant, and then he hand-fed me sushi."

"In the restaurant?"

"The woman next to me leaned over and asked, 'Did you have eye surgery?' 'Yes!' I said. 'As a matter of fact, I did.'"

A smile swept across her face with the memory of it. Jordan had never been to a sushi restaurant, or ever had sushi, for that matter.

"You want me to blindfold you, then?" he asked.

"No, I don't want you to blindfold me. Not yet, anyway."

"You're kidding," he said. He sensed it was a sex thing, the blindfold. It felt as though he were being asked to evolve right there on the spot. "But why did he blindfold you?"

"Novelty, I guess," she said. "It was exciting. A lot of the time, when you're eating, you don't taste the food. Not when you're blindfolded. Your senses are heightened."

"I don't know," he said. "A guy who wants to blindfold you on your first date is somebody you got to watch out for."

"It was fun!" she said, and she sounded downright girlish when she said it. "I'll always remember it even if it didn't amount to anything."

"What'd this guy do?"

"You mean for money?" she said. "He taught art at a high school."

"Figures."

"What do you mean, 'figures'?" She imitated him and made him sound oafish.

"I don't see a normal guy doing something like that. I just don't."

"Ah, normal," she said. "People always want you to be normal. Do you consider yourself normal, Jordan?"

"Yes, I do," he said.

"Normal Jordan." She laughed, and he felt a punt of fear that the date would go south, but her laughter felt light, not so pointed as it might have been, and he relaxed. He was going to spend a lot of money tonight, he knew, not just because Cyndi directed him to a clapboard-sided restaurant with tropical plants framing the doorway, but also because he had an end-of-the-road feeling about his life, so he might as well set a couple of hundred dollars on fire in the hopes that he'd have sex again. It had been a year and a half.

Outside, the Gulf was black except for the blinking red light of an oil platform in the distance. A sea wind beat on the windows so the air inside smelled deliciously of salt. The votive candle at the center of their table cast a gold light on Cyndi's face, and Cyndi held her menu up to her nose—she had eye trouble, he realized—and then peered over it with an expression he couldn't place.

"Jordan," she said. "What would you order if BP was paying for this?"

"What would I—" he said, and then he realized she meant the credit card he'd found. "I don't know for certain that it's BP's money."

"Don't be dense," she said. "It's just a question. What would you order if you knew BP was paying for your meal?"

The drink menu's tropical theme matched the restaurant's décor—pastels and banana plants, a coconut garland over the doorway, and a woodcut banner that read WELCOME TO THE CAJUN BAHAMAS. The other diners were better dressed than he was and clearly had more money. He looked around at all the other women and decided, happily, that there was no woman in the place he'd rather be with. The other couples were sucking down brightly colored tropical drinks in tall, shapely glasses. The drinks cost more than he usually paid for a meal.

"What the hell," he said. "I'd get a Dead Man's Float. I've never had a fruity drink in my life, and I don't think I'd like one, but what the hell. What about you?"

"Ocean Breeze," she said, flopping the menu down. "And the Surf-n-Turf. So, why don't you tell me about your family?"

"Tell you about my family?" He realized he had a habit of repeating the question she just asked him, and it was because the questions were so unusually direct for him, or perhaps no one asked him much about himself. Cyndi asked about his mother and about his falling-out with Doug Babies, whom she'd seen at the bar without him. When a tall, harried waiter arrived, Jordan handed the man their menus and announced that they'd both have the Surf-n-Turf and the tropical drinks. She didn't bat an eye, as if she'd known all along, and he loved her for that.

Over their shapely tropical drinks with toys in them, she asked after his business and his ex-fiancée, and he sensed, in her questioning, that she wanted to get a feel for his financial security; this pleased him, because he knew he could provide that much.

"You're not really going to use that credit card, are you?"

"I might," he said. "If BP is going to ruin my season, then I might as well get a free dinner out of it."

"No, you won't," she said. "You're too good."

"I might," he said.

She smiled disbelievingly. "Jordan, isn't there something you want to know about me?"

"What do you mean?"

"You haven't asked about me."

She looked disappointed, so he said, "Why don't you just tell me everything?"

She liked that. When the waiter brought him a steak that bled when he cut into it, he nearly wept with joy. Any fear about the date dissolved as he discovered how easy it was to talk with

Cyndi—how much effort she put into making him feel interesting. He didn't even care that Cyndi only ate half her meal.

The harried waiter returned more often as the diners thinned out and the tables were cleared. Topping off their water glasses, he asked, "Another round, you two?" The answer was always, "Yes," though they'd switched to beer by the time Cyndi was telling him about getting married right out of high school to, in her words, a dumb kid, because she'd gotten pregnant. They tried to fool themselves into love, or even getting along, but they had no real reason to do it. She'd just turned seventeen when her son was born.

"And if you want to know everything, I gave him up for adoption. My parents are selectively religious," she said. "They hardly went to church, and in many ways couldn't care less about what's in the Bible—but they cared a whole lot about me getting married and having that baby. It really didn't feel as though I had a choice. I was so young. I felt so trapped and scared, I could have screamed. Instead, I took to hating Billy, my husband. I knew he was feeling the same way, which was why we bickered all the time. We gave the baby up. My son went to a white family in Arkansas. The adoptive family didn't want me to visit, and we've had our battles about that, but I keep telling myself that someday, when he's out from under their wing, he'll want to have a relationship with me, and things will get better."

"How old is he?"

"Twenty-two."

"God," he said.

"God?" She worried the tablecloth between her fingers, and for the first time, she seemed nervous.

"I could have a kid or three by now at my age," Jordan said, scrambling, "but I don't. It's not that I didn't want kids."

"And how old are you again, Jordan?"

"I'm thirty-four," he said. "Do I look it?"

"That's what I'd guess." She shook her head. "Anyway, that's everything, or that's everything by way of the worst thing about me. I wasn't going to tell you that yet, but put a few drinks in me, and I'll just come out with the worst of it."

"I don't think it's bad," he said. "That's life. It just happens to you."

He could tell that Cyndi felt exposed, and so he talked a little more about wanting to fix up the bayou-facing office into a proper house and settling down now that he felt he was doing a good job running the business. That's if the oil didn't come inland.

She smiled sleepily and yawned with her mouth closed, only perceptible by the slight flare of her nostrils. There were only a T-bone and shrimp tails left on his plate, and he realized it was time to leave. The restaurant was empty, and he felt then how stupendously drunk he'd become, how elated and horny and sleepy he was. He wondered if he could get them back to Golden Vale without a DUI.

"I didn't know there was so much kick to those fruity drinks," he said.

"We could get a room," she said, looking past him as though something very interesting were happening at the empty bar.

"We could get a room," he said gratefully.

"Do you think BP would get us a room?" she said.

"I think they would," he said. "I think they'd even get us a good room, one with a view of the Gulf and a couple of chairs out front, so we could watch the waves in the morning."

"What about a Jacuzzi?"

"A Jacuzzi?" he said. "I think they could manage a Jacuzzi."

The waiter appeared at their table again, looking so tired his eyes seemed to be lower on his face. He left the credit card jacket on the table's corner nearest Jordan and then retreated.

"Is it bad?" she asked, watching Jordan look over the bill. Never before had the paper needed to be folded in order to fit into the bill jacket.

"We did great," he said. He pulled out Bolingsworth's credit card, held it up dramatically, and folded it in the bill jacket, not knowing he was going to do this until it happened.

"You wouldn't!" she said.

The waiter swooped in like a bat diving for a bug and took the card away.

"I can't believe it," she said.

It didn't feel like theft at all. It felt as though he were finally getting his due. They were elated, and the knowledge that they'd soon have sex passed between them like a second wind. Cyndi's face seemed to be singing to him, and soon they tore through the parking lot like a couple in cahoots. Jogging across the street to the only place in sight where they could stay, the Tropical Motel— which sat on wooden stilts like all the houses on the island because of the hurricanes—he didn't let go of her hand. He thought, Maybe I'm having the best night of my life.

He only reluctantly released her to buzz the motel office bell over and over like a maniac because Cyndi thought it was funny. It seemed all the doors of his life would remain open now. A hand-written sign above the desk said that cleaning fish in the rooms was strictly prohibited. Cyndi asked the clerk if the rooms had a sea view, and the woman clerk looked perplexed. They'd woken her up when they rang the bell. "You can see the Gulf from the top stairs, but not from the room."

"What about a Jacuzzi?" Cyndi said.

The clerk, a woman about Cyndi's age, frowned at Cyndi's obvious drunkenness. "Nothing like that here."

"They don't have a Jacuzzi, Jordan." She said this in a whiny voice, like a child, but she was kidding.

"Do you want the room?" the clerk asked.

"Yes, we do," Cyndi said.

Jordan slapped down Bolingsworth's credit card on the desk. The clerk picked it up and rattled her desktop mouse to wake up the computer. Cyndi had latched on to his waist, fitting snugly under his shoulder.

When the clerk asked to see Jordan's ID, he jolted a bit at his own stupidity and feigned a search through his shorts and the bulge that was his wallet in his back pocket. He looked at the camera pointed at him over the desk and almost walked out the door out of a certain fear that the clerk knew it wasn't his card.

"He'd forget his head if it wasn't attached," Cyndi said. "Don't you mind him. I'll pay cash."

"I don't want you to pay," he said. "I can't let you."

She smiled wanly at the clerk and reached into her purse for the wad of small bills. "You'll pay me back," she said, not looking at him, and the way she laid out the bills neatly in a row to count them out just about killed him. He could feel her bristling under the gaze of the clerk, who clearly thought that they were lowlifes. But once she surrendered her tips, he looped his arm around her waist and steered her clumsily to the stairwell, so poorly that she almost fell twice and Cyndi, laughing, pushed him off.

→ Twelve ←

Benny might not have known what he was doing, Kiki told him, but his actions said that he wanted out—that he wasn't fully ready to be in a relationship. Sitting with him on his bed, Kiki talked alternately to her nubby yellow socks or to the ceiling. Benny was willing to accept any psychoanalysis if it meant that there might be a way forward, and so he smoked cigarettes and ashed into a beer can cinched between his thighs while trying to actively listen. When she finished talking, they both cried and held each other and then they made doleful, impassioned love again. Then she left and she blocked his phone number, and he felt the bottom drop out. The grief and longing he felt were epic. The only moments he didn't cry were when he was sleeping—twelve, thirteen hours for the past couple of days—waking up and then remembering what he'd done and then lighting his first cigarette of the day in renewed misery.

Stani, his roommate, brought him tamales from the corner store twice and gently told him to lay off the cigarettes. He would smoke himself sick. Stani was newly bald, which had something to do with his dedication to Buddhist philosophy. Stani sat with Benny in the living room, smoking weed but not as much as Benny, as Benny kept steering the conversation back to Kiki. "She says I sabotaged the relationship," Benny would begin again, as if Stani didn't know this already. When Benny apologized for being self-centered and boring, Stani told him that his pain was also Stani's pain, the universal suffering of attachment, or, in other words, Don't worry about it. The presence or absence of love was all-consuming. Benny began to cry again.

Three days into his grief his phone rang. Benny had the volume turned up to the limit. The phone had been within arm's reach in case Kiki changed her mind. Benny lurched for his phone on the coffee table, startling the cat asleep by his feet. Stani watched him with interest and rubbed his bald head as if the missing hair still surprised him.

Jordan's name flashed across the screen. Jordan never called him, except for one other time on the day of the protest. Benny had assumed it was a mistake. They had nothing to talk about. But his mind quickly turned to his mother. Maybe she was sick. For a moment, he believed with his whole heart that his mother was dead, that everything bad in his life had happened all at once. He answered the call.

Benny laid his head back and stared straight up. There were two large wooden accent panels in the ceiling the size of adult coffins. "Everything all right, Jordan?"

Jordan asked how he was. Benny said his girlfriend had just dumped him.

"Damn," Jordan said, as if it couldn't be helped. Benny waited to hear more, a condolence, but nothing came.

"Right," Benny said. "Is Mom okay?"

"She's fine," Jordan said. "She's the same."

"Jordan, what's up? You call me for something?"

"I guess I did. I don't suppose you want to come out here and be a deckhand on my boat for a while?"

"Work for you?" Benny said. "Is this a joke? After you cut me out?"

"I'll pay you."

"I haven't talked to a lawyer yet."

"You'd be wasting your time. Talk to Byrdie if you want to."

Benny could not access the anger he felt at Jordan just a week before.

"Why ask me?" Benny laughed. "Because you know what a man of the bayou I am?"

"It's true," Jordan said. "You're worthless on a boat."

There was a long silence. Jordan was a heavy breather on the phone.

"Is it the spill?"

"I've tried everyone else," Jordan said. "Every alcoholic deckhand in this town has signed up to work for BP. There's no one left." Jordan had more emotion in his voice than Benny thought possible. "And this oil just may come inland and shut me down. It could get to my reefs."

Another long silence. Benny thought the call was dropped.

"Jordan?"

"People don't want to eat Louisiana seafood now. They think it's already tainted. I need to be fishing every minute I can, but my buyers are starting to get nervous too."

"You're getting all worked up."

"I don't know why I called you."

The oil spill hadn't been on his mind since the protest, and even then it wasn't out of concern for his family, just the unfortunate backdrop for one of the most miserable days of his life.

"Listen," Benny said, feeling unusually tender. "I'm surprised, is all. I mean, you never call me, least of all for help. I'll come hang out for a while. I don't have any money, anyway, as you well know."

"I'm not asking you to hang out, Benny," Jordan said, sounding more like himself. "You need to work."

Benny said he would drive to Golden Vale that evening and go out on the boat with Jordan in the morning. Jordan thanked him and hung up. Stani smiled at Benny in a knowing manner, in that contented way he had now, and Benny sank back into the couch. It was Kiki he wanted to call next. Maybe his leaving would give him an opportunity to meet with her. It would give her the chance to miss him too. If not actually improving himself, it might make him look as though he were improving.

Stani, off to his part-time gig stocking grocery shelves, stood up for a stretch, remarkably tall and long-limbed and reminding Benny suddenly of a greyhound, and then he locked Benny into a long hug. Stani was a soothing presence, even if he met your eyes in a way that suggested he saw everything coming. A modern-day bodhisattva. "Well, now," Stani said. "I guess we're both off, then."

→ Thirteen ←

Benny didn't arrive in Golden Vale until five a.m.—the hour that Jordan had told him they would embark to harvest oysters from the bay. He'd ruined a dinner his mother had planned by not showing up the night before, failing to meet a biologist she'd wanted to introduce him to. Benny's radio silence scared Jordan into thinking Benny wasn't coming at all. But Benny found he could make himself leave New Orleans only in the early-morning hours, when he could abscond like the rat he was. He'd gone back to bed after he said he would come home. He found one of Kiki's coiled black hairs in his sheets, and he put it on the tall stool next to his bed. He marveled at its existence in his room, a piece of Kiki DNA when Kiki no longer wanted anything to do with him. Then he drove through the middle of the night, cursing the long-haul truckers whose bright lights assaulted him, with the windows down, so the marsh air thrummed through the car as he lit one cigarette after another.

In the jarring light of the kitchen, Benny couldn't explain himself to Jordan, who was pouring them coffee into thermoses. Their mother was still asleep. The worry from the spill made Jordan talkative. Outside, it was still nighttime, an hour of the day Benny associated only with raucous nights. In his family's living room, there was a stack of boxes by the back door, and the living room looked barer, as if someone had died or was moving out. His dad's fishing trophies were gone from the shelf, as were quite a few other things that he couldn't remember yet. Benny wanted to ask his brother about this, but Jordan was talking about the Coast Guard.

"Dad never cared much for the Coast Guard," Jordan said, snapping a lid on his coffee. "The Coast Guard doesn't help when the poachers are on our oyster leases helping themselves to our oysters. No, the Coast Guard doesn't lift a finger when you need them. But Dad would be turning over in his grave if he knew how bad things'd get with them. There's no honor anywhere."

Jordan knocked on his chest. It was the third time that morning Benny noticed it, but he didn't say anything. Jordan slid a thermos across the counter to him. He looked wild-eyed with sleep deprivation, unshaven, and was it Benny's imagination or had he gotten thinner in the past two weeks?

"You'll have to fill me in later, chief," Benny said. "I've been on a bender, and I don't care if I live or die."

Jordan frowned, trying to get a read on his brother.

"I'm joking, Jordan."

"The Coast Guard works for BP now," Jordan said patiently. "The Coast Guard is lying about how much oil BP is spilling. Scientists know that more oil is coming out of that failed well than BP says. And it's the Coast Guard giving press conferences on BP's behalf—lying to everyone about how much oil is out there. Downplaying the disaster. The government is as bad as BP."

"Slow down, man," Benny said. He wasn't too surprised by this news. Governments lied when it was convenient. Could his brother be so naïve? "I'm afraid I'm going to have to ask you to hold off on all this information until I've woken up a bit."

Jordan picked at something in his teeth and Benny could feel the sting of Jordan's lifelong disappointment in him. They hadn't been any closer than cordial since they were boys.

"We should get on the water. Alejandro's waiting," Jordan said. "And just so you know, it's supposed to be what the Coast Guard is calling a 'bad air day.' This means that the wind is pushing that burning oil and dispersant our way. If you feel anything funny, like you can't breathe, let me know." Jordan laughed darkly at his own delivery of this news.

"Christ," Benny said. "Is this even safe?"

"They haven't closed down fishing in Caminada Bay yet."

Benny followed his brother through the backyard and the singing insects, past the empty pool, home now only to frogs, past his father's office, where Jordan had cut him out of the business only two weeks before, and across the street to the bayou road where he'd shown Kiki his father's oyster boats as if they were relics from another time. Now the oyster lugger named after his mother, *May's Day*, sat like a judgment in the water. He felt a soul-sinking depression come, looking at that boat. There was a short man in a baseball cap waiting by the hull. This was Alejandro, Jordan said, the deckhand.

Alejandro seemed to consider Benny quizzically when they were introduced and didn't hide his amusement at the way Benny was dressed. Benny touched the crown of his fedora, aware of it anew in Alejandro's eyes. He didn't own clothes for working in— his wardrobe came from swap meets and thrift stores, and he doctored them to his liking: cutting the women's jeans into shorts, tearing the sleeves from his T-shirt to make it a tank top. He took some pride in his Italian leather shoes, though they needed to be re-soled.

"Mucho gusto," Benny said, shaking Alejandro's hand.

Alejandro smiled wryly, and then Alejandro made himself busy with the boat's rope lines, untying them from cleats for the day, lassoing lines onto pilings, and Benny followed Jordan into the boat's cabin. It smelled of marsh and body odor and stale cigarette smoke from the ashtray. Benny sat on the bunk bed a few feet from the helm and watched Jordan start the boat engine with a cigarette in his mouth. But his attention drifted outside, where he was awed by Alejandro's launching the last rope expertly at the wood piling.

As they glided southward down the bayou toward the Gulf, the sky flushed violet, silhouetting the houses and boats lined up along the bayou.

"Caminada Bay is just inside of the barrier islands, so it's a salty oyster," Jordan said. "Some people in New Orleans know to request Caminada oysters by name."

Benny was not completely indifferent to his brother's plight, but the physical unease he felt around Jordan made caring about his business difficult. Plus, this might be the end of a business that he'd been cut out of, and Benny still had not reckoned with how he'd pay his rent now. As the boat traveled downstream toward the Gulf, Benny watched the squat houses perched close to the water, and he wondered, Why the hell did anyone want to save this place anyway? It was being so remote that made people backward, so bored and hateful toward people they didn't think were like them or deserving of their sympathy.

They passed a Vietnamese American family rigging their shrimp boat for the day. The woman sat with a net on her lap, mending it, and with the way it was spread over her, it looked like a kind of skirt. The father was busy with something in the cabin, and their boy, a teenager, had his cheek to a pole, looking dreamily at Benny as they passed. The teen waved guilelessly at him, and he waved back. He knew this boy likely would have had a rough go of it at Golden Vale High. Benny had had it rough because he was different—a difference people quickly assumed meant he was gay, which seemed to them the most shameful thing one could be. Not that Benny hadn't fooled around with boys before and had a great time doing it, but he'd never fallen in love with a man, and he didn't think he ever would. What he felt when he was young was that the whole town was out to kill him and that they would have succeeded if he hadn't left. He would have had a worse time if he'd been Vietnamese. There was a reason, he knew, that so many of his Vietnamese classmates had left the area. Facebook told him that a number of these classmates went off to more illustrious futures than he'd ever dreamed for himself—medical school, business school, law school. His first kiss, Annie Nguyen, was at Stanford Law now. He'd seen a picture of her, a svelte, stylish woman with oversized red glasses posing with the Golden Gate Bridge in the distance, a place he figured he'd never see.

The boat's dashboard was littered with curiosities. A crystal teacup. Sun-faded Mardi Gras beads. A logbook of some kind so warped with the humidity that it was a semicircle. Benny plucked the old logbook from the dashboard and flipped through the parabolic pages. Jordan stiffened when Benny grabbed it, as if he were defacing a shrine. He recognized his father's handwriting—a square serious print. The logbook held a record of oyster trip tickets dating back to the early 2000s. This probably hadn't been touched since Al had passed on the boat to Jordan. Benny wanted to find something personal of his father in the book, some record of those thoughts that were so opaque to him, but there was nothing in the margins to tell him who his father had been.

Jordan was looking down the bayou, which was swelling with the colors of dawn, the clouds shaped into peaks. Jordan's shoulders seemed more bowed than they had a couple of weeks before.

"You're probably right about me being worthless out here," Benny said. "I'm sorry about what's happening."

"Every day, I'm losing money," Jordan said. "Doug Babies really fucked me by quitting when he did. And then there's Alejandro. He needs to get paid."

Benny looked at where Alejandro was lying on the deck. He had his hands behind his head and his legs crossed.

"I can't stay long," Benny said. "I've got things to take care of in New Orleans."

"I haven't got long, Benny. I can't believe they haven't closed that fucking well. If that oil comes in, I'm closed for good."

Benny walked onto the open deck of the ship with his cigarette. He watched a few bats zip by in the half dark. The marsh grass shone green-silver, and the skeletons of long-dead cypress trees were black against the early light. He thought of his father, who took it so personally that Benny did not want to inherit his life that it left them little room for affection. The beauty of the landscape his father loved was so evident he felt walloped by a kind of tenderness at the sight of it. For a moment he had a reflex to take a picture for Kiki, but remembered that she'd blocked his phone number.

He wondered if he could actually use her fondness for the laboring classes to elicit forgiveness. It was such a feeble plan he was surprised it had occurred to him at all. Kiki romanticized the workingman, all the activists did, but it was a muddied romance because they also looked down on them. Benny almost flicked his cigarette overboard but thought better of it. Instead, he stubbed it out on his shoe and then slipped it into his pocket.

He felt Alejandro observing him from where he lay on the deck, so he went and sat on the pile of coffee sacks by Alejandro's head, sacks that would be filled with oysters later.

"So, you're the one who's going to save my life, huh?"

"Sorry?" Alejandro said.

"Jordan told me you'd tell me what to do."

"I thought this was your company," Alejandro said.

"I'm the loser in the family," Benny said. "Come back on my lowly horse."

"You don't look like you're dressed to work." Alejandro indicated the soles of Benny's leather shoes, the tips of which were open like little mouths.

"Alejandro, these are Italian leather shoes. They are from Milan, handmade. They may require a little attention at the moment, but they are otherwise fine shoes for all occasions. For work and for play. They also happen to be the only shoes I own."

Alejandro nodded like a confidant. Benny knew almost immediately when someone would be his friend. It was a gift of his. He liked Alejandro—who thought a lot more than he let on, whose wide-open face could have been carved from a beautiful piece of teakwood.

They both jumped at the suddenness of Jordan's voice.

"Benny," Jordan said from the loudspeaker. "Look starboard. That's where BP has a cleanup center. You see all that yellow tubing on the platform? That's boom to soak up the oil."

On the dock, the tubing was coiled up as tall as a house. It looked from the distance like yellow sausage links. He knew it was filled with an absorbent material that floated on the water's surface and corralled the oil so it could be burned or skimmed up. It was tremendous to see it—how tall it was—and to think for all this boom onshore, there was oil out in the Gulf. People bustled about the marina wearing vests. The marina normally housed charter fishing boats, but now the place was clotted with shrimp boats, and where the shrimp netting should hang, there was fat yellow boom.

"It's a joke," Jordan said into the loudspeaker. "They're using that dispersant to sink the oil. The boom doesn't work if the oil's not on the surface of the water. Somewhere out there is my old deckhand."

"Chief," Benny said. "You don't need to use a loudspeaker. I could hear you fine without it."

The beloved Caminada Bay of their father's didn't look like all that much to Benny. It was just bamboo poles as far as he could see, which marked where one oyster lease ended and another began. The bamboo poles were a visual cue to let other fishermen know they were on Pearce leases. This made it easy too for any friends in the area to keep an eye out for oyster poachers on the family reefs. Benny knew poaching was easy enough to get away with because they couldn't watch the reefs around the clock. He could smell the saltiness of the Gulf but was vigilant for something sharper and more chemical. As Jordan circled the oyster lugger in the water, Alejandro explained to Benny that they would drop the oyster dredge together.

"We will count to three, and we drop, but most important is that you watch out for your hand when the dredge comes up. You stay out of its way."

"I can't imagine I'd like to be in the way."

"This dredge wants to eat your hand." Alejandro gave the dredge a pat. It was a steel cage with teeth to scrape the floor of the reef. The oysters would tumble into a chain-link sack.

"You will need these," Alejandro said, tossing a set of gloves at him.

Once the loud droning noise stopped, the pullies began to turn. Together, Benny and Alejandro dropped the oyster dredge, which smacked the water so violently it scared Benny. It was like they'd dropped an anvil. The boat rolled slightly portside as the dredge scraped the reef below. After a time, Jordan lifted the dredge, and the cage rose, full of oysters and streaming water. Alejandro counted again to signal when they'd spill the oysters onto the culling board. The oysters thundered onto the table, spilling water and soaking Benny's loafers. Alejandro laughed when Benny stepped back, frowning at his shoes.

A small crab no bigger than Benny's thumb was on top of the oyster pile, and Benny watched the bewildered thing skitter over the mound. Benny marveled at the creature—how beautifully made it was. Its tiny russet claws topped its perfectly segmented legs. The crab was snatched from another world and had escaped death by a hair. It could have easily been crushed in the tumble of oysters. He picked up the crab. The creature seemed to consider Benny and the threat he posed. Delicately, Benny tossed the crab back into the bay.

For an entire hour, Benny was convinced he'd been wrong about everything: he was right where he belonged, working with the fruits of the sea, and he was ready to admit his misconceptions about oystermen's work. Alejandro taught him how to hold a cluster of oysters in his hand and where to hit the cluster with the oyster claw to break it up. "You hit the oyster here and not here. Be careful, or you'll cut your hand in half." He showed Benny the acceptable oyster size—a three- to five-year-old oyster was the size of the base of his hand to his thumb. Any oyster smaller than that you tossed back into the water. Alejandro filled his buckets of oysters four times as swiftly as Benny.

"So, Alejandro," Benny said. "I saw you tossing the boat lines earlier. You seem to know your way around a boat. How's that?"

"How do I know boats?"

"I guess that's the question."

"I repaired boats once, but I did not spend much time on them. Before I left El Salvador, I had a fiberglass repair company."

"A company?"

"That's right."

"You had your own company."

"That's right," he said, breaking up two fused oysters with a swift hit. "Small. Just me and four workers. We did cars, motor homes, tubs."

"And why did you leave?" he said. "If I can ask that."

"I had no choice," he said. "I could no longer pay—la extorsión."

Jordan told Benny over the loudspeaker to pick up the pace. His plaintive voice seemed to imply, We just don't know how much time out here we have left.

"If that guy speaks into the loudspeaker again, I'll kill him," Benny said.

Alejandro said nothing.

"I say we mutiny."

"I don't know this word."

"It's when the ship's crew overthrows the captain. Sometimes the guy gets lucky, and they just imprison him belowdecks. Other times, it's tough luck, Captain." Benny drew a line across his throat.

It was Alejandro who spotted the bird—a big limp brown mass, wet and furry. At first Benny thought it was a nutria, one of those rodents eating up the marsh grass, but they were too far out in the open water for that to be the case.

The pelican was like a prop. It floated on its back, wings outstretched in the water.

"Is it dead?" Benny said.

Alejandro hooked it with a net in one swoop, and he pulled the wet, mangled thing in, straining with the unusual weight of it.

"It looks dead," Jordan said.

Jordan cut the engine. They put it on the deck. It was not dead, but writhing grotesquely—too near death to be afraid, even, of them, of their net.

"Put it out of its misery!" Benny told Jordan, shielding his eyes. "I can't watch this."

"I'll call the Coast Guard," Jordan said, but he didn't move.

"What will they do?"

"It's got to be the oil. They're collecting the oiled birds."

"I don't see any oil on it," Alejandro said.

"Somebody kill the poor thing."

"Don't look at me," Alejandro said. "I will not."

"It probably ate some bad fish," Jordan said.

"Bullshit."

"I mean it probably ate some oiled fish. Pelicans dive with their mouths open. The water's killing it."

Then the bird convulsed like it was having a seizure.

"Somebody, stomp it!" Benny slowly lifted his leather loafer.

"Stop it, Benny. You're not going to do anything."

The bird thrashed its head without a sound. There was just the rustling of its body on the deck of the ship. Its eyes squeezed shut.

"I can't watch this," Benny said. "I'll lose it."

Benny walked back into the cabin and took his brother's cigarettes. He watched Jordan and Alejandro's backs as they stood next to each other on the deck, looking down at the bird. Benny doubted if he'd ever rid himself of the pitiful sight.

Jordan returned to the cabin. He took a cigarette too and lit it.

"It's dead," he said.

"Those evil motherfuckers," Benny said.

When Jordan called the Coast Guard—on speaker, so Benny could hear—a husky-voiced man answered, "Dead birds? I've got a number for live birds, but not dead birds."

"Do you want me to bring it in?"

"What am I going to do with a dead bird?"

Jordan did not appreciate his tone, and he said so. "I thought you'd want to document it."

"These calls are recorded," said the man. "It's documented."

Jordan suspected the man was lying. It sounded as though he were talking to a real person, but he wasn't. He hung up. "I don't know what I was thinking."

→ Fourteen ←

After the pelican died, they were quiet and uneasy with one another on the boat ride back to Golden Vale. They had no plans for the bird's body but agreed not to throw it back into the water. Benny said there might be an organization that would want to test the bird for exposure. They ought to make some phone calls. Jordan wasn't so sure. As for the bird, Benny and Alejandro stowed it in an oyster sack. Alejandro held the sack open as Benny lowered the bird's body into it. The bird's head hung lifeless like a telephone dangling on a cord. Alejandro knelt when he tucked the bird's body away under the culling table.

Benny felt mildly sick to his stomach, but he assumed this had to do with the pelican or the "bad air" he was breathing. The day's heat seemed to burn off the bayou's loveliness. The oyster-laden boat seemed to crawl up the bayou no faster than a rowboat would. The boat topped out at ten miles per hour with eighty sacks of oysters on its deck. He prayed for a breeze. The reflection off the water was so bright that Benny saw spots when he closed his eyes.

May said that his father's eyesight deteriorated because he never wore sunglasses on the water. "He burnt his eyes up," she said. But it seemed his father had gotten sick so suddenly, and so totally, that his body just gave out on him.

How strange that he should be on his father's boat, cruising up the bayou at a time like this, when he thought he'd never again set foot on it. Life bludgeoned him with mystery. A week before, the idea would have been absurd. He was thirty years old and hadn't even made a foothold in the world. He was a good musician, but his music had no currency outside of New Orleans. Kiki said he'd sabotaged their relationship. What a word, *sabotage*. He wondered how it was that other people were able to see themselves into the future and he could not.

A series of planes roared overhead on their way out to the Gulf. Benny could see Jordan in the cabin, watching the sky as he steered with anxious consideration. The bellies of these planes were filled with chemical dispersant, which they would mist onto the oil slicks in the wide-open Gulf like crop dusters.

As they neared the family dock, Jordan explained the unloading process. Alejandro would lift the hundred-pound oyster sacks onto the conveyer belt, and Benny would then load the sacks onto a cart that he'd wheel to the walk-in cooler parked in the driveway, some of which would be shucked, others sold intact, depending on how restaurants wanted them. Benny had forgotten about the unloading while he was culling oysters. His arms already felt useless and Jordan seemed to sense this.

"Heaviest thing you had to lift was a guitar, eh?"

Benny might have said this about himself, but he didn't like it in Jordan's mouth, even if Jordan was trying to joke with him.

"I've never believed that hard work in and of itself improved a person. I think that's some religious bunk the capitalists want you to believe." Benny was huffy, and he heard it in his own voice. He tried to soften his tone. "I just think there's more to life."

"You got it all figured out, then, don't you?"

"I won't stay long if this is what it's going to be," he said. "You picking at me. I can think of better things to do."

"You did good today," Jordan said. "You're not as slow as I thought you'd be."

"Thanks," Benny said miserably.

Benny took his cigarette and sat in the shade beside the dead pelican sack. It wouldn't look this way to Jordan, but he'd figured out one thing about life, anyway. His time was worth more than anybody wanted to pay him for.

Alejandro did the heavy lifting without complaint. Benny was on the dock with the wheelie cart, gasping after finally piling bags of oysters onto it. The wheelie cart had a mind of its own. It took a whole-body effort to steer it across the two-lane bayou road between the dock and the houses. The road was busy with passing trucks, so he'd have to wait for a long enough break in traffic to jog the cart across. He'd never seen so much traffic on the little bayou road before. Then a news van passed, driving slowly, and Benny realized that all this traffic was because of the oil spill. This news van was likely headed to the BP spill response center down the bayou. Benny crossed his arms over the cart handle and laid his head down, so tired he could cry. A green anole skittered over one of his shoes. He jolted at the sound of a car horn, and he looked up to see a bald man in a van had stopped in the middle of the road, his window rolled down, to take Benny's picture with his telescopic lens.

Benny gave the man the finger, and the man looked wounded by this, as if there were no harm at all in taking someone's picture while he was working. On top of this, the picture would have been false: this was Benny's first day on the job, so whatever portrait the man thought he was taking was a fantasy.

Hoa and Linh came out of their oyster-shucking station to flap their gloves and coo for Benny to come over, but he was too tired to go to them. He knew he'd feel bad about snubbing them later, and he did. As Benny was unloading, he heard Jordan muster false cheer when talking on the phone to a buyer about the oysters. Jordan was pacing up and down the dock. "Yes, the oysters are fine. There's a bumper crop from Caminada Bay. We haven't had a good crop there since Katrina."

When all the sacks were finally in the cooler, Benny put the dead pelican in the corner by the door, for what purpose he didn't know. He lingered in the cool air that tumbled out into the hot day like a stage effect. Jordan shot him a look, even as he talked on the phone, that Benny understood was a command not to let the cold air out. He obliged, and as he was locking the cooler, Alejandro came up behind him and put his hands on Benny's shoulders, a surprisingly tender goodbye, as if this were the most normal thing to do in the world.

Then Alejandro set off homeward in the stagnant heat of the late afternoon. He walked along the bayou road. As he walked away, Benny recalled being a child killing time on the bayou, the boredom and loneliness of the long afternoons, and his perpetual longing to be somewhere he couldn't imagine yet.

At the kitchen door, as Benny peeled off his sodden leather loafers and socks, he smelled something burning. Inside, he saw the oven belching smoke. He dashed in and turned it off, calling for his mother. The smoke flooded his face when he cracked the oven door. There was a casserole inside, the top of which was charred.

His mother appeared beside him, flapping the air with a dish towel, saying defensively, "I set a timer! Where's my timer?"

"Didn't you smell the smoke?"

She tossed a towel at him.

"Fan the smoke detector before it goes off." She turned on the roaring stovetop vent. She opened the kitchen window. "Jordan's going to think I've lost it. He thinks I've got dementia."

She fanned the air out the window with a towel. Her hair was half-curled where she'd been styling it.

"I've always been this way," she said with a laugh. "One screw loose."

"You can stop fanning," he said. "It's fine now."

"Well, welcome home, honey," she said. "And it was your favorite. Baked ziti."

He heard the radio playing in her bedroom, some classic rock. Then his mother swept across the room and hugged him. She smelled wonderful, like the perfume she'd worn all her life. She told him he looked sunstroked. Her accent was at its most halting when she was animated.

"Sunstroked?" Benny said, imitating her accent. "Do I look sunstroked? I can't say a day of honest work agrees with me."

"I don't sound like that!" she wailed.

Jordan walked in the back door.

"Jordan, you worked him too hard." When she looked at Jordan, she knew he wouldn't play along. She turned to Benny. "You'll adjust. There's beers in the fridge. I didn't know what kind you like so I got a few kinds, and I figured we'd have a fine time sampling them. I could have killed you for missing dinner last night." She looked at Jordan meaningfully. "We had a guest!"

"What burned?" Jordan said.

"The timer didn't go off," May said, guarding herself against a suggestion of wrongdoing. "The ziti burned. I'll make grilled cheese. I'm sorry, Benny."

"Don't be silly," Benny said. "I don't care. I'm so tired I don't know if I could eat."

May looked at Jordan.

"He did all right, actually," Jordan said. "Not too bad. He didn't throw a fit like the last time he was on the boat."

"I was twelve," Benny said.

"I knew it," she said, patting the new curls she'd just put into her hair.

"Here we are," she said happily. "Back together again, under terrible circumstances, but back together nonetheless. I'm going to finish getting ready. We're going to a talk tonight at the gym by a lady scientist."

"We are?" Benny said.

Jordan went to the refrigerator and took out a beer. He seemed puzzled by the label.

"This lady was in Alaska during the *Exxon Valdez*. She's going to talk about that and about the oil spill. It might be good for your activism."

He felt the sting of her drawing out the word *activism*.

"The gym? Like the high school gym?" Benny did not want to return to his high school.

"Where else could they fit all those people?"

Jordan grimaced, looking at the beer after he'd had a drink. "There's fruit juice in this."

His mother ordered them to "Go clean up," the way she had when they were boys, and then she bounded off to her bedroom.

"She's so happy," Benny said, surprised. He got himself a beer. "I haven't seen her so happy in years."

"This kind of thing happens often," Jordan said, studying the charred ziti.

"She's always been like that. Remember when we drove all the way to Baton Rouge to ice-skate and she forgot the skates? Or went to Alabama to camp, and she forgot the tent?"

"That's what she says."

"It's just a casserole. It doesn't mean anything. The spill has got you so gloomy you think everything's a calamity. God, I feel it too."

"Maybe so."

"I feel disgusting. I'm going to shower."

Benny went into the bathroom, turned the shower on cold, and slumped to the bottom of the tub, where he let the water rain on his face for a long time, not thinking about anything. He drank his beer in the shower. He'd been a baby in that tub.

After his shower, he sat down in an Adirondack chair with his second beer and smoked another cigarette. He killed a mosquito on his cheek, fat with his blood, and then one on his shin. The bayou at sunset was the least hospitable place in the world because of the mosquitoes. He batted the air lethargically as if he could shoo them away. He'd been awake too long. He wanted to fly off to New Orleans and leave them all to their "bad air" and poisoned sea life. If he could do this without speaking to anyone else, not to mention explaining himself, so much the better. He was not in the right shape—physically or spiritually—to return to Golden Vale.

His mother leaned out the back door and Jordan's old dog, Cypress, appeared immediately. She set down a bowl of burned ziti. "Don't tell Jordan." She laughed, watching the dog devour the food. "I'm making you a sandwich," she said, and then slipped back inside.

He wasn't worried about his mother's memory. He couldn't tell you the contents of a book he'd read three months before. What did strike him as strange was her bubbliness. This was more than her joy at having him home. He'd long been aware of her fragility.

As a child, he'd pick her flowering mustard or bring her the amber cicada husk he'd found in the grass. He'd done this without knowing she'd depended on him to.

Cypress padded over to him, looking for love, and carrying that open-mouth expression in a golden retriever that always seems like a smile. She licked Benny's leg as he petted her.

Then his phone rang, and to his stomach-sinking delight it was Kiki. He stood and jogged to the bayou for privacy.

"I heard you're in Golden Vale," Kiki said.

He tried to discern some disappointment in her voice, but her tone was light, chatty.

"Who told you?"

"I ran into Stani," she said. "You're working on the boat?"

"My brother couldn't get anyone to cull oysters," he said. "Apparently the BP cleanup work pays better than deckhand work."

"Unbelievable," she said.

"Which part—me on the boat or the cleanup work?"

"Both, I guess," she said, the delight in her voice buoying him.

"We pulled in a dead pelican this afternoon."

"Jesus. The oil's already there?"

"No, there wasn't any oil on it. But you can only imagine where it had been."

Kiki had many questions, which he was pleased to answer. Yes, they'd seen the boats with boom to soak up the oil. They'd passed an oil cleanup response center. He told her about the "bad air days," and the Coast Guard acting as a kind of police for the oil company, as Jordan had told him. Her interest was so total that their rapport was easy.

"Can I ask why you called?" he said.

"It's stupid. I just heard a song that reminded me of you. I miss you, of course."

A surprise that she would hazard as much.

"It still feels unnatural not to call you and tell you about my day."

"So, tell me."

Her favorite trainee at the café, a young man named Michael, got a good job as a line cook in a French Quarter restaurant, which was bittersweet because she'd miss him. The one-eyed café cat caught a rat outside and brought it into the kitchen and then set it loose, so it could be hunted again. It turned out that everyone in the kitchen was afraid of rats. There was Tariq, whom Kiki could not bring herself even to pity, he was such a bad influence on his coworkers. And he made her feel like a schoolmarm because she'd have to nag him into working. And she saw Maria—the girl Benny had slept with—biking by in the street, and she said, "Well, I hated that."

"Kiki, I'm sorry."

"I'm glad you're gone. I don't have to think about running into you."

He sat down in a plastic chair on the dock. One hind leg of the chair was broken, so it bowed with his weight, and he swayed on it back and forth like a rocking chair.

"It's probably good for you," she said, "to get out of New Orleans, and temptation, for a while."

"The only thing I'm tempted to do these days is camp out in your backyard until you forgive me, but I know it wouldn't help. Would it?"

The mosquitoes descended on him again. He looked down and they were all over his legs. She laughed this off. "There's a talk tonight by a marine toxicologist somewhere by you—Dr. Nikki Blau. I wanted to go, but I only just found out about it."

"I'm going," he said.

"You are?"

"It's at my old high school gym."

"I've watched interviews with her on YouTube," Kiki said. "She's great. You could write about it for the alternative paper."

"I might."

"Well, I'm proud of you," she said.

"Don't be proud of me, Kiki. You're not my mom. Be in love with me."

She laughed. "Okay, I won't be proud of you, then."

"Can I call you?"

"No, I can't handle it," she said. "But maybe later. How long will you be gone?"

"Until the oil comes in. We don't know how long we have until that happens. A couple of weeks, maybe."

"Good," she said. "Take care of yourself."

"Get another urge to tell me about your day," he said. "Just call."

"Sure," she said.

There was more than a hint of melancholy in her voice, maybe even a potential for tears. He waited for a while listening to her breathing before she said goodbye. It was a game they played when they'd first started dating—neither one of them wanting to be the first to hang up. One of them would laugh and say, 'You hang up first,' as if to hang up was to be the less interested one. 'Limerence,' she'd told him. 'This must be what it feels like.' He'd had to look up the word.

"Bye, Benny."

He looked back at the bayou, the brown moat of water he'd watched on its slow meander to the Gulf since he was a child. A spiderweb between two pilings in the water winked silver at him as the light touched it. A bullfrog smacked into the water from the grass. Sitting here, despondent as a teenager, he was mired in that old hopelessness he'd felt when young.

When he returned to the house, his mother could tell he was feeling low, and mercifully didn't ask why. She gave him a grilled cheese sandwich wrapped in a paper towel, which he ate while cramped into backseat of his brother's truck on the ride to the talk at his old high school. His mother turned from the front seat too often to watch him eat, and he felt a childish desire to ask her to stop staring at him, but he did not. Instead, he thanked her for the sandwich.

⟶ Fifteen ⟵

The high school parking lot was full, so Jordan had to park on the median. They'd all have to tramp over the rain-soaked grass to the gymnasium, where a surprising number of families were funneling in. They might as well have been attending a basketball game or a graduation.

Benny opened his door and landed in mud up to his laces. His shoes hadn't dried yet from the day on the water, and he paused for a moment, frowning at his feet once again. May smiled at him as if he'd been foolish. "Will you let me buy you new shoes?"

"No way," he said, rubbing one shoe against the other in vain. He only spread the mud around.

The public briefing was called "Protect Yourself: Your Family's Health During the BP Oil Spill." Jordan waited, hands on his hips, for a break in the traffic to cross the road. The three of them hadn't gone somewhere together in years, and Benny imagined it felt just as odd to them as it did for him. The sound of car doors slamming in the evening and fireflies blinking in the trees by the school track added to the sinking feeling that he'd gone back in time.

"Will BP be here?" Benny asked.

"This is just the Alaska people telling us what to expect," Jordan said. "They call themselves the 'survivors' of the *Exxon Valdez*."

Jordan's tone had some incomprehensible scorn in it.

"Maybe they did survive the *Exxon Valdez*," Benny said. "What do you know about it?"

Jordan huffed.

"My friend told me about the talk," his mother said. "I think it's in all our interest."

Jordan crossed the street too soon before a maroon SUV, making their mother shriek. He glared vengefully at the driver, who, Jordan seemed to imply, was driving too fast. He'd walked in front of the SUV on purpose. "Hit me," he said to the driver, standing a few feet from the bumper. A nearby family on their way into the gymnasium turned to watch.

"He's got a death wish," Benny said.

With Jordan out of the road, the SUV accelerated in rebuke.

"Fucking Texans," Jordan spat.

His mother scolded Jordan for being bullheaded, in a manner that he was accustomed to and could ignore.

"Dear god," Benny said.

It hurt her when he used the Lord's name.

"My wayward boys!" she sang, oddly upbeat.

Benny was surprised by May's interest in the event. She shared his dead father's mistrust of the government and government studies. She didn't follow politics at all, voted only in the interest of what she called "the unborn" or whoever his father had told her to vote for, though she would never admit as much. He didn't even need to inquire into what Jordan believed. In what Benny considered a kindness, he wouldn't talk politics with any of them after his father got sick.

The oceanic sound of voices inside the gym betrayed the large crowd, and Benny went rigid at the entrance, his mother and Jordan continuing without noticing he'd stopped. The smell of it. The heady wax on the basketball court and the rubber of basketballs and the plastic sports equipment and the dried sweat. Hours earlier, this gym had teemed with adolescents. Just the thought of it gave him chills of aversion.

There were national news crews, CNN and NBC, stationed by the door, and other crews on the opposite side of the gym. Men preening over their camera equipment, and hot reporter ladies adjusting their outfits. The event organizers had pulled out the wooden bleachers from the wall, which yawned like accordions into the middle of the room and were nearly full. Some enterprising minds might have sold refreshments, and before finishing that thought, he saw a couple of boys with a roller cooler selling off-brand sodas.

The crowd was mixed age and mixed race. Some serious-browed high schoolers sat up front with notepads as if on assignment. The groups mostly self-segregated according to race, he noticed. Black families sitting together and the Vietnamese families in the front rows. Benny knew many of the older generation didn't speak English, and so relied on their children or their friends' children to translate for them. He was relieved to see Hoa and Linh were not there with their husbands. He didn't have the energy to interact with them.

There were the local Indians from French-speaking tribes scattered across the coast. The Houma Nation. These tribes had been looked at with skepticism by Benny's father, who liked to roll his eyes at the epithet *Indian*. Al seemed to imply that these people were not truly Indian. Why would anyone make up being Indian? Benny wondered now. That was the thing about having parents;

you hold on to all their ideas, you're shaped by them, and you don't realize until later the scope of their influence—if the realization comes at all.

Then there were the rough-and-tumble commercial fishers with their hats on indoors. Of course, the fishermen were all but indistinguishable in dress from the oilmen. Some oilmen were out of work now because President Obama had put a moratorium on new oil drilling, and they were all furious, so he heard, likely more furious at Obama for closing down drilling than at BP for its oil spill. Some of these men were Cajuns, red-faced and authoritative and quick to laugh, just like his father had been. They had wives and children with them. Some of the housewives sat together—zippy, exasperated women who felt most comfortable operating on the level of feigned scorn. He felt as exposed and vulnerable as a child among these people. He was surprised at the old fear that bloomed in his chest being inside this gym, as if the whole crowd might suddenly rally together to ridicule him. These were his people, and he was scared of them.

Benny knew his hometown to be a big government–hating, Confederate-flag-toting haven. It made less sense to him the older he got. These people voted against their own interest in every election. They fervently believed in deregulation and the trickle-down economy when it seemed obvious, to Benny at least, that wealth would never trickle down to them and that deregulation had brought about the very disaster they all faced. What he feared most was that a community that had taken the party line, or, worse, the Tea Party line, as gospel, just couldn't change. He wished that Kiki could be there: Kiki, who looked at everything as if it were an opportunity for study, for uplift.

All these people had something in common, which was more than they might normally say. They were all being exposed to toxic airborne chemicals, and they wanted to know how bad it was.

Benny vaguely recognized some of the aged faces of his high school classmates, people he had little interest in interacting with. He tried not to look too intently and invite their attention. Everyone seemed to have put on weight and become dowdy. A woman with fried blond hair pointed Benny out to her husband, and they seemed to be talking about him. Benny walked on, and then a man stopped him by touching his bicep.

The man smiled at him familiarly. He was heavyset, balding, but something about his comportment announced sophistication. Benny didn't recognize him, and told him so.

"I'm a photojournalist," he said. "I took your picture today. You didn't seem to appreciate that, and I wanted to apologize."

His mother and Jordan were sitting in the bleachers near the front. The man looked at him intently. Benny shrugged. "Forget it. People don't like to be photographed without consent, but I'm guessing you know that."

"I do," he said. "Sometimes I get worked up when I see a good shot and I can't help myself, but it's no excuse. The shot is the best one I've taken all day. If you want, I can show you."

"I don't really care, to be honest."

"Are you an oyster fisherman?"

"My family is."

"We're trying to find fisherfolk to talk to. I'm working with NPR. Would you talk to us?"

"Fisherfolk, huh?" Benny had never heard this word before. "My brother is the one who knows everything, and he's no talker."

"What's his name?"

"Jordan Pearce."

"Pearce?"

"Yeah, Pearce Oysters."

"We've tried calling him. We heard you're the only oyster farmers left in this parish. Most of the oyster farmers are not young.

Who knew?" The man shrugged, seemingly charmed by the mystery.

"Jordan doesn't like reporters."

"Why is that?"

"He thinks they're out for their own good, probably."

The man laughed uncomfortably. "You seem nice."

"I'm the nicest guy you'll ever meet," Benny said. "I gotta go find my family now. I lost them."

The man smiled at him again, and Benny didn't know whether he was being flirted with.

A gray-haired woman approached the lectern, which Benny recognized as his old music teacher's, and glanced with impatience at the gaggle of kids playing half-court basketball. A handful of parents swept onto the court and herded the children toward the bleachers. The children's faces gleamed with sweat like new pennies.

Benny found his mother and Jordan separated by a rotund man in a Hawaiian shirt who was whispering to his mother and touching the inside of her wrist intimately as he made a point. The man beamed at him when he sat down, as if Benny should know who he was. Beside them, Jordan looked pained. The gray-haired woman at the lectern had begun to speak, and the man leaned forward to shake Benny's hand. He mouthed the words: Nice to see you. Benny, in his surprise, just stared back blanky. Was he mistaken, or was this big-necked man with his paw on his mother's forearm her boyfriend? His mother was looking ahead at the speaker, but on her profile was the prim smile of a secret. She clutched a pink pamphlet on toxic exposure.

The gray-haired woman had the no-nonsense demeanor of someone who has devoted her life to study. The woman began by telling the crowd that she wasn't there to alarm them, which jolted everyone a little straighter in the bleachers.

She was a marine toxicologist. She'd been studying oil spills, she said, since being "on the front lines" during the *Exxon Valdez* oil spill in 1989. She'd studied the effects of oil spills on the ecosystem and on the people.

"This spill, as I'm sure you all know, is not a spill at all. A spill has an end. This is a hemorrhage. This is an ongoing environmental disaster."

There was an affirmative murmur from the crowd that made Benny uneasy. He didn't trust this crowd to hear what the toxicologist had to say. He thought with a pang, again, of Kiki, who might one day speak to a gym full of people, which made him all the more receptive to whatever was happening in front of him.

"This disaster has already surpassed the *Exxon Valdez* spill in volume. It's only been two weeks, and I don't have to tell you that BP does not have a plan. It boggles the mind! How can you be one of the wealthiest multinational corporations in the world and not have a good backup plan for when the blowout preventer fails?"

There was a less enthusiastic murmur here. You don't come into oil country and spit on oil. She said she was experiencing some "déjà vu." She said BP was using a playbook that Exxon had written in how to respond to oil spills, and Louisianans needed to be aware that it was in the company's interest to mislead them about the spill, to obfuscate, and to make it very difficult for people to be compensated.

"It has been twenty years since the *Exxon Valdez* spilled eleven million gallons of oil in the Prince William Sound. Let me tell you, two hundred thousand seabirds died, twenty-two killer whales, the herring population collapsed, fishermen suffered greatly, and twenty years later, the ecosystem still hasn't recovered. In fact, in some places the oil is just as toxic as it was twenty years ago."

The crowd grew silent. Benny leaned forward to see how Jordan was taking this. He was staring at the ceiling where his name was displayed, along with some of his teammates' names, on a banner for winning the 1998 basketball state championship. Old glory.

"I'm here to talk to you about protecting yourself from toxic exposure," she said. "BP is using the same toxic chemical dispersant—Corexit—to disperse the oil into the water column. What we know about this chemical is that it's toxic to marine life and to humans, and when it's combined with oil, it becomes even more noxious. We're fighting tooth and nail to make the company stop using it."

The crowd let out a collective grumble now. This information wasn't sitting well with the families. Benny turned to study the faces. They looked skeptical.

She went on: "BP and the government are going to tell you what you want to hear. They're telling you it's soap, but it's not soap." She put her hand on her heart. "My conscience wouldn't allow me not to come here and talk to you all. Corexit is an industrial solvent. It's a degreaser. As unwelcome as this news is, we're dealing with a broken system. The EPA is not even testing the air adequately for the chemicals that we're all breathing in. Yes, they are measuring air quality, but they're going to give you an average, and depending on wind direction, toxicity will vary over the course of a day, so that the numbers, averaged over the course of a day, won't reflect the real toxicity present."

An old coot stood up and booed her. Everyone turned to him to judge how reputable this jeer was. There was some uncomfortable laughter in the crowd. The family members of the man urged him to sit.

The speaker continued, seemingly unfazed. "In Alaska, people working on the water and doing cleanup developed cancers that were toxicant related. They breathed it in. They had skin contact. They ate contaminated food. They started to cough, had trouble breathing. They got rashes. They had brain fog. They had trouble remembering things."

Benny watched his mother, who had her hand on the forearm of the man in the Hawaiian shirt. She unfolded the pamphlet on toxic exposure and began reading it—aloud. She spoke in a low voice, seemingly unaware that she was narrating as she read: "The properties that facilitate the movement of solvents through oil also make it easier to move through skin and into bodies."

He'd always been the odd one in his family, but as his mother mouthed the words, he was unsure of his standing.

"Mom," he whispered.

She glanced at him, gave her head a little embarrassed shake, and then refolded the pamphlet.

Her companion watched her with fond surprise. This was the friend she'd wanted him to meet last night, no doubt. The dinner he missed. She'd not told him she had a boyfriend. He wondered when—in the apocalyptic past two weeks—she had time to get a boyfriend. And the forgetfulness that worried Jordan—and, frankly, so terrified Benny he could not consider it—was that just preoccupation with a new man?

The speaker paused for what seemed a dramatically long time.

"And these people went to doctors, and the doctors told them they had colds, they had flus, they had staph infections, and they had asthma. They were given antibiotics. Very few of these people, the men and women who worked spill cleanup, are still alive today."

The man in the Hawaiian shirt shook his head sadly and said, "She's doing this all wrong."

"So, what can you do?" she said. "You need to document what you see. We have journals for you, so you can log your symptoms. If you're going to get compensated by the oil companies, you're going to need to have documentation. You need to educate yourselves on the signs of toxic poisoning. I need you all to know that if you're working cleanup, if you're on the water, you need to be wearing respirators. BP doesn't want you to have respirators because it doesn't look good on camera."

A family stood and noisily tramped down the bleachers. The mother, talking to some friends or neighbors as she passed, said, "She's scaring the children. What gives her the right?"

"I'm very sorry this is happening to you all. My suggestion is that vulnerable people—senior citizens, pregnant women, and children—should be moved inland if possible."

Another family stood up. A child, rushed by her father, fell and began crying. The woman with them scooped the child up and glared at the scientist as if she'd tripped her. The news cameras, which had been trained on the speaker, swiveled to capture the crowd's unrest.

The man in the Hawaiian shirt stood up. Benny worried he might jeer, but he put his hands out in offering to the audience. "This woman is here to tell us what she knows," he said. "Now, let's hear her out."

This had a comforting effect on the crowd. Whoever he was, he was respected in the community.

Of course, Benny thought, the poor people were turning against the woman. She was the bearer of bad news—the news that was so painful it could only be false. How could it have gone any differently? To her credit, the scientist did not seem too harried by this response. She seemed saddened. She apologized again for their circumstance, which Benny thought made her seem obliquely responsible for the spill. The BP officials were always on television apologizing.

"Pamphlets on toxic exposure are on that table by the exit," the woman said. "Take these with you to the doctor if you fall sick. Even very good doctors aren't aware of the symptoms of toxic poisoning."

A man with a walker struggled to row himself across the floor amid the clunk and squeak of his aluminum walker on the court. The man's walker had an oxygen tank attached. He had gaunt skin with white downy hair, his head sunken between his shoulders. He was wearing a red polo shirt, and the way the man labored to breathe after transporting himself across the court was harrowing to watch. To everyone's horror, this man, between tortuous breaths, said he was a fisherman who worked doing cleanup for Exxon after the spill. He introduced himself as Randall Sutherland.

"I was in a rig spraying hot water on the oiled beach," Mr. Sutherland said. "Worked ten-hour shifts. The steam of the oil would coat the glass windows of the rig I was on, but I never thought about it. I never thought about how I was breathing it too. I got a cough, thought it was the flu, but it stayed." The man sucked on his oxygen mask. "Lot of guys got a cough. We called it the '*Valdez* Crud.' Doctors gave us pills, but a lot of the cleanup workers got cancer. Exxon wouldn't pay. People went on disability." He paused to catch his breath. "There's not a day I don't wish I could go back and get on a plane and go far away from that oil spill. Not a day. I got paid out by Exxon, but I'm the only one that did."

May looked stricken. She grabbed Jordan's knee and Jordan leaned toward her to speak. He was pallid. They were all being handed a death sentence of sorts. It was one thing to know that you were breathing bad stuff, quite another to look at the future in the labored breath of Mr. Sutherland. Jordan's face was alight with agitation. He was angry, his eyes slivered. "I can't stand this anymore," he said, and he stood up.

Clutching his pamphlet on toxic exposure, Benny wondered precisely who his brother was angry with. BP? The organizers?

The look on Jordan's face signaled that he was ready to do something brash. It was a look that Benny remembered from childhood. He reached over and touched Jordan's hand, shaking his head solemnly, trying to appeal to reason.

"Buddy," he said. "Sit down. Don't interrupt the man."

His brother stomped down the bleachers so loudly that he drew the crowd's attention. He walked right up to the lectern. Mr. Sutherland stepped backward, bewildered, as if afraid Jordan would attack him. There, with everyone watching, Jordan tore up the pink pamphlet on toxic exposure, and the pieces of it drifted to the floor. A smattering of applause followed his act of defiance. People could disbelieve anything, Benny thought, if it's too painful. There are no limits. He swiveled to see who was clapping for his brother—people who seemed to think Jordan was being brave. This was fear masquerading as heroism, but it was the only form of heroism available at the moment.

When he walked outside, Benny saw that his brother's truck was gone, just as he knew it would be. His mother kept saying, "I can't believe it."

After Jordan's stunt, there was no mass walkout. The organizers carried on the event. The faces in the bleachers seemed racked with disbelief. They had been told repeatedly, in the news, by the Coast Guard, that they were fine. The air was fine. It would be a decision people would make for themselves, who and what to believe. On his way out of the auditorium, the photojournalist put a business card in Benny's palm. "Call us if you want to talk."

The night was ringing with insects and frogs, like it always was, but it all seemed malevolent now. Benny was overcome with the feeling that he should protect his mother, move her upstate.

Benny was in the backseat of a car being driven by the man in the Hawaiian shirt. He still didn't have the slightest idea who the man was. His mother was in the passenger seat, looking out her window, and thinking, no doubt, about Jordan. She was at ease with the driver, even if she was shocked by what had just gone on.

"Isn't it a shame, the way that went? Dr. Blau really bungled the delivery."

"But is it true, Doc?" his mother said. "The woman said we should evacuate."

"If I had a pregnant wife around, I might ship her up to the in-laws', and I wouldn't let the kids play on the beach right now. Do I think everybody needs to evacuate the coast? I do not."

"Excuse me." Benny leaned forward from the backseat. "Who are you?"

"Oh, I'm Fred." He laughed. "What a way to meet you! I'm a friend of your mom's."

Benny felt some touchiness at this word *friend*, and it surprised him.

"Call him Doc," his mother said. "That's what everybody calls him. He's a biologist. Doc was a friend of your father's. He's been over to the house. Don't you remember him?"

Benny took this in for a moment. He looked again at the man's profile. He had no memory of him. "I'm sorry. I can't say I do."

"It's been a few years," Doc said. "I see you got your braces off."

Benny saw Doc's tan, hooded eyes in the rearview mirror. There was a bald hope in the glance to see if Benny was amused. Doc wanted to sail past the discomfort of the situation—that he was trying to see Benny's mother naked. Benny didn't know what to make of him.

"Okay, Doc," Benny said. "What's your take on this whole thing?"

"It's bad as I ever seen," Doc said cheerily. "It's a disaster, all right. I'm on BP's environmental advisory board, totally powerless though, and I know for a fact that three dead dolphins washed up already on Grand Isle. It's enough to break your heart. I get spitting mad like everyone else. But I think people tend to lose their heads about this kind of thing. The Gulf was not pristine to begin with, as much as we like to pretend it was.

"Like right now, we're driving on a road," he went on. "When they pave this road, there's all sorts of chemicals, carbons, PAHs, and when it rains, these chemicals run off. They seep into the ground. They get into the bayou. They get into the Gulf. That's happening all the time. You got industrial runoff coming down the Mississippi. You got all the farms the length of the Mississippi with their DEET and their fertilizer, and that causes hypoxia, a dead zone in the Gulf, not a living thing, no oxygen, for an area the size of Delaware. And then you got the seepages, oil just seeping up from the Gulf floor naturally. You got bacteria in the Gulf whose job it is to eat oil. That's one thing that puts us at an advantage over Alaska. They don't have oil-eating bacteria up there."

He seemed like a guy who knew what he was saying, and Benny wanted to believe him.

"I worked as an extension agent in South Carolina for NOAA for fifteen years. Here's what I know about trying to disseminate new ideas to people. You can't scare anyone into thinking anything for long. People don't like to hear that times are changing—that they gotta change the way they net for shrimp or whatever. What you have to do is convince them it was their own idea. You have to hustle them. Besides, I'm a man of faith. I like to take the long view. This won't last forever."

"I wish Jordan could hear that right about now," his mother said, looking doe-eyed at this big man. The whole world felt so strange to Benny, he thought he'd been transported to a different dimension. Faith didn't sit well with him. He wanted a rational, scientific person to tell him what was what.

Finally, they were back at the Pearce family house, but Jordan's truck wasn't there. Jordan was gone, and he wasn't answering his phone. "Oh geez," his mother said. "Now I have to worry about him."

Doc shook Benny's hand congenially and instructed them to call him if they needed anything. Like what? he wondered. But it was just a thing to say. Benny couldn't imagine ever having to call him. From inside, Benny watched as Doc tried to reassure her. His mother hadn't had anyone to reassure her about life in a long time. Doc touched the back of her head while they kissed chastely, and Benny felt queasy.

His mother came inside, all smiles, and sat down on the couch opposite from him, clearly eager to talk. "Doc was who I'd wanted you to meet last night," she said.

"I pieced that one together on my own," he said. "How long have you been seeing him?"

"I don't know if I'm seeing him. I don't know what it is. He stopped by shortly after your visit. I hardly have words for how strange the past couple weeks have been. Every day surprises me. And now Jordan . . ."

"He'll be all right," Benny said.

"I can't believe it."

"Don't worry about him," he said. "I'd stay up with you and talk, but I'm so tired I'm already dreaming."

His mother clutched and hugged him good night. His childhood bed made a familiar groan when he lay down. It smelled of the detergent his mother had used all his life. He drifted off to sleep the moment he shut his eyes.

Sixteen

After Jordan left the gymnasium, he'd driven slowly past Bayou Bud's, and, not seeing Cyndi's car, he kept driving until he'd made it to her neighborhood. She lived in the same neighborhood as Doug Babies—by the drive-through seafood joint that had closed for good that week. When he pulled into Cyndi's driveway, he saw blue light from the television moving on her white curtains. He hadn't spoken to Cyndi since he'd dropped her off the morning after their date two days before. Her mouth had tasted like the motel coffee when she kissed him goodbye in front of her house, wearing her work sneakers and carrying her heels in her hand. It was a one-bedroom manufactured home she'd bought after Katrina tore through the neighborhood. Her yard had one of the few grand oaks left in the area, and Cyndi had set a rainbow lounger out front beneath its wayward limbs. That had been one of the best nights of his life, and he'd thought about it often in the days since. Yet, he hadn't called her.

Cyndi opened the door in an oversized T-shirt hanging well below her thighs She asked him why he was banging on her door like that. She didn't seem happy to see him.

"Is this an okay time?" he said.

"You know it isn't, Jordan." She looked down at herself in her pajama shirt as if offering this up to him for an answer. "You can't just come over when you get the notion to. What's going on?"

"'What's going on?'" he said. He was shaken by her demeanor, the hard wrinkle between her brows. He had expected she'd be glad to see him. Their date had gone so well. He'd expected she'd welcome him in. What had he meant to say?

He mumbled an apology and then turned to leave.

"No, you don't," she said. "You better explain yourself."

Holding the door open, she said she would put some pants on.

"Go get some water. You look like you're dying."

He sat on her couch and waited. She'd been watching the *Nature* show. On the television, a dolphin pod off the coast of Florida encircled a school of fish, corralled them by beating the sand with their tails. A camera shot from above captured a haze of sandy water encircling the fish like a lasso. The dolphins had made a trap, and then the dolphins had a feeding frenzy. He thought about the dolphins, the ingenuity of them, how social they were and altruistic even, and then he got up to turn it off.

Cyndi came out of her bedroom in old jeans with her big shirt tucked into them. She had her hair pulled back in a scrunchie. It wasn't that she was pretty; it was more than that. Her face was singing to him.

"You know," she said, "when I sleep with someone, and then they don't call me afterward to say, 'That was nice,' or 'Let's do that again sometime,' I usually write them off. That's a basic emotional intelligence thing for me." She'd had her arms crossed but dropped them. Her voice went soft. "You've been crying."

She climbed onto the sofa next to him, her legs folded under her. Words were getting caught in his throat. She looked at him pityingly. He pulled her toward him, and she didn't resist this like she might have when he first showed up. As she lay back on his chest, he stared up at the ceiling and said he was about to lose everything on account of the spill. And it was going to happen so slowly—that was the worst part. If it all came at once, it'd be better. Once he started blubbering, he couldn't stop.

"That's why you came?" she said. "Jordan, you are just a mess of a man." But she said it kindly, and she stroked the arm that was around her.

When he caught his breath, he said, "I don't know what's come over me. I'll go if you want."

"No point in you running away now. You're here, and I was feeling lonely anyway. I always watch the *Nature* show when I'm feeling down."

Then she went and got a cold bottle of vodka from the freezer and a jar of pickles. She liked to take shots and chase them with small fancy pickles, a curiosity that had charmed him, even if it was evidence of some man she was with before. After a while, they were loosened up and laughing again, folded into her couch together. His phone kept ringing, but he turned off the sound. He didn't know what to say to his mother, and he didn't want to explain himself in front of Cyndi.

"You just don't think it's possible," he marveled, petting her hair. "That you can lose everything. I thought I might do something crazy in that gym."

She laughed. "Men act like that all the time. I think I've always known there's not a thing you can hold on to in this world."

"I feel like someone just balled my life up and threw it in the trash."

He wanted to have sex now more than ever, more than he ever wanted to have sex in his life. He wanted to have sex like it might save him. If he could just have sex every few minutes for the rest of his life, he might be able to stand losing it all. He started to tug at Cyndi's clothes, but she stopped him.

"Aren't you going to say you're sorry?" she said.

"Cyndi." He put his hand on his heart like his father used to do when he was apologizing to his mother. "I'm a perfect fool. I'm sorry."

After they had sex, they lay on her bed, peeled apart from one another under the weak breeze from the overhead fan. Cyndi worried the drapery fabric between her fingers and became sullen. She seemed to think he'd be unreachable tomorrow. He was just another no-count guy, even though he came from a nice family, even if he did have a little money. She said she only ended up with no-count guys. She searched them out, she said miserably.

"Tomorrow," she said, "I know well enough what's happening tomorrow, and that's nothing at all."

Jordan promised her it wasn't true, and in that moment it didn't feel true. He would have promised her anything to stop the feeling that his organs were on the move. She wouldn't look at him. He got up on her bed and bounced, though the vodka destabilized his footing.

"Look at me," he said, gesturing at his naked body. "I'm all hanging out, and I promise to do right by you this time."

She refused to look, and so he started to jump up and down. He was chanting her name. The bed protested underneath him, but he kept on, thinking, If I'm willing to do this, it must be love. Maybe I'm in love. She still wouldn't look at him, went so far as to drape her arm over her eyes. She told him to stop. He jumped in earnest.

He heard a crack and then he fell, stupidly and slowly, onto the floor. He'd busted a leg of her bedframe.

He sat up, and they looked at one another like stunned children, and then they laughed. He crawled over to her, laughing, hardly able to stop long enough to tell her he'd buy her a new one. He'd buy her three new beds if she wanted.

Seventeen

Benny woke with the feeling that someone was staring at him, and there in the darkness was Jordan with a vacant look on his face. He sat in the papasan chair in the corner, as still as a statue; the crack of hallway light under the doorframe was the only light in the room. Benny pushed himself up in bed. Maybe Jordan had sleepwalked, he thought, but Jordan wasn't asleep and clearly hadn't slept at all. With the sunken face of a hangover, he looked as troubled as he'd been the night before.

"Jesus," Benny said. "You scared me."

"I was just thinking." Jordan rolled his neck.

"You've picked an odd place to have a think, chief."

"We ought to put a tarp up on the roof," Jordan said, feeling the scruff on his face with one hand. "So the guys up there see what they're doing to us. Send them all a message."

He must be drunk. "We'll talk in the morning," Benny said.

"It's gotta be a big sign, so they can see it from the air. See what they're doing wrong with the dispersant."

"I'm not awake yet!" Benny cried, and pulled the covers up over his face.

"It's time to go to work anyway," Jordan said, walking toward the door.

Outside, it was raining vengefully, a big storm emptied itself on top of them. Benny heard Jordan thump into the kitchen and start knocking things around. He heard May stirring, the scrunch of her bed as she rolled over. She probably hadn't slept well. Benny didn't feel rested either. He sat up miserably and looked around his bedroom. Thunder rattled the windows.

His mother was at the kitchen table making a list on a notepad when Benny emerged in search of coffee. It was still dark outside, rain slapping the windows. His mother mumbled something about paint while Jordan spread peanut butter on white bread. As Benny grabbed a mug, he got a look at Jordan in the light and noticed his neck was bruised from kissing. That was an interesting development. As if to herself, May said she'd look in Meemaw's house for the white latex paint she'd used to touch up the bathroom.

Benny interrupted her. "Are you not going to ask what happened to Jordan's neck?"

His mother lifted her reading glasses and squinted at Jordan, frowning. There was such an odd privacy between them. Jordan pawed at his neck as if he could rub the marks away.

"It's nobody's business," he said.

"I leave for a couple of weeks," Benny said, "and everybody has a lover except me. I just get dumped."

"But you were so enamored with one another," his mother said. It was more a statement of surprise than sympathy. She didn't sound unhappy about it.

"Nobody to blame but myself," he said.

"That can't be," his mother said, in complete sincerity.

"You think too highly of me. I don't deserve it." Benny blew on his coffee. "What about the fact that we're all being poisoned to death? That I won't live to see age forty-five? That I won't be able to see my children graduate from high school?"

Jordan had a wad of peanut butter sandwich in his cheek. He'd stopped chewing.

"And are you going to apologize for leaving us last night?" Benny said.

"I'm sorry," he said.

May put her pen down. "Doc says it needn't be as bad as that lady says. We don't have to evacuate. The Gulf is a lot different than the Prince William Sound. We've got to keep our chins up."

This sounded unbearably grim, and unconvincing, to Benny. A silence passed among the three of them that allowed Benny to hear the rain again. He wasn't sure if his mother even believed what she'd said.

"I wake up this morning," Benny said, wanting to change the subject, "and Jordan is sitting in the corner—staring at me with a dead look on his face."

"He had a great idea," she said.

"What's that?" Benny said.

"I told you," Jordan said. "I want to put a sign on the roof to send a message to BP. To get them to stop spraying that dispersant."

"A sign," Benny said.

"Yeah, the size of the whole roof, so you can see it from the air."

"I thought you didn't think it was a problem," Benny said. "You tore up the pamphlet in front of all those people."

"It's not that," he said, and took a sip of coffee, so they had to wait for him to respond.

"You didn't make a spectacle because you were mad?" Benny asked.

He could feel his mother tense beside him, worrying that another argument would erupt.

"Let's move on," she said.

"I was mad," Jordan said. "I'm tired of people telling me what's going to happen to me."

Benny crossed his arms. "Like the environmentalists?"

"Everybody," Jordan said. "BP, the government, the science people, everybody. What about me? Don't I have the right to say, 'No. You can't fucking do this to me. I won't take it'? Everybody's got that right."

"Yeah, sure."

"'Yeah, sure,' he says." Jordan was mocking him. "You like to raise a big fuss about the spill in New Orleans when your girlfriend can see, but when I do it, you don't care."

"Don't raise your voice, Jordie," his mother said. "It's early."

"Is that what you're doing?" Benny said, smiling. "Raising a fuss?"

"I've got to do something," Jordan said. "Maybe you won't help, and that's fine. That's normal for you, but then you should just go back to New Orleans."

"I'll help," Benny said. "I'm here to help."

Benny could see some color return to Jordan's face. He seemed weary, but his eyes were bright with enthusiasm, which Benny had not seen in a long time.

"Was a muse sucking on your neck last night?"

May squawked in surprise. Evidently she thought that was hilarious. She could hardly catch her breath. Jordan started blushing, and couldn't contain his laughter either. They were all there together in the small, warm kitchen with the rain thrumming outside. It was a fine feeling, the coffee going to work on his mood, and they talked about how they'd do it and what they'd need. They brainstormed possible messages: "DISPERSANT IS TOXIC TO MARINE LIFE" and "STOP SPRAYING NOW." Benny offered up "PLEASE DON'T POISON US." His mother wrote down their ideas and was excited to elicit more from Doc. She wondered where they'd find a tarp.

"You probably know someone, Jordan. One of your father's old friends? Who's the man from the marina?" his mother said, looking at Jordan. "I can hardly remember a thing! I'm in a brain fog."

"I wonder if they sell gas masks on Amazon," Benny said.

In that way, because they had to, they made light of it all. Jordan couldn't join in, but he seemed less stolid than usual. The rain outside was lightening up, sounding softer now.

"This is a fine thing to do," Benny said soberly, "but it's not going to stop the spill."

"We've got to do something," Jordan said.

This was not an unfamiliar argument to Benny. It was how all the activists talked. Kiki believed that if you raised enough of a fuss, people in power would need to listen. She had an index card taped above her desk with an old chestnut from Margaret Mead: "Never doubt that a small group of thoughtful, committed citizens can change the world. Indeed, it's the only thing that ever has." He'd heard her repeat this more than once in conversation. Jordan set about making another peanut butter sandwich. Benny was touched to realize that this sandwich was for him.

"I met someone last night who's eager to talk to you, if it's attention you want," Benny said. "A photojournalist with NPR. I bet we could get on the national news."

"See?" his mother said, patting Benny's thigh. "That's just what we need. Aren't you glad you came home?"

→ Eighteen ←

May had a date. She would drive to Doc's oyster hatchery for dinner, which meant Benny would be alone with Jordan for the night. Benny's past few evenings had looked much the same: watching the sun sink into the treetops over the bayou while his mother cooked for them. After five days harvesting oysters, his body ached uniformly in a way totally foreign to him, as if something noteworthy were about to happen, like his body would crack open and a new body would emerge from it. Something to that old idea about the curative power of work. He longed to inform Kiki of this, or anything. He checked his phone over the course of the day, but most often at night when he sat smoking outside. He was most desperate to hear from her in that lonely hour before dinner.

Benny was keen to use his NPR contact to set up an interview. If they made it on NPR, he imagined, it would reach Kiki, regular listener that she was. They'd not found a tarp large enough to cover the roof yet. Over dinner, the three of them brainstormed messages to use but hadn't landed on one. Once the tarp was up, Benny maintained, they'd need to set up an interview. Jordan acted cagey, kicking back his beer when the subject came up. Benny realized the reluctance was not about the business. Jordan was simply afraid of being interviewed—afraid he'd make a fool of himself.

After they'd finished eating, Jordan pulled out a map of the company oyster leases and a pencil, and busied himself with projecting the oil's approach to his holdings. May auditioned date outfits for Benny as he sat on the living room couch next to a box meant for charity—the family's old VHS collection. Jordan offered no opinions about the outfits, which could have been due to his discomfort with their mother dating, or Doc specifically, or the spill's prominence in his mind. She'd tried on two dresses already, narrating the merits of each. The black dress was most forgiving of her hips. The floral-print dress was dated, but she liked the neckline. She flew back to her bedroom to try on a third, and emerged in a floor-length denim dress with cut-off sleeves, brown buttons in a line down the front.

"Are you serious about that one?" Benny asked.

She nodded, smoothing the denim over her stomach.

"Hello, 1992," he said.

"It's a classic!" she cried.

"Absolutely not."

Traipsing around the room on her tiptoes—she wasn't wearing her heels yet—she paraded the ugly dress around. She was only fifty-four years old, he realized, with maybe a whole other life ahead of her. Little gold hoops in her ears, her doll-like face was a portrait of geniality. Benny was glad to see her happy, and found it endearing that she was visibly nervous. She had foundation on that kept her face white while her neck was splotched with red.

"Maybe you should come with me, Benny," she said. "You could see Doc's oyster hatchery and Grand Isle."

"You want me to go on your date with you?"

She was embarrassed then and changed the subject.

"You ought to call Rollo for the roof tarp," she said to Jordan. "He used to run an ice and bait shop, and he holds on to everything. Some might call him a hoarder."

"It's a good idea," Jordan said, not looking up from the map.

She rubbed the faded denim fabric between her fingers. "Maybe I shouldn't go."

Jordan looked up at her, scratching his head with his pencil. "Your going won't change anything," he said.

Jordan's weary smile at their mother touched Benny. He found himself moving toward the kitchen to put a pot of water on the stove for macaroni and cheese.

His mother was out the door before the water was boiling. She wasn't the woman Benny recalled growing up, running the house with tireless enthusiasm, but perhaps he was just too young to understand her then. Or perhaps she was the kind of woman who needed the structure of a husband and kids to operate, to understand herself. Whatever it was, he felt protective of her now, acting like a teenager on a first date. Jordan seemed to be thinking something similar as she fluttered out the back door in her floral-print dress, blowing kisses, but he kept those thoughts to himself.

The house shuddered, the macaroni quaking in the colander, and Benny verified this shudder by looking at Jordan. Yup, a low-flying plane. Now that it'd passed them, they heard the roar of it. Jordan flicked his map with his pencil with increasing violence. They knew the plane was filled with dispersant.

"We should just have the tarp say NO FLY ZONE," Jordan said.

"That's not a bad idea," Benny said, shaking the colander. "Really, though."

While Jordan was away in the bathroom, the house phone rang in the kitchen. Benny stared at it, that old gray relic on the wall. It wasn't his house anymore, but since Jordan was indisposed, Benny answered. At first Benny assumed it was a prank call. The man sounded like a cartoon to him. "I'm sorry?" Benny kept saying. "I'm Jordan's brother, Benny. No, didn't catch that. You're bringing something over?"

The man said something else. It was English, but it was unrecognizable.

"I'm sorry?"

Jordan came back. Benny extended the phone to him.

"That Rollo?" He was amused. "Put him on speaker."

The man repeated his garbled drawl, and Benny was delighted when he realized that Jordan could decode it. They'd been around Cajuns as children, but Benny only understood every third word the man said. Rollo had grown up in some little place in the bayou where they only spoke French, and those places didn't exist anymore. Cajun French was just something that confused college kids minored in. The man said something to the effect of "Shooting them all dead in their beds."

"The thought's crossed my mind." Jordan leaned on the counter, scratching his unshaven face. "Okay, Rollo. See you in a minute."

For a seventy-year-old, Rollo was an imposing figure, with a lean, muscled body from a life spent working. He had gapped teeth, rheumy eyes, the waxen red skin of a body too long in the sun. He seemed to Benny the kind of man who might have once enjoyed picking a fight, maybe still would pick a fight, though he had a noticeable limp. He spat when he talked, and seemed to be talking about their father, at one point turning to face Benny: "Your daddy could drown a turtle" was what Benny heard, and he nodded stupidly at the man.

The tarp was heavy and smelled vegetal, like it had long lived in a tall pile of grass. After Rollo drove off, they unrolled it onto the driveway. "Tough old bird," Benny said.

"Rollo said he's building a cemetery in Grand Isle."

"For who?"

"No, like a statement," Jordan said. "He's making a lot of fake tombstones for things that are dying in the spill. He's writing things on the tombstones like: SEA TURTLES, TUNA, SNAPPER, SUMMER FUN."

"Genius," Benny said. A firefly winked at him. "I know artists in New Orleans who'd die to think of that. What I want to know is how in the hell can you understand him?"

"It's 'cause I never left, I guess," Jordan said, chasing an anole off the tarp with his shoe.

Normally Benny would take this as a jab, but Jordan appeared to mean nothing by it. He looked down at the tarp and squinted at it like he was already painting it in his mind. "NO FLY ZONE," he said to himself. Benny killed a mosquito on his arm. He turned back to the house, thinking of the macaroni becoming gelatinous in the pot.

"Coming?" Benny asked.

"In a minute."

Benny was on the couch texting Stani when Jordan came in with plastic pails in each hand and a roll of newspaper tucked under his arm. Benny lifted his feet from the coffee table. He knew immediately what Jordan meant by this. During their lunch break on the water earlier that day, Jordan gushed again about Caminada oysters, at which Benny had just shrugged. Tired as he was, and maybe unfeeling, he'd said that all oysters tasted the same to him. Jordan had been appalled by this.

Jordan set the pails down on the coffee table. He brought saltines and Tabasco next.

"I've got three bays here," he said, sitting down. "I want you to try all three and tell me again you can't taste a difference." With the shucking knife, he pried open the oysters as effortlessly as popping a beer cap. Benny broke open a sleeve of saltines, but

Jordan said, "Eat the first ones naked, so you can taste them. The whole point of an oyster is where it comes from."

Benny put the shell to his lips and was about to kick it back like a shot.

"Oh my god, that's not how you do it! Dad is rolling over in his grave," Jordan said. "Act like you been here before. Lean over to drink it up. That way you get the liquor but not the grit."

"Am I supposed to chew?"

"Yeah, you're supposed to chew. It's not a pill."

The oyster slipped into his mouth. He bit into it—a burst of seawater—followed by a hint of metal.

"Okay."

Jordan handed him another.

This oyster was fatter—saltier yet somehow sweet—like summer had slipped down his throat.

And then a third, smaller oyster, puckered inside with a purple rim. This one was creamy, buttery, but less salty. It tasted more like the fresh water.

Jordan watched him with pleasure. "You can tell the best one. Which one is it?"

"The second one," Benny said. "It's subtle, but I like that one best."

Jordan slapped him on the back, elated. It was a shock. His brother hadn't touched him in years.

"That's them. Caminada Bay," he said. "The whole point of an oyster is where it's from. Okay, now you eat them with the crackers. I don't care. I just want you to know there's a difference. It's like this—oysters and saltines, a little hot sauce, and a beer. A real beer—not that shit with fruit in it. That's just heaven for me."

It dawned on Benny: Up until this point, he'd had no idea what was heaven for his brother. He'd been a mystery since they were children.

"We're gonna fish out the leases in Bay Courant tomorrow."

"What do you mean, 'fish out'?"

"I mean we're going to fish them until there's nothing left for next year. I've never fished out that lease before, since it's a wild-growing reef. But there's no point leaving oysters for next season when that oil's coming in to kill them."

"Isn't that a little drastic?" Benny said. "We don't know if the oil will make it that far."

"It would be a miracle. The oil's almost at Grand Isle. You know what that means."

"Yeah, I know," Benny said. He knew a week ago that the oil would eventually reach the bays and the oyster reefs, but since he'd joined Jordan on the boat he began entertaining some impossible thinking: every day it did not happen, maybe it never would.

"I just want you to know what they taste like," Jordan said. Jordan reached for the remote control to turn on the television. It would be the news again. Benny snatched the remote from him.

"Better not," Benny said. "It won't make any difference."

Benny extracted the VHS film from the box meant for charity, *City Slickers*, and Jordan grunted, but he did not object as Benny popped it into the ancient VHS player.

At that moment, his mother was forty-five minutes away on Grand Isle, a mile-wide barrier island that separated the Barataria Basin, and Jordan's prized oysters, from the wide-open Gulf. Benny knew his mother wouldn't be home right after dinner, and yet it still surprised him that she wasn't back by ten o'clock. He wanted to know what Jordan thought about it, recalling what Kiki had said—that Jordan and his mother were "symbolically a couple," disgusting as that was to think about. She could do worse than Doc, Benny thought. He expected his mother to be attracted to some mouth-breathing franchise owner who'd both worship her and boss her around. Watching Jordan crack open oysters and sliding them onto saltines with a dunk of Tabasco, he thought better of bringing it up. Jordan guffawed when Billy Crystal ended up in a tree clutching a coffee grinder because he'd started a cattle stampede.

There was a young Helen Slater in the film, all caring eyes and feathered hair, and down-on-her-luck charm, so Benny asked, "What's up with your girlfriend, anyway? How come she doesn't come around? And does she have a name?"

"Cyndi," he said. "She works nights."

"Like as a stripper?"

Jordan looked at him.

"Listen, I just don't know why the fuck you're so secretive about it. It's not unreasonable to ask unless there's something you're embarrassed of."

"She's a bartender, okay?" He took his feet down from the coffee table and then he put them back up. "She works most nights, so I don't see her, and business is up for her with the spill, and she's at her dad's house right now anyway. He's a shrimper out in Terrebonne Parish, Pointe-au-Chien Indian."

Benny watched as Billy Crystal lassoed a cow, to the applause of his friends.

Later, Benny said, "Wait a minute. Hold the phone. You're telling me that your girlfriend is Native American?"

"Guess so," Jordan said, not looking at him.

"Huh."

"What?"

"It's not bad. Of course it's not bad. I'm delighted, really. I just didn't expect it. You're so much . . ." Benny slowed himself to consider his brother's feelings. "Like Dad. I didn't know you even had any Native American friends."

Jordan cracked his knuckles. "She's a good girl."

"Hey," Benny said, "good for you. Any future in it?"

"I can't say I'm too optimistic about anything right now."

They kept watching the film. These city slickers feel most alive when in nature, out in the arid scrubland, where the risk and uncertainty deliver a kind of macho pride in "making it" against the odds. It's an old trope of the West, Benny knew, but the movie sold it well. There was even a surprising liberal Hollywood plea worked in advocating for animal rights, and vegetarianism, even. Benny found that he wiped away a tear at Crystal's reunion with his family.

"The Hollywood machine does it again! Look at me!" he said, laughing at himself. "Why in hell did we like this as kids?"

When Benny looked over at Jordan, he noticed that Jordan stared at the cheerful cartoon credits with dejection, clearly thinking about the spill again, but to avoid saying so, he picked up his phone and looked at the time—almost midnight.

"I can't believe she's staying over there," he said.

"She's grown." Benny shrugged. "She seems better, really, than she did after Dad died."

"I don't like the guy," Jordan said.

"You wouldn't."

Jordan grabbed three empty beer bottles by the necks. "I've got to go to bed."

"Me too, I guess." He looked at his phone on the table, which had not lit up all night like he'd hoped it would during the movie. "Nobody loves me in New Orleans."

⤳ Nineteen ⤶

May hardly saw a thing on her way to Doc's oyster hatchery on Grand Isle. She hadn't driven over there in years. It was where the rich tourists went to rent "fishing cabins" on the Gulf that were bigger than her own home. Everyone in Golden Vale hated that, that people called them cabins. The cabins were on stilts and painted tropical colors—a lot of these places new after Hurricane Katrina. People named their cabins things like SEA BREEZE and HIS RETIREMENT FUND. They were like Easter eggs on stilts. Normally she'd be jealous. Now the owners were making a killing renting them out to people in Louisiana for the spill—scientists or whoever. May heard that tar patties were washing up on the sand, but not the oily crude yet, which would shut down fishing in the estuary. That hadn't reached them. Once she reached the island, May noticed there were no children around. Normally, in summer like this, there would be gangs of children running about. Her hands were wet on the steering wheel, and she flipped through the radio stations as if she cared what was playing. It wasn't her first date with Doc, but he'd made some innuendos about what they'd do after dinner, and she had laughed knowingly, a good sport, but didn't know if she could go through with it.

The hatchery looked, to May's surprise, like all the rich people's vacation homes. Doc paraded her around, and she nodded too enthusiastically at the tanks with the algae in them, cooing, "How interesting! Wow!" at the baby oysters while Doc was going on about off-bottom oyster aquaculture. She'd been very formal with the Salvadoran man who was cleaning one of the pumps for the algae tank. So formal that Doc had laughed and said, "Let's get you a margarita, May. Do you like margaritas? I've already had one myself. Just to test the tequila out, of course."

He winked and then led her up the three-story wooden plank steps.

"The steps are so new!" she cried, as she climbed. "This is a climb that'll keep you fit."

She was helpless to say anything at all. Thinking all the time, What would Al think if he could see me now? With Doc, who'd been a friend. They climbed until they reached the top deck—an expansive covered porch overlooking some shallow oyster beds below and an unobstructed view of the Gulf with very nice, sturdy patio furniture and even a porch swing. Doc's house, perched on top of the oyster hatchery, was a new-smelling two-bedroom, clearly decorated by a man, without a lot of care, but with nice couches on laminate wood floors. An oil painting of a sunset on the mantel and an enlarged poster of Doc himself with Mardi Gras beads around his neck and a straw hat on, mugging for the camera. The poster was signed in gold marker: "We Love You, Capt. Fred! Kelly and Donald."

"Former students," he explained, dipping her glass in lime and then in salt. She'd forgotten that he was a professor too.

She didn't expect a place as nice as this for an oyster hatchery and she said so. He brought the drinks out to the porch, and she was so delighted and nervous that she laughed. Doc was a marvelous talker; she hardly needed to say a thing. The margaritas went down like juice. She couldn't figure out just what she was doing there at all.

Doc made a jambalaya he seemed very proud of, listing all the ingredients off to her as if she'd never had a jambalaya before. He said they could eat whenever they were ready to. The sun had gone down, but the sky was sorbet, thin wisps of purple clouds. She couldn't imagine eating. She kept thinking, But is this me? Who is it talking now about Benny's ex-girlfriend? Who is going on about the beauty pageant she lost in 1972?

He smiled and said, "I, for one, am surprised you ever lost a beauty pageant."

There, he'd said it.

And she blushed. "That was a long time ago. B.C.," she said. "Before children."

"You could win one tomorrow," he said. "I think you're a beautiful woman."

"You're very nice."

"It's not niceness," he said.

All of it like it was out of a script! She couldn't even look at him. She put her face into her margarita, but there was none left. And then he was off with her glass, the blender roaring in the kitchen. She pulled her phone out of her purse to see if the boys had called, desperate to hear from Benny or Jordan so she might again have a role she understood.

The jambalaya was too spicy, the rice undercooked and crunchy. He'd used so much cayenne her nose dripped, and she kept having to stop her nose up with her napkin and pretend nothing at all was happening, her eyes watering. He was talking about how these were his oysters in the jambalaya, plus shrimp from Tien, a friend of his. He bought up all the alligator andouille from another friend who lived in Larose. She was nodding. He seemed to know a lot of people. Al had been like that, a friend in every town. Every time they stopped for gas, it seemed somebody was coming up to them, "Look who it is. Al Pearce!" Al might not have been as smart as Doc—Doc had a PhD, after all—but he was well liked by everybody too.

Once they got onto the topic of children, she was relieved that his kids were not without their troubles. He had a son who'd gotten into drugs, opiates, and had been to rehab. A boy younger than Benny, just twenty-two. He was back in college now at Tulane. Doc had been a professor at Tulane, so he had his friends keeping an eye on the boy. What the boy liked most was video games, Doc said, so he hoped the boy could get involved in that.

Doc himself had been a troubled teen, and got into his share of jams. A nun at his school had called him into her office. She'd asked him, "What do you enjoy most, Freddie?" He imitated the shrill nun. He couldn't tell her the truth, which was drinking beer with his friends and fondling his girlfriend, so he said fishing and trapping turtles. She told him to study marine biology, which he did on probationary status at a Christian college in South Carolina. The rest was awfully straightforward.

May liked listening to him talk. She felt tipsy, and almost relaxed. She tented her napkin over her plate to hide the fact that she could only stomach half of the jambalaya he'd served her. Doc stood up to get a bottle of wine, and she told him she liked any kind of wine, which was a lie. She rarely drank it, but didn't want to say so.

When he returned, he started talking about his ex-wife with affection and distance.

"After the kids left the house, we looked at each other and thought, Now, who are you?" he said. "The ol' magic was gone. We tried to get it back, but we'd grown apart. Now, I'm a Catholic man, and I don't take divorce lightly, but I figure we've got enough time to have full lives with other people if we have the heart to look. She didn't like that I was here so much at the hatchery, living with my students. She got very suspicious about that."

May sipped her wine. "Al wasn't easy to live with," she said. "He wasn't always considerate, but he brought me a lot of joy."

She didn't want to think about Al too much. Al with his parties. Al with his demands. Al was the only man she'd ever slept with. Doc seemed to be waiting for her to say more.

"He traveled to New Orleans a lot, huh?"

"He did. He was on the Louisiana Oyster Task Force—that brought him to town a lot, plus all the buyers, the restaurants. He was well suited for his work. People liked him. They invited him to dinner all the time. He was a good salesman."

"Did he fool around?"

"Al?" she said. "*Al?*"

"I'm just asking."

"Why would you ask me a thing like that?"

"Aw, shucks," he said. "I've offended you. I didn't mean to do that. I just thought we were getting to know each other for real. No bullshit. But I shouldn't have asked you that, I see."

"I don't know why you'd ask me a thing like that," she said.

In the bathroom, she felt sick, and she wanted to go home. But she couldn't drive. He'd trapped her there. Doc knocked on the door and asked if she was okay. She kept telling him she was fine. But she felt she could vomit. Her skin was hot and itchy. She scratched her neck and noticed that there were raised welts on it. To her horror, the welts spread to her chest as she scratched them. Then her thighs itched. She began looking through his drawers for some anti-itch cream, some hydrocortisone. The drawers were empty. Doc knocked again.

May told him that she was feeling sick.

"You're upset, and that's okay. You don't need to lie about it."

He turned the door handle. She couldn't believe it. She'd locked the door, thank God. The welts crept up her neck onto her face. "I need some Benadryl, I think."

"Let me see," he said. Again he tried the door handle.

She sat down next to the toilet. Something was very wrong with her. She put her cheek on the cool plastic lid. "Would you go away, please? I'm going to be sick."

"Don't be dramatic," he said.

"Do you have some Benadryl?"

"Just open the door. Will you, please, May?"

She vomited violently and with a force that meant food poisoning. Up came the jambalaya, up came the shrimp and the oysters, and the cayenne pepper. Her vomit was bright red from the cayenne, and it burned the entire way up, lips burning, eyes watering again. She lay on top of the toilet seat, resigned to whatever was happening. She stopped listening to what Doc was saying on the other side of the door. She couldn't even hear him trying to come in. It was like that for a long time. She vomited until she felt it all was out of her, but there was a fist gripping her stomach and it squeezed.

The nurse was a woman her age, with a soft, worried face, who called May "sweetie" when she woke her up to take her vitals. They'd given her a walloping dose of antihistamines that knocked her out. "You had some kind of food poisoning!" the nurse said.

Doc was there too, in the same clothes he'd been wearing for dinner. He'd driven her to the emergency room in Graceland when she vomited up the Benadryl too. Her memory of getting to the hospital was fuzzy. She couldn't keep anything down, he told her, as if she'd forgotten. He looked pummeled with remorse.

"You said you're not allergic to anything? I wish it'd been me. I don't know how I'll make it up to you."

The nurse was entirely sympathetic to him. She said, looking at May as if interceding for Doc, "People often develop allergies later in life. One day, suddenly, they can't eat shellfish!"

May frowned at the nurse. "I eat shellfish all the time."

She felt entirely exposed. She must look wretched. Now that she was feeling normal again, the shame set in. She'd been out of her mind with illness. When someone has seen you compromised, she thought, you resent them after the fact. She just wanted Doc to go away.

Neither of the boys was very polite to Doc, especially not Jordan, who'd glared at him as if he'd intentionally poisoned her. She felt some comfort in this. On the way home, the boys played her favorite Joni Mitchell CD, and they told her they had gotten a tarp adequately sized for the roof. She sat longways in the backseat of Benny's car, which had been her car once, with a blanket draped over her body and her head against the window. The backseat of Benny's car was littered with the debris of his life, spent matchbooks and rocks from faraway places, flyers for a BP protest and an empty wine bottle rolling forward on the floor at every stop. When she didn't come home last night, Benny said, he couldn't believe it. "I thought, Mom is putting out!"

"But, really, in all seriousness," Benny said, "what if it was the seafood that got you sick?"

"Doc didn't get sick," she said.

"Or the dispersant," Benny said.

"You'd better not see that guy again," Jordan said.

She laughed and said, "It could happen to anybody," which wasn't quite dissent. She didn't know how she felt, except weak and cared-for in the backseat. It was such an unfamiliar feeling she could have cried.

→ Twenty ←

After he and Benny returned with their mother from the hospital, Jordan unfurled the tarp in the driveway. They decided to skip harvesting to keep an eye on her, despite the discharge nurse saying that May would be "just fine now that all the bad stuff's out." Benny recalled the lady scientist telling the gymnasium of scared people that the oil was in their bodies now. It had been three weeks since the explosion on the *Deepwater Horizon*, and the oil company's latest plan was to try to clog the leak with garbage — shredded tires and golf balls — dubbed their "junk shot." His mother hadn't eaten bad seafood. She'd eaten poisoned seafood. For all Benny knew, their oysters might already be tainted, even if this wasn't something Jordan was prepared to admit.

Benny stood in the living room, sipping coffee and watching his brother work. Jordan had set about hacking the tarp down to a manageable size, with an aggression that seemed meant for his mother's maybe-boyfriend. A fine mist churned over the bayou behind Jordan where their father's boats sat. It was seven o'clock in the morning, and in the early light, Jordan's body gleamed silver with sweat. Jordan was a natural workhorse. Benny found himself feeling generous toward his brother. He no longer felt the need to resent Jordan for cutting him out of the business, though if things had gone differently, at that moment he would be corresponding with his brother through an attorney.

Benny's phone rang, which always delivered a jolt of hope, but it was never Kiki calling. A woman introduced herself: "I'm Vanessa Sanchez, a reporter with NPR. My colleague Edward gave me your number. Is this a good time to talk?"

She sounded young—somewhere in his own age bracket. Benny sat on the couch.

"Hi. Sure, Vanessa of NPR."

"Edward said he met you at the talk on toxic exposure."

"Were you there?"

"No," she said. "I couldn't make it."

"Quite the event," he said. "Awfully bad news, if you're us. Most people there didn't take it too well. So, you're looking to do a story on fishermen who've been affected by the spill, right?"

"That's right. You're an oysterman?"

Benny did not feel this was true, but on paper it was. "Yes," he said. "My brother and me. The family's been in the oyster business for ninety years. The Pearce Oyster Company."

"And you're still harvesting oysters now during the spill?"

"Until we hear we can't," he said, surprised that he felt a tad defensive. "That oil hasn't reached the estuaries yet. But we have every reason to think it's just a matter of time."

"It's awful. I'm so sorry for your family."

"Thanks," he said. "It's a sorry situation. But after that briefing, my brother decided to send a message to the BP planes carrying dispersant to the Gulf. We're putting a tarp on the roof."

"Really? What's the message?"

"We thought about DON'T POISON US, but we decided to put NO FLY ZONE up instead."

"NO FLY ZONE," she said. "I love it."

"He's outside working on it now."

"Listen, I'd like to come out there and interview you, if you're interested. Edward would come too and take photographs."

"For the radio?"

"Well, it'd be an audio story, but it would also go up on our website. I'll talk to you and your brother—"

"Jordan."

"—Jordan. About the spill and your message for BP. And the oysters, of course. Oysters are quintessential New Orleans cuisine. I think a lot of people would like to hear your story."

Jordan would not enjoy an interview. Not only was he gruff, and generally bad with strangers, he thought that giving interviews was unseemly. As if it equated with crying about their lot rather than stoically enduring it.

"Great," he said.

"What about next Wednesday?"

"We'll have the tarp up by then."

"Can we go out on the oyster boat with you and watch you work?"

This, Jordan would hate. Benny watched him stop cutting to slap a mosquito on his arm.

"Sure," he said. "Why not?"

"I think it will really fill out the piece. The photos too."

He then gave Vanessa their address. They arranged to meet at six in the morning. He had a good feeling about it. It was rare that he had a chance to do something decent for his family.

As soon as he hung up, he reflexively dialed Kiki again, which he did maybe twelve times a day, mostly at night. Each time, the phone rang once and then went to voicemail. It comforted him to call, even if he didn't expect a different outcome. If she heard him on NPR, maybe she'd call him. He wished that she was less equipped to accept change. She seemed to think moving on from love was part of a journey that life demanded of you over and over. He did not. His stomach flipped in consideration of Kiki icing him out for good, and sent him checking on his mother to see if she needed more tea.

Her bedroom was dark, with the blackout curtains drawn, illuminated only by a night-light next to her bed and *Design on a Dime* on the television. Around the room was the evidence of her date preparation from the night before, the dresses she had tried on and decided against, a whitening pen she'd used on her teeth, lipstick and face creams in disarray on her vanity. This evidence must have seemed accusatory to her now. She'd scrubbed her face, cranked the AC to sixty-five degrees, and had her comforter pulled up to her chin.

"That one is my favorite, that designer." She pointed to the screen. "He is the most fun to watch, but it is the builder that pulls all the weight around there. I'd like to hire a designer to make over my space. I have some ideas, but I know I'm not thinking of everything."

On the screen was an immaculate white living room that looked like it was ordered out of a Target flyer.

"I want this place to feel more modern," she said. "Your father wanted everything to look the same. But I have a little playing money your father left me that I haven't touched yet."

Beneath her cheerfulness, he sensed a misery beyond words, and he knew the feeling well.

"Are you still stomach-sick?"

She pulled the comforter tighter around her body. "I feel like I haven't slept, but I can't make myself."

"Do you want me to make you some tea?"

"You're not going to oyster today?"

"Not when we've got a sick mom on our hands," he said. "It wouldn't be right."

This pleased her. "I'll be fine! No need to worry yourselves over me. I can always call Lucille if I need something. She won't believe me when I tell her what happened."

"NPR just called. They want to do a story on us."

"NPR, that's . . ."

"National Public Radio," he said. "They're coming out with us on Wednesday."

"That's wonderful, honey," she said. "Really."

He could sense the strain of her enthusiasm due to her state.

"Let me go put a kettle on. It's an icebox in here."

Through the window he saw that Jordan had finished cutting two sides of the tarp and had started on the third. Benny did not look forward to pitching in. Jordan had already told Alejandro they might get a late start, but they'd not called to tell him they decided not to work at all. While Benny waited for the water to boil, he called Alejandro again.

"No work today, buddy. Our mother was poisoned by her beau, and she needs us to watch over her." He could hear the disappointment in Alejandro's voice at the news. Alejandro needed the pay more than anyone did.

"Beau?"

"Boyfriend. I think that's a French word. *Novio*. She just got out of the hospital."

"You're kidding," Alejandro said, but there was a question in his voice. Alejandro was sometimes still unsure of Benny's sense of humor.

"I am," Benny said. "I mean, she was in the hospital. She got food poisoning from something he made her, some seafood, but as far as we know, he didn't mean to do it. Listen, sorry for the late notice about work. But we're making a tarp for the roof today. You can always hang out over here if you're bored."

"So you want free labor?"

Benny liked Alejandro. They'd had an easy rapport since the moment they met, and they shared a disdain for Golden Vale. A few nights after work, he and Benny had lingered by the docks, passing a joint as the sky darkened. Benny brought a guitar down, and Alejandro shocked him when he picked it up and played a fine tune without a fuss. He'd never mentioned that he played guitar.

"Yes," he said. "After you've had a few beers, if you feel inclined to pick up a paintbrush, I'll put one in your hand. But no pressure. Only come if you miss us."

"Are you leaving soon?" Alejandro asked. He meant for good. Their conversation had never ranged further than a day or two into the future, outside the general ending of the world in a fiery way.

"If I had a reason to," Benny said. "She won't give me a reason."

Alejandro was silent on the other end for a moment. "So, not leaving?" he said.

"No, not today. Today I'm painting a tarp. And if it's just me and Jordan at it, I'll probably be painting without any conversation to pass the time with."

There was an awkward silence. Benny already guessed how badly he would feel for Alejandro when finally he did return to New Orleans. Alejandro had said he was unprepared for how lonely he'd be in the United States, and how much worse it was in this small town, among the tight-lipped fishermen and marsh dwellers.

"Are you there, Ale?" Benny asked.

"Yeah, I'm here," he said. "Sorry."

"I've almost got you persuaded, don't I?"

"Maybe so," Alejandro said.

"Like I said, only if you miss us, or if you get bored."

"Okay," Alejandro said. "I'll come if I miss you."

Benny set down the steaming cup of peppermint tea next to his mother. She caught his hand when he set down the mug and squeezed.

"I'm sorry your date went so badly," he said. "When you stayed out so late, I thought, Mom is a liberated woman."

She looked scared. "I think the Lord is trying to tell me something."

"You don't believe that." He'd forgotten how religious she could be.

"I don't believe in the Lord? You're wrong there. I don't know what happened." She shook her head. "We raised you Christian. You don't believe?"

"I don't believe the Lord struck you with food poisoning because . . ." He couldn't fathom the source of her sin. "Because— what?—you went on a date?"

"He makes all things happen," she said, slowly and defiantly.

"Oh, Mom," he said. "There's nothing wrong with going on a date."

"In sickness and in health."

"Al's gone. Nobody would say that you can't go out on a date or, hell, even remarry if you wanted to. Don't be so hard on yourself."

"He wouldn't like it," she said. She was angry with him. "Al was your father. He's no Al to you."

Her voice broke then, and he feared she was going to cry. She was humiliated, he figured, by what had happened. He knew the prick of the old childhood injustice of being made a scapegoat for his mother's feelings. There was no point in saying so. She was too fragile.

"You drink your tea, and try to get some sleep, okay?"

"I've gotten so old!" she cried. She flipped onto her side and buried her face into her pillow. Her little shoulders were shaking.

"You're just tired. You're not old. You're just tired, Mom." He touched her shoulder. She flinched. He sensed she wanted him to sit down, but he wouldn't. She had her face in the pillow. From the doorway, he said, "I won't call him Al if it bothers you."

She looked up at him, her face red.

"The seafood was bad," he said. "Nobody wants to say it, but that scares the hell out of me."

In the living room, he tried again to call Kiki. Again, no answer. Benny heard his brother arguing with someone on his phone outside. He was calling the person unreasonable. At first he thought Jordan was talking to a buyer, someone bailing on an order, but no, his tone was more personal—a spat with his girlfriend. "You do what you want," he heard him say. And then Jordan looked at his phone to confirm what he already knew. She had hung up on him.

Benny went out for a cigarette. He pulled a folding chair into a triangle of shade thrown by the garage. Jordan took the folding chair next to him.

"How's she doing?" Jordan said, looking at the house.

"She's in the shame chamber."

"What?"

"The shame chamber. It's the morning-after feeling you have when you've gotten too drunk, or betrayed someone, or otherwise embarrassed yourself."

"I didn't know it had a name."

"It does to me."

Jordan huffed. This was the biggest reaction Benny could elicit with one of his jokes, but it pleased him all the same.

The tarp was spread out in front of them. The outline of NO was traced in white paint.

"NO FLY ZONE," Jordan said. "It gets the message across. Plus, we've got to consider what you can see from the air."

"I thought it was a good idea, and I still do." Benny went on: "Listen, I'm glad I caught you in a good mood. NPR called, and I set up an interview."

"You're kidding."

"Nope."

"They'll be here Wednesday."

"The tarp's not up."

"It will be."

"You didn't think to ask me first? That didn't even cross your mind?"

"You'd try to put it off. You wouldn't want to do it."

"Everybody is trying to get on TV now, crying to reporters about how hard they got it." His knee bounced as if in an earthquake.

"They do have it hard. They're not making it up for sympathy."

"I don't want to be on TV," Jordan said. "I just want my life back the way it was."

"This isn't TV. She's with the radio."

"Whatever."

"But this will be good for the business. And it might even help with the compensation we get from BP. Like, once it's documented how we're affected by the spill, it will be harder for them not to pay out."

"Don't be ridiculous. BP isn't going to feel sorry for us."

"That's not the point. The point is visibility. Why else make a sign?"

Just then a dim-faced youth appeared in the driveway holding a bouquet of flowers. He glanced at the tarp and then at them, uncomprehending. Benny looked knowingly at Jordan.

"You got some flowers for me?" Benny said.

"Maybe," the boy said, and his free hand searched his pocket for an order slip, which it appeared he'd lost. "Were you expecting flowers?"

"A lady always expects flowers," Benny said in a coquettish voice. Jordan huffed.

"I left the order slip in my car, I think," he said. "Just wait."

Before the boy could turn around, Benny pushed himself up from the folding chair. "I know who they're for. You can hand them over. She's sick in bed."

The boy didn't know what to make of Benny, but he handed him the bouquet nonetheless.

"If you want to go back and check, that's fine."

He turned to walk away, and Benny watched him go—the blockish size and shape of the young men who'd given Benny a hard time for sports in high school. Benny said, "Hey. Are you worried about the oil spill?"

"What's killing this area is that moratorium on drilling," he said. "Just 'cause BP spilled doesn't mean everyone's going to spill."

"So, your daddy's an oilman," Benny said.

"Benny," Jordan said.

The young man looked like he'd been slapped. Benny felt guilty for picking on him, but he said, "You think that we should still be drilling oil during an oil spill?"

"You all got cars, don't you?" the boy said, looking at Jordan's truck.

Benny smelled the bouquet. Snapdragons. No smell at all. "You got us there."

The young man stomped away up the driveway and out of sight.

"Why'd you do that?" Jordan said.

"I'm polling the locals," Benny said. He smoothed the paper wrapping of the bouquet. "I'm glad he sent flowers. She needs cheering up."

Jordan picked up his paint can and brought it to the edge of the tarp. He knelt, starting on the F in FLY. "Might as well finish this today if we're not fishing."

"Alejandro said he might come over and help too."

This surprised Jordan.

"We ought to have an unveiling party. Bring over this schlub," Benny said, indicating the bouquet. "Have your girlfriend over, even. I know Mom would be tickled to meet her. She's waiting for it to happen. This'd be a low-stakes way to introduce her."

"You said the interview was Wednesday?"

"Yup," he said. "A party before the interview."

"It's not a bad idea," Jordan said. "What time are they coming?"

"Six in the morning." Benny walked to the back door. "I better hand these over."

"We have to work then. What were you thinking?" Jordan asked. "Call them back and tell them to come at the end of the day."

Benny had one hand on the doorknob. "They want to come out on the boat with us."

"Hell no," Jordan said. "It could be our last day on the water until who knows when."

"Better for the piece, really."

"Goddammit, Benny." He sank the paintbrush back into the can of paint. He had purple crescents under his eyes. "Why didn't you ask me first?"

"I knew what you'd say. I didn't want to give you the chance."

Jordan sat on the driveway next to the tarp. "Fine, then. Whatever."

"It's for the best. I promise you'll be glad we did it."

"Hoa and Linh are nervous there won't be any jobs left for them."

"Maybe there won't be," Benny said. "Better invite them to the party."

Their mother read the note from Doc with a smile on her face and asked Benny to grab a vase from the kitchen. Later, through the wall, he heard her humming to herself.

Twenty-One

On Tuesday morning, the boys were out fishing for oysters in Bay Courant, and May got the party in order. It had become, for May, a kind of coming-out party—the first time she'd host a party without Al. Benny had said she was a liberated woman, and though in the past she could only have said the phrase "liberated woman" with sarcasm, she did feel liberated from a long gloom as she dusted paprika over deviled eggs and swayed her hips with the chorus of "Could You Be Loved."

She thrilled in party preparation almost more than in a party itself. And she was pleased that the family business would be in the news again. The national news, at that—National Public Radio. In the past, reporters had called the house phone asking to speak with Al. He'd commented on this or that development in the oyster industry, such as a proposal to change the inheritance of water bottom for raising oysters. In one book, a travelogue about oyster regions around the world, the writer called Al Pearce "the most famous oysterman in Louisiana." Though Al was the first person to say "famous oysterman" was a contradiction, he wasn't unhappy about it. And neither was May.

Doc had been over that afternoon to lend her speakers for the party. He'd helped May move patio furniture from the garage into the driveway. He'd given May a foot massage. He'd read Sunday's *Times-Picayune* in Al's old easy chair while May boiled potatoes for potato salad. May looked at Doc in the easy chair as she bustled about the kitchen and she felt a surprising jolt. Amid this great misfortune, a sense of well-being. Romance had filled her up and, at that moment, her boys were sailing up the bayou on their way home from working together. It felt like the fortune of the family was being righted. She had not taken an anxiety pill in four days, and her feelings were more vivid, her emotions more apparent in her body. She'd not known that turning down the volume on her worry had dampened other emotions. She felt her insides churn with a kick of excitement, her heart knocking in her chest, and there seemed to be no ceiling to her joy. May had even taken the liberty of inviting Doug Babies and his family to the party. She saw no reason that Jordan should hold a grudge against Doug when his quitting had brought Benny home.

When Hoa knocked on the back door with a cooler full of jumbo brown shrimp, instead of the usual tense politeness the women shared a laugh about a sign Benny had made for the party. He'd listed drink specials based on the methods BP had used so far to close the open oil well.

END OF THE WORLD DRINK SPECIALS:
CONTAINMENT DOME
THE TOP HAT
JUNK SHOT
THE RELIEF WELL

Hoa even winked at May when she spied Doc with the newspaper in the living room. It seemed, paradoxically, that the party was for the spill, but the party had also made the spill seem far away, and maybe it would stay that way for a while. Doc refolded the paper, hiding the aerial shots of the black-and-blue Gulf.

May balked at the black streamers Benny had brought home from the dollar store. She called him morbid. But Benny taped them up anyway with Alejandro's help. They stood on chairs in the living room and tacked the streamers up the length of the room in waves that fluttered with the AC.

May overheard Alejandro say, "The black streamers overhead are like oil floating on the water's surface. I think this means we are all underwater."

May had never seen Benny so delighted by a comment.

"Maybe then we fill the living room with dead fish," Benny said.

"Or our big dead bird," Alejandro said. "The pelican."

May had not known many of Benny's friends since they lived in New Orleans, and she was mildly unsettled by the quick, obvious bond that had formed overnight. Alejandro was just a deckhand, but he stayed for dinner twice that week. She found him to be so fastidiously polite, quietly kind, offering to help her with the dishes when her own sons did not, that she was glad to have him around.

The three boys had squabbled over how to attach the tarp. They were up late the night before, standing on the roof, in a sudden thunderstorm, tying it in place. May draped towels over their shoulders and brought them hot toddies in the living room after they'd climbed down.

All had been going well until Doc called late Tuesday to tell May he was requested at a last-minute meeting for the spill. It was all a big joke, he conceded, but he couldn't get out of it. He would be over as soon as he could. Her mental calculations for the party had revolved around Doc's introductions to Lucille, to her neighbors, to Jordan's new girlfriend.

"You're not going to miss the party?" she said.

"Not if I can help it."

She poured herself a wine cooler, turned up the music even louder, and then set about doing her makeup for the night.

Jordan sensed his mother's disappointment and wanted to be helpful to her. He offered to man the grill. He told her she looked beautiful. It seemed that the spill was aging them all, but she was looking younger, wearing clothes that suited her and pink rouge swiped across her cheeks. Jordan poured charcoal in the grill and kept a watchful eye over the driveway for Cyndi's arrival.

A few days before, Cyndi complained that Jordan didn't take her out, that they only holed up in her house at night as if he were ashamed of her. He could not fathom where he might take her. Didn't she recall that they were amid the worst oil spill in history? That's what the news was now calling it. He was working every available moment, he told her. His voice raised. "I could be working right now!" he said. "But I'm not. I'm here. With you." She patted his leg as if he were a dog, and they let the issue slide. But later, while they watched a rerun of *Friends*, her legs snaked around his, she said, "Are you embarrassed that I'm Indian? That I'm a bartender?"

He immediately denied this because he knew any hesitation was an answer in itself. But it was true that his ex-fiancée had been young, white, and a nurse. This did not mean he was embarrassed by Cyndi. Still, he had not hurried to introduce her to his family, and he didn't know why.

Over the next few days, she claimed to be "too tired" to see him. He had not heard from Cyndi all afternoon, and he was mired in sudden doubt that she was coming at all. Then he heard the unsteady clomping of heels up the driveway, and there she was, trotting toward him, hugging a quaking bowl of Jell-O salad to her chest. She was zippered into a pink halter top dress that constricted her movement. Jordan almost felt as though he needed to scoop her up, and he wanted to. Cyndi was normally self-assured, but he was moved terribly by the fact that he sensed some worry in her face. She was nervous to meet his family. Her black hair was down and tucked behind her ears. It shone silver in the sun and matched the silver eye shadow on her eyelids.

"My Indian princess," he said, and then laughed at himself.

"Oh, no, you don't with that," she said, but she beamed. She handed him the bowl. "Take this."

"You look so good," he said, and landed a kiss on her cheek.

"Here we go," she said, looking over Jordan's shoulder and watching as a smiling blond woman made a beeline for her.

May had her locked in a fierce hug almost immediately, one that swayed from foot to foot, even though she was considerably smaller than Cyndi. May thanked her excessively for the Jell-O salad, talked about the traffic on the town throughways what with the spill. And did she find the house all right? As if they didn't live in one of the only neighborhoods in town.

"So, this is the sign?" Cyndi said. The three of them looked up at the roof. "I've heard so much about it."

"It's sort of hard to read at this angle," Jordan admitted. "But it's for the planes most of all. I get a kick out of it whenever I hear a plane fly overhead and I remember it's there."

"Well, it's something. You've got to do something," Cyndi said. "That reporter tomorrow is going to eat it up."

Jordan frowned. "It's not for publicity. It's about the dispersant."

"But even if it's about dispersant, it's still good for the reporter's story, right?"

"But that's not why we did it. I don't want people to think we're just hungry for attention."

If May sensed some awkwardness, she was eager to blow past it.

"He's so private, Jordan!" May said, in a conciliatory tone. "He's always been like that. And here you are, finally. Jordan has stopped hiding you from us as if you were this big secret."

May chattered so much that Cyndi barely had to say a word, except that she was a bartender, at which point May frowned faintly. Cyndi clocked this, as did Jordan, who touched Cyndi's back protectively.

"Well, maybe you can make us some drinks!" May said, well-meaning, though it didn't land well.

"I'm pouring drinks tonight," Jordan said. He steered Cyndi past May and to the back door.

"We'll get to know each other very soon, I hope!" May chimed.

Jordan ushered Cyndi into the living room. They looked at each other as if to say, Well, we're doing it now. He apologized for his mother's comment, but she said she knew May hadn't meant much by it. His mother had everything arranged—all the cups, soda, and liquor options in a comically attractive fashion. Cut hydrangeas were in a vase on the table. Cyndi admired a top-shelf bottle of tequila that Jordan didn't recognize. He wondered aloud if Alejandro had brought it.

"Who?" Cyndi asked.

"The deckhand," he said, and pointed to a very dapper Alejandro in khakis and a button-up, the most well-dressed person at the party. Jordan thought he looked ridiculous dressed up like that, as if he'd never been to a BBQ, but Cyndi made a face when she saw him that surprised Jordan. Was Alejandro attractive?

Cyndi asked if she could make a pitcher of margaritas.

"You don't have to do anything," he said, but he sensed that she would be more comfortable making something, so he let her.

Cyndi squeezed limes for margaritas while Jordan pointed people out to her—the Black woman hugging her mother was Lucille, his mother's best friend. With Lucille was her son, Roland.

Cyndi laughed at the black streamers in the living room. She said Benny must be a real character, and then she pointed him out across the yard. "That's him in the hat?" He was playing shuffleboard with Hoa and Linh. "How is he recovering? Is he in withdrawal?"

Jordan had forgotten that he'd told her that Benny was an addict. In the weeks that Benny had been home, he'd seen no evidence of hard drug use. Benny's reasons for dressing and acting the way he did were more mysterious to him than that. He wanted to fly past his misapprehension without admitting it.

"You know, I think physical labor has been good for him. He's got more color on him now."

"Anybody would have color on them if they worked all day in that sun," she said. "You two hardly look like brothers. Then again, you have the same eyes. But not your mother's eyes."

"It's hard to imagine that we came from the same people at all," he said.

Benny felt cagey about the shrimp that Hoa and Linh brought, though this should have been brown shrimp season. After his mother's food poisoning, he started bringing sandwiches for lunch on the boat. He looked down miserably at the plastic plate of steamed shrimp they'd handed him.

"Shrimp catch is down!" Linh said. "But this shrimp is still good. My husband wouldn't sell bad shrimp. A fisherman knows."

NOAA had instituted a "smell test" for the shrimp, and on the news he'd seen assembly lines of men dressed in white smocks, leaning over bowls of shrimp and wafting the aroma toward their faces. The men had trained their noses by sniffing vials of diesel.

Linh told him that her husband was out on the water at that very moment for the evening trawl.

Benny brought the women big margaritas, which had them loose and chatty because they rarely drank. He played shuffleboard with them in the driveway. When Hoa gave a determined thrust to her puck and knocked Benny's puck off the board, he said, "Hoa's a ringer! Watch out!" And they laughed like schoolgirls.

Hoa wore a wrap dress with Hawaiian flowers on it and dainty pearl earrings. She bragged to Benny again about Annie's budding law career. She said Annie was handling all their paperwork for the BP claims process. Hoa leaned forward, and Benny realized that she was truly feeling tipsy then, a sly smile on her face as she motioned for Benny to bend down to her. "But Jordan is not helpful with our paperwork," she said. "It's a problem."

"I'm sure we'll get it straightened out. I'll hold his feet to the fire."

Hoa puckered her lips and shook her head. No, he couldn't imagine Jordan was a very communicative boss. It likely was a problem. He thought of Annie, whom he'd gone to a middle school dance with, who'd been a wallflower in high school but nevertheless possessed a quiet and alluring intensity. He remembered a forced cheerfulness in her that hid some melancholy. He wasn't at all surprised she'd done so well. Benny couldn't understand why, with such successful children, Hoa continued to work as an oyster shucker.

"Does Annie need a secretary?" Benny said. "Tell her I'll send over my résumé."

Hoa giggled. If he'd somehow managed to end up with Annie, he could imagine what a disappointing son-in-law he'd be. She wouldn't find Benny so amusing then.

"She will take care of me when I'm older," Hoa said. "She will move back."

"I think it's pretty hard to get the kids back from California, Mama."

"She will come," Hoa said, pleased with her own certainty. "She's a good daughter."

Benny set Hoa and Linh up with another round of drinks, this time to escape them. He suddenly felt some judgment from them about his absence during Al's illness. And he didn't want to think about his father.

May was telling everyone about Doc and his nice oyster hatchery on Grand Isle. He was bound to arrive any minute, she reassured them, though no one seemed too concerned about it. The blender was whirring in the kitchen, and a handle of frightfully green margarita mix had materialized with one of the guests, though she wasn't sure who. This was a first, margaritas in their house, and it seemed to May a step up in the world from the coolers of beer they used to have at crawfish boils and barbecues.

May roped Benny in from browsing the CD collection and reintroduced him to Lucille.

"Well, if it isn't the freewheeling Bob Dylan," she said. They got on immediately.

Lucille had brought Roland, whom Benny recalled from his childhood. A statuesque Black man who'd gone on to play football for LSU and still bore the evidence of it, the armored shoulders and thighs threatening the girth of his Bermuda shorts. He had movie star good looks. Roland had been fond of Benny as a child, when he'd been so runty. Benny said, "When we played capture the flag, you threw me over your shoulder like a sack of potatoes. I loved that."

Roland knew exactly what he meant.

Benny was disappointed to learn that Roland was a deputy sheriff, though he shouldn't have been surprised. Roland looked as though he could play a cop on TV. He was maybe ten years older than Benny, which had seemed a lifetime older when he was a child. Roland was telling them that he'd recently been assigned to guard a beach access road like some kind of Walmart stooge. He had to stop people, but mostly the media, from going to the beach and taking pictures of the beaches dotted with tar balls or, worse, some pathetic dead wildlife. Some of those people got in his face about it. "Why are you guarding the public beaches?" they cried. "You work for the people! You don't work for BP."

He was proud of his response: "I work for Sheriff Alan Battieux, and if you want to talk to him, you're welcome to call the station."

Lucille beamed at this remark.

Benny admired a guy who could spin a good yarn, but he couldn't admire the thoughtless adherence to orders. He disliked cops, he disliked managers, and he disapproved of the military. It was all the toxic masculinity stuff he grew up with. When he opened his mouth, Lucille sent Benny a warning look that shut him up. Of course, those people were right. Why should the deputies guard public beaches? It was only because the whole state seemed to work for BP now, and BP controlled the optics of the spill. He looked down on Roland for not recognizing this.

Alejandro tugged on his sleeve and leaned close to whisper, "Smoke break?"

They absconded down to the bayou.

Benny and Alejandro sat in chairs next to the water, passing a joint. The party continued at the house some forty feet away, where the music and the voices had a pleasant distant quality. The mosquitoes died down at that hour of the evening. Benny pulled his phone out of his pocket.

"There you go." Alejandro laughed. "Has she called you?"

"No," he said, putting his phone back. "It's a habit. These have been the longest weeks of my life, and I wonder if that's also true for her. Has she moved on already? I have no idea."

Alejandro leaned over with the joint. Benny noticed that Alejandro's hair was growing out and was curlier than he'd have guessed. It suited him.

"Now imagine it was your whole family," Alejandro said. "And they were three countries away."

Benny was embarrassed into silence. He was stoned. The evening air pulsed with crickets and frogs.

"What will you do when the spill shuts us down?"

"I'll go back to Texas, maybe. Their oyster harvest starts in November."

"What do you mean, 'go back'?"

"It's where I crossed. McAllen, Texas."

"Right, I forgot," Benny said. "But don't go to Texas. Come to New Orleans with me."

Alejandro put his hand on Benny's thigh to get his attention.

"Hey. Pass it over."

Benny had twice pulled on the joint without passing, he realized.

"Sorry."

Then the hand was gone, but Benny's thigh was alert where Alejandro had touched him. And there it was—attraction. He'd known immediately that Alejandro was handsome, but he'd not sensed that Alejandro might be inclined. In his high state, the insect noise began to take on a house techno beat. Benny couldn't be sure if he could trust the electricity he'd felt. The touch was just long enough to be noteworthy, but he was inwardly terrified by the attraction he now felt, and not just the inconvenience of it. He'd never exercised much in the way of self-restraint. He didn't know if he had it in him to resist attraction.

"I don't know anyone here," Alejandro said. "These have been the loneliest years of my life."

Jordan found he could not keep himself from talking about the oil spill. Kept spouting off depressing things, like the fact they were likely breathing in the dispersant at that very moment, that BP's latest containment dome had failed, and about the most recent thing the CEO of BP had said: "There's no one who wants this thing over more than I do. I'd like my life back."

"I can't talk about this all the time!" Cyndi said. They were standing by the pitcher of margaritas, which was now empty. "You've got to stop."

"It's taken over my life."

She softened. "I know it's hard for you. It's just, it's hard to hear about too."

"Do you want to see the boats?"

Jordan was unsurprised to find Benny and Alejandro smoking under the aluminum tent by the bayou. For the past few nights, they'd planted themselves there in the evenings and not once asked him to join.

"You're going to get us arrested," Jordan said. "You're always smoking. It's going to fall back on me one of these days. I know it will."

Benny ignored him.

"Cyndi," Benny said, "would you like some of our peace pipe?" Benny extended the end of the joint her way. It was hardly larger than his pinched fingers.

Jordan gasped. "Shut up, Benny."

"Are you saying that because I'm Indian?" she said.

"Did I offend you?" Benny said. He seemed genuinely sorry. "It was a dumb thing to say. I'm always saying the wrong thing."

Alejandro shifted in his chair.

"It must be genetic, then," Cyndi said, looking askance at Jordan, and Benny laughed. "But I would like some. If Jordan talks any more about this oil spill, I'm gonna scream."

Jordan chuckled uncomfortably.

Benny stood to hand her the joint.

"What is Indian to you Americans?" Alejandro said. "I'm confused by this."

"Oh, it's like . . ." Benny began to explain, but then he stopped himself, sitting back down. "I'm sorry. Cyndi, you say . . ."

"Indians are the native people who lived here before the white people came. As we learned in third grade, when Christopher Columbus pulled up, he thought he'd landed in India. Hence, 'Indians.' White people call us Native American now. And after they pretty much killed all of us, they like to dress up like us for Halloween. Or put our baskets in museums."

Alejandro nodded. "At least they want something from you now," he said. "From us, they want cheap goods, and to stay out of their country."

Cyndi surprised them all by inhaling expertly, holding it in.

"You look like a cousin of mine," Alejandro said. "Ana."

She surprised them again by responding in Spanish. Alejandro answered her, and they shared a hearty laugh.

Benny winked at Jordan, who looked ill at ease. He clearly didn't know she spoke Spanish.

"Cyndi, where'd you grow up?" Benny said.

"In a mostly Indian bayou town, Montegut," she began. "I grew up around French speakers, fishermen, crabbers, some oilmen. We were self-sufficient once." She went on to tell them that her tribe, the Pointe-au-Chiens, were not federally recognized by the U.S. government and so didn't receive the same support and protections that other tribes received. Her mother, before she passed away, had worked doggedly to collect the necessary tribal history to correct this. "White people were happy to call us Indians during segregation to keep us out of their schools, but now that's over, and we're no longer real to them."

Cyndi stubbed the joint into an ashtray and told them about the blessing of the boats that happened before shrimp season. A priest aboard his own boat, armed with incense and holy water, cruised down the line of fishing boats to bring good tidings, and everyone got drunk, including the priest, who, one year, fell as he leaned over to sprinkle the holy water. Into the water he went, white robe and all, and afterward he claimed he lost his balance and got all touchy if you suggested otherwise."

"Did you fit in?" Benny asked.

"I did until I didn't," she said.

"Ay Dios mio!" Alejandro said. "That sounds like a story."

Jordan hooked her arm and seemed to be indicating bodily that they needed to go somewhere."

She looked at him with slight annoyance, but consented. She turned to Alejandro. "Embarazo adolescente."

Alejandro stopped smiling. "Qué fuerte, hermana."

Then Jordan and Cyndi plodded across the driveway to the music and lights of the house to rejoin the party. Cyndi had to shake him off her, she said, because he gripped her too tight. It made it difficult to walk.

May had read somewhere, and this was true of her and Al—that each couple was its own vaudeville act. It was odd for May not to have a man at the party. She had never thrown a party without a partner. She drank down two margaritas that Jordan's girlfriend had shaken up. Jordan was parading the bartender around like she was a prized cow. Before May knew it, she was having some trouble walking without a sudden misstep to one side.

Benny caught one of May's missteps. "You doing a dance step, Mom?"

She had to laugh at herself. "Those margaritas are too strong." She looked mischievous. "But they are too good!"

Lucille had had a couple margaritas herself and got to bragging about her boyfriend taking her to Rome. But May knew it was never going to happen. She had met him once—a man so handsome May assumed he'd date younger women—and she had always been somewhat jealous, even though he was a cold fish. He rarely came to see Lucille in Golden Vale, a place he looked down on. A moody man, all charm and then quick-tempered when the waitress took too long with the soda refill. He'd looked around the restaurant and said, damningly, "This'd never happen in New Orleans."

"Oh, but I thought you were going last summer," May said.

Lucille looked stung. She made eye contact with Roland, who weakly smirked.

Now, why had May said that? Something she knew would hurt her friend. Because Doc wasn't coming. That was why.

May scrambled to cover herself. "But this summer will be better anyway. Now that you've got the knee surgery out of the way. It'll be so much better for you to walk around Rome."

Lucille recrossed her legs with distinct disapproval. May felt awful.

Jordan turned as he heard someone walking up the driveway. He hadn't seen Doug Babies for weeks. He didn't know his mother had invited him. As Babies walked up the drive, Jordan had his arm around Cyndi so tightly that she was almost in his armpit. He had been drunk and gleeful, watching his mother dance poorly with

Benny to a Pete Seeger song. The music hadn't stopped, but Jordan felt as though it did. Jordan forgot his anger at Doug, he was so surprised to see him. Doug had lost weight in the past couple weeks, and his ruddy coloring. He looked like he had a cold. He smiled roguishly as always, as if he knew something Jordan didn't.

It was Doug who spoke first: "My god! I wouldn't have guessed that!" He indicated Cyndi under Jordan's arm. "I never thought she'd go for it."

Cyndi pulled away from Jordan and took a step toward Babies, arms open for a hug.

Doug shook his head, stopping her. "You'd better not," he said. "As much as I'd like it, I've got a bug. It's going around the crew. Summer flu, they say."

May stopped dancing to welcome Babies. She was obviously tipsy. "Doug, you're looking very trim!"

Jordan wondered if she noticed how ill he looked.

"Yeah, yeah," he said. "I'm getting over a flu. If I got a flu every year for the rest of my life, I'd be a much fitter man."

They welcomed Doug in, put a beer in his hand. They pulled their chairs into a tighter circle to listen to him. One of the tiki torches went out. They wanted to know about the oil spill. And Doug told them, sparing little detail. Jordan had to wonder how much Doug was making up to keep their attention. His job was hauling oiled boom in and out of the water. He said that the boom was supposed to be gotten rid of as toxic waste, but it wasn't. His brother-in-law was given paperwork in which he had to pretend that the boom was not soaked in oil but simply "weathered." That way, BP didn't have an extra expense in getting rid of it. He said that maybe the weight loss was because he was in a hazmat suit on the water—his own private sweat lodge. Men had fainted, they got so hot. After handling the oiled boom for hours, his gloves would disintegrate on his hands, but he only got one pair of gloves a day. He said that he watched Guy Rally, a new friend of his, have a heart attack on the boat. Doug twirled the beer in his hand, looking solemnly at the ground. "It was terrible," he said. "The Coast Guard came for him right away. And all the guys on the boat were thinking, 'Do we need to be wearing gas masks?' But no one wanted to say so."

The group had circled around Doug, pulling in closer as he talked. Jordan didn't want to believe any of it. He wanted to think Doug was vying for attention. This was the same man who, as a boy, lied on a school field trip and claimed to have seen the floating orbs of dead Confederate soldiers. Then Doug pulled out his phone to show them a picture. In the photo, he wore a bright yellow suit smeared with black oil down his chest and across his arms. He was smiling brightly.

"We're just covered in the stuff," Babies said.

May launched herself from her chair and draped herself around Doug. "You take care of yourself, all right? My God, you take care of yourself." She was drunk. She wiped her eyes, possibly because she'd teared up.

And, while Jordan might normally have been jealous, he wasn't. His mother thought of Doug almost as one of her boys, and her worry for him felt like worry for Benny or Jordan.

Someone asked, "Is that a phone ringing?"

May went inside to fetch the phone, knowing before she even answered that it would be Doc. She told him, somewhat spitefully, not to worry about coming over at this late stage. No, the drive over would take him another hour, and they'd all be cleaned up. She suddenly didn't want him sleeping in Al's house. It still felt like too much of a betrayal.

When she came back, it was clear the party was over. A silence had fallen over the group, perhaps because they were thinking about what Doug had told them. Perhaps they were simply filled with drink. Alejandro had left while she was inside.

"There's Vanessa Sanchez in the morning," Benny said to his brother.

"I didn't forget," Jordan said.

Benny pushed himself up. "Mom, let's get the speakers inside before I go to sleep."

Benny and Jordan moved them together, wrapped up the electrical cords delicately around the speaker bodies. Benny did not come back outside after. Jordan went off with Cyndi. Little was said, after all, about the unveiling of the tarp. It had become just a reason to have a party. They might have lingered on this if they all hadn't been so tired.

It was May who stayed up late with Doug when everyone dispersed. Doug smoked cigarettes and coughed terribly, and she sipped warm white wine while he told her he'd been fighting more with his wife. His wife was so regularly unhappy with him that it didn't even feel strange anymore that she slept in his daughter's room. May was unsurprised. There was something familiar, even comforting, in how predictable this was. Ah, Doug. He'd made such a mess of things. May consoled him, offering suggestions for reconciliation, flowers or a thoughtful surprise, none of which Doug would attempt. May asked him, "Is Cyndi a good girl? She's a bartender." And Doug said that she was a very good girl. She had a good heart.

May had something to dish herself. She told him about Doc and her disappointment. Doc had been annoyed with her when she hung up on him, but he'd ruined her whole party. She felt her sympathies were safe with Doug, and so she told him that she was very happy with this new man but that she felt she was betraying Al. She couldn't help feeling her life was filling up again after a yearslong drought. She would later regret telling him this, but she'd had so much to drink. They approached something like intimacy, sitting alone together in the warm evening, talking about her life in a way that she didn't feel she could with her own sons. She told him this too, leaning over and resting her head on his shoulder. She was twenty years older than him. She knew it was wrong as soon as she'd done it. Neither one moved. He didn't stiffen under her as if it were unwelcome. She left her head on his shoulder for a few long minutes.

And a little later, after he'd left, she wouldn't be able to sleep with the shame of it. The next morning, when she checked her cell phone, she could not believe the text she'd received from him in the middle of the night. A text so lewd she assumed he meant to send it to someone else.

→ Twenty-Two ←

The morning after the party, Jordan and Benny waited in the driveway to meet the reporter and photographer. It was six-fifteen, an hour that Jordan normally saw on the water, and the team was fifteen minutes late. In the steamy half dark—it was already in the mid-seventies—the sun flirted with the horizon and made the sky purple over the houses. When that sun turned on its brilliance, it would be another boiler of a day. The day's high was forecast to be ninety-seven, and Jordan imagined that the NPR team, unused to the sodden heat, would roast on the water with them. Jordan didn't want to invite them onboard. A conversation in the cool of the business office after work was preferable, but according to Benny—and Jordan shouldn't have let Benny make the arrangements—the reporter felt the piece would be "fuller" if she could watch them work. They wanted to see the oil spill cleanup if they could, Jordan realized—the whole disaster unfolding in the bay.

His stomach was audibly in tumult. He anxiously watched the driveway as if he were about to submit to a physical examination.

"So you remember," Jordan said. "If she asks about the oyster business, just bring her to me. I don't want her printing anything false about the business."

"Have a cigarette," Benny said. "It'll make you feel better."

Benny had dressed up, in his way, for the reporter. He wore a tattered button-up shirt, which he'd tucked into his jean shorts, and he seemed to have messed up his hair intentionally, so he looked as though he'd emerged from a windstorm. Jordan wore what he always wore to work, a T-shirt and cargo shorts.

"I know you have a lot of opinions about what's wrong with the world," Jordan went on. "But let's keep the focus on the business. This interview is about the business. And the oysters and the oil spill."

"You know how I love the soapbox," Benny said, lighting his cigarette.

"I don't want to hear you lecturing anybody about capitalism. You're my business partner."

"Now I'm your business partner," Benny said dryly.

"You've been here all along. Right? That's the story."

"I don't see why you care where I've been if the focus is the oyster business."

"I want us to look respectable. We haven't been in the news since Dad got sick. It doesn't look good—your tramping around New Orleans."

"I'm going to ignore that because you're nervous," Benny said, ashing his cigarette. "But you know very well I'm a musician. I wasn't 'tramping around.' What does that even mean? But, fine, I'm an oyster farmer and have always been one. I set this interview up to raise awareness about the business. Not to embarrass you."

"I know," Jordan said, looking down at his work sneakers. He smoothed the T-shirt over his chest. It was the same one he'd been wearing for days. He hadn't given any thought to being photographed, he'd been so tortured by the thought of what might go awry in the interview. "I think I'll go change."

Then they heard the quiet crunch of car tires over gravel, and Benny lifted his foot to grind out his cigarette on his heel. "Too late," he said.

The rental car pulled into the driveway, a car so new the house lights glided over the hood like liquid gold. A short, exuberant woman popped out of the passenger side as soon as it stopped. Vanessa Sanchez launched into the story of the speeding ticket they'd just received, which she described cheerily as a means of putting everyone at ease. "My god, I thought he was kidding when he said the speed limit was fifteen miles per hour." She was TV-pretty. She wore tight, expensive-looking blue jeans and a crisp white collared shirt. Teeth so white and perfect they were like a sculpture of teeth. She looked to be about thirty years old and a harbinger of only good things.

"I should have warned you," Benny said, extending his hand. "We have a reputation as a speed trap."

Jordan shook hands with Vanessa and the photographer, Edward, in an NPR cap, who winked at Benny and said, "Nice to see you again."

"Would you look at that?" Vanessa said, pointing at the tarp.

They craned their necks to see the NO FLY ZONE tarp on the roof.

"It's bigger than I imagined," she said.

"Had to be sure they could see it from the air," Benny said. "That was our intention, anyway."

"I want to hear all about it," she said. "But I know we've kept you waiting already. You must be more eager to get on the water than we are."

The four of them walked toward the bayou, past the empty family swimming pool, past the cooler for storing oysters, past the shed where Hoa and Linh shucked oysters, past the business office. Benny announced then that he'd forgotten something in the office and bounded off. They watched him charge up the steps. With Benny gone, Vanessa turned to Jordan expectantly and said, "These oysters we're harvesting today, I hear they're prized in New Orleans."

"They were," Jordan said, straightening up. "People aren't eating Gulf seafood in the restaurants right now. They don't trust it. So, we're selling more to canning factories. They pay us less than the restaurants would, so even now, before we close, we're taking a hit."

She cocked her head as she listened, a kind of invitation to go on, but he felt a painful shyness fall over him. She was so attractive he was certain she could read his mind. Thankfully, Cypress padded over to them, and Vanessa bent down to the old girl, talking to her as though they were old friends. Cypress shed profusely as Vanessa petted her. To Jordan's dismay, Benny emerged with his banjo slung over his shoulder. God help me, he thought. He's going to serenade her. Benny was a showboat; he couldn't help himself. Of course, she had to be a beautiful woman. It would strip away whatever allegiance Benny had to the business. God knows what he'd say to her.

Vanessa stood, smacking the pet hair from her hands on her thighs, and smiled at Benny. The two of them walked ahead toward the dock. She seemed eager to fill the silence with goodwill, crooning about the beauty of the mist billowing into the air over the bayou, and the sounds of the frogs and crickets and cicadas.

As Benny and Vanessa walked, Jordan noted a rip in Benny's shorts under one butt cheek. His pale skin was exposed like a smile with every other step. There was no way Benny was unaware of this, but why he'd want to show his butt to the reporter was a mystery. Benny explained to her that the oysters they hauled in that morning would be shucked the next day in the shucking station.

Vanessa seemed enthralled with him already. The photographer stopped to snap a picture of the shed.

The photographer peered at the digital image of the photo on his camera. "Just garbage," he said good-naturedly. "I ought to know better than to take a photo with light like this."

Jordan knocked on his chest and followed his brother onto his oyster boat, where Benny was introducing Vanessa to Alejandro.

Jordan guided the oyster boat down the bayou as Benny entertained the reporter. She was on the deck with him. He'd overturned two buckets for them to sit on. When Alejandro cast off, looping the ropes onto the pilings, Vanessa cheered, inexplicably, "Yee haw!"

Over the sound of the engine, Jordan could not hear what Benny was saying to her. Benny pointed to the houses and the trees. The sky was lit pink and then orange. Normally, at this hour of the day, they'd have already started harvesting. But Benny said they couldn't ask the reporter to arrive at four-thirty in the morning; they'd just have to get a late start. The photographer paced the deck of the boat and snapped photos so frequently that Jordan could not imagine what the man was looking at.

In the shade of the canopy, Benny and the reporter seemed to be having an easy time talking. It was an advantage of his charm that people felt close to him quickly. Vanessa threw her head back and laughed often. Benny clearly wasn't talking about the oil spill or the business. His banjo lay on a stack of oyster sacks nearby. Jordan noticed Alejandro loitering by the boat's stern. He was pretending to be busy with something.

After she'd spent a good hour sitting on a bucket talking with Benny, Vanessa stood, stretching her back, and wandered into the cabin with Jordan. She surveyed bunk beds and the cluttered dashboard. She had an audio recorder in her hand. He sensed her selecting the details that she would report on—the ancient logbook, crushed cigarette boxes, the ashtray he'd not thought to empty, the plastic Virgin Mary his father had glued to the dashboard. She smelled like no woman he'd ever encountered. He didn't have words to describe it, something herbal. She petted the sun-faded Virgin Mary with one finger, and he noticed her nails, lacquered red, and a wedding ring. He hadn't taken note of the Virgin Mary in a long time.

"Does she protect you?" Vanessa asked.

"I doubt it," Jordan said. "It was my father's, but I doubt he'd thought so either. Then again, there have been times on this boat when I thought I'd die, getting caught in a squall, getting nailed so long that the boat nearly capsized. I've seen less than that make a guy pray for his salvation."

"My family is very Catholic," she said earnestly. "We hit the church hard when something bad goes down. Somebody gets sick and then we're all lined up in the pews like a bunch of backsliders, looking up at God, like, Okay, we need you now!" She gave a self-deprecating chuckle.

"It's like that for us too," Jordan said, and then pointed out a tricolored heron for her.

"Oh," she said.

"Well, I guess not entirely," he said. "After Dad got sick, Mom stopped going to church." He didn't know why he'd told her this. He'd betrayed his mother in saying so. But she wouldn't report that, would she? She hadn't asked about the spill yet.

"So, we're on your father's boat," she said. "What was he like?"

"This was my grandfather's boat," Jordan said. "And then it was Dad's. He renamed it *May's Day*."

She nodded vigorously as if she'd known this, or to beg his pardon for forgetting.

"Dad was well known. He was probably the most famous oysterman in Louisiana. As a kid, he used to have to sit under a tree by the LA-1 and sell oysters for two dollars a sack. He had an eighth-grade education, but people listened to him. People respected him. We were proud of that."

"You're a part of a long legacy, then. Fourth generation. Did you start young too?"

"I was on this boat before I could walk." Jordan looked at Benny on the bow, hugging his arms to his chest and talking to the photographer. "Both Benny and I grew up on the boat. Dad tied my stroller to that canopy pole right there when I was a toddler. He had to keep an eye on me when my mom was busy."

"And how does it feel to have the family's ninety-year-old oyster business close?"

Having a reporter on the boat made his life seem alien to him. She seemed to find everything quaint. The way she spoke told him so, her voice sounding like she was from another country, but no, she was not from another country, only California, she'd said.

"I guess I don't believe it's happening, you know?" he said. He knew it was true. Their business *was* closing down. "Oil spills we've had. But not like this."

The reporter looked at him with a face so sympathetic it seemed a kind of trumpet flower. Not only sympathetic, but interested. Before Cyndi, he'd rarely experienced the pleasure of feeling interesting. It made him feel like talking.

"This work," Jordan said, "it may not seem like a lot to most people. We don't make a lot of money. We make enough, but this, this quiet, the sunrises on the water. For me, it's enough. A lot of people just think of this as work, like, it's just oysters, you fish them like you would trawl for shrimp. But that's not true. We're oyster farmers. There's pride in that—that we grow a great oyster."

"And what does it mean to farm oysters?" she asked. "What does that entail?"

"We care for the reefs. We don't overharvest from our beds. We've got wild oysters growing on some plots that seed themselves. Every year there is an oyster spawn. It happens every summer, and you get your baby oysters, as many as a hundred baby oysters on one shell. They don't all live. There are a lot of obstacles for them—the predators, the drumfish, the sea snail, pollution—but some of them survive each year, or they used to."

Benny said his name in the way that meant something was wrong, but Jordan had already seen it. When they arrived in Caminada Bay, there was a charter boat—a boat that would normally take men out fishing for swordfish and red drum—unspooling bright orange boom into the water around a marsh island the size of a basketball court. Right next to his oyster leases. If they were putting the boom down, it meant the oil was coming in.

The men unloading the boom waved to Jordan, as men on the water tend to do. They could have been vacationers. As if this were all entirely normal. They were not wearing hazmat suits like Doug had been in the picture. The men seemed unbothered by what the boom meant, concerned only with the task itself. Jordan pulled the boat alongside them and slowed. The workers were not locals, Jordan didn't know them, but this was unsurprising to him.

"So the oil's coming in, then, huh?" Jordan asked, aware of Vanessa perched on the side of the boat, listening.

A man in a large straw sun hat cupped his ear, indicating that he didn't hear Jordan.

"You know when the oil is coming in here?" Jordan said.

The man was about to speak when he saw Vanessa and the photographer.

"You got press with you?" the man hollered, indicating the photographer in the NPR hat who was, at that moment, snapping his photo.

"When's it coming in?" Jordan said.

The other men working turned their backs to the camera. Jordan knew this was BP's unspoken rule. Keep the public from seeing the spill or documenting it. The man in the sun hat shook his head. "Don't know," he said. "Probably soon."

"I haven't heard anything about the oil coming here yet," Jordan said. "Not in this bay."

"We don't decide where to go," the man said, looking over his shoulder to the boat's cabin. "We can't talk to the press."

Another man walked out from the cabin. He held himself with authority, as if his chest were filled with air.

"I'm not press," Jordan said, but he knew it was pointless. He clearly had a reporter with him. He was grateful that Benny and Vanessa weren't hemming in as they might have, asking questions, making things worse. He never knew what Benny might do.

"You better get a move on." The man folded his arms across his chest. "You gotta be a hundred yards from oil spill cleanup activity, or you'll get a fine."

"When is the oil coming?" Jordan's voice was raised.

"It's illegal to interfere with oil spill cleanup." The man thrust his chin forward. "You gotta stay back a hundred yards."

"Interfere?" Jordan doubted there were any laws to this effect. "I've got rights here. My oyster leases are here."

"All right!" the man said, throwing his hands in the air, as if he'd been reasonable. "If you want me to call the Coast Guard, I will."

Jordan kept pace with the charter boat. The men continued unspooling the boom, which was coiled up on the deck. The boom itself looked rigid and heavy, only flexible because it was cinched between segments like a sausage link. The photographer snapped pictures with abandon. The smiling man in the sun hat shrugged at Jordan as if to say, No hard feelings, and then he relieved a man who was guiding the boom into the water behind the boat.

"You're not cleaning anything up yet," Jordan said, realizing what a useless point it was. The man was on the radio in the cabin, making eye contact with Jordan. He didn't know why he was lingering, other than the fact that he didn't want them to think they were in control. But, of course, they were. When the oil came in, he would need to ask men like them for access to his own oyster leases.

Benny walked up behind him and said gently, "I don't think there's much to be gained in hanging around here, chief."

Jordan steered the boat into the middle of the bay.

There had been plans to fish for oysters, to demonstrate their work, to show the reporter what would be lost, but Jordan was livid after the interaction. He didn't want to smoke in front of the reporter, but found he had a burning cigarette in his mouth as he overturned a bucket to sit on. Benny and Vanessa were mirroring each other, hugging their crossed arms to their chests as they watched the men in the distance ringing the marsh island with boom.

Vanessa adjusted her recorder on a bucket between them. "So, those men laying down the boom we just saw. That means the oil is on its way?"

"That's right," Jordan said. He looked at the men in the distance, and she followed his gaze.

"They want to have this big cleanup effort to keep people quiet, if you ask me," he went on. "They're paying well, big bucks every day. But as you saw, if you work for them, you can't talk to the press. That dispersant breaks up the oil. That's what it does. Now, if the boom catches the oil on top of the water, and the dispersant spreads it in the water column, how much good is the boom gonna do? And I'm supposed to be the dumb fisherman that doesn't know anything." Jordan fumed.

"Here's the tell-all portion of the interview." Benny pulled a cigarette out too. "Do you mind if we smoke?"

"That's fine," she said, but she pushed her bucket back a few inches. The morning heat was rising, and though they were in the shade, as Vanessa pulled her hair back into a ponytail Jordan noticed her neck glistening with sweat.

"Tell me about the dispersant," she said. "As oyster farmers, what's your perspective?"

Benny started to speak, but Jordan interrupted him. He was suddenly hungry to keep Vanessa's attention on him.

"What right have they got to spray all these chemicals out here that we don't know anything about? The stuff is banned in England. We know it's toxic. What's going to happen? They're hiding the oil, and we're all letting them hide it." Jordan laughed dismally. "You wouldn't see them spraying this stuff in your California. No way."

"And why do you say that?" She smiled at him knowingly, and he felt this delicious jolt of approval spur him on.

"Because we know it's bad. What a lot of people don't know is that oil owns Louisiana. If an oil tanker dumps drilling fluid on your lease, you know, there's no recourse. And if they bring their tugboats, they're gonna crush your oysters, and there isn't a thing you can do about it."

"But then why put a tarp on the roof that says NO FLY ZONE?" she asked.

"Because they're shaking the house!" he said. "They're poisoning the Gulf. And we're reminded every time they fly over. That's why we're talking to begin with. I don't like airing my dirty laundry. I'm no crybaby, but this is wrong, and people need to know about it."

Benny looked at him in agreement. His hands rested on his unruly hair, elbows out.

"It's true Jordan didn't want to do this interview," Benny said. "It's rare to hear him talk this candidly."

"Even with you?" she asked. "About the spill, you mean?"

"Maybe especially me." He laughed. "The spill has people questioning things."

Vanessa turned to Jordan. "Like what?"

"We're losing the wetlands now," Jordan said. "Those dead cypress trees you saw on our way to the bay—the twisted ones with the Spanish moss on them?"

"I remember."

"Maybe ten years ago, those were alive. We got salt water coming in from the Gulf now, and it's killing them. The marshland is dying or washing away. That means coastal towns like ours are vulnerable to hurricanes. And salt water in the estuary—it changes everything. All of a sudden you've got new predators in the bay—the sea snail. Enough salt kills my oysters too, makes the reefs worthless. It's a huge problem, and the state isn't acting. They want to flood the estuaries with Mississippi River water, which would kill us the other way. It'll drown our oysters. They need brackish water."

Benny watched him and, he could tell, was pleased with him. Jordan was touched by that.

"But tell her why it's happening, Jordan."

"There's a lot of reasons." Jordan pitched his cigarette into a bucket on the deck. "They starved the marsh of sediment when they locked the Mississippi in place."

"Yeah," Benny said. "But what about the shipping canals?"

"Okay," Jordan said. "You tell her."

"The oil companies," Benny said, "going back to the 1930s, have been digging shipping channels through the wetlands. They were supposed to fill in the channels afterward, but the state didn't make them. So those channels deliver salt water into the wetlands, and it erodes the marsh islands. Maybe we didn't know, back in the thirties, how valuable the wetlands were, but we know now. So why aren't we fixing it?"

"We're not against business," Jordan said. "Not at all. But these oil companies. They've got carte blanche to do as they please. It doesn't hurt their business if they kill every fish for a hundred miles. Maybe it'd be better for them. Then the fishermen would leave them alone."

She nodded and then produced a handkerchief from her pocket to dab at her neck.

"When we get back to the house," Jordan said, "I'll show you a map of Golden Vale from the thirties. You'll see all the business that used to be here—the people used to be fishermen. It used to be full of little businesses. Now everybody's got a family member in the oil industry, because that's the only thing that's here."

Jordan couldn't believe how easy it was to talk to her—freeing, even, to say just how he felt for a change, and wasn't it his responsibility to say so? Not only for his business, but for the estuary. That whole delicate web that connected him to the lowliest creatures on the Gulf floor. The photographer hovered nearby. Jordan heard a click of the camera from time to time. Alejandro was somewhere on the back deck. Benny leaned over and pulled his banjo into his lap. God help me, Jordan thought, watching him begin to pluck.

"Oh, lovely. Mood music," she said. "BP is starting this claims facility, and they are going to compensate fishermen for their losses. What do you think about that? Have you applied yet?"

"I've got a lawyer," Jordan said. "But they want all sorts of paperwork that I got to track down. I can hope that BP pays me, but let's be real. They make a living ripping people off."

Not one to be outshone, Benny added, "You have to consider too that we're on top of our oyster reef right now. When that oil and dispersant enters the bay, we don't know how long it will affect the oysters. If BP compensates fishermen for one lost season, will it compensate for future losses? You know, an oyster is a filter. It feeds by filtering the water, and whatever's in the water becomes a part of the oyster's body."

"Are you worried that makes oysters unsafe to eat?" she asked.

Jordan jumped in before Benny could.

"I'm worried that makes them defenseless. Oysters don't have fins. They're stuck to the ground. What they can do is close up if the water is bad. That's one of the only things that gives me hope these days—the thought of the oysters staying shut until the worst is over."

Benny plucked thoughtfully at his banjo, looking over the bay. Jordan had to stop himself from telling Benny to put the instrument away.

"But I feel like we're not talking about the bigger picture here," Benny said. "And why oil spills happen."

"Okay," she said. "Why do they happen?"

"We've defunded the regulatory bodies, so they're powerless. People around here, every election, they vote for politicians who receive huge campaign money from the oil industry. So they don't raise the tax rate on oil. Most of the profits leave the state entirely. It doesn't enrich the state of Louisiana like people think it does. It doesn't pay out in jobs like people think. Fuck, Walmart employs as many people as the oil industry."

Vanessa smiled at Benny.

"Benny," Jordan said.

"What?"

"Can we focus on our business, please?"

"You said yourself, oil owns the state," Benny said, looking down as he plucked. "I was just adding to what you said."

"And you really don't talk like this?" Vanessa asked. "Working on the boat all day long together?"

Benny chuckled. "I guess you'd better come out here every day to keep us talking. We'll get the whole country set straight before that oil comes in."

Vanessa blushed slightly at Benny's obvious flirtation. But he flirted with everyone. In this way, he was just like their father.

"To be perfectly honest," Benny said, looking down at his banjo, "I think Jordan and I are prone to disagree more often than not about politics."

Benny winked at Jordan.

"Okay," Benny said. "This is the last thing I'll say."

"Christ," Jordan said.

"We're dependent on oil and gas in this country, but that's not our decision—yours and mine. That's the government. That's the subsidies it provides. We're so dependent that we're sending kids to the Middle East to fight for it."

"We're losing the plot now, Benny," Jordan said.

"Thousands of Americans have died. Hundreds of thousands of Iraqis and Afghans. Just senseless loss of life to protect our oil interests."

"Knock it off."

"That's the last thing I'll say about it."

Vanessa fanned herself, seeming amused by the disagreement. She glanced at Jordan's knee, and he saw that it was bouncing.

"Here's what I figured out," Jordan said. "If I was born into the oil business, I'd be fighting for oil. I understand that—but I wasn't born in the oil industry. I was born in the seafood industry. And that's a much healthier business."

He stood and walked to the back to use the head. Inside the sordid little stall, he was dizzy in the heat and with the amount they'd said. He'd lost control of the interview, just as he knew he would. What would their neighbors think? Neighbors on either side of him worked in the oil industry. He had no idea what kind of story she'd tell about them. On the bow, he heard Vanessa laughing and then the twang of Benny's banjo.

Jordan emerged just as Benny began singing an old blues tune. Jordan watched from the boat's cabin as Benny's plucking hand jumped over the strings. Vanessa sat two feet away, rapt. Benny lifted the neck of the banjo when he whaled on it. The melody clear, his voice used to good effect. He was better than Jordan remembered. Jordan hadn't heard Benny play in years, not since he played for their father when he was ill. Al tapped the beat on the kitchen table with his infirm hand. Benny did not come back until the funeral.

Benny had probably planned to play for the reporter all along. It may have even been why he had suggested they contact her in the first place. He realized, watching Benny, that Vanessa could open doors for Benny. A new life for Benny could begin, just as Jordan's might be over. Jordan kept his distance while Benny played two more songs, feeling the irritation constrict in his chest. He noticed Alejandro leaning on the taffrail, watching the scene.

"You've been scarce today," Jordan said.

Alejandro folded his arms. "Not an accident."

"Camera-shy?"

"It's my asylum case," he said. "I don't want to be on camera."

It hadn't occurred to Jordan that Alejandro would be on camera. On the deck, Vanessa whooped in applause when Benny put the banjo down. He patted his pockets for his cigarettes. The photographer was clapping too.

Vanessa swept into the cabin, eyes wide with delight. She had her recorder on a lanyard looped around her neck. "Oh, he's wonderful!" she said. "A banjo-playing oyster farmer. Who knew? You're lucky to have him to entertain you all the time."

Jordan felt a pit in his stomach imagining the headline she'd write. The picture of Benny online, eyes closed as he plucked his banjo. The portrait it would paint of his sorrow at the failure of their oyster business.

"I told him, 'We ought to get you on NPR's *Tiny Desk Concerts*,'" she said.

Jealousy whipped through him, and then he blurted: "Benny hasn't been on the boat too much, to be honest." He hadn't planned to say this, but there it was.

"Not lately?"

"Not at all," Jordan said. He couldn't stand this portrait of Benny as some troubadour of the bayou. Jordan would look ridiculous if she reported that. Everyone would know it was untrue. And it was a disserve to all the work he'd put into the business. "My father left us the business, but Benny didn't want any part of it. He stayed in New Orleans to focus on his music. Yes, he's my partner, but I ran the business by myself. To call him a banjo-playing oyster farmer, that's not exactly right."

"Oh," she said, her face falling. Benny had led her to believe otherwise. Just as he and Benny had discussed.

He shouldn't have gone on, but he did. "Benny didn't even come out here when my father was dying. Not that we didn't ask. He was always too busy in New Orleans. Not too long ago, I thought Benny was addicted to drugs."

Alejandro, whom Jordan hadn't noticed lingering in the doorway, turned on a heel and walked onto the deck.

Vanessa nodded. She shifted her weight uncomfortably, looking over the dashboard at the blinding bay. She seemed embarrassed for him. He wondered if she was thinking, Why is this man being such a shit to his brother? And, truthfully, he didn't know. Jordan was suddenly ashamed of himself.

"He's been a big help these past few weeks, though," Jordan added, but it was too late. She'd made up her mind about him.

Benny appeared in the cabin then, smiling, exhaling smoke over his shoulder. Had Benny heard him? He had not—not from the smile still on his face. Benny fingered a strand of his carefully tortured hair, and then smiled at Jordan. This was the happiest Jordan had ever seen him.

Twenty-Three

A plane passed overhead in the direction of the Gulf, and it was almost possible to ignore the meaning of the plane—drinking, as May was, her second-and-a-half margarita overlooking the Gulf from Doc's oyster hatchery. The sunset refused to be sullied by the ongoing disaster. Doc and his friend had finished their third performance of "House of the Rising Sun" that evening. A performance more endearing for its mediocrity. It was the only song they could play together, and now they admired the delicate colors playing on the water, Doc red-faced from the hours he'd spent in the sun, and Willy, a dismally drunk conservationist from the Louisiana Department of Wildlife and Fisheries, cradling his guitar like it could love him back.

Doc told her that many of the vacation homes on Grand Isle were now filled with BP's disaster response teams instead of the usual vacationing families. Unbelievably, Doc reported, you could see these people walking around tar patties on the beaches at the end of the day almost like vacationers.

"Scum suckers," Willy muttered.

Only those who couldn't afford to leave Grand Isle, or had no place left to go, remained, and this meant the island was quieter than it ever had been. May had seen evidence of this, the streets empty of children, and footage of incoming waves frothed with the orange foam that she now knew was emulsified oil.

"How unfair!" she said to them, her tongue loose with tequila. "It's the worst summer of so many people's lives, and here I am— having the loveliest time."

Willy guffawed, disgusted by her comment, but seemed surprised that he'd responded out loud. He hugged his guitar tighter to his chest. He'd brought over his own bottle of paint-thinner vodka that he was using to doctor his margaritas. The whites of his eyes were angrily red. If Willy didn't look so pitiable, May might have been stung. All evening he looked at Doc, and not May, when he talked. He'd hardly said a word in her direction.

"What'd BP ever to do you?" Doc said to Willy, his tone improbably light.

"Today I carried a juvenile dead dolphin from the beach in my arms." Willy threw his hands up in mock surrender, slurring. "But it's not personal, bud, it's business!"

Doc reached over and squeezed her thigh in consolation. His wet hand from his sweating glass left an imprint on her dress, and she found herself laughing immodestly. Laughing at what? At Doc, who was so unabashed about his lust. Or maybe at herself, because she didn't know it would excite her. She felt as if something long held in her chest unhitched itself and let go. In such a mood, she could forgive anyone anything.

After Willy nearly killed himself descending the stairs on his way home, he bowed to them like a ruined dignitary. Doc said, "Willy's beside himself about the spill. He's usually much better company. He was in such a bad way when I saw him this afternoon, I thought maybe he'd do something he'd regret. It's why I invited him."

May waved this off like she hadn't noticed. She'd realized that Doc was the kind of man who got a kick out of people, even difficult people. He was jovial and self-assured and a bit ridiculous, but she now found that charming too.

"He might regret breaking his neck on the stairs," she said.

"You're funny, you know that?" And he patted his lap like she was a dog that knew to hop up when called, and up she went and plopped down on his lap as if she were a teenage girl, and a small one at that. He groaned facetiously and then he nuzzled his chin stubble into her bare shoulder, and she became a teenager again, just like that—a mother with two grown sons. It would be the third time she'd spent the night at Doc's oyster hatchery.

May told Doc about the text that Doug Babies had sent her the night of the party—"Isn't that disgusting?" she said.

"Not disgusting, no." Doc shook his head. She was pleased to see a flare of possessiveness in him as he petted her thigh. "That would mean that you were somehow disgusting."

"But I could be his mother!" As she said this, she was surprised at the pride this stirred up in her. Pride she hadn't realized was part of the equation.

"He just doesn't have any class," Doc said.

The morning after required a whole rigmarole of subterfuge. She felt a bit nauseated, her head announcing its protest to so many margarita top-offs that she was unsure how to tally the night's drinks. She'd lived her entire life as a woman who only had a drink on special occasions, but overnight she'd become a woman who had a drink several days a week. A plane had jolted her awake. Her eyes were burning. Why were her eyes burning? She took stock of her surroundings—the sparsely decorated bedroom here at the oyster hatchery. A portrait of Jimmy Buffett beamed at her from the opposite wall. Next to her, damp and snoring, was Doc's bear-like body.

She had to quietly exit the bed and ease the bathroom door closed slowly so the latch didn't click. She ran the water at a trickle, so as not to wake him, so as not to let him know how long this whole operation took. The key to her success was making him think that she didn't have to consider these things and that, if she did, she needed such minimal sprucing that it might be cinched in five minutes. Doc had not yet seen her without makeup. She opened the conspicuously large tote she kept by the bathroom for this reason, so she could use her gentle foaming cleanser, and the four layers of products that required time to slather and then set—serum, primer, SPF, under-eye cream, and then foundation. Plus eyelash curling and mascara. Plus the time it took for the pillow wrinkles to leave her face. All of this completed with an eye twitch that troubled her and she hoped would fade with the first cup of coffee. My god, her eyes stung! And how red they were. What was irritating them? As soon as she'd finished the mascara, her eyes watered and burned, the mascara running down her face, so she had to mop it up with bathroom tissue.

She peeked into the bedroom at Doc, still asleep in the nude. This had seemed outrageous to her—that anyone slept in the nude—and he had laughed at her surprise, which he said was probably a holdover from her Baptist childhood, and she couldn't argue. She used to think sex was wicked too, and that, of course, was part of its pleasure. Later, when life demanded that she be a kind of house manager, and her body, which had once seemed her own, felt its ownership transfer to the institution she and Al had built together, the children they'd made, the house they kept, the friendships they maintained, her body became a vehicle in service only of that institution. She forgot about it entirely unless something hurt. How unlikely that she would get to be reacquainted with the body again now. The sex she had with Doc made her wish she could have sex with Al again, and in this way it was as if she weren't betraying Al. If she didn't let herself investigate these thoughts too much, it was as if the sex were for Al somehow.

Doc was a big man and his was not a beautiful body, not in the way Al's was, but it became attractive in its bulky earnestness. He communicated a lot in bed—pleas for more, thoughts on how things were going, wishes, regrets, all delivered pantingly. They had not done anything fancy the first few times, but last night he sat her up very seriously and reminded her of Doug Babies's text. I WANT YOU TO SIT ONY MY FACE, the text had read. Appalled, she'd responded: I think you meant to send this to somebody else . . . ? Babies had taken the out and said he was very sorry. Maybe he had sent it to her in error, but maybe not. She told Doc that she couldn't possibly do that, and he said that he was willing to bet she could. She found that she didn't resist his positioning her on her knees, despite her laughing, saying, "No! you can't be serious," as he maneuvered himself between her thighs and then lowered her down, all while she fretted that she'd crush him, feeling huge and unwieldy, like a sea mammal. She looked down at his prone body, headless and with his feet pointed upward, and he looked like a man working on the underbody of a car, which made her feel like a big, beautiful car, and she bore down on him, feeling electric and filled up, as if she'd been put in control at long last.

In the morning, she sat with her coffee and looked out over the blinding Gulf in the still-merciful hours of the day. She watched the seabirds diving for fish, and it pained her to think about what was happening to them. Did the waves look funny this morning? She couldn't tell. The birds' wings were untouched by oil, but was there something unsteady in their flight? Were they weakened? At the thought of this, she texted Jordan to see if everything was all right at home. Jordan responded to her in one-word responses only. He always had, but still, she was ready to find indictment in the "Yes" he sent this time, as if his terseness were a judgment on her absence, her betrayal of Al.

The spill had coincided with a kind of stupor that had befallen her. She worried, instead, about penciling in her eyebrows. She watched YouTube videos by a girl who could be her daughter, instructing how to shave the peach fuzz from her face, which left her with a cut on her forehead that she could not explain to anyone. She checked her cell phone incessantly. When she was not with Doc, she wanted to tell Doc what she was having for lunch. She wanted to tell Doc that she was going to paint her nails. That she was organizing books at the library for a book sale. He occasionally sent her texts with smiley faces: Dying for you. She wanted to know what he was doing all the time. Was he teaching his grad students? Did he smell anything chemical over there? It snuck up on her, this feeling.

One day, she thought, I'll wake up to what's happening here, and I'll be horrified, but not today. Not today. It pained her to even look at Jordan's hangdog face. The spill was changing him. He'd lost some weight, which would have suited him if his face wasn't also so drawn, his eyes vacuous. May had imposed a no-news-during-dinner policy. Appetites shouldn't be ruined by their circumstances.

Doc emerged through the sliding door with his coffee, sloshing it on the deck and chuckling at his clumsiness. He was wearing a short terry-cloth bathrobe, his bare legs hairy and muscular as a young man's. "What a dream you are! Imagine me, waking up alone and thinking you gone, only to find you out here, having made coffee and looking like a sea siren. The mosquitoes aren't getting you?"

"They're better here than in the bayou," she said, but he knew this already. He'd said so himself. "Do my eyes look red to you?"

"Nope." He sat next to her on the swinging bench. He sighed loudly, looking at the morning water, seeming to say, Isn't this perfect? In daylight, you could look over Doc's experimental lease of oysters that grew in floating cages. The local oystermen, Al included, used to jeer at Doc's floating cages. It seemed to Al that floating cages would just invite poachers, already a problem, so it was an extravagant waste of money. But Doc maintained that this was the only way to adapt to the rapidly eroding wetlands.

"That's a tern," Doc said, pointing at the bird that had landed on the far side of the porch.

He pulled his phone from the pocket of his bathrobe and set it on the swing between them. "If this doesn't make a sound in ten minutes, I'll buy you dinner."

May heard someone crunching on the gravel below the porch. A man stopped on the rocks overlooking Doc's floating oyster farm. He had a baseball cap on and a lanyard around his neck.

"Now, who in the hell is that?" Doc said, without any malice, but not inquiring after the man either. "These BP people—they think they got license to go anywhere they want."

The man looked at the water and then up, trying to locate the voices. "Dr. Merritt?" he called. "Dr. Merritt?"

"Who wants to know?" Doc called down.

"Go on." May pushed him. "Go talk to the man."

Doc stood and took his coffee to the railing. The man told Doc that he was there to collect some samples for the study on chemical uptake in oysters.

"You came at a bad time." Doc said. "I'm not decent."

"You aren't open?"

"I'm open, I'm open. Just hold on, and I'll change. I don't want you messing with my reefs unsupervised. Not that I don't trust you. You want to come up for a cup of coffee?"

Doc winked at May as the man tramped up the stairs. She felt he was performing for her, and she wondered if this meant something was required of her.

She was surprised that the person who came up the stairs was not a man, really, but a young person in his twenties wearing khaki shorts and a peach T-shirt. He had zinc sunscreen painted on his nose. The young man was uncomfortable talking to Doc in his bathrobe and looked instead at May. She, at least, was dressed. Doc seemed to get a kick out of this. The young man was a graduate student from the University of Alabama, and Doc knew his dissertation adviser. "She's an old battle-ax, isn't she?" Doc said.

The young man shifted from foot to foot, looking back at the oyster leases. "Didn't they tell you I was coming?"

"You come here to ruin a perfectly good morning with my girlfriend?" Doc said.

Girlfriend. It was the first time she'd heard him use the word.

"It should only take twenty minutes."

"All right, have it your way!" Doc gestured to May with his coffee cup. "May will get you coffee if you want some."

The grad student made small talk with her, kindly refusing to sit down or to have a cup of coffee. He had good manners and delicate features, and he must be smart if he was in a master's program. She wondered about the kind of household he came from, calling her ma'am. "No, I don't need any coffee just now. No, thank you, ma'am." She pleased herself with thinking that Benny was far more sociable than this boy, who looked at the water as if something interesting was happening out there, but Benny had dropped out of college. Except maybe now he'd take on the responsibility he was meant to have. The boys were getting on better than they ever had before.

Doc's phone began dinging on the seat beside her and a picture of a girl with a dazzling smile and science goggles strapped to her face popped up. This was Camilla. Doc's graduate student, the one who studied algae. Doc was very casual with her too, teasing her like he was her father. May wondered if Doc had taken this picture of Camilla. She was holding up a sample of green water for the camera, like, Look at this! The cuteness of the picture did not sit right with May. She reached over and silenced the ring. *Goodbye, Camilla.*

Twenty-Four

For three nights following the interview, Jordan did not sleep well. His mind was a churning gyre of fears, and he lay awake in bed recalling Benny bent over his banjo, and the way Vanessa's face fell when he'd told her that Benny was not an oyster farmer. He thrashed from one side to another in the middle of the night, as if he could turn away from the thought. In the mornings, he noticed Cyndi curled up on the opposite corner of the bed.

He couldn't determine how much of what he'd said mattered to Vanessa. What he said wasn't untrue, but he'd been motivated by pettiness, and he was ashamed. She might even report everything he said, making them both look terrible.

Somehow the interview had carried on afterward. Vanessa kept close to Benny and Alejandro on the deck as they pulled up oysters from the bay. And after they returned Vanessa to the dock, they talked for another half-hour, touring her around the untidy office and the oyster-shucking station, which smelled like the gut of the bayou. Vanessa edged away from Jordan when he spoke. At the end of the day, the NPR pair looked weary and nearly embarrassed by their desire to leave. But Vanessa had said, finally, that theirs would be a great story. She felt honored to cover it. It would really wake people up. Put a human face to the environmental disaster. Hadn't they all shaken hands ceremoniously on parting, grinning like fools?

Still, the thought of what he'd said plagued him—so much so that he prised Vanessa's phone number from Benny, claiming he'd misspoken in the interview about the amount of acreage they leased. Benny shrugged and read the number aloud to Jordan slowly as if he were a half-wit. Benny still didn't know what Jordan had said, and Alejandro, Benny's new shadow, hadn't told him. Jordan avoided Alejandro's gaze while on the boat, and it seemed Alejandro was always lurking about on the periphery of his vision, idly inspecting some piece of equipment or another, the chain link of an oyster dredge.

Jordan decided to call Vanessa after work when he was alone. He was at Cyndi's house. She was showering before she went to the bar, and Jordan slipped outside to make the call, walking circles in Cyndi's driveway. The chorus of cicadas in the tree overhead stung his ears like a weed whacker. He got her voicemail. Not knowing what to say, he hung up. He smoked a cigarette and decided to call again. This time he left a message.

"Hi, Vanessa. Jordan Pearce calling you. Thanks again for coming out the other day. We really liked having you. Anyway, I'm calling because I'm worried I gave you the wrong impression about something. Well, it's Benny. I don't know why I told you what I did—about our father and all that—and Benny not working on the boat and all. I hope you don't put that in your story. I hope your story is about the oyster business and the oil spill. Though, now that I hear myself talking, it seems crazy. You wouldn't want to put that in your story. You're a nice lady, and Benny is really excited about the *Tiny Desk* thing. He says he hasn't heard from you about that yet, but we know you're busy. We're grateful for your time. Thanks again for coming out and doing a story on us. Just give me a call when you have a minute. Thanks."

He groaned upon hanging up, knowing immediately how he sounded, groveling. He would need to make a better impression when she called him back.

Jordan found Cyndi in the kitchen, freshly showered, microwaving a bag of popcorn, which she'd eat for dinner before she went to work. The orderliness of her kitchen, her whole house, imposed order on his inner life, and for the past couple of weeks her house had been a refuge from the oil encroaching on his livelihood. Her hair wet the shoulders of her T-shirt and back. He noticed some fatigue in her eyes that he figured was his fault, his tortured sleep. She'd not mentioned it like she might have. She loved razzing him.

"Private call?" she said.

"Just the reporter from the other day."

"You hardly mentioned what she was like."

"She was fine," Jordan said. "She was a sharp girl from California."

"She was pretty, wasn't she?" she said, smiling.

"I guess," he said, pretending it made no difference one way or another.

She poked him in the ribs in that way she so enjoyed, to indicate that she knew him better than he thought, and then turned to face the microwave. The kitchen filled with the smell of butter. As she watched the inflating bag spin inside the microwave, she began braiding her hair behind her back. He noticed the muscles in her arms jump as she braided. She was humming a Neil Young song. It felt as though his whole life was shaky except for those arms.

"I got a notion to ask you something tomorrow," he said, deciding it was true only as he heard it aloud.

"Why not ask me now?" She spun to look at him, smiling.

"I just think you'll want to be wearing something nice."

"Wear something nice so you can ask me a question?"

Jordan nodded. The kernels were popping all together now above the low hum of the microwave. "If you don't want me to ask it, then you'd better tell me now, or else I'll just embarrass myself."

"I'd have to know what kind of question it is before I can say one way or the other."

"The kind of question that goes better with a dress," Jordan said casually, as if they were speaking of anything else, the weather report, what they'd have for dinner. He opened the refrigerator door, took a look around, and closed it again. Cyndi watched him carefully.

"Don't play." She dropped her braid.

"Who's playing?"

The microwave started screaming at them. The last few kernels popped in the bag. She had a deep wrinkle between her brows as she searched his face over.

"You wanted to know if I was serious," he said, as if he were trying to convince them both.

"Not what I meant." She turned and pressed the button to pop open the microwave door. She shook the bag up and down, keeping her back to him purposefully.

"You don't want me to ask you, huh?" Jordan said, pulling her to face him.

"Oh, no, you don't. I'm not going to beg you ask to me anything," she said, "if that's what you're thinking. It wasn't my idea."

The room had become distinct, the yellow walls, the ivy trim, the yellow tea kettle, the smell of buttered popcorn, and Cyndi, her braid unraveling, brown eyes wide with alarm, or maybe excitement. She may have been right. It put his stomach on the move again.

"You wear something nice tomorrow," he said. "And you see whose idea it is."

"Oh Jesus." She smiled at him, showing her teeth, the crossed ones up front.

"No need to bring Jesus into it yet," Jordan said. "Just the dress will be enough."

"Oh Jesus," she said again, laughing now and lit up with all her loveliness. Jordan watched her smiling. "I need to get ready for work."

"What about your popcorn?"

"I'm taking my popcorn," she said. "I need to get my pants on."

"So get your pants on."

"Are you off?" she said.

"Just about."

Cyndi kissed the ridge of his jaw and squeezed his hand as she passed into her room, where she stepped her sweatpants off. He watched through the open door as she pulled her jeans on and swapped for a clean shirt. Just like that, Jordan thought, not even asking the question, but the question of the question, and everything seemed to have changed already. The future was real again, and it was his if he claimed it. He understood, it was not a question you could ask halfway. Broach it just a little, and there it is. But he was glad. He thought he was glad. He watched her see herself in the mirror, see herself smiling.

Later, when he returned home that night, his mind swam with the implications of what he'd said and could not take back. He plodded through the unmown front yard. The grass reached up to his shins. But how was it possible? He'd mown for the reporter team's arrival. He realized with a start that he'd mown the backyard, but not the front, and he'd been so out of sorts he hadn't noticed.

What riled him was that neither Benny nor his mother had noticed. His mother, who obsessed over appearances. She'd been with Doc at his oyster hatchery. His phone was ringing. He hoped it was Vanessa, calling to reassure him that Jordan wasn't terrible for disparaging his younger brother. In fact, she hadn't given it any thought.

But it was not Vanessa calling. It was Rollo, who was calling to tell Jordan that the governor opened up freshwater diversions from the Mississippi. They were flooding the Barataria Basin and the Breton Sound with fresh water. No warning. No public forum. Just went and flooded not only the public oyster grounds east of the Mississippi, but also all his leases on the west side. That was sixty percent of his leases poised to drown in fresh water.

"Why?" Jordan said. He stopped in the yard. The house lights were all off. "Why the fuck would they do that now?"

"They want to keep the oil out of there," Rollo said. "They're trying to do a counterweight to the oil coming in. Of course, it doesn't make any sense. The amount of oil coming in—it's not going to be pushed back with a little fresh water."

There was a once-red camping chair in the front yard. Jordan sank into it. He was quiet for a long time.

"You still there?" Rollo said.

"But why did they do it?" he said. It felt like the fabric of the chair was giving out underneath him. "It's like they want to wipe us out."

"They've had a bone to pick with us since we demanded they not raise the prices on the oyster leases. Your daddy had something to do with that lawsuit, if you remember." He paused for what seemed like a moment of reverence for Jordan's late father. "The state wants us to bend over. They want to sell all our oyster leases to Big Oil. It's just a cover-up, pure and simple."

Was that true? He figured the state didn't care one way or the other for oyster farmers, but this decision felt so shortsighted it smacked of ill will.

"These people," Jordan said. "Didn't they think what this'd do to the estuary?" He kept saying, "I can't believe it." But he did believe it. His fortunes had turned in such a way that every bad thing that happened to him felt inevitable, personal. If his house burned down in his absence tomorrow, he wouldn't be surprised.

"They do what they want, baby," Rollo said. "Me? I'm gonna get a lawyer. You got yourself a good lawyer?"

"You're going to sue the state?" Jordan said, disbelieving.

"I'm gonna make BP pay for every dead oyster. God help me."

"They won't pay," Jordan said. "Nobody is getting paid."

"Ain't that the truth," Rollo said. "You gotta make them pay."

Rollo said his wife was calling him to bed. "I just can't sleep to save my life this summer," Rollo said. "Down here, on Grand Isle, we got the dispersant blowing off the water, and we wake up with our eyes burning. My eyes are burning in my own home. The air-conditioning is sucking it in. I'm calling everybody. I'm so mad I could spit." They shared a long moment of silence. Rollo hung up without ceremony. "Okay, then. Okay, I'll see you," Jordan said.

Jordan lit a cigarette and let it burn down to the filter in his hand before he thought to take a drag of it. Sixty percent of his oyster leases. He was being done in not just by the oil industry but by his own state government. He threw the filter on the grass and lit another cigarette. As he was sitting, he began to drop through the fabric chair. It was giving out on him. He knew then they'd shut him down for good tomorrow. He looked at his phone. Cyndi was asleep. Vanessa might like to hear about this, though. It was too late to call, but this was breaking news. He called her anyway and reached her voicemail again. The light in Benny's room was off. When the fabric gave out completely, like a sigh, he sank through the chair, his butt touching the grass, leaving him netted in the fabric. He made no effort to change things, feeling his jeans soaking up the dew on the grass, feeling the will to change anything at all leave his body.

Benny had noticed a new charge between him and Alejandro following the party, when Alejandro had set his hand on Benny's thigh, and Benny had felt his body light up like wick to a flame. He became aware of Alejandro's lithe movements on the boat, the amount of space between their chairs at night, and all the subtleties of nonverbal communication that are heightened when two people are attracted. This development came as a surprise to him, a delight, even as Benny tried to push the flirtation from his mind. He still pulled his phone from his pocket routinely to check for a message from Kiki. He loved Kiki. And yet his body was keeping time with Alejandro's movements on the boat.

Alejandro had already begun searching for other work. Alejandro told Benny as they culled oysters that he'd called a man he met in immigration detention in Texas. Huascar worked on a construction crew in New Orleans and said he would inquire about a job. Alejandro admitted he didn't trust Huascar too much. Huascar had lied pointlessly and vehemently about the pettiest of things while they were in detention—what he'd said to the guard that morning, what he'd heard the lunch would be that day. Still, this was the only lead he had so far. Benny sensed Alejandro gently testing to see if Benny would want to see him in New Orleans.

"You'll like New Orleans much more than Golden Vale," Benny said. "Plus, we can hang out. I'll introduce you to my friends."

"Maybe," Alejandro said, smiling. "I have a feeling, no. I won't see you much in the city."

"You think I'm going to give you the cold shoulder in New Orleans, huh?"

"I think so," Alejandro said. "I arrive, and you're suddenly busy, busy all the time. You'll be with your band and your girlfriend. And I will be on a rooftop."

"Then I'll be looking up all the time."

Benny was watching Alejandro. One of Alejandro's eyes sometimes wandered on its own like a stray thought. He had a scar on his temple that was peach-colored. His eyes were honeyed brown. During lunch, Alejandro sat watching an ant navigate the forest of hairs on his arm. He looked at his arm with consternation and said, "He went the wrong way somehow, ending up on this boat, and here we are in the middle of the bay. He won't make it back to his colony."

Benny wondered if Alejandro had always been so thoughtful, or if his circumstance, the tolerance for uncertainty that was required of him, had made it his nature.

It happened the night after they'd seen the oil on the water. They could smell the crude oil before they saw it. Their heads filled up with it. It felt like asphalt filling up their mouths. Their eyes felt warm in their sockets. It was like a dream they shared—the three of them—crossing the floating barrier as if there were no more authority to it than the line of rope it was. No one in sight in the bay. The quiet once Jordan had cut the engine and they floated closer and closer to the slick until they realized they were going in it.

It wasn't black like they'd thought. It was marbled brown and red and orange and black. They floated into it. They were burping, and it was like they were burping up the oil, as if it were already inside of them. The oil slick made the world look upside down, as if the night sky were where the bay should be. The blue on top when it should be on the bottom.

The boat moved the oil as they floated into it, undulating the colors around them, causing the stripes to bend and billow in arabesque shapes. No one in sight to stop them. Maybe Jordan had known the oil was in the bay all along but had not told them.

Jordan leaned over the side of the boat like he was about to dive in, but no, he was dipping a rag. The rag oozed an orange puddle on the deck around it. Jordan had vomit on his chin where he sat with his back against the side of the boat.

They were on top of the oysters their great-grandfather had farmed. The quiet of it. No buzzing of flies or mosquitoes. Nothing alive in the air.

Benny sat so close to his brother their shoulders were touching. He could feel Jordan breathing through his arm, his chest expanding and deflating. They sat that way until a plane streaked overhead and rained dispersant down on them. They saw the mist floating down. It was cool on the skin. Benny held out his arms, disbelieving. He turned them upside down, a stranger's arms. Then his arms started to burn.

After they docked, Jordan walked toward the house without a word to either Benny or Alejandro. He climbed into his truck and drove to Cyndi's, lost in black thoughts. He could still smell it, the oil. He could feel it ache behind his eyes. The skin of his arms was tender with the sting of the dispersant. He'd watched his own life pass into metaphor right in front of him—the blackness on the water, the planes burning overhead. Suddenly he understood all had been lost for some time now, but he'd only just noticed. And then Cyndi's little house appeared through his window. He killed the engine and sat for a moment. Then he carried himself to Cyndi's doorstep, wearing an old shirt of his father's, heaped in misery. Cyndi answered the door in a green dress.

Benny and Alejandro had showered with a hose on the back of the boat, stripping down and sudsing up with a bar of green soap. Their skin felt tenderized, as if they'd been sunburned. Was Jordan thinking, just as Benny was, of Randall Sutherland? The man's labored steps, the man drowning as he breathed? He did not know where Jordan had gone in his mind or where he'd gone with his truck.

He might have told Alejandro about Randall Sutherland. "I didn't think about what I was breathing," the sick man had said. "They've stolen my life. Stolen it. It don't matter how much money they give me now. I'm still dead."

Would it be a kindness to tell Alejandro this? He thought not. He insisted that Alejandro stay and shower again in his bathroom. Benny balled up their clothes and put them in the trash can.

Alejandro came into the hallway with a towel tied at his waist. "You've thrown away my clothes?"

"They're contaminated," Benny said. "They'll make you sick!"

He offered Alejandro a David Bowie T-shirt and a pair of cargo shorts that he'd worn in high school. Alejandro's hair dripped on his shoulders as he hugged the clothes to his chest. They looked at each other. It felt wrong to be in his mother's empty house at that hour of the day with the light heating up the windows.

"You're going to stay, right?" Benny walked into the steaming green bathroom. "You won't leave?"

Benny found himself rushing through the shower, soaping himself up three times, digging his nails into the bar of soap and picking all the grit from beneath his fingernails. He came out of the shower raw and pink-faced but feeling like a weight had been lifted from him. He called Alejandro's name. Fearfully, he realized, because Alejandro was laughing at him.

"I'm right here," he said. "I'm in your room."

Because Benny and Alejandro had nowhere to go, and it was too hot to go if they had, they set about killing the afternoon the only way they knew how, with a guitar and a twelve-pack in the roller cooler down by the bayou. Besides, it was there, by the boats, where they always sat. It was where they'd become friends. Next to them, the oyster boat was ringed with oil still. They heard Jordan's truck return from somewhere, not that he'd come down to see them. Alejandro sang Benny a Zapatista song that he'd heard in the detention center in Texas. He sang it again and again until they could sing it together, nearly shouting the anthem's end, and feeling as though they'd gotten away with something.

It occurred to Benny to ask, "They let you have guitars in there?"

"No, man." Alejandro laughed. "They don't let us have anything in there. You had to sing."

He hadn't meant to, but Benny found himself telling Alejandro about Randall Sutherland anyway. He told him about the woman in the auditorium, about how poisonous the dispersant was that they'd been sprayed with that morning.

Alejandro made a slingshot from a tall weed and shot a seedpod into the water. He shrugged. "Something will have to kill me," he said, and he took a cigarette paper and pinched a wad of tobacco in it, rolling it up expertly. "I don't think it will be a mist."

"It wasn't just mist."

"We have heart attacks in my family," Alejandro said. "That's how I'd rather go."

"And I'd like to go in my sleep at ninety-two. It's not like we choose."

"Then why worry?"

Benny didn't know if this was a macho put-on, but it was what he wanted to hear all the same.

As the day wore on, their chairs gravitated closer to each other, and the sun's light softened in the sky. The sprinklers in the yard started and swept over the lawn in graceful arcs. The frogs and crickets turned up their volume. It's true that he missed this sound when he was in the city. A car would pass by occasionally, its headlights blinding them, invading their intimacy. They were sharing a joint. Alejandro told Benny that he'd been on a truck hiding for four days on his way across the border. Everyone pissing and shitting in a corner of the truck, the smell terrible. Babies crying or, worse, not crying, because so much had happened to them. He thought, I am illegal. Why is anyone illegal? It made no sense to him, nations and languages and borders. All of world history. Why had the world been the way it was? The world's powerful took from the less powerful—dominated them—and then made justifications later. The human animal was a sad one—perhaps he too was like this, but he hadn't had the chance to know. Was he any different? Alejandro was embarrassed of himself for his philosophizing. Alejandro hiked one leg up on his thigh, and maybe because of his embarrassment, or maybe because he was a little stoned, he fell silent, listening to the thrum of insects.

Alejandro screamed, starting up from his chair. And Benny saw the snake, a water moccasin, zipping over Alejandro's bare ankle as if it were a log. Benny screamed too and jumped upright, grabbing Alejandro's shoulder.

The snake did not strike at them, but slithered on to the water's edge. It plunked into the bayou. Alejandro jumped up and down. "Shit, fuck!" he said, laughing. They both laughed. And then Benny looked at Alejandro's beautiful laughing face and pulled it to his. They kissed more fearfully than Benny had ever kissed in his life, as if when they pulled away and looked at each other they might have to reckon with the decision they didn't make. It was teeth-knocking, hungry kissing that set their whole bodies in motion, fumbling for one another, grabbing, stroking, until they wordlessly decided, when a truck passed, holding them in its light for what felt like an eternity, that they ought to move to Benny's bedroom.

They pulled apart then and looked at each other. Alejandro had a goofy smile on his face. They tottered across the street like giddy children, but when they reached the house, through the window they saw Jordan on the couch with the lights on. They would have to pass him on their way to Benny's bedroom. The TV was on, but Jordan wasn't watching it. He had his head back on the couch, so far back that he faced the window. The way he was staring, Jordan looked like a possessed man, his face drawn and his eyes vacant. Benny hadn't realized he was holding Alejandro's hand until he dropped it. He felt himself shrink. But Jordan couldn't see them. In a lit house, Benny remembered, someone could see from the outside in, but not from the inside out.

Then Alejandro pulled Benny to his own car and opened the rear door, which was always unlocked. "Is this okay?" he asked. The Volvo had hardly the room for two men on their knees, however tightly they pressed into one another. Benny leaned over, elbowing the door panel. Alejandro labored above him, crooked and neck bent beneath the low headliner, taking Benny's waist in one hand and his thigh with the other, firmly, gently pressing him farther into a strained and ecstatic geometry. "Is this okay?" Alejandro asked. "Yes," Benny said. Everything was okay. Headlights came once around the curve of the road and swept them over brightly and then continued and left them again in the dark. And in this darkness, they hurried on like fugitives. Benny was overcome with affection for Alejandro. He found himself stopping himself from saying, I love you, I love you, when they were entwined, but had no idea why. He didn't say much of anything out loud.

When it was over, Alejandro stroked Benny's face. No one had ever stroked his face after sex. They were a man's fingers on his face, and he hadn't had a man's hands on him in a long time. They lay entwined in the backseat, sweating and sour-smelling from day-drinking in the sun, and Benny's head rested in the crook of Alejandro's neck, looking down on Alejandro's statue of a body. Alejandro was singing a song in Spanish. Benny didn't know what it meant, but it all seemed so sweet and sad that he might cry on the spot.

It was two o'clock in the morning. They had to use their shirts to wipe down the foggy windows before Benny could drive Alejandro home, to a trailer he shared with a couple who Alejandro said fought frequently. Benny feared the comedown that was already in motion in his chest and so did not look over too often as he drove. Before Alejandro got out of the car, he took Benny's hand and kissed it. "Don't worry," Alejandro said. "I don't have any big ideas."

Alejandro had forgiven his cowardice before he had the chance to act on it. He watched Alejandro fumble with the broken knob of the trailer because a junkie had kicked it in. Alejandro had to hide his savings outside of his home because he couldn't trust his roommates, even if he liked them well enough. Why had Benny never driven him home before? It was probably that he hadn't wanted to see how Alejandro lived. Into the dark of the trailer he went, and Benny looked after the trailer, momentarily dumbfound, then he looked around at all the other trailers, sodden and dark, people sleeping inside them. The trailers seemed like witnesses to his cowardice. He had not offered Alejandro any reassurance, but he could have. What might it have cost him? Benny drove home with the music loud enough to outrun his thoughts—and yet, I love you, I love you, he'd thought, and maybe Alejandro had felt it.

Benny slept for a few hours and then snapped awake at five a.m., his whole body buzzing. There was no work left to do—the oyster lugger would remain docked in the bayou until who-knew-when—but his body told him to wake up anyway. He was hungover, his stomach sour, and he replayed the previous day's events in his mind, ending with Alejandro. He couldn't place the true source of his illness—what he'd put into his body, or what had been sprayed on it, or if this was the pang of betraying Kiki again, or having slept with a man. The only relief he could imagine was returning to New Orleans, where his life made sense.

He checked his phone, hoping to hear from one of the women who could change his life—Kiki or Vanessa—but he'd received no messages overnight. The NPR piece would air in two days, and he wanted to be in New Orleans when it happened in case Kiki called him. He weakly hoped Vanessa would put him in touch with her friend who worked on the *Tiny Desk Concerts*. He'd never put much effort into creating an online presence. He'd not uploaded a song to Bandcamp in a couple of years, and now he wondered why. That he might establish himself beyond the parties and bars in New Orleans was not a development he'd entertained. Though he knew it was unlikely, the wider world, in the form of Vanessa, had announced some interest in him and planted a feeble optimism in his chest.

Benny found Jordan awake and prone on the living room couch. Jordan had been watching the news at a whisper so as not to wake Benny. He swung his feet to the carpet, stretching his arms over-head and groaning. They'd passed the age when a night on the couch was spent without consequence. He smiled upon seeing

Benny, seeming aged and mired in a doom that would cocoon him for days. Benny sat his duffel bag of clothes on the carpet.

"You're leaving," Jordan said.

"Kiki called me," Benny lied. "I need to go back to New Orleans."

Jordan nodded, seeming unsurprised.

"I proposed to Cyndi," he said.

"Is that happy news?" Benny perched on the arm of their father's easy chair. "I can't tell."

"Spur-of-the-moment," he admitted. He extended his feet on the coffee table.

"She said yes, then?"

"Not exactly, but it's on the table."

Benny dumped yesterday's coffee into the sink and started filling the carafe. "I like Cyndi. She's spicy. Not what I'd bet on as your type, but I like her."

"Have you heard from Vanessa about that *Tiny Desk* thing?"

"No word yet," Benny said. "She's probably busy. God, she was a babe, wasn't she?"

"I keep calling her, but she won't call me back."

"Why?" Benny said. "You're still worried about misquoting the acreage?"

He spooned coffee into the coffee maker, the sharp scent churning his stomach. He didn't want coffee, he realized, but he would need it for the drive.

"I just want to make sure she doesn't print anything inaccurate."

"She probably won't. Anyway, it's too late. The piece is supposed to air soon. You're just in your head about it. I get it. Yesterday was a nightmare. I'll never forget it. We took a toxic chemical shower. Everything seems doomed right now."

Jordan was looking at him. He seemed to actually be listening to him.

"Don't worry about what you said," Benny continued. "She just wants a basic piece about the oysters. It won't get too specific. I'm sure it won't even get too political. I know I pissed you off—talking about the Iraq War. I couldn't help it. I guess I was thinking about Kiki the whole time."

"Forget it," Jordan said.

"I was proud of you—baring your soul like that." He smiled at Jordan. "You know, you sounded almost like a liberal."

Jordan chuckled miserably. "I don't trust the government any more than I trust BP." Then Jordan told him about the freshwater diversions. "The state of Louisiana may have just fucked us more than BP did. Or at least they're competing for the title."

"Maybe this is a dumb question, but can they close the—what are they?"

"Diversions," Jordan said. He knitted his hands on the top of his head. "Easy to open, hard to close. Like a fool, I even called the governor's office. They said they'd get back to me, so that settles it. It's all taken care of."

"What will you do?"

"The way I see it?" Jordan said. "Run out of money? Lay everyone off. Wait around for the lawyer to call with news. I'm glad Dad isn't alive to see this."

"I am too," Benny said. "It would've killed him. Not that I'm glad it's happening to you either."

Outside, a light rain began and pattered the window. Benny knelt for a thermos, filled it, and then poured a mug for Jordan.

Jordan looked at Benny's meager bag of clothes—all he'd arrived with. "You're not saying goodbye to Mom, then?"

"Is Mom here?"

Jordan shook his head.

"Then I guess not," he said. "I'll be back." He carried Jordan's mug to the coffee table and sat opposite Jordan in the easy chair with his thermos. "Can we talk about money? I need some."

"Like right now?"

Benny nodded.

Jordan took his feet from the table. He shifted onto one haunch and removed his wallet. He opened it to show Benny it was empty. "I'll have to write you a check. How much do you want?"

Benny said the largest sum he could think of. "Five thousand dollars."

"All right."

"Really? I expected you to give me a headache about it."

"I guess I'm too tired to." Jordan was bent forward, with the heels of his hands dug into his eyes. He didn't look up as he spoke. "I'd feel so much better if she just called me back."

"I don't believe it's her that's bothering you."

Benny's stomach churned as he sipped the coffee he did not want. The rain tapped on the windows. He looked at his feet on the teal carpet, which was browned from decades of their walking on it. When he was young, the family business was like a fortress in his mind—dependable and enduring. They relied on an estuary and an organism that seeded itself if you ensured the right conditions. Over the course of his time in Golden Vale, weeks that felt like months, the business was dismantled. Jordan looked up at him, finally, and shrugged.

"Let me get my checkbook," Jordan said.

When Benny approached his car in the driveway, he was struck still with remembering Alejandro in the backseat, and he couldn't bring himself to open the rear door to toss his bag there for fear of seeing the bodily evidence. He set his duffel bag on the front seat and laid his banjo on top of it, waving to Jordan in the driveway. He left the quiet neighborhood as the sky lightened to gray and the rain slushed under his tires. It was careless of him to sleep with Alejandro, cruel even, considering how vulnerable Alejandro was. If he'd not complicated matters with sex, he might have taken Alejandro with him to New Orleans and helped him find work. He'd made a predictable mess of things. He should have stayed to say goodbye to his mother.

He called her from the road, but she did not pick up. When she did call him back, she was crying. Not about him, but because her boyfriend was sleeping with his graduate student, a girl younger than Benny, who lived at the oyster hatchery with Doc part-time. She was crying so much it was hard to get the full story out of her. When Doc was in the kitchen making breakfast, she said, she'd gone through his phone and saw a damning text message. Something not overtly sexual, but overly familiar enough that, when presented with this evidence, Doc didn't deny it.

"Oh, Mom. I'm sorry."

She was crying openly into the phone. The connection wasn't good, and he couldn't hear her too well. It looked like a storm was going to dump on him. He had her on speakerphone.

"The son of a bitch!" Benny yelled into the phone. "I never knew what to think of that guy."

"I'm such a fool!" May cried. "When I think about him now, I see all kinds of evidence. He talked about that girl like she was his daughter, but I ignored it. What'd I know about what grad school professors are like?"

"He seemed sleazy," Benny said.

"What?"

"He seemed like a sleaze," Benny yelled.

"I can barely hear you. Where are you?"

"I'm driving to New Orleans. There's a storm coming."

"What?"

"I have a gig," he yelled.

"This is terrible," she said, but he didn't know if she meant Doc's infidelity or his leaving. "Once he admitted it, he wouldn't say it was wrong. 'She's an adult,' he kept saying. 'She makes her own decisions.'"

"Did you call bullshit on that?"

"What?"

"Bullshit! She works for him! Maybe she thought she had no choice."

"I couldn't think. I was so mad, I couldn't think. I have been humiliated over and over again in my life. Your father—"

The first wave of rain slapped his car, and he braked too hard, the back of his Volvo fishtailing and then righting itself. "Fuck, fuck, fuck," he sang.

"What?"

"Nothing."

"I thought your father was sometimes unfaithful in New Orleans."

"Mom," Benny said. "There was that woman who came for money after Dad died."

"That was just her word," May said. "Against his. I think she made it up. I don't think Al would get involved with a low woman like that. She was a dirty liar."

"Oh, Mom."

"I could just die," she said. "I could just die of humiliation."

Benny could picture his mother, doubled over in grief. The whole world seemed to be concentrating its grief in the part of the world where he grew up, and he was driving away from it as swiftly as he could. It was unbearable, thinking of his mother like that. He told her to make herself some tea and go to sleep. She was well rid of Doc. Benny knew that Doc was exciting, he said, but she would see that Doc was just a footnote in her life. She would find someone more worthy of her. She didn't want to hear that, and as he said it, he realized that someone had probably said this to Kiki. She was well rid of him. It was why his phone number was still blocked.

"I'll be back soon," he said. "You just try not to think of it too much."

⇢ Twenty-Five ⇠

Jordan had never done violence to another man, but he was now on his way to do just that, he realized, driving down to Doc's hatchery in Grand Isle. When his mother came home with the news of what Doc had done, her face was a mess from crying, and he'd carried a spark of rage in his chest ever since. He struggled now to marry his truck to the double line. My will be done! he thought. He parked cattywampus next to Rollo and Alpharetta's defunct ice and bait shop on Grand Isle—a modular home painted so cheerily light green it looked like a child had done it, and they were pleased to see him, glassy-eyed as he was.

Rollo loved a brawl, and perhaps that's why he'd stopped. Alpharetta, Rollo's wife, had a tidy round face, wide dimpled arms, and icy blue eyes that shone from her sun-ravaged face. She said, "You ought not to drive when you smell like this, baby, or else someone will get the wrong idea about you."

Jordan lowered himself with the help of a deck railing onto a cooler.

"What are you doing here, Jordan?" Rollo asked.

"I'm on my way to have a word with Doc."

"How's that brought you here, then?"

"I wanted to talk to you about the business I got with Doc."

"Well, what business have you got with him?"

"I'm after his head," Jordan said.

"That's an ugly business."

He came to be dissuaded, maybe, from his hateful thoughts about Doc, about BP, and what little there was to separate them—what right did they have? Nobody had the right to treat a person like they didn't matter. His mother had refused to see Lucille when she came by. She claimed to have a migraine. She had a sopping-wet washcloth on her eyes, wetting her pillow. She spoke weakly. She'd call Lucille when she was feeling better. Lucille, bless her, knew when to honor someone's plea for privacy, but on her way out the door she grabbed Jordan by his bicep, and she said, "I know it's hard for you now too. Are you all right, Jordan?"

"Fine," Jordan said. "I'm fine."

She tightened her grip on him. "Everyone around here thinks they can give me the slip, but if you aren't fine, will you call me? It's times like these you've got to know that you can call your neighbor. In case you're ever thinking something crazy. Not that you will. But if you do, you just call me, okay?"

Lucille, a retired nurse, who'd hollered his name at sporting events his whole life, who didn't seem to favor Benny like everyone else did, a woman so seriously, unshakably devout it made you think she had a direct line to God. He was ashamed to look the way he did—he couldn't recall if he'd brushed his teeth that day.

"You take care of yourself too, okay?" she said.

"Thanks, Lucille. Okay."

Jordan realized the source of her concern when he caught sight of himself in the hall mirror, which he'd tried to avoid. He thought, Who is this deadbeat in my house? The man was a stranger—stoop-shouldered, unshaven, disbelieving. He wore dried mustard stains on his shirt from his two-hot-dog lunch. *Bankrupt* was the word that came to mind. There was Cyndi, at least. Wasn't there Cyndi? His shower shared a wall with his mother's room, and he heard her crying in there—the low whimper of it. It killed him because he knew she did not want him to hear her. The violence he wished upon Doc then was a relief. It relieved him of his own worries for a moment. He would go over there and have a talk with Doc about how you can't treat a person.

He sat down in the shower and let the water splatter his face until there was no heat left in it. He'd paced all morning with a letter from BP open on the coffee table. It was his claim for financial compensation for his losses—and this was even baffling for him—because how could anyone calculate his losses when he didn't know how long it would take him to recover? How long to come back from nothing? Five years? Twenty? He was not young. The letter from BP told him that someone else had filed for compensation under his name, another Jordan Pearce, and now his claim was under investigation. "Fraud is illegal and punishable by law," it read on BP letterhead. They were threatening him. Jordan called his lawyer and left two messages with the secretary, sounding hysterical, he realized, because the woman said, "All right, now. Just calm down." What made her think he was not calm? Dispersant had rained down on him, and for all he knew his days were numbered. Who was going to take care of his mother? Doc had dishonored her, treated her badly—like a worthless thing. You can't do this to people, he wanted to say to this man. His mother was a vulnerable widow, just opening herself up to life again. What a time to be so careless with someone. What right have you got, he wanted to say, to treat people like they matter nothing at all?

———

"Let's take you for a walk," Rollo said. Jordan did not want to walk, but he let Rollo lead him down the steps, following Rollo's wicked limp. His home was lifted onto pilings to protect him from the storms. There was a wraparound deck. He'd never met a person more proud of his deck.

The limp was painful to watch. Jordan followed it down the steps and into the plot next to Rollo's place. Cut grass exploded into the air with each swipe of his leg. Jordan was sweating through his shirt. When Jordan looked up, they were at the edge of a graveyard with knee-high tombstones. Rollo's graveyard. He'd cut the tombstones from wood himself. Rollo led Jordan around the lot, reading them aloud to him. SUMMER FUN. OYSTERS. CRAWFISH. CLEAN GULF WIND. REDFISH. OYSTER SPAGETTI. SWORDFISH. TROUT. BLUE CRABS. GUMBO. KIDS ON THE BEACH. BROWN SHRIMP. WHITE SHRIMP. MY RETIRMENT. And this was silly, maybe. Yes, there were misspellings. Rollo had a fifth-grade education. But could there be a more earnest cry of grief? Jordan felt himself moving like he was contending with a hazardous wind. He should not have driven. Alpharetta was right.

Earlier, Cyndi had popped in on her way to work and returned from his mother's room, asking him, "Do you know where she keeps her pills?"

Jordan could not comprehend. "Her anxiety meds?"

"She's really out of it." Cyndi sat down on the coffee table to tie the laces of her ugly orthopedic runners.

"Well, that man humiliated her."

"I've been around the block, babe. You ought to keep an eye on her," Cyndi said. She looked tired. She'd told him that the out-of-work bar patrons drank with growing desperation that was hard to watch. "If I weren't making so much money, I'd say we take a vacation until this is over."

This *we* was the only silver lining he'd heard all day. Before he could stop himself, he sat down on the couch and pulled her onto his lap. Cyndi resisted this at first but gave in, letting her body relax. He wanted to feel the weight of her. She was so tough all the time, rebuffing him, making cracks at him. It was only when she was close to sleep that she could let herself be nakedly affectionate. "Where's Jordie?" she'd say in a baby voice, seeking out his back and hugging him to her chest like he was a life preserver. This was so out of character that it elated him. But that afternoon, he'd gotten hard immediately. He wanted to jump right out of his skin one way or another, and she scoffed, straightening up to lace her second sneaker. He did not ask his mother about any pills.

Rollo's graveyard was in a plot next to his bait shop. The air was crisp with the smell of cut grass, and Jordan's ankles itched from the mosquitoes that triumphed at that hour. The sky was purple up to the clouds and blue above them, a palm tree waving in the wind. He loved this part of the world more than any other. He'd been to a distant cousin's house in the mountains of Tennessee once, and he'd stood on a mountain looking at those peaks. "It's nice," he'd said to her, but it didn't touch the bayou, the ground so low to the sea it felt like you were in the sky, the clouds fat and climbing high like mountains, and the smell of the brackish water. He had that water in his blood! He ate from that water every day of his life. They were trying to kill him. The cicadas were screaming, the frogs walloping, the mosquitoes whining. They were trying to kill him forever.

In his cup Alpharetta had poured the wine cooler she was drinking, because that's how people were—if they didn't have any extra to give, they'd give you some of theirs. Rollo's limp led him down the rows of his graveyard, this man who'd cradled each tombstone in his lap to paint it with his arthritic shrimper's fingers. Jordan could hear Gulf waves breaking on the shore.

Jordan had not seen the oil on the beach, and Rollo was disappointed that Jordan didn't want to see it. But Rollo led him down to the beach anyway, just fifty yards from Rollo's trailer. NO TRESPASSING, a sign said by the entrance.

"No trespassing on a public beach!" Rollo howled.

The beach was blanketed with reddish globs of oil, splashed in fan shapes at the water's edge. And the waves—there was timber in the waves coming in. Long poles like telephone poles, and he almost asked Rollo, Why are there poles in the water? But, on a better look, no, it wasn't timber. That was the oil cresting in the waves, coming in looking like logs of oil. Again the smell of crude oil filled his head. He bent down and took a thick pancake of it in his bare hand, massaging it with his fingers. It was heavy. It'd come from the core of the earth. The heat of the earth had made it. It wasn't like blood, this red was too brown, but he wanted to say it anyway, "It's like blood."

Rollo nodded as if this were true. There, a dead little seagull, its body in an oil pancake the consistency of marmalade. Its legs up and stiff.

Alpharetta had hidden Jordan's keys, and Jordan said some ugly things to her before he fell asleep on their couch. He'd made her cry, he remembered, but what had he said? He woke in the early morning regretting what he couldn't remember. He was forty minutes from home and trapped there on the island.

He dreamed of the woman who had come to his father's funeral. The woman who'd come to upset his mother in her ridiculous floppy hat with its overlarge sequined flower. The woman's teeth long in her mouth. She might have been the jazz singer his brother had mentioned. A New Orleans accent. The woman had clomped up to his mother at the funeral reception and told her that Al had made her certain promises, which she hoped May would keep. She said this to his mother leaning in, as if offering a condolence. Jordan escorted this woman out. "Your father made some promises to me," the woman said. "You didn't know him," he'd said, never more certain of anything in his life. She was just a loon, he decided.

In a few hours, Jordan snapped awake with panic, and as he felt his resolve failing him, he descended the stairs of Rollo's mobile home and was out in the dark, humid summer night. Not a car passing on the street. He had more of his wits about him, but his body felt like a sack he was dragging around. The fishing cabins were dark, some with their storm shutters drawn. He walked by a sno-ball stand painted rainbow with a sign nailed to the door: SEE YOU NEXT SUMMER! THANKS, BP! ☹ And a large plywood sign that put a wry spin on the Jimmy Buffett song about tourists covered in oil. He tried to summon the rage that had fueled him earlier. He would throttle the man. Go at him like the chimpanzee who had disfigured its owner's face. Doc would be asleep. Could he throttle a man in his sleep? He might be asleep with the graduate student.

He walked through a fence gate left open and up the gravel driveway, past a truck. This might have been Doc's truck, with crab pots in its bed.

Doc's lights were on. Jordan stood and looked up at the burning lights. He couldn't see movement in the upstairs windows. There was a long stairwell up to the door. Would Doc hear him climbing up? His designs dissolved as he stood there. He could not imagine what was going on in there or why the man was up so late. He could not imagine attacking a man in his kitchen. He stood looking up at the door when he heard his name.

"Jordan!" Doc said, and there he was in his black waders and suspenders, standing a few feet from him. "My god, Jordan. What's the matter?"

Jordan was stunned. "Nothing's the matter," he said dumbly.

"You come over to talk to me?" Doc was holding his suspenders. "Come inside."

Jordan followed Doc up the stairs. They were noisy stairs. Doc would have heard him climbing had he been inside, but then again, it had never been Jordan's plan to attack him in the night. He could kick him now. He could punch him in the back of the head and run away. But he wouldn't and Doc seemed to know this, which made Jordan resent him. They did not speak as they climbed. Doc asked him to take off his shoes before he came in. Doc unhitched his waders and stepped out of them, leaving the rubber legs outstretched on the deck. In the fluorescent kitchen, the lights burned his eyes and perhaps alerted Doc to how bad he looked. Doc stepped out of arm's reach to fill a glass of water in the sink, and he set it down on the bar for him. Now Jordan could not imagine how to begin.

"Well, the oil's here. It's here, all right," Doc began. "My oyster beds have become a big ol' science experiment on oil and dispersant exposure. They're just for testing now. And tonight the pump on my algae tank gave out. Just died. Five-thousand-dollar piece of crap. Mechanics is not my thing, but I wish it was. It would have saved me thousands of dollars over the course of my life. Tell me, have they shut you down yet?"

It happened two days ago, Jordan said. He heard that Barataria was oiled, but he'd wanted to see for himself.

"And then the state of Louisiana opens the freshwater diversions on you," Doc said. "I called them screaming. *Screaming.* Who was your consult on this? I want the names of your engineers, and I want them to tell me they'd talked to a biologist before they opened up the pointless, destructive diversions. You know what I heard on the other line?"

Jordan did not know.

"Silence. They're in crisis mode. I can't find an engineer who can tell me that those diversions will keep the oil out. It's criminally reckless behavior, is what it is. This is how people act when they are in crisis. Let cooler heads prevail? No siree. People just slam their hands down on the detonate button."

"I called the governor's office," Jordan said. "Nobody will talk to me."

"That's just it!" Doc said. "You better believe they won't. You're just a dumb fisherman to them. You know a lot better than those people with their degrees. You can't mess with the ecosystem. You can't mess with the ecosystem! I don't need to tell you that. They need to talk to the fishermen. Don't get me started on the Vessels of Opportunity program."

"They won't call me in to work. I'm on the wait list."

"And you better believe that there are folks from all over Texas and Arkansas working that program. That's nepotism for you!"

Jordan was nodding. It was true. He saw the out-of-state plates whipping by on the highway by his house. Jordan watched the whirring bubbles in his water glass float and settle.

"I want you to know something," Doc said. He slid his body forward on the kitchen island, leaning on his forearms to be frank with Jordan. "What you're going through isn't easy. You've lost everything, okay? I know it, and you know it. It isn't your fault, we both know that, but you've gotta know that nothing is going to be as bad as it is right now. This is the worst that has ever happened to you and will ever happen to you. This is a test of what you're made of. What you do now matters."

"I don't know what to do."

"You will," Doc said. "Your life may seem like it's over, but it isn't, you hear me? You're going to figure something else out." Doc pointed at the dark windows facing the Gulf. "In a few hours that sun is coming up, baby, and do you know what that means?"

Jordan did not.

"It means that another day of your goddamn life is starting—pardon my French. You can squander it if you want, but you won't. You won't because you're made of better stuff than that. Are you hurting? Yes, you're hurting. You'd have to be crazy not to be, but you're going to be okay, Jordan."

The room became indistinct to him. He could not look at Doc, who was speaking to him. Doc had looked right into him and seen the dark place where he was living. He'd needed to hear this, and Doc was the very last person he expected to tell him as much. He was moved despite himself.

He felt himself nodding, but quickly stopped. This was how his mother was won over. This man got you on his side with the incredible force of his personality. Doc recognized why he'd come. Jordan was not someone who could keep his thoughts from his face.

"But I suppose that's not why you came over here at three a.m., to talk about the spill. Am I right?"

Jordan agreed that it was not.

"Well, I trust you're not some kind of caveman," Doc said. "You can ask me anything you want. I'll tell you anything."

Ask him? Jordan had nothing to ask him.

"Did your mother tell you she went into my messages and got certain ideas about me and my graduate assistant?"

"She did."

"What kind of a person goes digging into another person's private business? Tell me, is that fair? Is it fair that she breaks a glass in the kitchen? Loses herself completely and accuses me of having sex with children? Because that's what your mother implied."

Jordan did not know how to respond to this. He could feel the argument slipping away from him. "You didn't treat her right."

Doc bowed his head reverently, crossing his arms and nodding. "I understand that's how she sees it."

"You made a fool of her by treating her that way."

"You're absolutely right, I wasn't honest. I regret that, but I think May ought to understand, and we've talked about this too, that when I say, 'I'm dating someone,' it doesn't mean I'm married to them. I object to her saying I made a fool of her. May is an adult. So is Camilla, for that matter. I don't enjoy being called a pedophile. Camilla is a fully grown adult. It's an invasion of my privacy to go through my phone. She had no right to do it."

"But that doesn't make what you done right."

"It kills me that I hurt your mother. I never meant to. I just didn't expect things to get so serious. We were having fun. Then she got an idea in her head."

"She's a widow. You scooped her off the floor just to toss her over your shoulder."

"Women your mother's age—they want too much."

No, he thought. Doc was wrong there. "You knew what she was expecting when you came to date her. You've got to take responsibility for that. You can't hurt people and then treat them like they're crazy for getting hurt."

There, he'd landed one. He surprised himself with his ability to say just what he meant, and he saw that this objection had reached Doc.

And there was Doc, hand on his heart, saying, "You're right. You're right about that, and I'm ashamed of myself. I'd say I'll make it up to her, but I doubt she'd let me."

A silence descended. Then they repeated this sentiment back and forth to each other a few times as if they were practicing lines of a play, until their roles attained their peak iteration, of offense and genuine remorse, and they were finished with it. Jordan was suddenly sleepier than he'd ever been in his life.

He didn't remember how he'd fallen asleep on Doc's couch, but it was daytime when he awoke to the smell of sausage in the kitchen, smoke filling the room and the sound of sizzling. He woke with a curious mix of surprise, hope, and a sneaking guilt.

Doc was at the stove, a spatula in his hand, gesturing toward an empty coffee cup next to the coffeemaker.

"The oysters," Doc said. "I've been hoping to talk to you about the oysters. The way you've been farming them. This whole system of leasing plots from the state and planting seed there. It's in the past. It's over with, Jordan. It's beautiful what your father did, but it can't be that way anymore. Growing in cages. That's the future. It just is. We've got to face it."

Doc was making him eggs. He said, "I'm making you eggs. Normally I'd go out in the surf and catch a fish to fry up for you, but I can't do that today. Breaks my heart to say it. Today, it's just eggs."

Jordan had a coffee cup in his hand. He meant to fill it with coffee. He set it down. He was in the enemy's kitchen. It all felt wrong. He'd failed to avenge his mother's honor. Drinking this man's coffee—talking about the future of oyster farming with him. Doc had a big head, and he could land a punch right there, on the man's temple. Couldn't he? No, the window for violence had long been closed.

But then he did it anyway. Lobbed Doc right in the temple. He was still holding the spatula on the floor. The pan had gone flying, uncooked eggs sloshed on the wall. Jordan watched the realization come into Doc's eyes as to what had happened, and he was sure that Doc saw the fear that Jordan felt seize him immediately, now that he'd done it. "Fuck!" Jordan said, and he ran to the kitchen door, jamming his feet into the shoes he'd taken off the night before. "Fuck!" he said again, scrambling down the stairs, trying to get away from what he'd done, but feeling, also, elated.

→ Twenty-Six ←

For two days, Benny turned his head to the sound of every whirring bicycle in case Kiki was astride it. The city delivered her face to him over and over. When he'd arrived back in New Orleans, his heart had swelled at the sight of his house. His street. Stani's one-eyed Himalayan asleep on his front stoop. He'd only been away for two and a half weeks. He hadn't thought longingly of New Orleans while in Golden Vale, but now that it was in front of him, he was awash in love for it. This was his life restored to him. Stani had answered the front door wearing a neon-yellow onesie.

"You pay rent here, don't you?" Stani had said, holding the door. "What are you knocking for?"

As Stani locked him in a hug—he was so thin—Benny was struck by the vegetal smell of the old house and the sense that there was nowhere else he ought to be.

Two days after his return, he still felt a sleep deficit making demands of him. He lay in his bed in the afternoon. He'd taken a cold shower, lathering himself with his roommate's oatmeal-studded soap, and then he climbed wet and naked into his bed.

His sheets smelled herbal, like the woman who'd been staying in his room. He did not feel the bed's ownership restored to him, but he was pleased to meet again the particular give of his pillow. The NPR piece would air today, he thought, though he'd still not heard from Vanessa. Mercifully, he felt the tug of sleep lapping at him, and as he let the tide of sleep take him out to sea, it seemed possible he would be reborn—he'd wake up with the energy and insight to change his life.

When he did wake, miracle of miracles, it was because Kiki was calling him.

Her voice had a playful lilt when she said "Benny," as if she were calling his attention from across the room. "I just heard you on NPR! I thought, No, it can't be, but then it was! Talking about generations of oysters on the radio."

"Kiki," he said, sitting up. "Hi."

"So that's what you've been up to in Golden Vale," she said.

"We put a tarp up on the roof."

"I know!" she said. "NO FLY ZONE. I love it. I went to the website and found the pictures. And there was a picture of you playing the banjo."

"They put that up too, huh?"

"You haven't seen it?"

"I was just taking a nap."

"But you know what really surprised me?"

"What?" he said.

"Your brother!" Kiki said. She was gleeful. "He laid it all out. There was a really beautiful clip when he talks about oyster farming and what it means to him. Maybe I underestimated him."

"You didn't."

"I'm proud of you."

"I hate it when you say that." She expected so little of him. "What are you doing for lunch?"

"I haven't thought about it. Why?"

"Will you have lunch with me?"

"You're here?" He could hear her pottering with something on the other end. He pictured her at her desk with its potted plants. "I've got all this work. I just wanted to call and tell you I'd heard . . ."

He sensed in her voice that there was leeway in there for him.

"Have lunch with me, Kiki. You can spare an hour for lunch."

"Where?"

"Viola's?"

"Okay, Benny. Goddamn, okay. I didn't think you were in town. I thought the coast was clear."

"The coast is soaked with oil," he said, and felt silly for it immediately.

"When?"

"What about right now?"

"This is an awful idea!" she said, hanging up.

The old flirtation was alive between them, and it seemed there might be a chance for him yet. He wanted to slip back into his life before the spill, as if his mishap with Maria and the spill was just a nightmare he was waking from.

He'd chosen Viola's Café because his check from Jordan hadn't cleared yet, and he knew that Ali, the owner, would let him work off their lunches if he played piano during the brunch rush that weekend. "Ragtime brunch," Ali called it, wheeling a corny chalkboard sign out to the sidewalk for tourists. Most breakfasters would chat over his playing, too engrossed in their shakshuka even to clap when he'd finish a song. Playing on the street was better. People at least gave you their full attention before walking away.

Ali was a friend—a thin, tireless Palestinian man who hand-painted Mardi Gras masks as a hobby and asked every pretty patron to pose with a mask for his website. He lived next door to the café and treated it like his living room. He played chess with neighborhood kids. He painted his masks by the dusty window plants. And he made a falafel platter with baba ghanoush that Kiki had a weakness for.

What a beautiful sight, to see long-legged Kiki roll up on her bicycle. To watch her swing one leg over and perch on one pedal before she rolled to a stop. She hadn't seen him yet, so he got to watch her lock up her bike before she noticed him. She checked herself in the window, adjusting her thick ponytail over one shoulder. She laughed when she finally noticed him, and then hugged him hello. He did not hazard a kiss, but gave her a squeeze when he had her in his arms.

"It's just like you to catch me with my guard down," she said.

"Thanks for coming."

If Kiki had been too friendly, he would have taken it as a sign for the worst, that she was already distancing herself in her friendliness. As they went to the counter, rather than talking to Benny, she directed her attention to the high school girl working the register, asking her where she'd gotten her tank top. The girl's shirt said MY ANCESTORS GOT MY BACK, and this opened Kiki's heart to her immediately. Kiki was good with young people. She knew how to deliver a compliment without embarrassing anyone.

"Just coffee," she said.

"Order something, please."

"I'm not hungry."

"I'm playing the ragtime brunch this weekend, so order anything you want."

"So you'll have to work it off?"

"Kiki, please."

"I'll have the falafel," she said.

Kiki chose a seat farthest from the counter. She looked at the old upright Baldwin in the corner and then back at Benny. He could almost see the memory turning in her mind. The last lunch they'd had at Viola's, six months before, she asked him about ragtime, so he walked over to the piano and started in on Scott Joplin's "The Entertainer." Kiki had clapped for him when he finished, inspiring a couple of other diners to clap. "That's not ragtime," she said when he sat down. "That's what the ice-cream truck played." He'd loved that.

Now she held her coffee mug on the table with her nail-bitten fingers, and he was afraid to touch her hand.

"Isn't it a little hot for coffee?" he said. His own stiltedness was killing him.

She asked if the oil had closed the family business down yet, and he told her how they'd floated into it and then they'd been sprayed. It burned his skin. The oil on the water. Her eyes widened, and she peppered him with questions. What about the wildlife? Had he seen any more oiled birds?

Then Ali appeared with their falafel platters, calling Kiki "my darling," because he called everyone his darlings. After he set down the plates, he tried to massage Kiki's shoulders, but she shrugged him off.

"I have asked everyone, 'Where is my favorite piano player, pretty boy Benny?' But nobody knows."

"I went home to help family because of the spill," Benny said. "My family are oystermen. The business just shut down."

"I'm sorry, my darling." Ali put a hand on Benny's shoulder. He looked genuinely troubled. "Are they going to be all right?"

"They've dealt with oil spills, but there's never been so much oil. It could be the end."

"It's a crime against the planet," Ali said. "They should be put in jail."

Someone called Ali's name from the kitchen, and Ali squeezed Benny's shoulder before leaving them. "See you Saturday," he said.

"You know, Benny," Kiki said, "you should write about this for the paper."

Benny shook his head. "I wanted Jordan to get some attention because it could help him. It's going to be hard to get money out of BP. He needs the attention."

Benny wanted to change the subject. He didn't want to talk about the spill anymore. He motioned to her plate. "Eat, please."

She tore her pita into shreds but only tasted the baba ghanoush. Kiki said she was coauthoring a piece about BP's track record. An explosion at BP's Texas City refinery in 2005 killed fifteen people. The Chemical Safety Board's report blamed production pressures, budget cuts, and systemic safety issues.

"Sounds really important, Kiki."

She frowned, and he realized how flat he'd sounded. He tried to brighten. "Did you say you're coauthoring it?"

"Yes, with Possum," she said, and then she popped a falafel into her mouth.

"Why him?"

She held up one finger while she chewed. "He doesn't have a lot of experience writing, and he wanted to collaborate."

"I don't have any right to be jealous," Benny said.

"We know you don't."

She had her elbow on the table, and at that moment she was looking very mature, almost older than him. He tried to push the thought from his mind, but it was unavoidable: It occurred to him how the intimacy between them had vanished. When you're in love and loved, you could reach over and pet a person any time you wanted without a moment's thought. Now he felt the gulf that was between them.

"You should really write a piece for the newspaper," Kiki said.

"I thought about you every day," Benny said. "Don't talk to me about the newspaper. Please."

"I thought about you too," she said.

Her pitying tone told him all he needed to know. She needn't have told him she was sleeping with Possum now. Maybe it wouldn't matter if he'd thought that she still loved him. Kiki looked at him as if she were already safely years away, looking at a photograph of Benny as he'd been, with his head hung low above the bright red table, wearing his old, ragged smile. She was already clear of him in her heart. Benny felt himself transform into a memory before her very eyes.

She sensed this realization and sat back in her chair. She glanced at the stray cat outside, Ali's cat, and he admired her profile, her elegant neck, the slope of her nose.

"I guess I don't know what I wanted from this," she said. "I thought this'd be a friendly lunch."

"It's not unfriendly."

"It was dumb of me to come. Your being back was a surprise. I didn't think about the emotional toll of it."

"We're friends!" he said. "I've missed you. It's not bad."

She stood up. "It's hard for me."

"You hardly ate."

She looked at the mostly full falafel platters as if they'd just appeared and she was trying to decipher some meaning from them. There, she was going to cry, but not for the reason he wanted her to cry. She shook her head as if he'd asked her a question. If there was hope of love, he would have boxed up her falafel and ferried it to her home. He would have written a whole book of articles about his father's doomed oyster farm for the alternative newspaper. He would have refilled the tea kettle late into the night as she typed at her desk. Now the inevitability of this turn smacked him in the face. There went luminous-skinned Kiki, out the door, ignoring Ali's goodbye, her hands shaky at the bike rack. She didn't need him anymore, if she ever had. He imagined Kiki telling

Possum about this sorry lunch, sitting cross-legged with him on her bed, and he wanted to puke. He did not get up. Through the window, he watched her strong back as she pedaled away on Royal Street.

The news broadcasters reported that tourism was flagging because of the spill, but Stani and Benny sat on a curb together on French-man Street and saw no shortage of tourists glutting the street, plastic beads around their necks, walking like all of their joints had been lubricated, looking around and at one another like big-eyed children in the sour-smelling night. Stani had biked to Frenchman with Benny, amplifier in tow, when Benny said he could use some cash until his check cleared. As he sat on the curb with Stani, underarms wet with sweat, Benny occasionally eyed the keyboard he'd brought with him, but he could not summon the heart to begin playing. Instead, he sat there hating the tourists and finding them undeserving of his performance. Alejandro had called him that afternoon, but his phone died before he could call him back.

"I need another beer to warm up," Benny said, though this would be the third beer. Besides, maybe a block away a brass band was in full swing—dueling trombones, a wicked trumpetist, and a snare drum. Even people walking away from the music were bopping in time with the bass drum.

A young college student stumbled past them, and he drew his friends to him, trying to communicate the big feelings he'd just had, wagging his head, saying, "That was the most intimate jazz moment of my life! I was in it! Fuck, even the cowbell killed me." Stani winked at Benny. Judging by the look of the young man, this was the only jazz moment he'd had in his life.

A man and his girlfriend stopped in front of them. The man wore a goofy straw hat he'd likely bought that afternoon and would never wear again. He had one arm hooked around his girlfriend's waist, and he pointed with his tall beer can at Benny. "Doesn't that guy look just like a young Bruce Springsteen?"

"He does!" she said, and she looked at him as if Benny should share in their excitement, as if it should mean something to him. "Play something for us, Boss?"

Benny swatted the air at them as if they were unwelcome strays, telling them to move along. He told Stani he had to get the fuck out of New Orleans.

"Look at this place," Benny said, extending his arms to the slow-moving flow of tourists. The brass band up the street had finished their set to great applause. He was juiced enough to believe he could share certain inalienable truths. One, he was a loser. Stani tried to object, but Benny went on: No, no, it was true. Two, New Orleans was a fucking heartless city. It didn't take care of its poor. Look at the wealth disparity, look at how racialized that wealth gap was. No one doing a thing about it. It was a city for white tourists. It was a city set up for people to fly in and drink until they puked pink juice on the streets. These dim-faced vultures come to suck the life out of whatever they thought was authentic. Jazz was music born from enslaved people. The blues had their basis in the spirituals that African Americans sang to console themselves for the hardships of their lives. That's where the beauty came from. It was an exorcism of pain! You couldn't just buy it! Now, look at all of these tourists, roving in packs, hungry for a good time, and feeling entitled to it. These people all seemed to agree it was the last night on earth and looked incapable of considering the poor bastard who'd have to sweep up their smashed daiquiri cups. These people. These people didn't care about the oil spill, about the generations living in the Lower Ninth Ward who saw no way out. The whole human enterprise was a pitiless shit show.

"Show me your titties!" someone in the crowd hollered, as if Benny had orchestrated it to make a point.

After Benny monologued as if doing Stani a great favor, Stani said patiently, "There's more to the city than Frenchman Street. I'm getting tired, Benny. If you're not going to play music, I'd like to go home."

Suddenly embarrassed, Benny pushed himself up from the curb to begin. He started half-heartedly playing a New Orleans classic, "When the Saints Go Marching In," and a crowd quickly congealed around him, clapping to the beat. It was the very theme song of New Orleans, and the tourists knew it instantly. Benny played the song with ironic distance, but then he looked at Stani, who did not find this funny, and Benny straightened up and played in earnest.

He did not pause for applause before launching into the next song. He saw a few bills leap into the wastebin he'd hooked to his keyboard. People like for you to look them in the eyes when they tipped you, and Benny gave them this. Yes, pretty mother from Kansas, I see you. Yes, shy boy in tight T-shirt. Yes, big tough man with a crucifix on his forearm and PURA VIDA tattooed on his wrist. Yes, I see you. He was playing "Tipitina" by Professor "Fess" Longhair. Benny loved the drama of the song's opening. The right hand jumping like a spider and the left hand responding with the bass.

Many piano players held their hands gently. But not priestly Fess, with his big square glasses, rocking back and forth as he played. He pushed and pulled the keys, lengthening their stride. Some players bent to the keys; Fess made the keys bend to him. And when he sang, he threw his head back for a guttural "Oola malla walla dalla," as if it were a sound deep inside of him that he needed only to let out. Benny could feel Fess's spirit lie down on him as he played. He felt his body loosening up with the sound, becoming gentler and nobler and feeling his hands had been freed from him. For once, he could say something good and true.

There was so much to dislike about people—how poorly they cared for one another and what they were doing to the planet—and then, when you watch them listen to music, their faces go soft and thoughtful. Unzip us from our skin suits! their bodies say. He got to watch this happen to them. Beauty was out there. He'd just forgotten, was all. My god, why else are we alive? It was obvious. Why was it he forgot this every single day of his life? If only he could play for them forever, they could take back all of their dollars. He wouldn't need anyone else to love him.

Twenty-Seven

Jordan listened to the NPR piece like a man listening to a verdict for his criminal case. He'd called Vanessa half a dozen times over the past week, but her silence told him well enough about what she'd publish. He listened acutely for confirmation of his guilt. It was a ten-minute segment on the radio and was published on NPR's website. Cyndi had her hand on Jordan's forearm as they listened, seated on her couch together with her laptop open on the coffee table, and each time his voice came on, she gave his arm a little unconscious squeeze. Vanessa had focused the piece on Jordan. Benny was just given a short clip at the beginning and at the end. The headline was "Brothers Protest BP's Use of Dispersant as 90-Year-Old Family Oyster Business Shuts Down."

As they listened, Cyndi clicked through the photos of Jordan and Benny on the oyster lugger together, one with Jordan's arm over Benny's shoulder. There was a picture of Benny and his banjo, eyes closed as he sang with feeling. Again, the clutch of guilt in Jordan's chest.

"That's a good one," Cyndi said.

She enlarged the photos of the men unspooling boom around the marsh island. Vanessa had dramatized the brief altercation between Jordan and the oil cleanup workers.

"If I was born in the oil business," she recorded Jordan say, "I'd be fighting for oil, you know what I mean? I understand that—but I wasn't born in the oil industry. I was born in the seafood industry. And that's a much healthier business."

Jordan groaned aloud at the sound of his voice, but he was relieved. She hadn't shared what he'd said about Benny.

"Stop!" Cyndi said. "You sound good, Jordan. You do. And just look at your photo here. You look handsome."

"No."

"Yes!"

She enlarged the photo of Jordan at the helm of the oyster lugger, and he did not look as vulnerable in the photo as he'd felt. The photographer had been beside him when he snapped the picture, so the photo showed his profile. The Virgin Mary on the dash was out of focus. Jordan gripped the wooden helm, his brow furrowed as he looked over the bay.

→ Twenty-Eight ←

May could feel Jordan watching her, inquiring too often if she needed more iced tea. Her bedside table was crowded with tea glasses. She'd spent the better part of the past three days in bed looking at the television, considering the excessively attractive lives onscreen, but not really watching it. She had been felled by despair; she'd fallen into a pit of it and could not see her way out. She'd known the pit was there all along, but in the past there had been so much to do—the laundry, the dinner prep, the book fair for the children's hospital—which allowed her to sidestep the pit, not even meeting its eyes. But now it was unavoidable. She was furious with herself for being such a fool.

Jordan came in and sat on her bed, which was unusual. They'd lived alone together for years since Al passed, but Jordan rarely crossed the threshold of her doorway. Perhaps because he was so private himself, he was reverent of others' privacy. She pushed herself up in the bed, trying to be chipper, but it felt like she was talking to him from the bottom of a well.

"Jordie," she said, "I'm feeling so much better, thanks. I don't need anything, honey."

"I proposed to Cyndi last week," Jordan said. "I got an idea in my head in the kitchen, and I just asked her. I think that's why she said 'Maybe.' I haven't brought it up again. Now we act like it never happened."

"You proposed, Jordan?" May said. "Do you want to marry this girl?"

"I think so."

"That's not a very good answer, son."

Normally he clammed up at the slightest hint of rebuke. Instead, this time he pulled himself farther onto her bed, so he could rest his back on the headboard. "I don't feel much at the moment, but I know that I need her. I probably wouldn't be talking to you right now if it weren't for her."

"Jordan, you don't mean that you'd have hurt yourself." It was beyond unusual, for him to be so candid with her. She'd been so preoccupied with Doc that she just left Jordan to fend for himself. "Was that on your mind, really? I wish you could tell me things. I wish that we could talk."

Jordan patted her leg. "Please don't cry, really. Or I won't talk to you."

"Okay, I won't cry." She found some relief in her glass of tea. "But I should have been here."

"You didn't spill the oil," Jordan said. "Besides, you're allowed to have your own life. I mean, I never liked that shitbag, but you can do what you want."

May choked on the tea, laughing. "What'd you say?"

"Shitbag?"

"I never heard that word before. It sounds like a Benny word to me."

Jordan thought about it. "Yeah, I think it is."

"It was good having him here, wasn't it?"

"I guess it was." Jordan crossed one leg over the other, and it was a comfort to feel the weight of him next to her, having his hairy legs on the bed. "BP thinks I'm defrauding them. Somebody put in a claim in my name, if you believe that. I just got my food stamps card in the mail today, though, so that will take care of everything."

The thought of using food stamps clearly pained Jordan. Like his father, Jordan felt there was no one lowlier than someone receiving a handout.

"There's no shame in it," May said. "That's what the government is for, to help people when they need a little help."

Jordan made a face that told her he disagreed but wouldn't say so. May relished this closeness. It had taken the oil spill to get here, but sometimes it takes a disaster. Then Jordan grew stern. He was thinking about something that made him uncomfortable. "Mom, those pills you were taking for your nerves, do you still take them?"

"No," she said, too quickly. "No, my gosh, no, honey. Not for a long time. It was just after your father died, and I was feeling so sad."

Jordan would not look at her. He nodded, maybe even hinting that he did not believe her.

"Why do you ask?"

Jordan patted the bed. "No reason."

"I've just been a fool, is all," she said. "And I've been so mad at myself for it. I'll get out of bed now. You'll see. Why don't you go to the store and get us groceries and I'll make you and your girlfriend dinner? If you're thinking of marrying her, I ought to get to know her better."

Then her cell phone rang, and she knew who it was. It was Doc. If she were being honest with herself, she'd kept her phone by the bed for this very reason, to see this name blinking at her on her phone screen. Jordan seemed to know this too, and he swung his feet to the floor.

"I wonder what he wants now," May said.

"I meant to tell you something else," Jordan said.

"What?"

Jordan smiled at the ceiling, and he looked almost boyish. She'd not seen this brand of smile in years. He'd done some mischief.

"Jordan, did you do something?"

He popped up from the bed.

"Jordan, what did you do?"

"Nothing, really. I'm going to take a shower," he said from the doorway. "Make me a list of groceries for dinner, and I'll see if Cyndi can come over. Oh, and the interview came out."

"Why didn't you say so?"

Jordan shrugged, still smiling, and then he left.

May watched as the screen went dark and then flashed with a missed call. She hated herself for wanting to talk to him. What she really wanted was a time machine, to wind back the clock to before she knew about Camilla. No, even further—before Doc had asked her to have dinner with him. She didn't feel betrayed by Doc so much as disappointed that he wasn't the person who would usher her into a bright new life. Hope is an unhappy thing to watch walk out of the door. She was sorry about smashing the glass in his kitchen, because she knew what people said about women who acted that way. She called him back. Doc was very cordial on the phone, asking how she was, and then he said, "Did Jordan tell you what he did?"

Doc described the incident lightly at first, but while describing it he grew more irritated. "I could have called the police!" Doc said when he finished. "I could have had him arrested—for trespassing and for assault."

May was mortified. "I had no idea! Really, Doc, I am sorry. You'll have to excuse him. He's beside himself because of the spill. He's out of work." It was what Doc had said to her about that conservationist who'd been at his house, and she wondered if he recalled this. "Are you all right, though? He didn't hurt you?"

"I'll be fine," Doc said. "But he could have really hurt me. I'm sure he intended to do worse, showing up in the middle of the night like he did. I understand he's upset, and I'm sorry for him, but there's no excuse for violence. He's lucky I didn't call the police. If I were another kind of man, I might have."

"Thank you for that," May said. "He's got enough problems right now. These are dark days indeed."

Silence. Maybe he was waiting for her to say more. If he was expecting an apology from her about what she'd said about Camilla, or the glass in the kitchen, he wasn't going to get one.

"It's water under the bridge, May. I have to say I'm sorry for the way things ended between us. I still think you're a wonderful lady."

"Thank you," she said coldly, but it was all she could venture. Being sorry for "the way things ended" was hardly an apology, and though she'd devoted hours of thought to the subject, it seemed suddenly pointless to talk about it with him. It certainly wouldn't change what had happened. "I'm sorry for what Jordan did. That's not how he was raised."

She listened to Doc talk for a minute about Grand Isle and BP, and then she told him that she had to get going. A timer was going off in the kitchen. He seemed to know what this meant.

"Okay, May, I hope to see you again sometime."

When she got off the phone, she felt her body fluttering, her nerves jumping and feeling that she couldn't live without another pill, so she went to the aspirin bottle and found that, thankfully, she had only a few left. Then it would be over with. She had no way of getting more. Her physician had retired, and she'd rather die than ask another doctor for pills.

She couldn't believe Jordan had gone to Doc's hatchery and punched him like that, but after he implied being so low as to consider taking his own life, she should be grateful that that was the worst of it. And maybe she didn't feel too broken up about Jordan knocking Doc in the head once. Where she grew up, it was not uncommon to hear about matters of the heart being settled this way. She pictured Doc again in his kitchen, and then she relived her humiliation.

When she confronted Doc about his obviously romantic text thread with a near-child, and she read aloud what he'd written to the girl, "I can hardly work knowing you're around," he had the gall to say, "That doesn't have to mean what you think it does."

Then she'd slammed a water glass on the tile floor. She'd never broken anything in anger in her adult life. It's just as well he's shown himself, she told herself again. It was like a dream she'd had—that she'd be taken care of again—and this had been such a balm to her nerves. Benny said that he was a sleaze. She'd been blind to it. Now Benny was gone and hadn't come right back like he'd said he would, and she regretted all the time she'd missed with him while he was home and she was away at Doc's hatchery.

That night she made eggplant Parmesan for Jordan and Cyndi, and she and Cyndi made Jordan walk them through his version of the story. He perked up as he told it, delighting in the details of the eggs splattering on the wall, the spatula in Doc's hand. They laughed and made him tell it again. Cyndi was very helpful in the kitchen, very agreeable, though maybe she drank her wine a little quickly, like it was water, and maybe she was a little coarse for May's liking. At the table, Cyndi told a crude joke about a priest in a bar that made Jordan blush because he knew May was the wrong audience for this kind of joke. Cyndi was a bartender after all. She was the kind of woman who liked to make lighthearted jabs at her partner, and this was a fine thing for a person to do, unless that person was May's son, in which case it was not fine.

Cyndi said she forbade Jordan from talking about the oil spill for the next two hours. But Cyndi also seemed eager to win May over, which was endearing, and Cyndi was a talker, thankfully, because Jordan certainly was not. Cyndi solicited details about Doc and the graduate student, and it surprised May how relieving it was to tell her. "I thought that he was overly familiar with the girl, but maybe this was what having a mentor was like. What did I know?" The night passed pleasantly, with Jordan looking between May and Cyndi as they talked.

After dinner, they watched *Under the Tuscan Sun* in the living room, and Cyndi, a little tipsy, advised May to forget all about Doc and go to Italy like Diane Lane and meet a sexy brown man like Raoul Bova. This made May laugh, to say *sexy brown man* to your boyfriend's mother, but also, Cyndi wasn't young, was she? She was more worldly. She must be five years older than Jordan, approaching forty years old. She'd never imagined her son with a woman older than him. Perhaps no mother did.

"I've never even left the South. Al and I had our honeymoon on Grand Isle," May said. The thought of traveling alone was out of the question.

At the end of the night, Jordan and Cyndi went back to her house, though May protested that Jordan shouldn't be drinking and driving. They could stay in Jordan's room. May asked Jordan why they had to go, and Jordan smiled at her as though she were being unreasonable. Ah, May thought. Of course. They wanted to have sex. Cyndi had one arm hooked around Jordan's waist at the door but broke away to hug her. Cyndi might have smelled like cigarettes, but she was a sweet girl, and she hugged with a lot of feeling.

Before May went to bed, she checked the aspirin bottle again. Yes, two pills left. Ah well, she thought, I'll have to make do. What else could be done? On a whim and before she could even think twice about it, she texted Doug Babies:

> Doug, I've hurt my back, and the Tylenol
> won't touch it. I wonder if you know where
> to find something stronger?

She sent it. She actually sent this. Oh, he was going to think she was an addict. What was she thinking? He'd think she was crazy. He might tell Jordan.

> Noooooo! Yeah, I got u, Mrs. P. I'll be right over.

> That's not necessary. I have one for
> tonight. But not tomorrow . . .

> Im up now. I work tmw.

> It's late. I don't want to bother you.

> No worries.

> Ok.

> See u soon!

She took the two remaining pills. Her hands were shaking. She paced around the house, twice almost telling him not to come, but she decided this seemed more damning, more suspicious. Maybe she could pretend to be asleep when he came. She'd never have sent that text if she hadn't had a bottle of wine in her. They'd had three bottles.

She was so consumed with her own thoughts that she yelped when Doug knocked on the door. He looked terrible, and this softened her up. His eyes were sunken. He still had the flu from the week before, he told her. He'd lost some weight too. He came in, looking around at the dark living room, the empty bottles of wine on the table, and smiled conspiratorially at her. "Jordan and Cyndi just left," she explained. They talked for a moment about Jordan and Cyndi—what a surprise it was to Doug that they got together at all.

May was prepared to make an excuse about her back, but she found she was reluctant to bring it up and embarrass herself by lying again. Doug gabbed with her as if there were nothing strange about his coming over at ten-thirty p.m. He looked deteriorated, but he remained very much the tubby boy who'd sat on her couch periodically throughout the years. She gave him a drink of whiskey as he'd asked and poured herself some tea. Just when she sat down and was ready to acknowledge his reason for being there, Doug reached into his pocket and put a palmful of pills on the table with some lint. The reality of the pressed white pills on the table was a scandal she could hardly bear to see unfold. They were oxycodone, Doug said, and he made one stick to his finger and brought it to his mouth. A gulp of whiskey came next. So this was what she was doing to herself, she thought.

"No, thank you," she said when he asked her if she wanted one, and he shrugged. The room started swimming, and she regretted the pills she'd stupidly taken before he came over. Her face went numb so that she was surprised she could form words, but it was important, first and foremost, that she did not betray this to Doug.

May told him that he did not look well at all. Doug said, "I'm making more money these last few weeks than I'd make in a month working for Jordan. I don't mind breathing in some diesel for a little while. A little cold isn't going to kill me."

He'd been on a boat deep in the Gulf for the past week. He wasn't far off from where BP was burning the crude oil on top of the water, but he felt good knowing that he was cleaning up the Gulf. That was important to him.

She almost asked where he got the pills from, but she was suddenly determined not to talk about them at all. She would pretend that they were not there.

May was drinking a cup of tea and slipping farther into the couch. Doug had moved to the couch with her, but she wasn't sure when this had happened exactly.

"Do you think Jordan is still mad at me about the cleanup job? He doesn't call me anymore."

"Oh no, honey," May said, shaking her head. "I don't think he's still mad at you. Too much has happened at this point. It's not possible. He's just preoccupied."

The course of events became hazier to her in recollection. Doug asked her if a back massage would help her back pain. He said he used to massage his mother's back when she'd get cramps in her wheelchair. Then he waggled his fingers at her and said he had magic hands.

No, she couldn't possibly allow him to massage her back, even if he'd meant nothing by it. He was like her own son. She'd been at his wedding. She'd babysat Patrice when his wife was away at a nursing conference. Doug looked older than her own boys, droopy-eyed, sipping the whiskey she should not have given him.

She was unwell herself, disoriented, and felt a couple of times that she'd lost the plot of the conversation. He laughed at her gently, and she imagined that he was dying like Al had been dying and she leaned into him. It had been such a long night. She could hardly believe all that had happened in the past few weeks. She hardly knew herself. She wondered if she could ever travel to a foreign country alone as Diane Lane had. She didn't think so. Maybe she'd said yes after all to the back massage, because it was happening. She had her cheek on the couch cushion. When they moved to the bedroom, she wondered, Is this me? Is it me doing this?

✧ Twenty-Nine ✧

Y ou aren't mad, are you, Mrs. P?" he asked. In the harsh morning light, there was Doug Babies's unwell face in bed next to her. He was right to suspect as much. He sat up in her bed and looked a little scared. They blinked at each other at the start of another sweltering morning. The little desire that had passed between them the night before was so feeble, it had no business showing its face in the daylight. She'd never forgive herself. Jordan would never forgive her either. She sat down on her vanity chair and held her head in her hands.

"Yes, Doug, but only at myself. I need you to leave right away before Jordan sees you. Please."

"I didn't know you liked to party," he said. Doug was laughing a little bit, and she knew, looking at him, that he was not to be trusted with a secret. She knew that she could rush him out of her house at that moment, but if she didn't confess to Jordan, some idiot in a bar, and possibly the one in her bed, would tell him she'd slept with Doug.

"Now! Please, Doug."

He went rooting around for his pants, and she listened for the sound of Jordan's truck. She heard a truck sputter by, but with the wrong sputter for Jordan's truck.

Doug had his pants on and looped his belt. "I'm on the last rung of my belt," Doug told her. "I've lost that much weight. Pretty soon I've got to buy new clothes."

He sat back down on the bed and was looking at his phone. "Well, shit," he said. "I missed the boat today. Regina's gonna kill me."

May did not care at that moment if he was unemployed for the rest of his life. "Please hurry, Doug. I can't have Jordan see you here."

"You called me, Mrs. P!" he said.

She could have screamed. "He'll be home any minute. Don't be foolish!"

"I'm hurrying," he said, but he was sluggish, and she despised him, but not nearly as much as she despised herself. She heard Jordan's truck in the driveway then. No mistaking it.

"Oh my god," she said.

Doug hustled out of her bedroom—to do what?—she was calling him back, but she did not know what she aimed to tell him.

May did not follow Doug out to the driveway to help him explain why he was there. She stayed in her bedroom. She heard Doug and Jordan talking outside. Dear god. Please don't tell him. Please don't, please don't, please don't. I'll do anything. She overheard their voices, but not what they were saying. The voices weren't raised in anger. Jordan slammed the screen door upon entering, calling her name. He came to her bedroom doorway. She was still sitting by her vanity in her bathrobe.

"Are you sick?" he asked. She could detect no anger in his question. "You look sick."

May shook her head.

Jordan surveyed her bedroom. She followed his gaze but saw no evidence except for the unmade bed.

"So he's fighting with Regina again?"

This flustered her. She said something nonsensical. "Oh, you know Doug!"

Jordan noted things were strange but did not leap to any conclusions. The truth of the situation was too strange to arrive at.

"Did she catch him again?"

"Uh-huh."

"Jesus," Jordan said, hanging on the doorframe. "Who was it?"

"I don't know," May said. "Some woman he met."

"Did you see his fucking new truck?"

May had not.

"He used his first paycheck to lease a new truck."

He hadn't guessed, then.

"I'm going to the BP claims facility now to prove my identity to them. Did you make coffee yet?"

When she said no, he gave her a dubious look and then went to make some. She nearly confessed, but it wouldn't benefit him any to know what she'd done. She listened to him moving around in the kitchen, cleaning up from dinner the night before, which he likely also found strange because she never went to sleep with a messy kitchen. She could have wept with relief when he brought her a cup of coffee in her room as if nothing unusual had occurred.

⤗ Thirty ⤖

The line at the BP claims facility, where Jordan had gone to assert his identity, gave him a chance to survey the economic uncertainty of the Gulf Coast in the sorry faces of the people waiting. These were people who looked like they didn't belong under fluorescent light, fishermen and some women speaking all sorts of languages—Vietnamese, Spanish, French, and others he'd never heard before. Everyone clutched their papers—deeds to boats and tax returns and bank statements. Some people flapped the paperwork on their thighs as they waited. The line snaked around a plastic chain-link divider, moving a few feet an hour toward a row of clerks. Jordan was three rows back in the line.

He was standing behind a talkative Filipino man from Buras, Louisiana, who said, "They're gonna say you don't have the right paperwork, man. I was here yesterday."

"How many times have you been here?"

"Three times, man. Yesterday there was a fight and they shut down early."

"What was the fight about?"

"Some bullshit," he said, and turned forward again to flip through the papers he'd brought. Jordan studied the tattoo of a fish skeleton at the base of his hairline. The line moved so slowly that the man ahead of him grew bored and turned around again. He pointed to the sour-faced blond woman at the farthest counter. "It matters who you get. They'll tell you it doesn't matter, but it matters. If you get that bitch on the left, you know you're coming back here tomorrow. *Bureaucracy* is the ugliest word I know."

Jordan agreed and was relieved to be united with this stranger.

He flapped the paperwork, thinking again of Doug Babies in his idiotic new truck and feeling enraged. He'd leased a new red truck as soon as his BP paycheck came in, like a fool destined to be parted from his money. He'd told Doug that morning he held nothing against him, but that his mother had her own problems, and Doug wasn't helping any when he came to cry on her shoulder because he was having problems with his wife. To Doug's credit, he'd sucked in his lip, nodded, and said, "I understand. See you around."

There was a high school boy of Vietnamese descent who moved from clerk to clerk, translating on behalf of a whole community of Vietnamese fishermen. The boy looked ungodly tired.

No one was leaving the claims facility looking relieved, especially not the poor bastards without paperwork. A lot of guys around there didn't make enough money to file taxes, or they didn't keep the receipts from their fishing trips. Or they were paid under the table, like Alejandro.

When it was his turn, it was with the woman he'd been warned about. Jordan paused for a moment, lingering, hoping another clerk would open. He sensed the line behind him shifting restlessly. Jordan made eye contact with the man from Buras who was talking to another clerk. The man shrugged as if to say, Tough luck, buddy.

Jordan trudged up to her window and flapped the letter from BP on the sill.

"I'm Jordan Pearce," he said. "Regardless of what you may of heard."

The woman blinked at him, confused, and then took the letter and read it over.

"So someone else filed under your name?" she said.

"That's what your letter says," Jordan said.

"I've heard that happens, but you're the first one I've seen. Some people think the claims process is a pot of gold. You've got your ID?"

He slid the ID to her. She looked at it and then up at him, squinting. She then set it back down on top of his paperwork.

"Y'all didn't pay the other person, did you?"

"I can't see into that," she said, gesturing to the computer next to her as if he knew what was on her screen. "But I doubt it. You see all these people? They haven't been paid. You got your documentation?"

He put the rest of his paperwork on the sill, and she picked it up, looking it over for completeness. He resented the boredom in her voice when she said, "Okay. Let me go make copies."

She walked off with his stack to a copy machine.

"Jordan!" someone shouted, and he turned to scan the line for the source. He saw Ted Abramovic smiling and waving at him as if he had no idea where they were.

"Hi, Ted."

"Some shit, huh?" Ted said.

"That's right," he said.

When the woman returned, she sighed and told him in a manner that inspired no confidence that they'd refile his claim. He gave her his banking information, and the woman told him he could expect an Emergency Advance Payment to cover his immediate costs while the rest was being calculated.

"And what about my claim for compensation for my losses?"

"Sure, well, that'll take more sorting out still."

"On whose part? Is there something I got to sort out to get this back on track?"

"Not you, no. I have your paperwork now."

"So you'll sort it out, then?"

"No, not me personally. I'll get the ball rolling. I have to send your paperwork along to processing."

"Where does it go?"

"That goes back to the team."

"Which team is that?"

"I'm sorry?"

"I just want to know who I should talk to next about it if it's not you."

"You won't have to talk to anyone else about it unless we call you about it."

"You'll call me?"

"I won't call you, no, but somebody from the team may."

"You keep saying *team*."

"Yes, I know."

"But I don't know who that is."

"I'm sorry, Mr. Pearce, I see this is frustrating. But, I promise, we have your paperwork now, and it's going to get where it needs to go. In the meantime, we've got a lot of people to get to."

"What's—can I ask what your name is?"

"My name's Shauna."

"Okay, Shauna. I know it's just your job, and I know there's other departments and, you know, processing, and you're telling me that a bunch of money is just going to appear in my bank account?"

He wanted her to hear how unlikely this sounded.

"If you're approved," she said.

"But when will I know?"

"When the money comes through."

This seemed hopeless to him. "How long does this usually take?"

"Two to six weeks for the EAP," she said. "The claim for compensation will take longer. I can't really say how long."

She seemed to clock his displeasure and said, in a voice approaching condolence, "At least you've got all the paperwork. Most of the people here don't even have that much."

Jordan lowered his voice, and in a near-whisper he said, "Can you help me get on with the oil spill cleanup?"

"What?"

Jordan looked back at the line of fishermen. He spotted Ted, head down, rereading his papers. "The Vessels of Opportunity program."

"Vessels of Opportunity?" she said, too loudly. "That's another program. We've got nothing to do with them."

He shouldn't have hated that dumpy-looking woman with the furry face, but he had no one else to hate in the moment.

"Well, goddammit," he said, pulling his paperwork back toward him. "Thank you very goddamn much!"

She balked in her chair as if he'd slapped her. He did not glance at the line of waiting men as he stomped out, paperwork clutched to his chest.

When he got home, Jordan hammered a sign into the front yard that said PEARCE OYSTERS 90-YEAR-OLD BUSINESS CLOSED BECAUSE OF BP'S OIL SPILL AND BOBBY JINDAL'S FRESHWATER DIVERSIONS. That afternoon, he saw a media truck parked on his lawn to take a picture of this sign, and he felt somewhat satisfied. Then he set about finding the missing W-2s for Hoa and Linh amid the years of god-knows-what-papers in his office. Annie Nguyen's name was more prevalent in his recent call list than his girlfriend's. He never answered and avoided even checking the messages.

He was making a cold-cut sandwich later when he noticed the carpet was changing color in the living room. It was wet. He went into the hallway. His mother's tub had overflowed, and she did not respond to his calls, so he had to kick in the door. She had a pulse, but he couldn't wake her up.

→ Thirty-One ←

In the morning, Benny sat at the table as Stani and Rachel moved about the kitchen. From the afternoon onward, the kitchen was the least hospitable room in the house. It cooked in direct sun all afternoon and had no window AC unit, so it was novel to sit there in the company of his roommates while an Allen Toussaint record spun in the living room. Stani washed up the dishes Benny had left in the sink, and Rachel scooped coffee into the French press. Benny was prepared to dislike this squatter, whom Stani brought home from his meditation group, but he found her to be a sweet, serious-browed girl in her mid-twenties with a nose piercing and unfortunate dreadlocks. Rachel set three coffee cups on the table in front of him, winking. A bowl of sugar had materialized, which Benny had never seen before.

Benny had wondered if Stani was involved with her, but he sensed no spark between them. They acted more like siblings.

"So, what's the story, Rachel?" Benny asked.

"Mine?" She had her back to him as she poured hot water into the French press. "Why I'm here?"

"Yes, the story of you here. Is it a you-and-Stani story?"

"Stani didn't tell you?"

"Wasn't my story to tell," Stani said.

"I just got in a mess with a boyfriend, is all."

"He kicked you out?"

"More like I flew out the window."

"Uh-oh," Benny said. "He's a bad one?"

"Oh yeah. Real bad. He's still hunting the streets for me."

"For real?"

"He's stomping around with a hammer out there."

"Christ," Benny said. He stood and searched out the window.

"Not out *there* there. Out there somewhere," she said. "Or maybe he's tired himself out by now."

Benny turned and saw Rachel up on her toes over the French press, levering her little weight down on the plunger. She looked over her shoulder. Benny had a hard time impressing his concern upon her when she seemed so disinterested in her own tragedies. She saw the vexation on Benny's face and shrugged.

"I've been in messes like that before. Now I need to figure out why I keep finding these guys over and over again."

She brought the French press to the table and sat down. Benny appreciated her candor. His shortcomings were more apparent to him daily, and he felt increasingly ready to confess them. He was eager to see a person turn her life around after she'd admitted a few ugly truths to herself. Rachel had started working as a barista at a coffee shop on Frenchman Street. Soon she'd have a little money again so she could pay rent somewhere. In the meantime, she'd taken up residence on the couch.

They drank the coffee Rachel had brought from the café, which was much better than the coffee that his brother and mother drank, and it seemed to him that this good coffee held in its citrusy notes some curative power.

"I couldn't believe that Stani was for real," she said. "He came up to me after meditation. After I cried like a baby in front of everyone. I didn't know him at all. He said I could stay in your room if I needed to. He could have been a creep. But he wasn't. It's the nicest thing anyone's ever done for me."

"Stani's a good one."

Stani shifted in his chair, uncomfortable with the compliment. "So, what will your brother do now?" he said.

"Wait for his BP money," Benny said. "If his oysters die? I don't know. He's not suited for much else."

"He always wanted to be an oyster farmer?" Rachel asked.

It had always seemed to him that his brother was going to be an oyster farmer, but he didn't know if this meant it was what he wanted. Maybe it had just been what was expected of him, his father's dream, and Jordan made his father's dream his own. It was likely more complicated than that. Their father had been disappointed that neither of them graduated from college.

Rachel said her coworker at the café applied for BP money for lost tourism revenue, and that she was thinking of applying for compensation too. Why not?

"I read that the whole BP claims process is a mess," Stani said. "The government is giving BP all of this authority, and you wonder why."

"Better to let BP take the hit for its incompetence," Benny said. "The government doesn't want to be responsible."

"We all talk about the spill in New Orleans, and about BP," Stani said, "but the truth is that it's still so far away from us. You see the pictures of these oiled birds, oil in the marshland, turtles covered in oil. It's terrible, but it's like a foreign war or something."

Benny was about to tell them that he'd been sprayed with the dispersant when Stani pulled the empty coffee cups toward him. Stani had class to attend. He was earning an associate degree at

Delgado Community College. Rachel had work at the café. The only item on Benny's agenda was to visit the bank and see if his check had cleared.

"I'll wash those," Benny said.

Stani placed a hand on the crown of Benny's head on his way out of the kitchen. The record had finished in the next room, and Benny heard Rachel turn off the record player. The overhead fan swayed as it circled in a way that made him think the fan would come down on him.

Once alone in the kitchen, he wondered how he would fill his days now. Benny had tired of his own cynicism. It had gotten him nowhere. The musicians he adored most had self-destructed, and he'd unwittingly followed this model, thinking that—what?—the world would reward his misanthropy with fame. Calling the whole human enterprise a shit show felt only half true. He suspected that he'd misjudged things along the way, that the world was a good deal more interesting than he'd let himself notice. Still, he didn't have a clue how to change the groove he'd worn his way into. He knew that Vanessa was not going to call and put him on the radio, but despite himself, he still wanted to check his phone.

He left the mugs in the sink and went to his bedroom. His phone had been off for two days. When he turned it on, his voice-mail box was full. Jordan had been calling him.

Jordan picked up on the second ring and told Benny that their mother had overdosed and was at the hospital in Graceland. Jordan had to repeat it three times.

→ Thirty-Two ←

Benny found Jordan in the waiting area of the emergency room slumped in a familiar angle of resignation. Their mother's handbag was on the seat next to him as if holding her place while she was in the bathroom. He pulled the bag onto his lap so Benny could sit down.

"Can't we see her?" Benny asked.

"They'll say when," Jordan said. Without knowing it, Jordan began to pet the bag.

"Why are your pants wet?"

"I found her passed out in the bathtub," Jordan said.

Benny winced. "She's unconscious still?"

"She denied taking the pills when I asked her. I thought I'd leave it alone." Jordan spoke to the clock on the opposite wall. He cracked his knuckles. "They say she tested positive for opioids."

"When?"

"This morning," Jordan said. "And I saw her this morning."

"It doesn't make any sense."

"Why was your phone off?" Jordan asked.

"It died."

They watched as a procession of new patients filed into waiting room. A man walked into the emergency room holding his bleeding neck, trailing a remorseful-looking woman. A boy cradling a broken arm was chased inside by his parents. A stretcher zipped by with a large man on it. He seemed to be in cardiac arrest.

"She can't die," Benny said. "People don't die from overdoses like this. That's ridiculous."

"I know she can't," Jordan said.

A thought occurred to him. "It was an accident, wasn't it?"

Jordan's leg was hopping up and down. "It was an accident."

A nurse called Jordan's name. Her demeanor betrayed nothing about their mother's condition. They followed the nurse into the ER theater, which was alive with a young woman's screaming for something to stop. The rooms were cordoned off with privacy curtains. At the center of the room was a station for the nurses and computers.

"She's awake?" Benny asked the nurse as they walked.

"Baby, I wouldn't be taking you to see her otherwise," the nurse said, not unkindly. "It didn't look good for a moment. People who don't regain consciousness right away sometimes hemorrhage."

It occurred again to Benny that his mother might have taken the pills intentionally, and that her despair had been as bad as he'd feared all his life. Benny knew the paralysis of self-loathing. He'd periodically been so despondent as to see no point in waking, but he'd never tried to hurt himself.

"Here she is," the nurse sang when they reached May's bed. She bent over May, adjusting the pulse reader on her finger. "We're going to move you to a room soon."

Their mother looked small in the bed, her hair pulled back from her dinner-plate-white face. A woman somewhere behind another curtain kept pleading for help, and their mother looked at them with alarm. Benny and Jordan stood rigidly, wondering what was happening with the poor woman. It went against all human instinct to stand so near to a wailing person and offer no help, but the nurse went about taking their mother's vital signs as if she couldn't hear it. Benny felt that the cries were issued on their mother's behalf somehow.

The nurse then tapped something into a computer stand by the bed. Benny had had questions for his mother, but when he saw her, the questions escaped him. Her hair wet, face drained of color. He and Jordan went to either side of her hospital bed and each held one of her cold, clammy hands. Her voice was small and hoarse. The nurse said she'd been intubated. Benny suddenly felt terrified of what their mother would tell them.

"I was so stupid," she whispered. The voice was unfamiliar to him in its hoarseness.

"Don't say that," Benny said. "It was an accident."

Jordan turned away and walked between the curtains into the ER theater. Benny watched him go. He thought Jordan was upset with her. It seemed that his mother thought this too. She gripped his hand like it was a knot of a tree she might try to climb.

"You're all right now," he said. "Don't worry about anything now. You're all right."

"How did I get here?" she whispered.

Did she mean: Where was the esteem of her neighbors? The love of her husband? The house they'd built and crowded with small children? Benny couldn't tell, so he responded: "I don't know, Mom. We almost lost you."

She grinned her old coconspirator grin and kissed his hand. Everyone in his family felt they needed to act so goddamn tough all the time. It reminded him of the faraway look his father had when he was embarrassed by someone's emotions.

Then Jordan came back with a blanket, which he flung open and tucked around her prone body like she had done to them when they were young.

"He's making you into a bedtime burrito," Benny said. "See, Mom?"

She made a face that was more remorse than it was smile. She had likely known what she was doing when she took the pills.

An addiction counselor spoke with them after they'd been redeposited in the waiting area. A sweet-faced Japanese woman with one ear pierced completely from lobe to ear-top asked if there were any more drugs in the home, in such a way that Benny didn't immediately realize she was asking if they took pills too. She didn't seem to believe him, anyway, when he said, "No."

"She got a prescription after our father died," Jordan said. "I didn't know it was a problem."

"Xanax is highly addictive. And, like in your mother's case, it often leads to experimentation with other drugs."

"Other drugs," Benny said, because he couldn't believe it.

The counselor gave them a blue handout with a list of drug rehabilitation facilities in the state. "Treatment *works*," she said, as if intending to get one step ahead of their denying it.

They drove their mother home from the hospital, led her inside, and turned on the lights. May turned her hospital bracelet around on her wrist and then asked for scissors to cut it off. The carpet was still soaked halfway to the kitchen, but she didn't acknowledge this. Jordan took a towel from the closet and laid it down over the carpet, and then, seeing that it helped not at all, broke down into unprecedented tears.

"I don't know what to do, Mom." He sobbed and could not be consoled. The sight of this was so foreign in their family that

Benny felt a rush of relief. He laid his head on Jordan's shoulder, felt Jordan heaving, and looked at his mother. Jordan let Benny rest there for a moment—longer than Benny expected—then he ducked out from under and stood, wiping his eyes.

"Just a minute," he said, then disappeared into the hallway.

Benny and May listened to the sound of the sink running.

"I didn't think he even knew how to cry," Benny said. "There's hope for him after all."

A small squeak came from his mother beside him. Benny thought he might have drawn a laugh out of her, but he turned and saw she was weeping too. Her hand over her mouth, eyes big with heart-break. He walked over to where she sat in the armchair and put his arm over her and pulled her little shoulder into his waist.

"Just two weeks," Benny said. "Humor us."

He felt her nod under his arm.

"Yeah?" he asked, looking down and seeing just the top of her head.

"Just two weeks," she said in her smallest voice.

"Two weeks is nothing," Benny said. "You can do two weeks of anything."

"I can do two weeks of anything," she said back to him.

"That's right. One time I spent two weeks in a friend's garage before I found out it wasn't even his house. The owners came back from vacation and chased me out with a broom."

"You didn't."

"No. But it sounds like something I would do, doesn't it?"

"It's a lot of money," May said.

"Oh, shut up about the money, Mom."

"It's like setting a few thousand dollars on fire."

"I don't want to be too dramatic, but I look around and I think maybe we're burning down already. Just look at the state of your carpet, Mom. My god."

She laughed then, tearful and ragged.

"See?" Benny said. But he wasn't exactly sure what he meant. See: life is still possible. See: laughter still lives in this ruined home. See: we can carry one another out of any rotten feeling. Then they saw Jordan emerge from the bathroom with his hair sopping wet, as though he'd just dunked his head in the sink basin. He had the usual look of confusion on his face, but none of the hardness.

"Two weeks," Benny told him.

"Yeah?" Jordan said.

"She's being a baby about the money. I told her to shut up about it."

Jordan stepped over the wet carpet in little squelches and took his mother's hand. "Shut up about the money, Mom," he said.

The three of them left the family home in May's sedan the following morning. A fine June morning, before the sun grew relentless in the sky and they'd need to cloister themselves inside. May was pensive on the drive, seated up front in the passenger seat, her purse clutched in her lap. They were headed two hours upstate to a town outside of Baton Rouge. Jordan drove her sedan too fast on LA-1, and as they left the bayou and entered the green-and-gold plains country of Louisiana, they passed chemical refineries spewing smoke and oil pumpjacks nosing the ground. On Benny's old CD, Brian Wilson was singing, "I Just Wasn't Made for These Times."

They were bereft, the three of them, like sails without wind, but they were easy with one another. The uneasiness to their conversations that made the silence painful had gone. In the car together, like a family on a road trip. Except they were delivering their mother to rehab, and the strangeness of this was felt by all.

Benny was in the backseat, and as they passed a refinery, he said, "Sometimes I think humans are a plague on the earth."

"I don't disagree," Jordan said.

"Doc said something like that to me," May said. Her voice still tight with irritation. "Or was it about man-made disasters?"

"Fuck Doc," Benny said.

"Don't say that," she said.

"Sorry," he said, and leaned between the two front seats to grab Jordan's cigarettes from the cupholder.

"You're killing yourselves with that stuff," his mother snapped at him. "I wish you'd quit."

He slid the cigarette behind his ear for later.

They parked next to the rehab facility. It did not look like a temple of wellness—a squat brown building with pebbles pressed into the concrete walls.

"It doesn't look so bad to me," Benny said.

"Let's not lie to one another, now," May said, looking into her purse. "I'm only agreeing to this because I feel so bad. These places are not for people like me."

May was short when saying goodbye to them. Jordan and Benny loitered around the bright, scrubbed lobby with her, taking in the bland abstract paintings of yachts and sunsets on the walls, smelling the astringent floor cleaner, and listening to the overly friendly old woman checking their mother in.

A man with half his teeth gone on one side walked by the front desk, scoping out the newcomer. "Howdy, motherfuckers," he said, looking at Benny and Jordan. Of course, they looked more the part of a new admit than their mother did.

May turned to them, a hint of punishing drama to her expression.

"Just go if you're going," she said finally, and they left feeling wholly unsure that they'd done the right thing, or if the facility was any good. It was the most affordable option, but they knew nothing about recovery or what to look for in a rehab facility.

"She acts like we're punishing her," Benny said on the drive back.

"She's terrified," Jordan said.

Jordan was right, and it was an insight that seemed out of character for him.

With May gone, they lit one cigarette after another. Benny thought they might have a heart-to-heart about things somewhere between Gonzales and Golden Vale. Benny, for one, was shocked as hell that their mother was an addict. Even the word, *addict*, seemed like an ill-fitting sweater, and he'd kept looking at her the night before with incredulity he could not suppress, like she might shock him again with news of an illegitimate sister or secret kleptomania or a confession of an unseemly affair. When he asked her where she'd gotten the oxycodone, she did not answer. She met his eyes in a way that suggested she would keep her secrets to herself. He felt that maybe as sons he and Jordan had failed her, not in the way that she'd implied—failing to get along and produce grandchildren—but that they'd failed to love her properly. Or maybe it was the gender role she'd had to play. He wanted Jordan's take on it all. He asked Jordan to turn off the news, but then the silence between them was so loud that Benny had to roll down the window and fill the car with wind. Benny studied his brother's profile while he smoked—Dad's nose, strong chin, bad haircut—and Benny could not figure out which combination of words would give him access to that mind. He failed repeatedly to ask Jordan how he was doing.

They drove south from the expanse of the mainland with its stands of cypress trees and tupelo into the soft green, shrinking marshland. The trees gave way to a series of refineries, each like a gray city unto itself, with flares and tall fences topped with barbed wire. These refineries exhaled voluminous clouds of gas, containing god-knows-what chemicals. The sight was more defeating than it had ever been. The refinery complexes towered over the landscape like gloating prizewinners.

As they approached Golden Vale, the traffic on LA-1 jammed up. They'd grown used to this strange busyness, the bustle of the cleanup. Ten minutes had passed of crawling behind a tractor trailer carrying oversized oil drilling equipment when Jordan began cursing to himself in a meditative rage. The truck took up two lanes, which prohibited passing. The longer they were stuck, the more obvious it was that they'd be stuck behind it the entire way home. They were moving so slowly that Benny could feel the sun burning the right side of his face. He looked down at his arm and saw the new smattering of freckles there, his forearm bigger than it'd ever been. He'd been a child just the other day.

Jordan's phone started ringing, and Benny had to fish it out from where it was wedged between the seats.

"It's Annie Nguyen," Benny said. "What's she calling you for?"

Jordan told him to ignore the call.

"Why?"

Benny nearly answered it anyway, but Jordan shouted, "Don't!"

Benny silenced the ring. "What's the deal?"

"She's calling because she wants me to find Hoa and Linh's tax returns and shit. She's been a fucking pain in the ass for two weeks now. She calls me all the time."

"Why don't you answer her, then?"

"I haven't found the paperwork."

"Do you know where it is?"

"If I knew where it was, she wouldn't be hounding me."

"They need their BP checks too, you know."

"Of course I know that."

"Relax," Benny said. "Did you know she was my first kiss, Annie Nguyen? Now she works in San Francisco like a real hotshot. I let all the good ones go."

"They let you go, Benny."

"Don't remind me."

The wet green grass stood as tall as a child in the ditches. The pipes on the truck bed ahead of them were so large it would take a giant to do anything with them, Benny thought. A giant would have to jam them into the ground.

In the house, Benny went down on his knees and tested the wetness of the carpet with his hand, though it was wet to the eye, and then he wiped his hand on the dry part of the carpet. It would mold, they decided. They'd have to tear it up, and why not put down a new floor as a gift for their mother when she returned? Jordan was surprised to hear Benny talk as though he were going to help with this project. They returned to Jordan's truck and drove to the home improvement store two towns away.

The particular woody twang in the air of the store evoked a memory from Benny's childhood so forcibly that he stopped walking. It was as if he'd stumbled into a scene from his past that'd play on a loop for eternity. He and Jordan monkeying around the lumber section like it was a jungle gym, testing their father's patience until he exploded at them, and their father's waterborne accent emerged. He called them *a couple o' couyons*, and Benny had mispronounced this all day as *coopulacoolons* to make their father laugh. Benny looked again at Jordan, and it seemed Jordan had felt this nostalgia too.

A woman in a blue vest, with her black hair curled into hardened ringlets, advised them to pick the snap-together vinyl plank flooring and showed them their color options. Jordan pointed to a tacky cherrywood color.

"Why are you making that face?" Jordan asked.

"I don't like it," Benny said. "And I don't think she would. Her stuff is all blue. I think you should pick gray."

"Wood isn't gray. That looks fake."

"It's all going to look fake. I think you need to consider her colors. It'll look modern."

"You want a wood floor to look like wood. It's dumb to pick gray. She'd think so too."

Benny had his arms crossed and shook his head.

"You don't live there," Jordan said. "What do you care?"

"I'm thinking of her," he said. "And what she'd like."

The woman tired of them. She shifted her weight from one hip to the other. Benny smiled at her, trying to win her to his side of the argument. "What do *you* think?"

The woman clucked her tongue. "It's not my floor. Why don't you call her?"

"We can't call," Jordan said flatly. "She's in rehab."

It was unlike Jordan to offer up a remark in a tone approaching humor. The woman's eyes bulged momentarily, but she suppressed any further expression like a woman with sorrows of her own and no time for theirs.

"Okay, fine," Benny said happily. "Pick the ugly one, then."

They moved the living room furniture into the hallways, and together with much effort, they moved the overstuffed family couch into the garage. Underneath the couch, they found a smattering of coins, one of which was Canadian, a child's spinning top, a well-fingered book of psalms, a mini–candy bar, and a half-full medicine bottle with their father's name on it for something unpronounceable. Jordan put this bottle in his pocket. The carpet was faded and discolored from the repeated passage of their feet, but it shone the bright original shade of teal where the couch and easy chair had been. Benny stumbled on some sentimental feelings about this and the foot traffic of his family, but Jordan wouldn't indulge him.

They started tearing up the carpet in large swaths. Benny pulled too hard and tumbled backward on his ass, and Jordan erupted in laughter. It was difficult work and oddly satisfying to hear the pop of staples as they came out of the wood. Benny piled the carpet and padding in the driveway against Jordan's advice that the rain would make a mess of things. But Benny didn't feel like listening to Jordan, who always felt entitled to tell him what to do. When a thunderstorm passed over and dumped water in slaps across the driveway, the pile of carpet and padding looked sodden and immovable, and Benny understood the objection.

They took a break during the storm and sat on the family couch in the garage to drink beer and watch the rain assault the driveway. The rain misted their faces, and they were grateful for its coolness. Benny said they ought to have always kept a couch in the garage for this purpose. They wondered about their mother's phone privileges and brought the house phone out with them in case she called.

"It feels wrong to be home at this time of day," Jordan said, "when I should be on the water. I'll never get used to it."

"Maybe you can treat it like a vacation," Benny said.

Jordan stared at him.

"I'm sorry," Benny said.

"I wake up at four still, thinking it's time to work, and then I remember, no, it's all over. And it hits me again, how fucked my life is, how little I can do, and I can't go back to sleep."

"Sometimes I think life just kind of grinds you up, and it isn't your fault. There are all sorts of structural reasons that people fail. Because they're born in a poverty-stricken country or their parents are cruel or one day a plane crashes into their house, scalding all the children. It can all go away at any moment. This sandcastle you've been guarding all your life."

"I know it's not my fault."

"I think sometimes the problem with Mom is that she let herself care about the wrong things."

"Maybe you care about the wrong things too," Jordan said.

Benny nodded. "I'm starting to get a whiff of that."

"Did Vanessa ever call you?" Jordan said. "About the little desk thing?"

Benny turned to Jordan in confusion, and then he understood. "Oh, *Tiny Desk*." He laughed. "No, *Tiny Desk*, no. That was never a real possibility. That's for musicians with albums, with names for their acts. Vanessa was just trying to flatter me. It was more than a long shot."

"Benny." Jordan shifted around in his chair. "I might have messed things up for you. I acted like a maniac—calling Vanessa so much. I'd been feeling so crazy. I said some crazy things."

"Oh shut up," Benny said. "Don't say anything else about it."

"I thought that was eating you still."

"No, it's dumber than that. I just had it in my head," Benny said, "that maybe it was going to make my case for Kiki. She'd hear me on the radio, and she'd see why I was worth keeping around. I don't know what I was hoping for, really. But then I was hardly in the interview at all. You were just too good. They didn't need me. And that's just as it should be. You're the oyster farmer."

A little brown anole slipped silently across one of May's planters, and Benny leaned over to watch it go. Jordan understood that he had never really learned to wish good things for Benny. It was as if Jordan had been waiting for something first. But what? Once he had everything he wanted, when he'd vanquished his doubts and his loneliness, once he didn't feel so small all the time—maybe that's when he'd planned to wish Benny well. He thought for a moment that he might come clean and tell Benny all of this, and about what he'd said to Vanessa too. Then Benny looked at him and shrugged.

"I just had it in my head, is all," Benny said. "I just pictured my life going off in a different direction. I see now there was never much difference to be made. Kiki wasn't going to change her mind. It was just nice to think about."

Then Benny stood and stretched and readied himself to return to the carpet.

"I never thought I'd ever like you," Jordan said.

Benny turned to look at him, but Jordan, of course, would not look at him while he spoke.

"And you still don't?" Benny said.

"No," Jordan said. Then he huffed. "Yes."

Jordan futzed nervously with his beer bottle. "I mean, thank you for coming back."

Benny offered to stay the week until the new floor was in place and promised to return when it was time to pick up their mother after her rehab stay. Cyndi came over a few nights, and they made dinner together. Cyndi could make Benny laugh, and Benny looked at Jordan with surprise when he did. It was Cyndi who said Doug Babies had likely filed that claim in Jordan's name.

"I mean, who else could it have been?" she said.

"It could have been anybody," Jordan said.

"He couldn't have thought it'd work," Benny said.

"I've just had this feeling it was him," she said, running a hand through her hair. "But I shouldn't go accusing him. The spill has me thinking the worst of people."

"But it's so stupid," Jordan said, not that he doubted it. As soon as she said it, he feared she was right. "He'd be a person I didn't know at all, and I've known him all my life."

"Forget I mentioned it," she said, standing from the table. "Should we have a smoke?"

Eight thousand dollars appeared in Jordan's checking account that week, and this gave him reason to hope more compensation might be on the way, as BP promised it would. Jordan found the missing paperwork for Hoa and Linh. If there had been a whole battalion of Annie Nguyens advocating for their mothers, then everyone would have gotten paid. The claims process was so grossly haphazard, Jordan would have preferred taking his chances with FEMA relief but, riding the optimism of this first deposit, Jordan helped Benny submit his paperwork too.

Alejandro came over to help them finish installing the floor. The catty-corner wall in the living room had given them hell. They struggled to cut the panels right, so they would lie flush against the diagonal wall. Alejandro made this look easy. He lingered late until after Jordan had gone to bed, and Jordan was surprised to find Alejandro alone in the kitchen the next morning by the coffee maker. There was polite embarrassment in Alejandro's smile when he said, "Good morning."

"One of those for me?" Jordan asked, pointing at the three empty mugs on the counter.

Alejandro slid it to him.

"Thanks," he said, straddling a stool, and poured his coffee. He looked back at the hallway where Benny was still in his room, and then at the floor that Alejandro had helped them finish. It had a faint luster in the morning light.

"I can probably find some little jobs for you on the boat," Jordan said. "Maintenance stuff. Not a ton of work, but it's something."

"I'm going to New Orleans," Alejandro said. "There's construction work there. I know somebody there."

"You're going with Benny?" Jordan said, shocked that he'd asked so directly. "You're staying with him?"

"Yes, with Benny." Alejandro looked down and then up, almost apologetically.

"I'll be damned," he said quietly. "I didn't know."

And then Benny emerged from the hallway—a little flushed, his shoulders hunched, realizing at that moment that Jordan understood, finally. He was boyish in his awkwardness walking toward them, but also somewhat relieved. Saying, jovially, more than a little forced, "There's coffee left for me, I hope."

They left together, as Alejandro said they would.

On the day Jordan was due to pick his mother up from rehab upstate, he rose from the couch when he heard Benny's Volvo arriving in the driveway. He had not expected Benny would return.

May appeared in the lobby in a new floral-print dress—a gift from a woman she'd befriended. May hugged this ruddy-faced woman goodbye under the awning, and the woman whispered something to May that made her laugh.

On the drive home, she told them one sordid, tragic story after another about her fellow patients. Her new friend Mandy Peters woke up to her boyfriend dead in her bed from a heroin overdose. Casper DeWitt fell from a second-story window and through the roof of a little tin shed. Garret Evans crashed a golf cart into his stepsister's wedding cake. Bo Silva passed out and lost seven toes to frostbite in a ditch in Idaho just before his first stint in rehab (this was his fourth attempt at sobriety). May was halfway through the story of Jesse Fontenot's kitchen fire when her sons led her inside the house. She had to stop and cry at the sight of the new floor.

In the months that followed, she drove forty-five minutes twice a week to see her therapist. She began writing notes to herself on the refrigerator. In the mornings on his way for milk, in the evenings for a bottle of beer, Jordan tried his best not to glance at his mother's notes. He now knew more of her private sadness than he had ever hoped to. *You are deserving of love,* one note said. It was unseemly to Jordan that she would confess all her woes to a stranger, but Cyndi told Jordan he was being unreasonable, and he figured that was his father talking through him. Al was growing shadowy in his mind, but the days of his father's illness did not have as much fidelity as the good ones. Some things were a blessing to forget.

What went first were the memories of his father diminished by illness, empty-faced in his chair at the TV. Or Al opening the door to the refrigerator only to be lost in the wilderness of his mind. And as those memories receded, the rest came back into view for a time: his father as a younger man, at an age Jordan now approached. He remembered his father just as he was when he returned from a sudden squall on the Gulf—a bloodied welt on his face, the sky bright with lightning. He remembered his father's whistle high and clear over the water; the familiar voice he used when speaking to any dog he met. He could see his mother and father at the old church banquet, dancing small circles after a brief quarrel in the car; he saw all this renewed for a time, without obstruction, and then those memories too began to recede into shapelessness, and he was left with just a few precious recollections that he would keep in perfect fidelity to the end of his days: The night, for instance, when his father came into his room after a football game and sat down on the bed. He was uneasy with this and his father was too. His father said, "The way you run upfield, the way you drive through the defense like that." He stopped. Jordan thought he was going to get criticism. "It's nice to watch. To see your grace." That word, *grace*. It troubled his father to say it, but he looked into Jordan's eyes to make sure he knew that he'd meant it. This was his troubled inheritance. He'd remember that for the rest of his life.

One evening not long after his mother returned, he sat alone in the living room with the TV running. It was June, and the oil had invaded the inshore bays and wetlands by then. The well was still open. He'd stewed too long in one spot and needed to move.

He walked out in the soup of air and insect sounds down to his dock, where *May's Day* sat still in the bayou. One of his neighbors down the way was welding in his driveway, the sparks a gold fan flickering to life.

He boarded *May's Day* and walked around, running his hand along the taffrail, nearly tripping over the coffee sacks he could not see in the dark. He sat on the culling table, the steel still warm from the day's roasting it. He finally owned it, the business, the boat—he wasn't sure when it had happened, the transferral—but there it was. Just when he was losing it, it was finally his.

⤳ Epilogue ⤲

The oil well hemorrhaged into the Gulf of Mexico for nearly three months—the largest accidental oil spill in the history of the world. What seemed to go on forever, the well spewing oil until the earth's core was empty, like a deflated balloon, had finally ended. The well was capped in July and sealed with cement in September. Could you call it relief that Jordan felt then?

Jordan was unable to check on his oyster reefs because the Coast Guard had blocked access to the oiled areas. He stayed home for another three months, performing small maintenance jobs on his boat, weathering little arguments with Cyndi. It often seemed as though he could do nothing that would please her. His sense of pride eroded as the weeks at home dragged on. He slept so little he felt drunk during the day. If not an oyster farmer, who was he? He had to tell the checkout girl at the grocery store "EBT" so she could ring up his groceries another way. The girl couldn't care less, but Jordan cared quite a bit.

Once he was permitted to reenter the bays, Jordan went to nearly every oyster lease he had and hauled up dead oysters. He shucked open the shells to find oysters inside as milky and form-less as snot. It was Jordan's luck that his reefs were vulnerable to both the deluge of fresh water and the oil and dispersant that reached the estuary. Oyster farmers in other parts of the state fared better, or else they leased so much acreage of reefs that they'd been insulated from the losses they suffered.

A year later, Jordan's lawyer got another one hundred thousand dollars from BP for the oyster business, but this sum would not cover his costs for making no profit for the next five years, which was how things went, and Jordan couldn't afford to pay himself a salary. He spent nearly every dollar rehabbing his oyster reefs, scattering boatloads of crushed cement on top of his dead oysters with the hope that new oysters would plant themselves on the cement since they were not growing on his reefs. A strange thing had happened in the wake of the spill. The new generations of oysters were not attaching to his reefs. Something about the water composition had changed, but no one could tell him exactly what. The baby oysters weren't surviving. For five years, he told himself, If I don't start making money, I'll have to do something else.

It took Jordan much longer than it might have taken another man to realize his oyster leases would not recover. The afternoon he accepted this was a cold one. He was back in the bay, and he watched his deckhand sorting the live oysters from the dead. Only a pittance remained. For a long time, he had maintained that he was as much a creature of the Gulf as any redfish. If you took him out of the water, he'd die. A Cajun has webbed feet. People liked it when he said this, and he'd said it more than once. He'd spoken to a boatload of reporters by then, and had gotten better at it, but it hadn't changed his prospects. A weak winter sun overhead, a near-stranger of a deckhand on his boat with him, and he thought, All right, then, it's over.

Jordan sold *May's Day* to an oysterman in another parish for next to nothing—a man who owned so many acres of oyster leases that he hired sharecroppers to harvest his oysters for him. The man never went out on the water himself. He had no business calling himself an oysterman—that was Jordan's opinion. Cyndi had left the pregnancy test out by the coffee maker for him to find one morning that winter. They hadn't been trying to conceive, and Cyndi had given him every reason to think that children were not in the cards for them. But all of a sudden he had something to look forward to.

When Benny returned to New Orleans, he devoted himself to music and to helping Alejandro settle in the city. Benny was invited to play the keyboard in a synth-pop band. The band enjoyed a brief success when one of their songs was on the radio and then bought by a hip kitchen utensil company for a commercial, but Benny didn't think of their dreamy heartbreak songs as art, and he couldn't muster his enthusiasm for very long. The traveling strained his relationship with Alejandro. They'd tumbled into a relationship—tender and fun—but ill-equipped to sustain distance. Alejandro never did feel at home among Benny's friends, though he'd received asylum in the U.S. and had adopted a threadbare look, and he felt adrift when alone in the city. While Benny was on tour, Alejandro applied for his own apartment in Houston.

After Benny left the band, he reenrolled in college at the University of New Orleans with the idea that he'd become a social worker. He played piano every two weeks at the ragtime brunch just for fun, and he enjoyed some notoriety around town for this. Kiki was gone by then, and the next time he thought to look her up, he found out she was a city councilwoman in New York. Benny watched a campaign ad on her website once—a little of her uprightness still affected her speech, but the years had softened her. He imagined she'd win a major election one day, and he would tap a sign with her name on it in his front yard in an instant. She'd be queen of his yard like she'd been queen of his heart once.

Jordan sold the houses to a man who worked in offshore drilling. The houses weren't worth much because coastal erosion had left them vulnerable to Gulf storms. Once, there had been so much land in that town that cattle grazed there. It was called Golden Vale because the fields shone yellow with pis au lit flowers in the spring. Jordan felt he'd buried his father again the day he signed the papers. He walked circles in his office past the Pearce family portraits, photos of deckhands, mountainous oyster harvests, oyster paraphernalia, and framed maps showing the wetlands as they once had been and were no longer.

May had always been afraid of the city, but Benny helped her find an apartment uptown, where she volunteered at the public library. She was introduced to a widower in Gentilly with a fondness for mythology, a gray ponytail, and an elaborate garden. May was overjoyed when Benny had a song on the radio and a modicum of success that looked like it might take him into a different sort of life, but it didn't work out the way he'd hoped. May sometimes couldn't believe what had happened to them—that the spill had split them up again, when she had been certain it was going to bring them all together. People say that time has a way of ravaging us all. In Louisiana, it's washing the land away. You can watch it happen. A wave will whip up and arrest a clump of marsh grass and pull it out to sea. The soil disperses, and like that, Louisiana dissolves into the sea like a biscuit into a cup of coffee.

Jordan and Cyndi had a church wedding one warm day in early spring. She had a baby bump and white flowers braided in her hair, and she wore cowboy boots. The whole affair was earthier than he'd imagined his wedding would be. Doug Babies's thirteen-year-old daughter, Patrice, attended with her mother because Doug was ill that day. His health had declined precipitously, and he'd be in and out of the hospital for the last two years of his life before succumbing, uncomprehendingly, to prostate cancer. All her life, Patrice would harbor the thought that the spill had killed her father, as she ran from the arms of one no-count man to the next.

At the wedding, the table platters were piled high with catfish and fried shrimp, though everyone knew the fishing nets were pulling in tar balls still. On a humid spring night, you do not think about the oil spill, not with so many people clapping for you while you cut the cake, not while you watch your brother in a suit twirl your mother under the bare-bulb lights.

Acknowledgments

I am grateful to the Baylor University Institute for Oral History, whose grant enabled me to record the oral histories of Louisiana oyster farmers, fishermen, scientists, community activists, and journalists in the wake of the 2010 *Deepwater Horizon* spill.

This novel was informed by my time in Louisiana and the source material I collected in the aftermath of the environmental disaster. It would not have been possible without the generosity and support of the people who allowed me to record their stories. They taught me about oysters and much more than I can qualify here. Thank you, John Supan, Alfred Sunseri, Sal Sunseri, Mitch Jurisich, Nathan Jurisich, Benjamin Alexander-Bloch, Byron Encalade, George Ricks, Daniel Nguyen, Theresa Dardar, Donald Dardar, Ever Martinez, John Tesvich, Tony Tesvich, Vlaho Mjehovich, Peter Vujnovich, Jules Melancon, Nick Collins, and Wilbert Collins. Anyone interested in hearing their oral histories can find them in full in the BUIOH online archive.

Additionally, I'm grateful to Wilma Subra for sharing her expertise on toxic exposure and its effects on communities.

I've been fortunate to learn from many great writers, and I owe much to them for their feedback, advice, and encouragement:

Robin Allnutt, Lucinda Roy, Alice McDermott, Jean McGarry, Dana Johnson, Aimee Bender, and Meg Wolitzer.

I'm grateful to the English Department at the University of Southern California, Stony Brook University's BookEnds fellowship, Virginia Center for the Creative Arts, Banff Centre for Arts and Creativity, and Blue Mountain Center for the gift of time and space to write. I'm grateful to Tulane University's New Orleans Center for the Gulf South for its support of my scholarly work.

This book couldn't have had a better editor and advocate than Jordan Blumetti. The thoughtfulness of his edits and his talent made this novel the best version of itself. My heartfelt thanks to Zibby Owens, my publisher, for giving me this wonderful chance. I'm grateful to Anne Messitte, Sherri Puzey, Diana Tramontano, Coralie Hunter, and Kathleen Harris for their help in shaping this book and launching it into the world and to the entire Zibby Books team for all the energy that went into this release.

I'm indebted to my incredible agent, Maria Whelan, for championing my work and finding a home for it.

For the foundation of love that made my life possible, I'm grateful to my parents, Robin Takacs and James Takacs. Thanks for encouraging my earliest work. You'll remember which one.

A few dear friends were essential readers, and shoulders, over the years. Thank you, Gwen E. Kirby, Rebecca Waldron, and especially Helena de Groot. You've been such a blessing to me.

No one spent more time with this novel than Taylor Koekkoek, who read this first over email, and then became the person I ask to read everything. A godsend for my writing, but much more so for my happiness. Thank you for your great love and for existing.

Again, for my father, James Takacs. I so wish we could have talked about this.

About the Author

Joselyn Takacs holds a PhD in Creative Writing and Literature from the University of Southern California and an MFA in Fiction from Johns Hopkins University. Her fiction has appeared in *Gulf Coast*, *Narrative*, *Tin House* online, *Harvard Review*, *The Rumpus*, *DIAGRAM*, *Columbia: A Journal of Literature and Art*, and elsewhere. She has published interviews and book reviews in the *Los Angeles Review of Books* and *Entropy*. She lived in New Orleans at the time of the 2010 oil spill, and in 2015, she received a grant to record the oral histories of Louisiana oyster farmers in the wake of the environmental disaster. She currently lives in Portland, Oregon.

@ joselyn_takacs
www.joselyntakacs.com